Praise for *Love*

Told in split time, *Love's Fortress* is a ca
ily, and faith. Readers will find this bea   d
story difficult to put down, intrigued by the historical as much as by the
contemporary.

—Eva Marie Everson, president of Word Weavers International
& bestselling author of *Dust*

Love's Fortress is an engaging, heartfelt dual-timeline story. Jennifer Uhlarik
skillfully explores the wounds of our nation's past alongside the wounds of
her characters' pasts. Romance, faith, and a satisfying ending complete this
lovely novel.

—Heidi Chiavaroli, Carol Award-winning author
of *Freedom's Ring* and *The Orchard House*

This dual-timeline just might be Uhlarik's best yet! In the present day,
an unexpected and unwanted inheritance leads to a journey of discovery
and truth, and God's grace and love. In the past, the revelation of dark
secrets leads to a place of courage in the midst of self sacrifice. By turns
heart-warming and heart-wrenching, this story touches some of the deep-
est places of the soul.

—Shannon McNear, 2014 RITA® nominee, 2021 SELAH
winner, and author of *Elinor* and the upcoming *Mary*,
books 1 and 2 of Daughters of the Lost Colony

Fans of dual-timeline fiction won't want to miss Jennifer Uhlarik's contri-
bution to the multi-author *Doors to the Past* series. Uhlarik sheds light on
a heartbreaking portion of American history and one woman's search for
the truth about her estranged father, weaving together the past and present
to show that things are often not what they seem. Readers will love the
satisfying way these two timelines tie together.

—Amanda Cox, author of the 2021 Christy Book
of the Year, *The Edge of Belonging* and *The
Secret Keepers of Old Depot Grocery*

Love's Fortress is a dual timeline that blends real history with a sweet romance, a clear faith element, and a contemporary mystery. I've read many of Jennifer Uhlarik's books, always historicals, and was very pleased with how strong her contemporary writing is. Her historical storyline is thoroughly researched and compelling, as always. There's something in this book for everyone!

—Pegg Thomas, award-winning author of *Maggie's Strength*

In *Love's Fortress*, Jennifer Uhlarik unlocks a fascinating and tragic door into the past, escorting readers back to the journey of the Plains Indians and their treasured ledger art. As the present-day characters in this time-slip novel chase after God's providence and the truth about the past, they uncover a number of surprises along the way. A beautiful portrait of hope in the hardest of circumstances!

—Melanie Dobson, Carol Award-winning author of *Catching the Wind* and *Hidden Among the Stars*

Doors to the Past

LOVE'S
Fortress

JENNIFER UHLARIK

BARBOUR
PUBLISHING

Love's Fortress ©2022 by Jennifer Uhlarik

Print ISBN 978-1-63609-181-5

eBook Editions:
Adobe Digital Edition (.epub) 978-1-63609-183-9

All rights reserved. No part of this publication may be reproduced or transmitted in any form or by any means without written permission of the publisher. Reproduced text may not be used on the World Wide Web.

All scripture quotations are taken from the King James Version of the Bible.

This book is a work of fiction. Names, characters, places, and incidents are either products of the author's imagination or used fictitiously. Any similarity to actual people, organizations, and/or events is purely coincidental.

Cover Model: Shelley Richard/Trevillion Images

Published by Barbour Publishing, Inc., 1810 Barbour Drive, Uhrichsville, Ohio 44683, www.barbourbooks.com

Our mission is to inspire the world with the life-changing message of the Bible.

ECPA Member of the
Evangelical Christian
Publishers Association

Printed in the United States of America.

DEDICATION

*To the seventy-three Plains Indians
who were held at Fort Marion*

ACKNOWLEDGMENTS

A hearty thank-you to the following people:

Ross Lamoreaux, who provided some much-needed help with historical St. Augustine details. You are always so gracious to answer my questions, and I appreciate it!

Leigh Anne Brown, who helped me with details on motorcycles. Girl, who'd have thought, nearly forty years ago, that I'd be turning to you for help with both costumes/historical clothing and motorcycle details!

Susie Dietze, who took time to help me sort out details on the missionary movement of the 1870s. You are such a faithful friend, and I appreciate you pointing me in the right direction to find the facts I needed.

Danine Gruber, who accompanied me on a whirlwind trip through the Castillo de San Marcos and who graciously found and purchased a book on the women of St. Augustine, which became part of the basis for my research. I love you, my friend! You are a blessing!

And lastly, Emily Kapes, curator of the James Museum of Western and Wildlife Art in St. Petersburg, FL (which I fictionalized in my story). Thank you for taking the time to read my rambling email and spend an hour on the phone answering my many questions on ledger art, forgery, and all things artwork!

You all played an invaluable role in making this story happen, and I appreciate each of you very much!

GLOSSARY

Hinono-eino—Arapaho
Kadohadacho—Caddo
Ka'igwa—Kiowa
Numinu—Comanche
Tsitsistas—Cheyenne

CHAPTER ONE

Franklin Sango's Home, St. Augustine, Florida—Present Day—Saturday

*H*ardly the best choice of mood music, you idiot." The evocative first lines of "Sound of Silence" had seemed appropriate when it came up on her playlist, but as Dani Sango pulled into the driveway, a thick blanket of melancholy threatened to smother her. She put her fourteen-year-old Kia Sorento in park, clicked out of her phone's music app, and unplugged the device from the charger. Cutting the power to the engine, she patted the dashboard.

"Thanks, old girl."

She stared at the tasteless brown ranch-style house, its only distinguishing feature the bright red door flanked by ornate sidelights. The house sat on a pretty tree-dotted lot. Some distance down the street stood a quaint commercial garage with vintage-style gas pumps and signage. Parked near the road, two restored classic cars straight out of the movie *Grease*—both in cherry condition—sported primo paint jobs. Between them stood a sign, JOIE-RIDES RESTORATION AND CUSTOM DETAILING. Behind the quaint building stood a much larger structure with numerous garage bays.

Dani sighed. Enough stalling. She dropped her phone in her tiny purse, extracted the key labeled HOUSE from the manilla envelope she'd been given, and stepped out of the car into the sweltering June heat. Draping her purse across her body, she pocketed her car keys and walked to the door. Her hand shook as she fumbled and failed to insert the house key.

"Get a hold of yourself, girl." She blew out a breath and, this time, accomplished the task.

Dani swallowed and pushed her way into the nondescript living room. A broken-down couch with a mismatched coffee table and end table sat on one side of the room. On the other, a small entertainment center of no particular style held a flat-screen television. A worn leather chair and a floor lamp finished off the sparse furnishings. Yet the walls were filled with pieces of artwork in varying styles and sizes—all framed canvases.

A shrill beep cut the silence. She followed the sound to a landline phone and answering machine combo on the kitchen counter. Who in the world still used an answering machine—or a landline phone, for that matter? The ancient machine registered fourteen messages. After glancing around as if expecting someone to challenge her, she punched the PLAY button. The recordings ranged from robocalls about extended car warranties to automated reminders about prescriptions, and several hang-ups. She listened with only half an ear until a pleasant male voice came across the line, his charming southern accent snagging her attention.

"Hello, Mr. Franklin."

Dani drew back in confusion. *Mr. Franklin?*

"This is Brad Osgood of the Andrews Museum. I'm sorry I haven't reached out sooner. I was out for a few weeks dealing with. . ." An awkward silence lingered. "Um. . .vacation." The man cleared his throat. "Anyway, I'd be very interested in speaking with you about the pieces you mentioned in your email. Please give me a call at your convenience." He finished the message with his phone number.

Dani hit the REPLAY button while reaching for a nearby pad of sticky notes and a pen. In the process, she knocked over a file folder wedged between the wall and the answering machine, and photocopies and lined notebook papers with dark chicken-scratch writing scattered. She huffed. Why was she even bothering to write this down? Not like *Mr. Franklin* could call this person back. Her throat grew thick, and she cleared it as the message replayed.

Brad Osgood—Andrews Museum. Calling about "pieces" "Mr. Franklin" mentioned in email.

She replayed the message once more and jotted the 727 area code number. St. Petersburg? Interesting. Just an hour from her Tampa-area apartment. The message's timestamp said five days ago. With a sigh, she gathered the scattered papers from the fallen file. Straightening them, she found bajillions of handwritten scribbles, an article about the arrest of one James Kenneth Knox, and an obituary for the same man.

"Keeping up with your jailhouse bestie, Franklin?" She shuffled the papers back into a neat pile, shoved them into the folder, and tossed them back on the counter.

She listened again to the message just to be sure she'd heard it all correctly. Did she dare wonder why Franklin Sango would be contacting a museum about *some pieces*—and using a fake name to do it? What pieces? She turned again to face the living room, giving each framed canvas more attention. One of these, perhaps? She circled the room, recalling some of the more famous paintings from her college art appreciation class—Van Gogh's *Starry Night* and Dali's *Christ of St. John of the Cross*. Her heart pounded. These couldn't possibly be the real things, could they?

"It's a shame I even have to wonder such a thing, *Mr. Franklin*, but then, that's what convicted art forgers get, isn't it?" An instant pang twisted her belly. "Sorry. I guess it's not right to speak ill of the dead—even if it's you."

Perhaps not right, but her father's conviction twenty-six years ago had forever changed her life. It had cost her a father, driven a wedge between her and her mother, and was the very reason she'd never allowed herself to explore anything of an artistic vein. She'd taken art appreciation in college to meet a humanities requirement, and that was the last she'd seen of the university's art department. Thankfully, none of her college classmates had recognized the name *Sango*, but her professor sure seemed to. Nice of him not to outright ask if she was the infamous forger's child, but the overlong, questioning glances were proof enough he suspected she was.

As Dani looked again at the art pieces in the room, a speeding motorcycle blurred past on the street outside. She glanced up—too late to see the speeding rider. *Moron! Great way to get someone killed.* Shaking her head, she wandered down the hall toward what she assumed were the bedrooms.

The hallway walls were decked with more art pieces, some large, some small. A few familiar, many not. Behind the first door, she found a large, bright art studio, sunlight streaming through a big skylight and two oversized windows. A paint-spattered easel took center stage, and a drafting desk sat tucked in one corner. Scattered across its wide surface were photographs of a motorcycle from various angles as well as a few scribbled notes in the same chicken-scratch from the folder. A sketchbook lay open, pencil resting beside it, but nothing graced the blank page.

Between the two huge windows sat a chest-high cabinet with louvered doors. She opened one side to find tubes of paint in every color, brushes, and other artist's tools. Shutting it again, she faced the only other thing in the room—a cheap folding table shoved against the far wall. An old hardcover book lay on its surface beside a crisp, new cardboard box, the inside filled with foam cut to the book's size. As Dani cautiously opened the cover, the binding objected with pops and crackles. The ancient, yellowed pages contained faint, preprinted lines forming rows and columns and rudimentary images of long-haired men on charging horses.

Had a child drawn this? It was far more simplistic than anything else in the house. And it was drawn in, what—an old bookkeeping ledger? Like a schoolchild might draw in a spiral notebook today.

"Not exactly your style there, Franklin."

"Who are you?"

Dani spun, heart pounding as she spied a stocky young man in a sleeveless shirt, colorful tattoos covering every inch of exposed skin from his jawline down.

"What're you doin' in here?" He glowered.

She shrieked and backed up a step, bumping into the table. "What do you want?" She clutched her tiny purse—just large enough to hold her smartphone, ID, and cash. Little good it would do in protecting her.

"I asked first." He punctuated the statement with a foul name, his nostrils flaring as he paced farther into the room.

Dani's jaw hinged open. Was this some meth-head come to invade an empty house? How in heaven's name had he gotten in? Or was he already here when she'd entered?

"Leave now, and no one will get hurt." *Be brave, girl!* But every fiber in her trembled.

"Hurt?" He loosed a derisive laugh. "You think you're gonna hurt me? You got no right to be here." He paced still farther into the room.

Oh, crud! Dani backed into the corner. How to extract herself from this situation?

"Get out—*now!* Or I'll call the police!" Hands quaking, she withdrew her cell and attempted to bring up the keypad.

"Call! I dare you." He stepped nearer, now only a few feet away. "You'll be the one in handcuffs!" He jabbed a finger in her direction.

"Gray!" An even deeper voice bellowed the word from the front room.

The tattooed man drew up, faced the door—started moving toward it. "Down here! Hurry!" He bolted into the hallway. "We got us an intruder."

Think!

Dani looked around. She couldn't escape down the hall—he was blocking her path. Instead, she dropped her cell back in her tiny purse and darted to the nearest window. Thankfully, the blinds were pulled up. Dani flicked the locks, jerked the window open, and, with practiced skill, popped the screen's aluminum frame out. Barely had it clattered into the leaf-dappled yard before she ducked through the opening. She scrambled for her car, nearly fumbling her keys as she jerked them from her hip pocket.

C'mon, old girl. Help me out!

She unlocked the Kia and crawled in, slammed the door, and hit the locks. As she did, the tattooed man darted out the door, followed by. . .a giant. She jammed the key into the ignition.

"Start, baby. Start!" She cranked the key. The engine ground and sputtered but wouldn't turn over.

No! Not now. . .c'mon.

The two men halted, the giant ordering the tattooed one to stay back. At Tattoo's curt nod, the big guy—a *very* muscled man of at least six-foot-five, with the back and sides of his hair shaved and the top pulled into a short, graying ponytail—approached the driver's door. His ginger beard hung in a thick braid, and his own tattoos peeked from under the V-neck and sleeves of his shirt.

Dani cranked the key again. Again, the engine sputtered and failed. Her eyes burned with unshed tears as the giant stopped a few feet from her.

"Are you Danielle?" he hollered over the sound of her third attempt to start the car. "Danielle Sango?"

She released the key, panic boiling through her. "Please leave me alone!" Her cell chimed, and she pawed to extract it from her purse. Drawing it out, she pushed the button to illuminate the screen and poised to dial 911.

"Gray didn't mean to upset you. And neither one of us is going to hurt you, Danielle. I promise."

She darted a skeptical glance his way but kept her thumb poised. "How do you know my name?"

"Your father was my best friend. I've been expecting you to show up since. . ." Sorrow flashed in his eyes, and her own tears came then.

"Who are you?"

"Matty Joie. I own Joie-Rides." He jerked his braided chin toward the garage on the corner. "Your dad and I worked together for many years." When she didn't answer, he held up his hands as if surrendering. "I'll show you." He produced a worn leather wallet and, after some digging, pressed a Florida driver's license and a business card against her window. The ID showed his photo with the name Matthew Louis Joie. The business card sported the same logo as the nearby garage's sign with his name and the word *Owner* beneath it.

Her pulse slowed just a little as she looked from his identification to him, and finally to the other man.

"Who's he?" She nodded in Tattoo's direction, speaking loudly enough to be heard through the glass.

"Sam Grayson. We call him Gray. He works for me." Mr. Joie palmed the cards he'd shown her. "I'm sure he frightened you, but he was just watchin' out for Frank's house. He didn't know you'd be showing up today." Mr. Joie glanced in Gray's direction. "Did you?"

Gray hung his head like a chastised pup. "Didn't know you'd be showin' up at all. Frank never mentioned having a kid."

Of course he hadn't.

Mr. Joie spun on Gray. "Get to work!" His voice dropped. "You're not helpin' here."

Gray's inked shoulders slumped. "Sorry." He glanced at his boss, then to her. *"I'm sorry."* He overenunciated the words before stalking off toward a motorcycle parked in the grass between the house and the garage.

Once Gray fired up the bike, Mr. Joie turned to her again. "Please, Danielle, I only want to help. Will you trust me?" Hope tinged his words.

What choice did she have? Her ancient car had apparently given up the ghost, and this giant Viking wannabe didn't seem to be going anywhere.

"I'll take a look at your vehicle—see if I can't get it running again."

Tears welled afresh. Was he reading her thoughts?

Gulping down her emotions, she stared at the house, still standing wide open, then shot him a sidelong glance.

She might just regret this...

Dani removed the key from the ignition, popped the hood, and reached for the door handle.

❧

In between watching Mr. Joie and one of his employees hook her vehicle to a tow truck, Dani stared at the artwork adorning Franklin's walls. Across the room, her phone chimed with the special tone reserved for her best friend, and dread spiraled through her. She paced to the beaten-down couch, withdrew her phone from her purse, and read Rachel's text.

FLIGHT GOT IN LATE LAST NIGHT. FAMISHED. WANNA GRAB LUNCH?

Her stomach growled. If only. Her fingers flew over the keyboard.

OH GIRL, YES! BUT...CAN'T TODAY.

WHY NOT? HOT DATE? ;)

Dani looked at Mr. Joie and his employee—and almost laughed—yet her recent panic quelled the urge. She discreetly snapped a photo of him through the front window. Rachel would freak. She attached the picture and typed a message.

I WISH. YOU MIGHT BE BETTER COMPANY THAN THIS GUY.

WHAT THE...? WHO'S HE? HE'S A LITTLE FRIGHTENING. A LOT FRIGHTENING. YOU OKAY?

CAR BROKE DOWN.

WHERE ARE YOU? I'LL COME MEET YOU.

TOO FAR AWAY TO MEET.

WHERE. ARE. YOU???

ST. AUGUSTINE.

AT FRANKLIN'S.

She pressed her eyes closed and held her breath. Three. Two. One.

The phone rang, and she clicked into the call.

"You're visiting your *father*?" Rachel's voice rasped over the line. "Is that him in the picture?"

"Not exactly visiting. And no, Franklin worked for this guy."

"Works for him. . .at what? Thuggery?"

"Mechanic."

"That's convenient, at least."

Wasn't it?

"How are you at Franklin's but you're not visiting?"

Dani's throat knotted, and she walked down the hallway so no one might see her if she lost it. "Rach, I got word two days ago. There was a car accident. Franklin's dead."

Silence hung thick on the line, then, "Oh, sweetie, I'm so sorry. Are you all right?"

Her shoulders slumped. "I don't know. How's a girl supposed to feel when the jerk who abandoned her dies?" She sniffled and wiped her nose with the cuff of her sleeve.

"You should've told me sooner."

"You were visiting your sister. Helping with her new twins. I couldn't intrude on all that joy." Not for a man she'd not seen since she was two years old—and of whom she had only one terrifying memory.

"Girl, we've been best friends for years. You know you can call me anytime, anywhere, with any kind of news."

The knot in her throat grew. "Thanks, Boo." She slipped into the studio and gulped a few breaths to get her emotions under control.

"So what are you doing up there?"

Voices floated through the open window where she'd escaped earlier, and she crossed to shut it. As she did, Mr. Joie glanced her way with a warm smile. She pressed her lips into a halfhearted grin at the giant, locked the window, then plopped into the chair at the drafting table. "An attorney contacted me. Apparently, I'm named in his will. The man never wanted anything to do with me, but he leaves me a rundown house with dumpy old furniture. So I had to come up and sign some papers."

"He left you his house?"

"Yeah. The official reading of the will is next week, but when I went by the attorney's office earlier this morning, he gave me the house keys and said the property was part of what I'd be receiving."

"Part. So there *is* more to come."

She groaned. "If this place is anything to go by, it's probably just a boatload of debt."

"What's it like?"

"Plain. No real style. The furniture looks like thrift-store specials, but he's got the walls decked out in all kinds of framed canvases. Really nice ones—beautiful, in fact—but at least two appear to be forgeries of some of the masters."

Dani described the art pieces.

"So he kept forging things even after doing time. . .for forgery?"

She closed her eyes and cradled her head in her free hand. "I don't know. It's all really confusing. I even found a message on his answering machine from someone at the Andrews Museum wanting to talk to *Mr. Franklin* about some pieces he'd emailed about. Why would a convicted art forger use a fake name to talk to an art museum about artwork unless he was up to no good?"

"Where's the Andrews Museum?"

"St. Pete."

"That's close." The faint tap of computer keys clacked from Rachel's end of the phone connection. "I've never heard of it. I'll see what I can dig up."

Outside, the tow truck pulled away, and a loud knock came at the front door. "I gotta go, Rach. I'll call you later, okay?"

"You better. I'm worried about you."

"Thanks, Boo."

Dani ended the call and headed to the living room. Through the ornate sidelights flanking the front door, she could see Mr. Joie's huge frame. She opened the door.

"Hey. Tim's taking your car to the garage, and he'll start looking for the problem. Hopefully, we'll have it up and running again soon, but. . . um. . ." His voice trailed off in a not-so-hopeful tone.

"It may be a lost cause?"

"Yeahhhh." He drew out the word into a sigh. "Cars with that many miles don't usually make it this long."

So she'd been told. "I've been holding the old girl together with chewing gum and duct tape for a while now."

Concern flashed in his eyes. "Have you been lookin' for something new?"

"I've—" She'd warned herself *not* to overshare with Franklin's friend, yet the words tumbled loose. "I've been trying to get some bills paid down. School loans. That sort of thing."

"School loans?" His voice grew incredulous, and his expression flickered with questions.

"Yes. College? I needed a degree—"

"I thought your family was—"

"Thank you for your help, Mr. Joie." The last thing she needed was this nosy giant butting into her messed-up private affairs. "It's kind of you. I'll find a way to pay you for—"

"No, you won't. It's the least I can do for Frank's daughter. And please, call me Matty. Everyone does." Despite his fierce Viking vibe, enhanced by the sheen of sweat and smudges of dirt dampening his skin after checking her car, his intense hazel eyes exuded a warmth and his smooth, deep voice a caring that she hadn't expected.

Drat the stupid lump in her throat. Dani forced a fleeting smile. "Then you should call me Dani." She shrugged. "Danielle is what my mother calls me. The name reserved for when I'm in trouble."

"Which is it, darlin'—what your mother calls you or when you're in trouble?"

"One and the same. I can never please her, so I'm always in trouble."

He chuckled, a wry grin parting his lips. "Surely not. You look like a nice girl."

Dani gave a noncommittal shrug. "I *am* a nice girl, but things are fairly chilly between me and my family. Have been for years." Particularly since she'd gotten into middle and high school and begun to understand how her mother and stepfather felt toward Franklin and—by default—her.

"I didn't mean anything by that, just so you know."

"No offense taken."

He smiled. "Mind if I come in and get a drink? It's hot out here."

She hesitated but opened the door wide and moved out of his way.

He ducked inside, closed the door, then headed toward the kitchen.

Dani followed. "I haven't looked around in there yet, so I don't know if there's anything stronger than tap water."

"Frank always keeps. . ." As he reached the kitchen, his footsteps faltered, and he braced a hand against the peninsula's edge. "Kept. . .Frank always *kept* the refrigerator stocked with drinks." He turned toward the sink and peeled two paper towels from the roll on the counter. After running them under the faucet, he squeezed the excess and mopped his face and neck. After a moment, he turned. "Sorry. Still getting used to a world without him."

Dani flinched. "Well, that makes one of us."

Emotions roiling, she stalked to the refrigerator, jerked the door open, and reached for a. . .Dr Pepper? *That* was unexpected. She'd always pictured Franklin Sango as a slobbering drunk, too inebriated to take care of himself, much less care about her. Dani snagged one of the umpteen cans, popped the top, and took a long drink.

"I'm sorry," Matty whispered. "That was insensitive."

"Yes, it was." She beelined to the living room, slumped into the couch, and set the can on the coffee table. Her phone chimed once with Rachel's special ringtone. Just a text.

In the kitchen, Matty leaned heavily on the counter and mumbled something she couldn't hear. With a sad shake of his head, he also retrieved a soda and paced to the living room. Blowing out a breath, he dropped into the mismatched leather chair. "Your daddy loved you very much, Dani." He popped his soda open and took a drink.

She loosed a disgusted chuckle. "Let's get something straight. Franklin was no *daddy*. That would actually require a relationship. And if he did love me. . . Well, he sucked at showing it."

This time, Matty flinched. "I understand why you'd say that. And I'm so sorry. He made some wrong choices along the line, ones he truly regretted, and he's spent a lifetime trying to make up for them."

A sassy retort rose on her tongue, but she let it die when his cell phone rang.

"Excuse me a minute." He rose and stepped outside, cell to his ear and soda in his fist. His warm, deep voice muffled as the door closed.

Dani stared around the room, her gaze landing on the coffee table as she reached for her drink. A stack of magazines and books in its center snagged her attention, and she grasped the corner of the bottom one and pulled the pile nearer. It easily slipped her way and revealed a thin, silver laptop hidden beneath. Before she could wonder about it, Matty stepped in again.

"I've gotta go. Customer waiting at the shop." He crammed his phone into his pocket, looking uncomfortable. "Do you need anything? With your car broken down, I don't want to leave you stranded."

"Thank you. I'll be fine for now."

"All right." He checked his watch. "I'll check in on you in an hour— around lunchtime. Here's my cell number if you need anything before then." He paced toward her and held out a business card. "If you need to go anywhere before we're done with your car, stop by the shop. I've got one I can loan you."

She took the card. "Thank you, Matty."

He departed, and she withdrew her phone and checked the notifications.

Andrews Museum of Western Art—St. Pete, FL Cowboys and stuff. Van Gogh and Dali hardly sound WESTERN (???)

Not at all! So weird!

Dani retrieved the note she'd jotted from her purse. Mr. Osgood's message had said Franklin *emailed* about the pieces. She squinted at the laptop, then drew it into her lap. If he *was* up to something nefarious, would Franklin Sango be so stupid as to leave an obvious trail?

"Criminals aren't known for being the brightest bulbs in the box."

She opened the computer, and it fired to life.

CHAPTER TWO

The Andrews Museum of Western Art,
St. Petersburg, Florida—Present Day—Saturday

Think, Bradley. Mind on your work."

It didn't matter how many times Brad Osgood chided himself. Still, the computer cursor blinked at the top of the blank screen as if mocking him. He blew out a frustrated breath, shook himself, and once more squinted at the two 8x10 photographs of the bronze sculpture he was trying to describe.

One photograph of the fifteen-foot-high statue depicted a herd of bison stampeding down a mountainside while a wizened Native American man watched from its peak. The second photo showed the opposite side of the statue where, on the same mountain, a lonely cowboy stood watch over a herd of moving longhorns. It depicted the passage of time in the wild western lands, but the ability to articulate anything more had eluded him all morning.

His cell buzzed, and he grabbed it. Unfortunately, not the notification he'd been hoping for. Fear and disappointment coiled in his gut like a deadly snake.

"Lord, if You're up there and You're listening, I'm begging You. Give me *something* today."

He brought up the text message app and scrolled to the several-week-old message from an old high school friend a few weeks ago.

Saw Trey and Jazz in town last night. I'm worried. Have you talked to them lately?

The attached photo of his brother and sister-in-law only knotted his gut further. Both wore that familiar "high as a kite" look. Glassy, sunken eyes. Multiple sores. Skeletal frames. They'd likely been living in that state for a while. A long while.

A soft knock startled him, and he spun, turning the cell facedown as he did.

"I'm sorry." The new museum docent shot him an apologetic look. "Didn't mean to startle you. I'm heading down for the Saturday Sneak-a-Peek. Are you coming?"

"Oh, um. . ." He jiggled his computer mouse and checked the clock in the screen's corner. The children's program would start in twenty minutes. As he turned, his silenced cell gave off the extended buzz of an incoming call, and his heart lurched. "Let me take this, and I'll meet you down there."

"Yes, sir."

"Shut the door, please?"

As it closed, he snagged his phone and accepted the call.

"Brad Osgood."

"Hi, Mr. Osgood. My name is, um, Danielle. Dani. . .Sango."

At the hesitant voice on the other end, he glanced at the incoming number. A Tampa area code. His disappointment spiraled. *Not* the call he'd been waiting for. He leaned his elbow heavily on the desk and cradled his forehead in his hand.

"How can I help you, Dani?"

"You received an email from a Mr. Franklin a few weeks ago—about some pieces of Native American artwork?"

Had he? Since learning that his brother had relapsed, he'd hardly been able to keep a thought in his head. Again, he jiggled the mouse to enliven the computer screen and pulled up his email. Trapping the phone with his shoulder, he hit the search function and typed in *Franklin*. He glanced at the single result, and his memory jogged.

"Yes, about the ledger art."

"Right."

"I need to supervise a children's tour in a few minutes, but I'd be happy to give you and Mr. Franklin a call back in about an hour and a half."

A moment's hesitation, then a gentle exhale. "I hope you will. I'm curious about these pieces and hope you might shed some light on them for me. And just FYI, I'm *only* seeking information. Nothing more."

His brow furrowed. "I'll do my best to provide what information I can, Dani. I'm sorry. I missed your last name."

"Sango."

He scribbled the whispered name on a scrap of paper. "Is this the best number to reach you?"

"It is."

"It'll help if I'm able to see what we're discussing. Are you or Mr. Franklin able to email me pictures of the artwork?"

"I can do that."

"Perfect. Thanks. I'll take a look before I call you back." He rattled off his email address, bid her farewell, and ended the call. Jotting the number and her first name on the same scrap, he stared a moment. *Sango.* The name rang a bell, but why?

"A question for a later time."

He wrote a reminder to check for her email, then pocketed his phone and headed for the office suite's main door. As he stepped out, a tot with long dark ponytails and panicked brown eyes stood feet from the second-floor elevator. He stopped short, the heavy door smacking his shoulder blades as it closed. At his soft grunt, the young child turned his way, chin quivering, and loosed a plaintive wail.

Something lurched in his chest. *Brynn.* The urge to pick up the poor girl and hold her close, provide her the comfort and love Trey and Jazz obviously weren't, bubbled through him. But this wasn't Brynn—this was a young museum visitor who probably wandered off from her mom.

He squatted before the upset child. "Are you okay, sweetheart? Where's your mommy?"

Soft sobs rippling through her, she answered with only a shake of her head.

"You don't know?" He arched his brows.

"Nooooo." Her tears came faster.

"Okay. We'll find her."

The little girl gasped for breath.

Withdrawing his keycard, Brad unlocked the office door and stuck his head in. "Wendy, call down to security and ask Steve to meet me outside the second-floor elevator. I've got a lost little girl who wants to find her mom."

The secretary grinned. "He just radioed a museum-wide BOLO on a lost child. I'll let him know."

He turned back to the distraught child. "Don't cry, sweetheart. Mommy will be here in just a minute, okay?" He pointed toward the bench beside the elevator. "How about we sit? C'mon."

The girl continued to stand, crying. He stared, helpless—helpless to comfort her, helpless to stop the demons chasing his younger brother and his wife. . .and most of all, helpless to know what Trey and Jazz had done with four-year-old Brynn. All he knew was that, when he'd arrived in Cawley three weeks ago to check in on them, she was nowhere to be found. All his attempts to learn her fate resulted in frustration and anger. He'd been forced to call the police and file a missing persons report. Brad had stayed as long as he could, searching Cawley and surrounding areas, but his beautiful blond niece had vanished.

"It'll be all right. I promise. Mommy's on her way." He held out his hand. With coaxing, she finally slipped her tiny palm in his. At the same moment, the elevator dinged, and the doors slid open. The uniformed security officer, Steve, and a young woman stepped out. Relief flooded the woman's face as she looked their way.

"Chloe. Oh, thank God." She rushed to her daughter and swept the child into a bear hug.

The little girl clung to her mother.

Swallowing around the knot in his throat, Brad rose and shoved away the worst-case scenarios that bombarded him. *Lord, please, I'm begging You. Let there be a happy ending for Brynn.*

"You found her?" The woman shook visibly.

"Yes, ma'am. Brad Osgood, acting curator."

"Thank you so much. I was purchasing our tickets, and when I turned around, she was gone."

"I pushed the buttons on the elebator, Mommy." Chloe sniffled loudly. "Just like you said."

A flash of exasperation dissolved into chagrin. "Silly girl." The woman rubbed Chloe's back. "You have to wait for me. Always."

Brad smiled. "I'm glad she's safe. I hope you'll enjoy the museum today."

"Thank you. We were going to do the Sneak-a-Peek tour, but I'm not sure I'm up to it after this."

He forced a smile. "I understand." All too well. "The tour's not scheduled to start for another ten minutes or so. If you're still not ready at that point, I'd be more than happy to have another docent take you on a private tour when you are. Or we'll get your name on the list for another day."

"Thank you." At her request, he directed her to the restroom and told her to meet him in the lobby once she'd had time to collect herself. As she and her child headed around the corner, Brad and the security guard walked toward the large staircase overlooking one of the many bronze statues in the museum's entrance.

"Thanks for your quick work, Steve. You did well."

Steve nodded. "Helped that you found her so fast. Could've been a lot worse."

He nearly choked on the innocent comment. *Lord, please. . .*

They reached the lobby and parted ways, Brad finding the docent in the midst of the milling group of parents and children.

"Nervous?" he asked in a hushed tone as the young woman watched the children interact with each other.

"I've survived subbing in classrooms with double or triple this number of kids, so this small group should be easy. I'm more worried about remembering the facts about the artwork."

At that moment, his cell vibrated against his leg, and he dragged the device from his trouser pocket to look at the number. A Cawley area code. His heart thudded heavily.

"Excuse me. I've been expecting this call." He barged through the front doors and out into the sunshine. There, he clicked into the call. "Brad Osgood."

"Mr. Osgood. This is Lieutenant Al Lipscomb of—"

"Do you have news about Brynn?" He headed to a shaded corner of the museum's wide entry and pressed his back to the tall stone wall.

"We've found her."

Oh God, please. . . He shot a pleading glance heavenward. "And?"

"She's pretty shaken up, but she doesn't appear to be injured."

His legs went soft, and he sat heavily on the sandstone bench a few feet away. "She's alive."

"Yes. We're transporting her to the hospital now, just to be certain she's unharmed."

"Good. Thank you." For a moment, he couldn't unjumble the long string of questions enough to find one to ask. Finally, a word settled on his tongue. "Where. . .?"

As the lieutenant rattled off the particulars of the hospital, Brad pulled the pen from his golf shirt's collar and scribbled the name and address on his left palm.

"I'm in Florida now. It'll take me several hours to get up there. Should I head straight to the hospital, or—?"

"If you'll call me when you're about an hour out, I'll give you further instructions."

"All right. Thank you." The string of questions unraveled a bit more, and he cringed at his next inquiry. "Where was she?"

Silence flowed from the other end of the line. "We're still investigating, but we got a tip based on news reports we've run. Someone called saying a young child matching Brynn's description was seen with the girlfriend of a known drug dealer in a neighboring town. We found her there."

Brad leaned an elbow on his knee and cradled his head in his hand as a bajillion what-ifs ran through his mind.

"Did you arrest them?"

"We've detained both, as well as your brother and sister-in-law. Like I said, we're still investigating."

Anger roiled through him at Trey and Jazz. "I need to tie up a few loose ends here, and I'll be on my way. I hope to be there by dinnertime."

"I'll be waiting to hear from you."

Brad clicked out of the call.

This would change everything.

Brunswick, Georgia—Later That Evening

"Brynn Osgood's room?" The colorful walls of the hospital's pediatric wing did little to calm Brad's racing heart.

"And you are?" The middle-aged nurse planted a fist on her ample hip. Could she not see his computer-printed visitor tag? "I'm Br—"

"It's all right, Luann." Lieutenant Lipscomb's familiar voice rang out, and relief washed through Brad. He turned to find the officer, dressed in plain clothes, striding down the hall toward him. "This is Brad Osgood, the child's uncle." Lipscomb came alongside Brad. "He's a good man, and you've got my permission to allow him in to see little Brynn."

"Well, then." She returned her focus to Brad. "Room 328, sugar. Straight at the end of this hall. I'll alert her nurse that you've arrived."

"Thank you!" Brad rushed from the desk, the small Minnie Mouse suitcase he'd bought for Brynn in one hand, his own backpack in the other. As the lieutenant fell in beside him, Brad shot him a sidelong glance. "Why's Brynn here? You said she wasn't injured."

"She's dehydrated, and the poor thing was so beside herself, she wouldn't stop crying, so the doctor in St. Marys chose to have her transported here to the pediatric unit for observation. Just overnight."

"Was that really necessary? She must be terrified."

"They sedated her before transport, so she's been asleep this whole time. And by keeping her, the doctor gave you time to get here and prevent her from the ordeal of an emergency foster care placement. We all thought that might be more traumatic than sleeping through an overnight hospital stay and waking up to a familiar face."

The words stalled Brad's charge as shame cascaded through him. He'd not thought of it that way. "Thank you, and I'm sorry. I've been out of my m—"

"No apology needed." Lipscomb shot him an understanding smile.

"What *did* happen to her? Has Trey said anything?"

The lieutenant's expression turned grim. "We've questioned your brother and sister-in-law, as well as the pair Brynn was found with—and we've arrested them all."

"For what?" He tightened his grip on both bags. "Were they so broke they sold their only child for another high?"

"I can't share the details of an open case, but I'll tell you there are multiple charges against them, and at least one of those charges carries a maximum sentence of twenty years."

"Twenty years?" He swallowed around the knot in his throat. "She'll be out of college by then."

Lipscomb clamped a hand on his shoulder. "She'll have the opportunity to *go* to college because you'll provide her a more stable home and better upbringing than what your brother's given her so far."

Fears bombarded him for the hundredth time. "You act like getting custody of Brynn is a done deal." He'd take her in a heartbeat, but would the court consider giving *him* custody?

"Between the signed affidavits I have from Trey and Jazz *asking* that you take custody of their daughter, your willingness to take her, as well as my testimony, I don't see much chance the courts would deny you."

He made it sound so easy.

Lipscomb nodded toward a door. "C'mon. Let's get you to your niece."

Inside, a woman in business casual glanced up from the tall stack of files on the room's built-in desk. At the sight of them, she stood.

Brad's attention flew past her to the bed where one tiny lump marred the otherwise pristine bedclothes. Brynn. *Lord God, thank You!* Her blond hair fanned across the pillow, and her cherubic face peeked from above the blankets. One spindly arm rested atop the covers, a tiny IV taped across the back of her hand. Ignoring Lipscomb and the woman, Brad made for the bed, dropping the backpack and suitcase on the foot of it.

"Brynn, do you hear me? It's Uncle Brad." He laid a hand on her hair and kissed her forehead. "I'm here now, sweetie."

"She's still sedated." The woman's voice was familiar. "The doctor said once you arrived, they'd consider tapering that off."

He turned her way. "Miranda Edwards?"

"Hi, Brad." She smiled shyly. "It's Miranda Dempsey now. Got married about ten years ago."

"You two know each other?" Lipscomb arched a brow.

Miranda shrugged. "We're old friends from high school."

"Don't you mean academic rivals?" He'd always been one step behind Miranda—one point lower on every test, second place in every way.

She hung her head. "I was rather obnoxious, wasn't I?"

Good of her to admit it—more than a decade late.

"What're you doing here?"

"I'm a social worker. When I saw the news reports about a little girl named Osgood who'd disappeared from Cawley, I figured it might be some relation of yours, so I asked to be assigned the case."

"Why?"

"The personal connection. Wanting to help an old friend. After all you've been through with Trey, I thought maybe you could use a friend in your corner now."

As much as she'd been a long-ago thorn in his side, her answer humbled him. "Thank you. I wasn't expecting this."

Lipscomb grinned. "You're fortunate. She's got a real heart for this job, and she's a bulldog."

Brad brushed his niece's soft curls. *If this is You, God, thanks. We could use a bulldog.* "So what'll happen next?"

"I'll try to get an emergency custody hearing on Monday. If not then, it'll definitely happen by Friday. But based on what the lieutenant has told me, there's no reason the judge would refuse you temporary custody."

"Temporary?"

"It's the first step. Permanent custody will take longer, but I'm sure you'll get that too."

"It's all right for me to stay here with her tonight—without custody?"

"Absolutely. Waking up to a familiar face will be her best medicine."

It would do *him* good too. "Thank you." He stifled a yawn. "Sorry." He'd not had a full night's sleep since the text message he'd received weeks ago asking about Trey and Jazz.

"Why don't you get some rest. The nurse can bring bedding for the sleeper chair." Lipscomb nodded toward the recliner. "Miranda and I can return tomorrow to cover everything else. Between nine thirty and ten?"

Miranda smiled. "Works for me."

With a brief farewell, the lieutenant departed.

"Do you need anything before I go?" Miranda's gaze was full of concern.

"No. . .thanks."

"If you don't mind, I'll finish the note I was making before I pack this mess and get out of your hair."

"That's fine." He opened his backpack and removed the hand-crocheted horse he'd bought from the museum giftshop and tucked it next to Brynn. After staring at her for a moment, he pulled his laptop from the backpack, sat in the recliner, and opened the machine. A scrap of paper with his handwriting fluttered from between screen and keyboard and landed on the floor. He retrieved it.

Dani Sango. Re: Native American ledger art. (Check emails.)

"Crud." He'd forgotten all about her.

Miranda's curious look caught his attention. "You all right?"

"I was supposed to return a phone call, but there's an email I need to look over first, and—" He waved a hand at the sterile-looking room. "I don't suppose there's much chance I'll be connecting to the internet here, is there?"

"Have you eaten anything today?"

"What?"

"Food." She pantomimed spooning something into her mouth. "There's a Wi-Fi hotspot in both the cafeteria and the coffee shop downstairs. If you want to grab a quick something to eat, you can download your emails. I'll stay with Brynn."

"I don't want to leave her."

"I understand, but you're not doing her any good if you don't take care of yourself. Please, Brad."

His gaze snagged again on the name. Dani Sango. Why was it so familiar? "You'll stay with Brynn?"

"Gladly."

After a moment's hesitation, he snapped the laptop shut and dropped it into the backpack's padded pocket. "I promise I won't be long."

He kissed Brynn's hair and navigated to the first-floor cafeteria. There, he purchased a light meal, parked himself at a table, and again fished the laptop from his bag. Once he'd connected to the Wi-Fi, he watched as emails began to download, then pulled up a search engine and typed the last name *Sango*.

The first handful of search results linked to articles about a recent car accident where a Franklin Sango died in St. Augustine. He squinted at the screen, then flipped back to his emails, typing the name in the search bar. Four results came back—the one from weeks ago, sent by a Mr.

Franklin—only days before the accident mentioned in the articles, and three in the newly downloaded batch from Dani Sango.

Returning to the search results, he skimmed articles for more detail. Late in one piece, a line thrown in almost as an afterthought triggered his memory.

Sango, convicted of art forgery in 1995, had turned his artistic talents to better uses in recent years, working for Joie-Rides Restoration and Custom Creations in St. Augustine.

So was Mr. Franklin the art forger, Franklin Sango?

He scanned for an obituary and read through the brief paragraphs for the information he sought. *Frank leaves behind one beloved daughter, Danielle.*

Or Dani for short.

The beloved daughter of a convicted forger—one he'd heard about in his college studies and within the art world afterward. Why, in heaven's name, would she be following up on an email her ex-con father sent days before his death? Had Franklin Sango been trying to play Brad? Was this some forgery scam? And was Dani Sango following in her father's footsteps? If so, why choose *him* as their dupe?

Mind warring with questions, Brad clicked into the first of Ms. Sango's emails and pulled up one of the attachments. He squinted at the unique specimen. Hardly like the examples of ledger art he'd come across before. He zoomed in to see more detail. Staring at the screen did little to convince him whether it was real or fake.

His focus returned to his surroundings. The hospital cafeteria. Better get back upstairs to Brynn. He blew out a breath, then rattled off a quick email to Dani Sango.

> *Ms. Sango, forgive my delay in responding. There's been an emergency in my family, and I've had to leave town unexpectedly. I will get back to you once things are more settled.*
>
> *Brad Osgood*
> *Acting Curator*
> *Andrews Museum of Western Art*

There. Hopefully that would hold this woman at bay until he could process what the daughter of a forger wanted with him.

He picked at the food he'd purchased and set his email to respond with an "out of town" message, then stowed his computer and trashed the remains of the tasteless sandwich. Returning to Brynn's room, he found Miranda had packed all but one file, which lay open in front of her.

"Get what you needed?"

"I did, thanks."

She tucked the file into an overstuffed leather briefcase. "The nurse made up the sleeper chair. If you need anything overnight, here's my card." She held it out to him. "I'll see you around ten tomorrow morning."

"Thanks."

After she left, he caressed Brynn's arm, smoothed her blond curls, and pondered just how his life would have to change with a four-year-old in tow—*if* the court awarded him custody.

Finally, he settled in the chair with his computer. Clicking on the first attachment from Dani Sango's email, he stared at the rudimentary depiction. If Franklin Sango forged the picture, he'd captured the very basic style of ledger art well. Brad zoomed in, moving the cursor around to see the various parts of the picture up close.

A long, single-file line of Native Americans, each with their hands and feet shackled, walked in between two rows of soldiers. Around the three lines of figures, a sea of featureless faces—except for two. A blond woman in a big dress stood in the path of the oncoming columns, blue eyes wide with surprise. Beside her, a taller man, also blond, with spectacles, pulled at her hand. To one side of the marching lines, multiple masts and ships' riggings rose in the distance, and to the other, a large stone wall—almost like a medieval fort.

He'd not seen another piece of ledger art like it, which made this more than intriguing. But the attachment to Franklin Sango soured his interest.

Maybe if he conveniently lost her number and email, Dani Sango would move on to another dupe.

CHAPTER THREE

Sarah Mather's Home, St. Augustine, Florida—Thursday, May 20, 1875

*H*e said he admired our hearts in the matter, but the church couldn't help." Sally Jo Harris bristled afresh at Father Simeon Gabler's words.

"Oh dear." Sarah Mather frowned and set her teacup on its saucer. "Did he say why?"

Sally Jo prepared to answer, though Luke Worthing beat her to it. "He said the w-war hit everyone hard, even in Florida. People are still struggling to get back on their f-f-feet all these years later."

By rote, she watched Sarah closely as Luke spoke. God bless her—the woman didn't react to his stammering in the slightest, though Sally Jo should've known better than to expect her to. Sarah had known Luke far longer than she. In fact, it was Sarah who'd introduced them by letter, seeing as they both shared the same dream.

Luke continued. "He said because of. . .that, the church coffers have grown thin, and there's no m-m-money to help sponsor us to a foreign mission field."

"He said he hesitates to ask the membership to give more when they're already stretched so tight." Sally Jo clamped her eyes shut. "I can't help but wonder if it's because of Luke's difficulty with speech rather than the coffers being thin."

"It might be." Luke laid his hand over hers. "I t-tried to tell you this wouldn't be easy."

Yes, and she should've listened. He'd written her across the last three years about numerous rejections he'd received in his quest to share the

Gospel in foreign lands. Why had she thought asking her own church would turn out differently? She'd let herself assume Father Gabler would see what was so obvious to her—that once she and Luke were married, they'd be ready for such service. That any difficulty he had with speech would be diminished as she came alongside him as wife and ministry partner.

Oh, how naive! She'd failed to prepare her heart for the disappointments Luke warned her would come.

Sarah's mouth thinned into a grim line. "I doubt Father Gabler is fibbing. I think we have no idea how much the war affected the men who fought." She pinned Sally Jo with a firm glance. "You've said yourself that you see it in your father. He came back a changed man. Surely that ripples into all areas of their lives."

"But Papa has continued to provide. I would dare say better than before the war." He was far more emotionally distant—something she lamented daily, especially since Mama's death almost five years ago—but no one could fault his earnings.

"Yes, my dear, but your father made connections during the conflict that led to his appointment as a federal judge. Men who returned ten years ago missing a leg or an arm, or those who still battle demons we can't possibly know—or families whose menfolk didn't return at all—they have had to pick up the pieces of their farms, businesses, and lives and are still struggling."

Heat washed through her at the gentle scolding. "I don't mean to be insensitive. Of course, you're right. Papa and I are very fortunate, I know."

The gentle squeeze Luke gave her hand was reassuring. "God has b-blessed you both."

"Yes. And I am sorry for allowing my impatience to rule. All too many *are* still hurting, and I have no room to complain."

Only she *could*. Papa was far moodier than when she was a child. He'd always been stern, but prior to the war, they'd shared precious moments, snuggling together while they both read, or sweet moments holding his hand while they walked to church. The pride that once shone in his eyes when people complimented her had long ago seemed to wane.

After his return from the war, he was more strict. Quiet and watchful. Rarely smiling. Even more seldom did he give any outward show of affection. He'd become far more concerned with how her actions appeared to others. He and Mama fought more, or perhaps she'd matured enough to be more aware of their fighting.

And after Mama's drowning accident, he'd withdrawn yet more, grieving alone, as if she hadn't also lost someone very dear. Sarah—one of Mama's precious friends—had been the one to help her through her grief, far more than Papa did.

"Do not fear, love. We serve a good God." Luke brushed the back of his hand against hers.

Sally Jo shook off the memories. "Are you telling me this doesn't bother you?"

"No. It hurts. But after twenty-five years of reject. . .tions, I have learned He will make the path clear."

She swallowed her frustration. "You're right. If God wants us to reach the mission field, He will provide the means and the way."

"Exactly." Sarah sipped her tea. "Did Father Gabler have anything more to say?"

Luke brushed Sally Jo's hand again as he straightened. "Yes. If we truly wish to s-serve immediately, he could recommend ways here in St. Augustine. We told him we would p-pray about it." He checked his pocket watch. "Come, love. I need to get to work."

Sally Jo forced a brave smile to her lips, all the while warring within.

Lord, it is not that I don't want to serve here—I would be pleased to help anyone I can. But You said every tribe and tongue and people and nation. Didn't You?

Tocoi, Florida, twenty miles east of St. Augustine—Friday, May 21, 1875

Arms full of his meager belongings, Broken Bow shuffled over the bobbing wooden plank that spanned the gap between the strange-looking raft with the giant red wheel at its back and the wooden platform that extended out over the water. He reached the platform and hobbled ahead, the iron shackles around his ankles making walking difficult. He ached to feel earth and grass under his moccasins once more. When finally he stepped on solid ground, he moved out of the line of other captives, dropped his pack, and sat, heavy chains at his wrists and ankles rattling with his effort.

His stomach roiled as he stared at the unfamiliar thing that had carried them downriver. A raft he was used to. The Tsitsistas used them on occasion when they crossed great rivers. This, though—it was like no raft he'd seen before. Not with its tall profile and even taller pipe that belched black smoke. Nor had he seen a raft with a great wheel to churn the water rather than strong men with paddles or poles to move it along. What turned the wheel to churn the waters? It happened by some strange and powerful medicine.

His brother, Painted Sky, shuffled across the wood plank and down the platform, finally reaching the grass. There, he ducked toward him. Broken Bow looked away, hoping Sky would go elsewhere. Instead, he circled to Broken Bow's right and sat.

"Do not tell me you are still sick, brother."

"Fine." He looked across the river, avoiding Sky's gaze. "I will not tell you."

Sky chuckled with humor and sympathy. "How can you ride a horse with great speed and face great dangers in hunting and battle, but traveling on this medicine raft or the iron road sours your stomach?"

"Why do you laugh? Were you not one leaning over the iron road, spitting up food in those early days?" He turned the full weight of his anger on his brother. "Many of us have been sick, I among them." Their lean frames and gaunt cheeks testified to that fact.

Maybe for some it was the strange motions and the speed on the iron road that caused the food to curdle in their bellies. For him, it wasn't the rocking or the *clack-clacking* that rattled their seats. Not after the first day or two. No, it was the knowledge that after years of warring with the white man over his broken promises, the Tsitsistas leaders had surrendered. *Surrendered!* They agreed that their people would move to a reservation—a bleak land with small borders and no way to hunt buffalo. It was no place to live.

Worse, he and these men had been separated, chosen as the worst offenders against their captors' ways. They'd been taken from the reservation—from their parents, wives, and children—to go even farther.

When anyone asked what land they traveled to, they were told *Florida*. Already, they'd traveled almost a full moon. Perhaps that was the price they were being made to pay—to always move for the remainder of their days with no rest.

White Chief Pratt approached with his translator, Rafael Romero, and both came to stand beside Painted Sky. The yellow-haired chief, a man of at least thirty summers, maybe more—he never could accurately tell a white man's age—smiled and spoke in his tongue.

Romero looked at them in turn. "White Chief asks if you men are well."

Broken Bow drew his knees up. "I was better before you two approached."

Romero, of Tsitsistas and Mexican blood, shot him a stern look. "That answer will not satisfy White Chief."

"Tell the chief—"

"Brother." Painted Sky caught his arm. "Speak carefully."

With effort, Broken Bow gathered his small pack and pushed to his feet. "Tell him I am tired and wish to know how long we must keep going."

To Broken Bow's surprise, the chief answered Romero's translation in a seemingly compassionate tone.

"He says your journey will end today after one more short ride on the iron road."

A seed of hope sprouted in Broken Bow's heart. Was it true? Would they soon be allowed to rest from this wearying journey?

"Today. . ." Painted Sky spoke the word softly as he stood.

"Well before the sun sets." Romero nodded.

A smile curved Painted Sky's lips, and his tentative chuckle bloomed to a full-fledged laugh. "This is reason to celebrate, is it not, Brother?" He elbowed Broken Bow. At the happy exclamation, others approached, crowding around to hear.

While the news filtered through their ranks and their excited chatter surrounded him, Broken Bow eyed White Chief Pratt, any momentary hope he'd allowed himself dying just as quickly.

"What is wrong, Brother?" Painted Sky whispered. "Why do you not celebrate this news?"

"You are a fool if you trust his lies. This promise that our journey will end today before sunset probably means that they will line us all up and shoot us at dusk."

St. Augustine, Florida—Friday, May 21, 1875—An hour later

The summer sun blazed across the Matanzas River. Sailing vessels of different shapes and sizes moved past, sails billowing and snapping. Still others sat at anchor, bobbing on the sparkling water, masts dancing lazily. Sailors bustled up and down the docks, some carrying crates or packs while others walked empty-handed in groups.

"I can't believe you were able to surprise me with this." Sally Jo breathed deep, filling her lungs with the salt air. "I've wanted to paint the river and the boats for—"

"As long as I've known you. And today's a g-good day for it. The *Mystic* is back."

"Mama's favorite ship. She'd get almost giddy when it came into port. We'd come down here to look at the boats when I was a little girl."

Sally Jo had very fond memories of those times. Papa never understood. . .always forbade it, especially after Mama's death. He said this was no place for a young woman alone. Maybe he was right. Maybe if Mama hadn't been alone, she wouldn't have fallen in and drowned. But in more than one of her letters to Luke, Sally Jo had spilled her frustration that Papa made it sound like the sailors themselves had done something to her, so he would never make time to accompany her on such an outing.

Yet Luke made the time. "How did you smuggle my easel, a canvas, and some painting supplies into the buggy without my knowledge?"

"S-Sarah helped."

"I should have known." When Papa became so overprotective after Mama died, Sarah had provided balance. The sixty-year-old woman was bold and opinionated enough to speak reason to Sally Jo's father, and she was one of the very few Papa would listen to.

Despite Father Gabler's disappointing answer the previous day, her heart was happy. *Indeed, God, You* are *good to me!*

Paintbrush in one hand, palette in the other, she drank in the sight of the docks and the river. She dipped her brush into the dollop of blue paint and mixed it with a hint of white, softening the intensity of the color, then applied it to her canvas in broad strokes.

Luke crowded in, peering over her shoulder. "Beautiful."

She chuckled. "I've barely started, silly!" Despite her thrill at his nearness, she nudged him gently, hinting to give her space. When he didn't back up, she turned. "It's a few blue streaks. Nothing more."

"I did. . .didn't mean the painting."

"Oh." She bit her lower lip. "Thank you." Could he be any more charming? "How has God gifted me with such a prize?" As she turned more fully toward him, a crowd gathering near Fort Marion caught her eye. Her focus on him, she stood on tiptoes to kiss his cheek.

"Some will think you a f-fool for thinking of me as a prize."

Her chest constricted at the truth of his statement. She'd seen, during three years of Luke's letters flowing with beautiful, descriptive language, just how intelligent and sweet he was. "Those who hear only how you labor to speak, rather than glimpsing the pure and lovely heart from which your words flow, can think what they will. It is their loss. You're a rare and wonderful man, Luke Worthing."

"Thank you for. . .seeing the real me."

She reached to cup his cheek with her hand, but her loaded paintbrush caught the tip of his chin, leaving a wide blue splotch in its wake. Her mouth fell open. "Oh! Forgive me!"

They both laughed, and she whirled to grab a rag from her basket. As she did, her attention shifted again to the growing crowd gathering near the huge coquina fort down the street.

"What're you doin' there, pretty lady?" Three disheveled sailors approached, the speaker taking a nip from a squatty brown bottle before passing it to one of the others. "You painting portraits, missy?"

"No, sir." She grabbed the rag and handed it off to Luke.

"Ain't you s'posed to put the paint on the canvas not on the person?" Another of the three guffawed.

Her heart rate rose, and Luke tensed beside her. The men were obviously inebriated.

"I'd planned to paint the river and the beautiful boats."

The first speaker trotted up to stand where he could see the beginnings of her painting while the other two struck ridiculous poses a few feet from her easel.

"Paint us, missy!" One of the others tilted the bottle to his lips as he threw his free arm around his friend's shoulders. The third fellow folded his arms, stilling his features into a smirk.

"Aw, she ain't painted nothin' but her fella!" The first stared at the canvas. "I could do better! I'll show you." He stepped nearer, the scents of rum and sweat washing over her as he grasped the edge of Sally Jo's palette. With his firm tug, her thumb torqued in the hole, and she yelped as her arm twisted painfully, the paintbrush falling to the ground.

Luke grabbed the man's wrist. "S-s-stop!"

Even as the startled sailor released the pressure without letting go completely, Luke slid between her and the drunken man. "Leave her alone. N-n-now."

For one stunned instant, the man stared before the trio burst into laughter.

"What are ye—an eejit?" the smirking third man piped in a thick Scottish burr as he grabbed the brown bottle from the second.

Her arm still bent at an odd angle, though not so painfully as before, Sally Jo wheedled her thumb free and straightened, her heart pounding. "You'll not call him that, you. . .you. . .addlepated dunderhead!"

The Scotsman balked. "What'd the wee lass just call me?"

She took a step around the easel toward him. "An addlepated dunderhead. And you, sir. . ." She turned back and stabbed a finger toward the one still holding her palette. "You are a boorish dolt. And you stink to high heaven!" She fanned the air in front of her nose. "Now return my things and be gone, the three of you!"

"Miss Harris." A familiar voice from the direction of the military barracks across the street rang out. "Is everything all right?"

Several uniformed soldiers trotted toward them, Sergeant Walt Pearson in the lead.

The sight of them sent a shot of calm through her, and Luke's posture eased as well.

"I *do* believe these men were about to leave, but perhaps you could escort them to their destination?" She nodded at the drunken bunch.

"Glad to, miss!" The sergeant and those with him picked up their pace.

The one holding her palette growled and jammed it toward Luke. "No need for that! We're just goin' to see the show at the fort!"

Luke barely received the paint-spattered wood before the boor released it and stomped off. His inebriated friends trudged after, the Scot stopping long enough to take a flourishing bow.

"Good day to ye both, *Your Hind Ends*—I mean, highnesses."

"Move along!" Sergeant Pearson gave him a shove.

He grumbled but didn't fight, and the soldiers herded them away.

Sally Jo studied her throbbing thumb.

"Are you all right?" Luke laid the palette aside and also studied the fast-bruising skin below the second joint of her left thumb. Spying the growing mark, he gently took her hand. "Y-you're not."

"I'm fine." She moved the offended digit and proved she still had the full range of motion. A grim attempt at a smile wobbled her lips. "I suppose this is why Papa never wanted me to come here alone." *Or at all.*

Luke nodded.

"Thank you—for stepping in."

"Miss?" An older gentleman with dark hair liberally streaked with gray approached from the docks. He was oddly familiar, though she couldn't place why.

Pearson returned then. "Are you well, Miss Harris? Unharmed?"

She looked first at the older man, then peeked around Luke's sturdy frame toward the soldier. "I'm fine, thank you, Sergeant."

"Did they cause any damage to your belongings? Should we detain them?"

"There's no need for that."

The young sergeant seemed unconvinced. "Judge Harris won't—"

"My father won't know any of this even happened, because none of us are going to tell him about it, are we?"

A quick lift of her chin set the man's head bobbing. "Absolutely, miss. The secret is safe here."

"I appreciate that." She smiled sweetly, then turned toward the other man. "Did you need something, sir?"

For an odd instant, he stared, his lips slightly parted. "No, miss. Just wanted to be sure my men hadn't harmed you." He growled at Pearson as he strode away. "Call off the dogs. I'll make sure they don't harass Miss Harris again."

Pearson sneered as he watched the soldiers herding the drunken sailors.

She arched a brow at him. "One of the men mentioned something happening at the fort. What's going on?"

"Oh, I was wonderin' if you and your, ah. . .friend?"—he glanced Luke's way—"were down here to watch the spectacle."

"Forgive me. Sergeant, this is my beau, Luke Worthing. Luke, this is Sergeant Walt Pearson."

"I am p-pleased to make your acquaintance." Luke extended a hand in greeting.

Pearson pumped Luke's hand, though his grin faltered—whether due to Luke's stammering or her pronouncement that he was her beau, she couldn't decide. "Mr. Worthing."

"You were saying, Sergeant? About the *spectacle*?"

"Surely you're joshin'. Your pa didn't tell you about the interesting newcomers we're gettin'?"

"It must have slipped his mind. Do tell."

At the sound of a faint train whistle in the distance, Pearson's smile faltered. "I've got to go. The train's arrivin', miss." He took a couple of steps but turned back. "Why don't y'all come. I'm just bettin' you won't have seen anything like it."

She squinted as he rejoined the other soldiers who'd come to their aid. As the six trotted off, curiosity gnawed. "He's piqued my interest. What hasn't Papa shared?" And why wouldn't he have told her?

Luke shrugged.

"Shall we investigate?"

"You don't want to p-paint?"

"I do, but I'm curious." Sally Jo faced Fort Marion. "I haven't taken you to see the fort yet, and how often will we get to experience. . .whatever this will be?"

At his tentative glance toward her easel, she gripped his hand. "I can't tell you how much I appreciate the sweet gesture to bring me here, but the docks will be available to paint on other days. Whatever might happen at the fort could be a once-in-a-lifetime experience."

He finally nodded. "A-all right."

She squeezed his hand. "Thank you!"

Luke loaded her belongings into the buggy again, and they walked the short distance to the fort, where the growing crowd gathered. By the time they reached it, they had to take up station near the fork where the path from the street split, one portion doubling back toward Fort Marion's entrance and the other continuing toward the river beyond.

Once in place, minutes ticked by before anything happened, and when it finally did, several wagons rumbled up the busy street and stopped. Beyond the thick crowd, soldiers buzzed about, helping people from the wagons—though at her distance, she couldn't tell who. All she could see was that two lines of soldiers formed, and the crowd seemed to hold its collective breath in anticipation of what was about to happen.

"Can you see?" she whispered to Luke, who was standing behind and to one side of her.

"N-no."

"Make way! Back up!" The cry came from far up the line where the soldiers had formed.

The crowd widened out, making space for the lines of soldiers to advance. As they moved, a metallic rattle sounded. Sally Jo shaded her eyes, straining to see who—or what—approached. As the lines neared, she finally saw that, sandwiched between the two lines of soldiers was a ragtag line of bare-chested men, each with dark eyes and long, black hair. Several wore white feathers at the backs of their heads, the tips peeking to one side or the other.

Indians.

Her heart ached in her chest at the sight of the gaunt, shackled men shuffling nearer. The first Indian's face was a stoic mask, but there was no mistaking the fact he was taking everything in, watching, prepared for danger from whatever direction he perceived it to come.

"What is this?" She whispered the words toward Luke.

"You don't know?" Athol Kemp, the storekeeper, turned on her from where he watched nearby.

Being the daughter of a federal judge, she was often one of the first to know things, but not today. "Enlighten me, Mr. Kemp. *Please.*"

"They're incarcerating the worst of the Indian braves—them that's brought war against the whites out on the western plains."

"Move back! Make way!" an approaching soldier shouted.

The crowd around them shuffled back several feet, and someone else sounded off. "Honest to goodness, I don't know why they didn't just lynch 'em out there and be done with it. Why go to such effort for a bunch of heathens?"

She gaped at the man. "You should be ashamed of yourself, sir."

Luke cleared his throat roughly. "Sally Jo!" He reached for her hand, tugging on it gently, though she wiggled free of his grasp to stare at the man beside Mr. Kemp.

"Are these not the very ones Matthew twenty-five speaks of? Are these not the hungry, the thirsty, the sick, the strangers, and the prisoners? If we feed, clothe, and care for the least of these, do we not do it unto Christ Himself?"

Mr. Kemp and the fellow beside him both stared, and each took two big steps backward, even as Luke swooped nearer and looped a strong arm around her waist. "Come. Now!"

When she turned toward the approaching line of soldiers and Indians, her stomach dropped. No longer approaching. Rather, they stood, waiting for her to move. Heat swept through her.

She gulped a breath as her gaze fell again on the first Indian. Tall and broad shouldered, his stoic expression had been replaced with contempt and distrust. Sally Jo locked gazes with him, recognizing the same haggard look she recalled from the soldiers returning home from war a decade ago. The poor man.

At the front of the line, an unfamiliar lieutenant in a pristine dress uniform cleared his throat.

"P-pardon her," Luke said as he ushered her out of the pathway.

For an instant longer, the line stalled there, soldiers, Indians, and spectators staring at her.

"Forgive me." If only the earth might open and swallow her whole.

"What is your name, ma'am?"

Oh, this couldn't possibly be good. "Sally Jo Harris, sir. And it's *miss*— not *ma'am*."

A flash of surprise rounded his eyes, though he quickly schooled his features. "Please give me one hour to get the prisoners settled, then meet me outside the fort. I have a matter to discuss with you."

He gave a sharp hand motion, and the sharp cry came again.

"Move back. Make way!"

Surely, she'd get two earfuls—one from the lieutenant and one from Papa. The only thing that might save her from a third was Luke's stammering.

CHAPTER FOUR

*A*larm gripped Broken Bow as the bluecoats herded him and the other prisoners toward the massive, high-walled structure. He'd never seen a place so large nor one made of stone blocks. Any white man's structures he'd seen were tiny in comparison, made from stacked squares of grass or sometimes wood. Nothing like this. What evils happened inside?

As they reached a sharp bend in the path, the line of bluecoats to his left stopped, though the other line, led by White Chief, continued on. As the first prisoner in line, Broken Bow shuffled beside White Chief. Once they made the sharp turn, the path narrowed so only two could walk abreast. The chief ushered him over a wooden platform, not unlike the one he'd crossed leaving the medicine raft earlier, only this one spanned grass, not water. The chief guided him toward a second, longer wooden walkway. On its other end, the gaping mouth of a dark cave cut through the stone structure. His heart stuttered, and he stalled. The rattling steps of the others also faltered. White Chief stopped and offered him a sympathetic smile.

The chief spoke a word in his liar's tongue and beckoned Broken Bow forward.

On the far side of the open-ended cave, bright sunlight shone on green grass, but still his skin crawled with dread. If he stepped into the darkness, passed through this cave, there would be no escape. He sensed it.

White Chief Pratt made the sign for *come*, then motioned to the black opening.

Behind him, Painted Sky settled his shackled hands at Broken Bow's shoulder. "What is the problem?"

"This is not a good place. I do not trust what waits for us inside."

His brother grumbled and gave him a gentle nudge. "You can see what waits—grass and sunlight. Do not let your fear hold everyone up."

"I am not *afraid*! I am careful."

"Go!" Painted Sky pushed him, causing Broken Bow to totter forward a step. "Before you bring trouble to us all."

White Chief Pratt signed again. *Come inside. You Eat. You Sleep. It is safe.*

Safe. He gritted his teeth. Nothing about white men was safe. They'd proven it over and over. Yet weariness pulled at him. He had fought so hard, moved for so long. Food and rest would be a welcome change. With a great sigh, he plodded forward, wary eyes roving the darkness ahead. Chills swept him as he plunged into the cave and, as much as the iron chains would allow, he hurried through, slowing as he stepped into the sunlight once more.

"Keep moving." Painted Sky gave him another shove and, feet tangling, Broken Bow staggered, nearly losing his balance. The fool! He glared at Sky, started to follow him, but when his brother's mouth fell agape, Broken Bow really looked at their surroundings.

Four high stone walls towered over them, enclosing this patch of grass. Square openings, large enough for at least two men to walk abreast, dotted the inside walls. Those openings appeared to lead to other caverns with more of a twilight appearance than the full black of the two-ended cave. He squinted at the nearest opening and saw wood boxes stacked high inside. Two bluecoats stepped out, carrying a box between them toward a cavern on the far wall. They set the box down and returned, only to repeat the process.

At each corner, armed bluecoats watched both from the ground and atop the walls. The now-familiar sight snapped him from his wonder at the sheer size of this fortress, their presence a stark reminder they were still prisoners. More prisoners now than on the arduous journey, for they were trapped in this stone-block mountain. He glanced at the many openings and tried to picture the outside of this place. There was only one way in or out that he'd seen—the way they'd just come.

"Tsitsistas and Hinono-eino," Romero called in a loud voice. "This way!"

His tribesmen moved toward the cavern where the two bluecoats had deposited the boxes. Over his left shoulder, George Fox, the interpreter for the Numinu, Kadohadacho, and Ka'igwa, directed their tribes toward a cavern along another wall.

Painted Sky sidled up next to him, but as he prepared to speak, Broken Bow held up his hands. "Silence. I tire of your happy words."

"As I tire of your angry ones." He shoved Broken Bow playfully.

"My anger is justified! They have removed us from everything we know." Broken Bow stepped near as he spat the words in his brother's face. "You are acting as if we should be celebrating and feasting!"

"Stop!" Romero approached with a couple of bluecoats. "No fighting."

He glowered at the interpreter but said nothing. One bluecoat herded Painted Sky off several steps, and he went willingly.

"This way, both of you," Romero beckoned them to follow. "All Tsitsistas will sleep here." He indicated one of the holes in the stone wall.

Heart thudding, Broken Bow went to the opening and peered inside. Sweat prickled across his skin at the close, still air within. His tribesmen, as well as the Hinono-eino men, settled blankets and arranged their meager belongings around the places they'd chosen to sleep. The cave-like room, with its high, arched top, stank of sweat and mold.

"We must sleep in there?" He indicated the interior.

Romero nodded. "White Chief has spoken." The interpreter stepped up and motioned for Broken Bow to extend his hands.

Once the man had unfastened the mechanism that held the chains on his wrists, Broken Bow stared at his feet, still shackled with the heavy chain. "What about these?" He rattled the bindings.

Romero shook his head. "White Chief says to loosen only your hands for now."

Of course he had.

Romero motioned for Painted Sky to come near to extend his hands. After Sky's chains were removed, Romero picked up a strange item from a wooden box at the door and offered it to Broken Bow.

Broken Bow eyed it with skepticism, unwilling to touch the thing until he knew more. "What is this?"

"White men call it a *book*." Romero lifted the cover to reveal crinkling leaves bound inside. "These are *pages*. White Chief wants each of you to have one. You can draw in them, like you did on animal skins back home. He wishes you to record your memories and what happens while you're here."

"He *wishes* us to. . . ?" Why would he desire such a thing?

When Broken Bow still wouldn't take it, Romero set the book on top of his small pack, then handed over several narrow sticks no fatter than his smallest finger.

"What are these?"

Painted Sky pressed in, taking the book offered him by one of the nearby bluecoats.

"White man's paints."

"You do not make sense! These are not paints."

A smile tugged at the man's lips, and gripping the bundle, he placed the pointed ends against one of the interior leaves. Dragging the tips in a circular motion, he made several lines in varying colors appear. "See?"

Stunned, Broken Bow stared at the marks, then took the fistful of paint sticks.

The interpreter jutted his chin toward the interior of the cave. "Find a place and make your bed."

Thoughts spiraling, Broken Bow shuffled past. "Why does White Chief give us these. . .*books*?"

"So you will not forget what makes you Tsitsistas. He looks forward to seeing what you will draw. He will wish to inspect your books at times, so get busy."

White Chief *wanted* them to remember their former life? That was an unexpected kindness. But at what cost?

Sally Jo stood on the second drawbridge spanning the presently dry moat, her back to the giant pitch pine doors separating the exterior of the thick-walled fort from its interior. She tugged at a loose thread on the cuff of her dress, then smoothed her skirt for the hundredth time. When she lifted a concerned glance toward Luke and patted her upswept hair, he held up his hands.

"S-s-stop. You are beautiful."

The sweet assurance did little to quell the roiling in her belly. "Thank you, but what is my father going to think once he hears about this humiliation? Surely by now word will have reached the courthouse." Papa would be furious she'd brought shame upon him. If only this lieutenant had given her half an hour more, she could've hurried home to freshen up and return. "If I'm going to be called out by the military for such a public shaming, then I at least need to look. . .not like a windblown—"

"Please breathe." He looked her in the eyes. "This will all turn. . .out."

She folded her hands to keep from fidgeting, though at the ache in her bruised thumb, she prodded the offended joint. "I hope you're right, but you're only just coming to know Papa. He has rigid ideas of what's appropriate, with no convincing him otherwise." And derailing a military parade would hardly be deemed appropriate, she was certain.

Behind her, the pine doors opened, and she turned, praying she didn't look as panicked as she felt. The lieutenant—a handsome, blond-haired man in his middle thirties—stepped out. Again, she found herself smoothing imaginary wrinkles from her dress.

"Miss Harris." He nodded politely, then turned to Luke. "Mister. . ."

"L-Luke Worthing, sir."

"Mr. Worthing. I am Lieutenant Pratt, the officer in immediate charge of the Indians."

Just lovely. Sally Jo gulped down her embarrassment. "So you're replacing Major Hamilton as the post commander?"

Pratt laughed. "I'm a lowly lieutenant. I haven't earned the rank for such an appointment. Major Hamilton is still in charge of the fort, but the army has placed the lives of these men in my care."

"I see."

"Am I assuming correctly, miss, that your father is Judge Edwin Harris?"

Oh, Lord above, this can't be good. "You know Papa?"

"No." His smile widened. "I haven't had the pleasure. Rather, I've done some research on my new post, surroundings, and the people in it."

Her chest constricted. If he'd researched who held the power in the town, surely he'd waste no time in sidling up to them. Better diffuse any tension quickly.

"Sir, I am so very sorry for interrupting the ceremony and pomp you were trying to create. I can't apologize enough."

The lieutenant's brows furrowed, and he chuckled. "I am not at all upset by that interruption, Miss Harris. I would have preferred to bring my Indians into the fort under cover of night with no spectacle. The last thing I wanted was a vainglorious display."

Perplexed, she looked at Luke, who offered an encouraging nod.

"Unfortunately, the train arrived in broad daylight, and the crowd had already formed, so there was little to do but to march them down the middle." Pratt's shoulders slumped slightly. "If there'd been any other way to get them inside, I'd have done it."

"S-so you're not upset with us?"

"Hardly. I apologize for letting you think I was."

Luke's gentle nudge landed softly against her back, eliciting Sally Jo's smile. "I'm relieved to hear it, sir."

He motioned toward the pine doors. "Would you mind joining me inside? There's an important matter I'd like to discuss."

She drew a steadying breath as excitement and curiosity collided within her. However, before she could nod, Luke broke in.

"Is it s-safe?"

"Quite. There are many soldiers inside, and we've not removed the Indians' leg irons yet."

"Then we'd be glad to," she agreed before Luke might differ.

"After you." Lieutenant Pratt opened the pine door and waved a welcoming hand toward the opening.

Luke's hand settled at the small of her back, and he guided her inside. Lieutenant Pratt led them to the courtyard where, just to their left, a group of twenty or so Indians sat in the corner, postures stiff and unnatural with the leg irons still in place. The lieutenant paused, allowing them to take a good look at the prisoners.

Her heart ached. While stoic, the captives were also watchful, dark eyes distrusting, even calculating. No one talked as they stared back. One in particular stood out as he balanced a book on his lap and marked on a page. As he lifted his eyes and scowled, she recognized him as the leader of the line she'd blocked earlier.

"These are but a handful. The others are still preparing their quarters. We're bedding the Kiowa Caddo, and Comanche prisoners here." He motioned to a door to their left, just past where the Indians sat. "And the Cheyenne and Arapaho on the north wall there." Movement flashed in the rooms he'd indicated as the Indians carried out their work.

Pratt beckoned them to follow him to the gun deck above. Again, Luke's hand settled at the small of her back as she gathered her skirts before starting up the steps. At the top, the lieutenant chose a spot half-way between the armed sentries watching the courtyard below.

"My true purpose today has to do with what you said to the man in the crowd, Miss Harris—about these Indians being the hungry, the poor, the sick of which Matthew chapter twenty-five speaks. Did you mean those words?"

Startled, she nodded. "Very much."

"You do realize, there are reasons these particular men were chosen to be incarcerated here in Florida rather than on the reservation lands out west."

She arched a brow. "Go on."

"Some might call these men the troublemakers. Either their actions against white settlers were particularly harsh or they've incited others to act out on the reservations."

She stiffened at his meaning. "War is harsh, Lieutenant. I'm sure I needn't tell a distinguished military man like yourself such a truth."

"No." He shook his head slowly.

"While I'm not knowledgeable about such things myself, I am old enough to remember how the war changed my father. He came home a much different man than when he left. Even today, a haunted look overcomes him when a memory grabs hold. He won't speak about his experiences, so I know they were terrible. Is it not the same for the Indians? Have they not experienced loss and tragedy, like the Sand Creek Massacre or Washita?"

Trying—unsuccessfully—to gauge the officer's reception, she plunged on. "I'm sure my thoughts won't be well received by a man like you, but while they've done harsh and terrible things, so have many during war. These Indians are no less God's creations than any one of us, and it angers me when people are too shortsighted to understand that."

Pratt turned to Luke. "Do you share her sentiments, Mr. Worthing?"

"I do." He gave a sheepish shrug. "Just n-not as. . .eloquently."

A fleeting smile came to the officer's lips.

Sally Jo's heart sputtered as she waited for the lieutenant's fierce rebuttal, though when he spoke, it was anything but.

The lieutenant's eyes drifted closed. "Lord. Thank You."

"P-pardon?" Luke narrowed a glance at the officer.

"Forgive me. My wife and I have discussed these very topics at great length, and we both have been praying. Unless you all greatly surprise me, you two might be the answer to our prayers."

She looked at Luke, then back to Pratt. "I'm not sure we understand, Lieutenant."

"Bear with me as I explain." His attention drifted to the growing crowd of Indians. "Miss Harris, you assume your thoughts wouldn't be shared by a man like me. I respectfully disagree. I have no desire to make the incarceration of these men harsh or unfair. They will be treated with the utmost dignity and respect. My hope is to implement programs to educate them in trades—blacksmithing or farming, for instance—so that they might work in the community, given time. I've pages of notes with ideas I'd like to implement—even the irrational idea that we might educate them in speaking English, reading, writing, and some simple arithmetic. Most of all, I want the Good News to be shared with them, so I've planned to speak with local ministers to ask for volunteers to help put such plans into motion. Then I came across you, and I found two like-minded people immediately."

As he spoke, she grasped Luke's wrist, her grip tightening as her excitement grew.

"Might you be interested in participating with such plans, or would you know of local women who might be of similar thoughts to help me?"

She shot Luke a wide grin, her mind spinning. "Yes, Lieutenant, Luke and I would love to take part—and I'm certain I could get my mother's dear friend, Sarah Mather, to participate. She is a distinguished teacher, a genius in the classroom. . ."

Oh sweet heavenly Father, thank You! You do *have a plan!*

CHAPTER FIVE

Matty Joie's House, St. Augustine, Florida—Present Day—Sunday

*H*ad she *dreamed* she'd placed a panic-laced, middle-of-the-night call to Matty Joie? Not a dream, given her present surroundings. Rather than the cheaper-than-cheap motel she'd chosen the previous night, Dani padded barefoot down a well-appointed hallway in some-body's spacious, upscale home. How she'd actually gotten *in* the house, well, that was a mystery.

With her head pounding and sleep clinging, she'd not been able to find her bag to freshen up so, still wearing her oversized sleep shirt and capris, she stopped at a wide opening and peeked into a roomy kitchen. Stainless appliances, pretty stone countertops. A wide island with bar-stools lining one side. There, Matty sipped coffee and read the newspaper, seemingly unaware she was up.

Nope, she hadn't dreamed that call. Would he be cool about it or. . . ? Whatever way it went, she needed coffee first. Spying a mug beside the coffeemaker, she beelined toward it.

As she entered, he looked up. "Morning."

She scooped up the mug. Thank God. It was clean. She reached for the full carafe.

"You look rough. How much did you have to drink last night?"

She cringed at the direct question. Dani turned slightly and held a finger to her lips. "Coffee first." But even in her hungover state, that sounded rude, so she met his eyes. "Please?"

He chuckled. "You're just like Frank. He always needed a whole cup before he could string coherent thoughts together."

Hardly the conversation she wanted to have. She poured a cup, doctored it with cream and sugar, then arced past him to sit at the far end of the island.

Once she'd had several swallows, Matty cleared his throat softly. "Kicking in yet? Safe to talk?"

Cradling the mug in both hands with its rim resting against her lips, she inhaled the warm scent. "Starting to. And maybe." All depended on how he wanted to play it.

Again, he chuckled. "Just like your father."

She shot him a scowling sideways glance.

He waved a hand. "I know. Last thing you want to hear, but the truth is the truth."

Dani took another swallow, choosing to leave his comments unanswered.

"So. . .what happened last night? Did you find some night life?"

"No!" She set the mug down harder than she intended, and coffee sloshed across the counter.

Matty grabbed a paper towel from beside the sink and passed it to her.

"I told you, I'm not a party girl."

"All right. But when I showed up at your door, you were about as drunk as if you'd swallowed your body weight in beer."

"Considering I'm as big around as a toothpick, that's not saying much. I had part of one bottle. I was tipsy after four sips and drunk at the halfway point." She wiped the spill, set her mug on the paper, and pulled one knee toward her chest. "And I'm twenty-eight. Hardly some underage drinker."

"I'm just trying to understand how you wound up drunk in a seedy motel in a bad part of town." Neither his tone nor his expression held any judgment, only concern. "Look, how you live your life is none of my business. I just want to make sure you didn't end up the victim of date rape or something."

Realization dawned. "Oh. No. Nothing like that."

Matty's expression flooded with relief.

"It was just. . .the whole day was weird, y'know? The guy who never wanted anything to do with me leaves me his ratty old house. I get to it and start looking around, only to get ambushed. . .by you and that other guy."

"Gray. And again, I apologize." His contrition was palpable.

"Then my car wouldn't start, and you hit me with the news it's unfix-able. And all that artwork in the house."

"What about the artwork?"

Did he really not know? "You *are* aware Franklin is an art forger? Convicted. Spent years in prison."

His jaw hinged open, then snapped shut. "I'm aware."

"So why does a man like him have forged copies of the masters hang-ing in his house?"

"He painted those in art school before his conviction, with the inten-tion to practice technique."

That shut her up a second. "Oh." It made sense if it was true. "But what about the book of artwork in his studio?"

"What book of artwork?"

"The Native American pictures? They look like a child drew them—at least compared to anything else he's got. He even contacted a museum in St. Petersburg about it, using a fake name. He called himself Mr. Franklin."

Matty shook his head. "I don't know anything about that. Next time we're over there, show me. But in the meantime, none of this answers how you wound up in that motel."

Dani rubbed at her throbbing temples. "Everything just added up on me. I was kinda freaked about staying at Franklin's, so. . ." She shrugged. "When I went out for food—thank you for loaning me the car, by the way—I bought a bottle of beer—one bottle—to go with it, found a motel I could afford, and shut myself in for the night." She wrapped her arms around her leg and rested her chin against her knee. "I didn't realize how rough a neighborhood it was until I was already halfway into my bottle. I figured I'd find someplace better come morning. But then someone started screaming down the hall, and I could swear I heard a gunshot, and. . .I spooked. You're the only person I know in St. Augustine, so I called you." She dragged her mug nearer though she didn't drink. "Sorry if I disturbed your sleep." If this was her stepfather, Alec, she'd get a royal butt-chewing for such a call. "It was stupid, I know."

"Not at all." He leaned against the kitchen sink. "Actually, I'm proud of you. And I'm really glad it wasn't what *I* was thinking."

She unfolded her leg as she twisted to face him more fully. "I'm not the type to pick up random guys. I've dated *maybe* three men since I graduated high school, and none of 'em for more than a month." She rubbed at her throbbing head.

Matty watched her, then went to a cabinet and removed something. On his return, he pushed a bottle of ibuprofen across the counter. "Also very wise to stay put when you knew you shouldn't drive. And I'm glad you called when you realized you were in over your head. There's a couple of the guys at my shop who could stand to learn those same lessons."

A healthy dose of surprise sprouted in her chest. She cracked open the pain reliever and dumped two gel caps onto the paper towel. "So, I'm not too stupid to live?"

He laughed out loud. "Girlfriend, if this is the worst you've got to offer, you've got a long life ahead."

How refreshing! Her mother, stepdad, and grandfather would've berated her for such decisions. Dani quirked a feeble smile at him, then swallowed the pain relievers with a gulp of coffee. "Thank you."

"But you might want to rethink drinking your way out of a rough day. That usually leads to more problems."

"You don't have to worry. I proved again, I'm so *not* a drinker."

"And I do wish you would've told me you weren't comfortable staying at Frank's. I've got more than enough space here, or—I'd have helped you find a better hotel."

She shrugged. "It didn't bother me so much until it started to get dark. You were already gone, and. . .I just don't have much free money to spend. Besides, I barely know you, and forgive me for being blunt, but you say you were Franklin's best friend. I couldn't count on him, so I don't know what to expect from you." She faced forward again and waited for the explosion that dart would probably elicit.

None came. Instead, Matty's cheeks puffed, and he whispered a few breathy words she had to strain to hear. Was he *praying*? Again, surprise wound through her.

"Dani, I understand all too well why you'd think so poorly about Frank, but there's so much about him you don't know. I hope you'll learn it in time. His life was much more than his conviction and prison sentence.

That said, after yesterday—and particularly last night—I hope you're able to separate me from him long enough to see that you can trust me."

Her throat knotted, and she tipped her coffee to her lips to cover her tears. She gulped the last swallow, now tepid, and blew out a breath of her own. "I can, and I do."

"Good. I only want to help." He checked his watch. "Do you have any plans today?"

On safer ground, she glanced his way again. "Until I meet with the attorney tomorrow, I don't really know what to do. I don't want to start going through things, then find out I tossed something that was supposed to go to someone else, y'know?"

"The attorney wouldn't have given you the keys to the house if that's going to be an issue. But if you don't feel comfortable to start before tomorrow's reading, then don't. I'll need your help getting the loaner car back from the motel parking lot, and I'd prefer we get it sooner than later. It's a rough area."

"Yeah. Sorry for the trouble I caused." Heat crept into her cheeks. "Do you know what happened to my bag?" Hopefully, he hadn't let her leave it behind in the hotel room.

"Oh. You'd passed out by the time I got you back here, so I dropped it by the front door and went back to carry you in. I'll get it." Matty disappeared, though he continued talking. "I don't know if you're feeling up to it, but I lead a ministry at my church. A motorcycle ministry." He reappeared with her bag and set it on the stool next to her. "The regular church service will have ended by the time we take care of the car, but if you'd be interested, everyone's going for a ride afterward. If we head straight there from the motel, we could make it in time."

She narrowed a glance at him, a perplexed grin tugging at her mouth. "What?"

"You're full of surprises."

"Meaning?"

If he hadn't gotten upset at her for anything else she'd said, hopefully he'd take this in stride too. "Not trying to be rude, but you look a little terrifying at first glance. I wouldn't have pegged you for the church type."

He smiled. "Everyone's welcome in God's kingdom, darlin'. Doesn't matter what you wear or how you fix your hair. It's what's in here." He tapped his chest. "You want to go?"

"I've never been on a motorcycle before."

"It's easy. You just hold on, lean into the turns, and trust me."

She stared a moment, then nodded. "All right. I'll go."

◈

Brunswick, Georgia

His back stiff, Brad roused. At seeing the sterile hospital environment, he sat up, folding the recliner into its upright position. Brynn still slept, one arm around the crocheted horse he'd tucked beside her. The rumpled bedclothes testified to the fact they'd weened her from the drugs. An untouched food tray sat on the table, and a clock on the wall registered nine forty-nine. Panic filled his mind, and he checked his watch to confirm.

"Oh, great." Miranda and Lieutenant Lipscomb were to return by ten. Casting off the blanket, he crammed his feet into his shoes, snagged his backpack, and headed for the bathroom. In the five minutes he took to wash his face, brush his teeth, and ready his clothes to change, voices sounded outside. Still in the basketball shorts and T-shirt he'd slept in, he stepped out to find Miranda chatting with a nurse.

"Morning, sleepyhead." Miranda giggled. "Just waking up?"

Warmth filled his cheeks. "Sorry, I finally crashed."

The nurse extended a hand. "I'm Brynn's nurse, Sandy. I was going to remove her IV and get her ready for discharge."

"Thanks." He shook her hand. "I appreciate it."

Once Sandy moved to the bed, Brad met Miranda's eyes and hooked a thumb toward the bathroom. "I'm just gonna change. I'll be out in a minute."

Miranda failed to stifle a teasing grin. "You might want to brush your hair. It's sticking up in the back."

"Of course it is." He stepped back into the bathroom, shut the door, and rolled his eyes at the lone sprig standing upright at the crown of his head. *Always. . .* She always found a way to embarrass him or show him up.

Brad tamed his hair and pulled on jeans. As he reached for the clean V-neck he'd packed, a terror-filled cry sounded in the outer room. He jerked the door open and burst out, tugging the shirt on as he rounded the corner. Sandy stood with her back to him, Brynn cowering against the far-side bed railing.

"Brynn, baby. . .it's all right!" He hurried past Miranda and around the bed. "It's all right. Uncle Brad's here."

Her panicked blue eyes sparked with recognition, and with a hiccupping sob, she reached for him. He scooped the tiny girl into his arms and settled her against his chest. Spindly arms circled his neck, and she wept.

"It's all right, Brynnie Bear. I've got you now." His throat grew thick with emotion. When he glanced toward Miranda, tears pooled against her lower lashes.

Sandy pushed the IV pole around the bed and whispered that she'd return to remove the IV shortly. Miranda accompanied her out.

"Shh, baby. It's okay." He sat in the recliner and crooned words he hoped might comfort her. It took several more minutes to calm her.

She clung to him as if her life depended on it. "I wanna go home, Uncle Bad."

Uncle Bad. He cringed at the nickname and cursed his brother silently.

He rubbed her back. "I know, baby. We'll leave here soon. I promise." But probably not to go to her house. He'd gone there on his way to the hospital, intending to pick up a change of clothes, a toothbrush, and her favorite stuffed animals. The house was in even worse shape than only a few weeks earlier. He'd quickly given up trying to find anything clean and instead went shopping to pick up the Minnie Mouse suitcase and a few changes of clothes. At some point, he'd need to clean the place, dispose of any drugs and paraphernalia, but not with a four-year-old in tow. Especially after what she'd already been through.

"Look, Brynnie. Look what I brought you." He snagged the handmade horse from the bed, and she latched onto it, though without her usual excitement.

A soft knock came at the door, and Miranda looked in. Brynn whimpered and clung to his neck all the tighter.

Brad's heart lurched. "It's all right. No one's gonna hurt you, baby."

At Miranda's questioning expression, he beckoned her inside. She and Lieutenant Lipscomb entered.

"We come bearing gifts." Lipscomb held up a box and a cup of coffee. "Thought Brynn might like donut holes better than this." He waved at the hospital fare.

"Want a donut hole, Brynnie?" Brad rubbed her back.

She only trembled.

Lipscomb placed the box on the desk. "That's okay, sweetheart. Maybe they'll sound better later." He handed the coffee to Brad. "It's black. I didn't know what you liked."

"That's fine." He rarely drank the stuff, but today was a rare day. He took an awkward sip, then kissed Brynn's temple. "Brynnie, if I find you some cartoons, would you let go for a minute so I can talk to my friends? We'll stay right here with you."

Wordless, she buried her face in his neck.

"It's all right." Miranda sat at the desk. "I won't know about an emergency hearing for tomorrow until early morning, so I'll need you to stay close. Will you take her back to Cawley, or. . . ?"

"Not to the...h-o-u-s-e." He spelled the word, not wanting Brynn to understand. "It's not an appropriate environment."

"I agree." Lipscomb nodded.

"Then maybe find a hotel around St. Marys and catch up on some rest. I'll call early tomorrow to let you know the hearing date and time."

"Could I maybe take her into Jacksonville, walk around the...z-o-o?"

"Sure, just keep your phone handy and stay near enough that you can get back here easily."

"I will. What about after the hearing, assuming it goes like we hope. I live and work in St. Pete, Florida."

"It's *going* to go your way. Once it does, we'll contact Children and Family Services and get you set up with a caseworker there." She paused. "Where do you work?"

"The Andrews Museum of Western Art. I'm the acting curator."

"Wow, I'm impressed."

"Thanks. I've fought hard to get there." He was so close to being given the full-fledged curator position, but when the situation with Trey and Jazz blew up weeks ago, he wondered if it might be lost.

"You were always willing to do whatever it took. Sounds like nothing's changed."

Sandy the nurse entered again, and after a lot of coaxing, Brad was able to convince Brynn to allow her to remove the IV. Once Brad signed the discharge paperwork, Lipscomb turned to him.

"I don't assume you've got a booster seat for your girl, do you?"

"Oh. . .crud. I—"

The lieutenant held up his hands. "Don't worry. The agency keeps extras on hand for this type of thing, so I grabbed one this morning. I'll meet you in the lobby with it."

"Thank you. Both of you."

They both smiled in return, and Miranda stood. "Keep my number handy in case you need to reach me for any reason. And be watching for my call about the hearing."

"I will."

They both departed, and Brad helped Brynn change clothes and brush her teeth.

True to his word, Lipscomb met them in the hospital lobby with a booster seat, then ran interference with the news reporters who'd camped out waiting for the scoop on Brynn being found. He provided enough of a diversion that they were able to slip past without being too bombarded with questions. At Brad's pickup, the lieutenant stashed their bags on the driver's side backseat while Brad started the engine and got Brynn strapped in.

"Can we go home now, Uncle Bad?"

"No, baby. You're gonna stay with me." As her eyes filled with tears, his chest constricted, leaving him almost breathless. "I promise, Brynnie girl. We're gonna have a lot of fun."

Her chin quivered, and her eyes turned misty. "Please, can we go home?"

Lipscomb touched his elbow, and Brad faced him.

"What do I do? I can't take her back there, but I'll go nuts if I have to sit in an empty hotel room going over things until the hearing."

"You'll probably do that no matter where you go. Give yourselves time. You've both been through an ordeal."

Brad shook the lieutenant's hand one more time, and once the officer departed, Brad shut Brynn's door, jogged around to the driver's side, and climbed in.

"C'mon, my Brynn. Let's find you some breakfast, and we'll figure out where to go."

CHAPTER SIX

*M*atty held the church door, and Dani entered, scanning the one big room as forty-odd people milled about in jeans and leather vests sporting the same strange logo. Odd that a *motorcycle* group would have a biker chasing a flying goose for a logo. Weren't they supposed to go for something fiercer than a goose—skulls or mythical creatures, maybe?

A woman in the nearest group looked their way. "Mattyyyyy!" Arms outstretched, she walked toward them. Behind her, the room rippled with similar greetings.

Dani glanced at him. "What is this, the church where everybody knows your name?"

He quirked a grin at her. "Isn't that pop-culture reference a little before your time?"

"In the rare moments when my mother's not hobnobbing at the country club or saving the planet, she wiles away her free time drinking wine and watching eighties sitcoms."

Chuckling, Matty met the other woman with a giant bear hug. "Good to see you, Lana." He released her. "Lana Quint, meet Dani Sango. Dani, Lana."

"Hi, Dani." The woman smiled.

"Lana, look after her a minute while I get this ball rollin', please." Matty excused himself and stepped away.

"Will do." Lana engulfed Dani in a warm hug. "So glad you came, hon."

For an instant, awkwardness enveloped her, but the embrace quickly warmed her like a soothing balm.

Out of the corner of her eye, she saw Matty flip a couple of switches in the sound booth off to the left, then head toward the front of the church.

Lana released her. "So what do you do for a living?"

Dani refocused on her. "I'm a bookkeeper in Tampa."

"Do you enjoy it?"

"Honestly? I hate it. I landed in that profession out of necessity."

"That's hard." She smiled sympathetically. "What would you rather do?"

She glanced toward Matty, then back. "Um. . .I don't know. Maybe equine therapy. Using horses to help people with special needs develop skills. Especially kids."

"So you have a heart to help others. That's really good."

The sound system gave a soft *pop* as Matty flipped the wireless mic on. "Morning, everyone."

People murmured their hellos.

"Sorry to keep you waiting. We'll start the goose chase in a minute, but I had two things to share before we leave. First, please welcome Frank's daughter, Dani, standing at the back with Lana."

As every eye turned her way and the room erupted into whistles and applause, she backed up a step, instinct urging her toward the door. Before she could run, Lana looped an arm around her shoulders.

"Stay, hon. We don't bite."

Even as she said it, Matty held up a hand to quiet the room.

"I do believe Dani's part jackrabbit. She spooks easily."

"Oh, good gravy." Heat flooded her cheeks, but Lana tightened her hold, giving her arm a reassuring rub.

"In fact, she told me this morning that I look a little terrifying." Laughter erupted, and he winked at her. "And half of y'all—especially you over here"—he motioned to a tight group to one side—"look more frightening than me. So try not to scare her off. Welcome her, but don't overwhelm her, all right?"

"He's doin' a fine job of that himself," she whispered.

Lana rubbed her shoulder. "Hon, with Matty, this is all good-natured teasing. And he loves it when you dish it right back to him, so don't be shy." Again, she tightened her hold and faced the front as Matty continued.

"And the second thing." He fished a paper from his back pocket and unfolded it. "You know little Brynn who we've been praying for."

Heads bobbed across the room.

"This article was in today's newspaper." He held up a clipping. " 'Toddler Found Safe, Reunited with Relative.'"

Again, the room erupted.

"She's in the care of an uncle, and her parents and the couple they found her with have been arrested. So let's celebrate her return, but keep praying for the family and the situation."

Dani turned to Lana. "Is he talking about a church member?"

"No. A few weeks ago, a little girl went missing in Georgia, an hour from here. It grabbed our hearts, so we committed to pray for her quick return."

"All right," Matty continued. "Let's pray, and we'll get this goose chase started!"

"What does he mean, goose chase?"

Matty cleared his throat and bowed his head, and Lana followed suit. What had she gotten herself into?

At the end of the prayer, she tried to ask again about the goose chase comment, but people filed past, welcoming her, some offering words of condolences about Frank while others told her how much he'd meant to them. Matty brought up the rear, and once he arrived, Lana slipped out, leaving them alone.

"You all right?"

She folded her arms. "You set me up, brought me here to prove what a great guy my father was."

"No, darlin'. I asked you to ride along because I didn't want you to be alone after the night you had. But anything I do is with people who worked with Frank or socialized with him. This group, in particular, has been praying for you for years, so I couldn't exactly hide that you're his daughter. Get used to the idea that you'll hear about him. It's not a setup. It's just a fact."

"You could have at least told me."

"Would you have come if I did?"

She swallowed. "Um. . ."

He shot her a knowing glance. "That's what I thought. Let's go. We're holding everyone up again."

Once Matty locked up, they started for the parking lot.

"Why has this group been praying for me for years?"

"You were Frank's daughter, and he loved you very much, whether you believe it or not."

Dani bristled at that answer, but before she could say anything, he led off.

"C'mon, darlin'."

As they passed through the parking lot, motorcycles roared to life. Once they were settled on his Harley, she heard Matty's voice in her ear as he spoke into the helmet mic.

"You ready for your first wild goose chase?"

"Why do you keep calling it that?"

"It's a reference to something Frank read years ago. The ancient Celts used to refer to God's Holy Spirit as "the Wild Goose"—an untamed, unpredictable bird. Trying to follow one is nearly impossible, and you can rest assured, it would lead to quite an adventure." He revved the motorcycle to life, and the seat rumbled under her. "This group isn't just a motorcycle *club*. We're a ministry. After reading about the Celts' thoughts on the Wild Goose, we began to change how we did our rides. Instead of mapping a course to a set destination ahead of time, now we pray and ask God to show us where to go. Once we get there, He usually shows us at least one person we can talk to or pray with. It's a whole lot like being on a wild goose chase, only it ends well most of the time."

Dani's skepticism burst out in a laugh. "Isn't that a little out there?"

"I used to think so too until I saw God work."

Brad pulled into a parking space outside the Castillo de San Marcos and glanced in the rearview mirror. Brynn sat in silence, clutching the crocheted horse, eyes watchful. Haunted. His attempts at drawing her into conversation had largely failed. She'd answer his direct questions but wouldn't engage otherwise. That wasn't like her.

Lieutenant Lipscomb's words returned. *Give it time.* She'd been through an ordeal. Should he just forget this whole outing to St. Augustine's fort—a suggestion from a helpful waitress earlier that morning? As much as he didn't want to sit in some boring hotel with nothing to do but rehash his own fetid thoughts, a quiet day to rest might be better for them both. He shifted the truck into reverse and began to back out.

"Uncle Bad?"

He stomped the brake. "Yes, baby?"

She craned her neck to see from the backseat. "Is that a castle?"

A spark of hope lit within him, and he pulled back into the space. "It's like a castle. It's a fort. Wanna see it?"

She pulled the stuffed horse closer to her chest and quirked her lips to one side in uncertainty, yet continued to stretch to see around the passenger seat's headrest.

It was the *only* thing she'd shown interest in since leaving the hospital.

Brad put the truck in park, climbed out, and waited for the car next to him to pull out. Once it drove off, he opened Brynn's door. "C'mon, sweetie. We'll go walk around a little while. Stretch our legs." He unbuckled her seat belt and hoisted her onto his hip. But as he shut the truck, she cried out and lunged for the door.

"What? What's the matter?"

A minivan pulled up, indicating a desire to pull into the empty spot.

"Peanut!" She grabbed the door handle.

"I don't understand, baby. Peanut?"

"My horsey!"

She'd named the horse? "No, baby, it's better to leave your horsey here so she doesn't get los—"

"No!" she shrieked. "Don't leave! *Please!*" She sobbed. "Peanut is scared!"

The terror in her voice grabbed him by the throat, and he jerked the door open. Brynn nearly lunged from his arms, though he managed to hang on to her even as he snatched the animal from the seat. "All right, baby. Here. Here."

She held on to the toy as if it were a lifeline, sobs and whimpers still flowing.

The minivan beeped, startling him, and he flung a hand to tell the driver to move along.

"See? Peanut's safe and sound. She doesn't have to be afraid anym—" *Wait!*

Peanut was the nickname Trey had given to Brynn when she was a newborn. His stomach soured as her frantic cries took on a whole new meaning.

Brynn buried her face between his shoulder and the toy, whispering words he couldn't quite grasp over the sound of the minivan's engine.

The driver finally accelerated and parked somewhere else.

Brad rubbed Brynn's back in an attempt to get her to quiet down. "It's all right, Brynnie. Peanut's safe. *You're* safe. You don't have to be scared now. Uncle Brad's got you."

She held tight to the horse, and he again debated abandoning this whole plan. Maybe touring the fort was too much, too soon. But when her attention continually strayed toward the huge fort, he opted to give it a minute.

"You want to go see it, Brynnie Bear?"

At her almost imperceptible nod, he locked up the truck, hurried across the parking lot, and once he stepped onto the sidewalk again, put her down and wrapped his arm around her tiny frame.

"See there? Isn't it big?" He pointed at the impressive square fortress, at least twenty-five feet high with bastions at each corner. "Know what it's made of?"

She shook her head against his shoulder.

"Great big blocks made of little bitty seashells. You like seashells, right?"

Another expressionless nod.

"Think you own the road in your big, shiny truck?" The sharp words, spoken from over his left shoulder, snapped his focus from Brynn. The speaker—a short-statured man in cargo shorts and a T-shirt—stood near a woman pushing a stroller with three young kids surrounding them.

"Excuse me?" He furrowed his brows.

"Pretty selfish of you, mister!"

"What are you talking about?"

The woman attempted to take the man's hand. "C'mon, hon. Let's just g—"

"The parking space? Pretty rude, dude."

Understanding dawned. "Oh. Sorry about that. I had a situation—"

"You couldn't step out of the way because of your brat's meltdown?"

Brat? Irritation crawled up his spine. "Butt out of what you don't understand."

"Oh, I understand tantrums. Piece of advice. Giving in to one is as effective as pouring gasoline on a fire."

"Obviously, you do understand them." Brad rocked to his feet, tucking Brynn in behind him. "You're pitchin' one right now, you dumb jerk." Over a parking space.

The man's face reddened, and the woman grabbed his arm.

"Honey, please. *We're on vacation.* There was no harm done." For one tense moment, the man glared. "Darren!" The woman spat his name under her breath. "The children are watching."

Brad straightened to his full six-foot-one height, towering at least five inches over the man. "Walk away, Darren. Right now."

Once more, the woman tugged at him, and this time, he went.

Brad turned and scooped Brynn up, adrenaline flowing. He kept one ear turned in that direction, but all he heard was hushed arguing between the man and woman. As he got a short distance away, Brynn's little frame shook in his arms.

"You okay, Brynnie?"

"Peanut was scared."

His feet stalled at her tiny words. Peanut was scared, but Brynn was trembling. He pulled her even tighter. "I'm sorry, baby." *Lord, if You're listening, please help!*

As they headed down the wide path toward the entrance, the green grass and sparkling river beyond drew his eye. Tall palm trees waved near the water's edge, and boats dotted the river. His mind sparked with familiarity. He glanced toward the nearest fort wall, then faced the river again. Was this. . .?

"Brynn, baby, get down for a minute. I need to look at something on my phone."

She whimpered and latched onto his leg. After massaging his fatigued muscles, he fished his cell from his pocket and pulled up his email, navigating to the ones from Dani Sango. He found the attachment he wanted. Angling the screen to see better in the bright sun, he studied the picture of the ledger art she'd sent. A stone wall to the left. Boat masts to the right.

And in between the two, three columns of people—soldiers surrounding Native Americans. His excitement swelled. Of course! Why hadn't he put this together earlier? This fort was where so much of the ledger art had been drawn. . .and this very walkway seemed to be the location depicted in this scene. Stupid of him not to realize it sooner. The only explanation was to chalk it up to stress and distraction.

But he squelched his excitement. Dani Sango was likely the daughter of a convicted art forger who lived and worked in this area. He could've easily known about the ledger art drawn here, might have dummied up authentic-looking fakes in an attempt to scam some unsuspecting idiot.

It wouldn't be him.

At the admission stand, he requested their tickets, then fished his wallet out of his back pocket.

"I haven't been here in about twenty years, so remind me, please. There were Native Americans held here, right?"

"Yes, sir. The Castillo was home to the Seminoles in the 1830s, the Plains Indians in the 1870s, and the Apaches in the 1880s."

"And the Plains Indians were known for their ledger art, right?"

"Correct. We have a room dedicated to that part of the fort's history, and the park rangers can answer any questions you might have."

"Thank you." He pocketed his wallet. "C'mon, Brynnie. Let's go see your seashell castle." He walked down the path, angled over the first of two wooden drawbridges, and stopped at one of the coquina walls. Finding a spot where the plaster coating had eroded to reveal the small shells beneath, he pointed to it. "See here?"

She touched the layered shells, then cuddled back against him.

"Uncle Bad, do they have princesses here?"

He laughed. "No, baby. This isn't a princess place."

"No pretty princess bedroom?" Her voice was flat, lacking her usual excitement and spark—but at least she was talking.

"I don't think a princess has ever slept here, but we can look around, okay?"

She nodded.

With a bit of coaxing, she agreed to walk rather than be carried, and he led her across the second drawbridge, through the tunnel, and into the grassy courtyard. Sightseers dotted the walkways, ducking in and out of the rooms along the lower level. At the direction of one of the National Park Service rangers, he led Brynn toward the first room to their left, but at the sight of its especially dark interior, Brynn put on the brakes.

"You don't want to go in there?"

With a fierce shake of her head, she wrapped her arm around his leg and clutched Peanut close to her heart. "Too dark."

She'd never been afraid of the dark that he recalled. Was this a childhood phase or was it because of what Trey and Jazz had done? Brad reversed course, heading back into the sunlit courtyard.

"How about if we just look in some of these other rooms?" They weren't nearly as dark. "Maybe we can find a princess bedroom."

At her timid nod, he walked toward the next room. A few tall signs and pictures depicted important people in the history of the fort from the time of the original Spanish rule.

"No beds, so this can't be a princess bedroom."

She didn't respond.

"Let's try this one." He ducked through an interior doorway. Again, a few large signs explained about people and conditions at the fort under the British rule. When they reached another room with a rustic tick mattress laid over a rough-hewn wood bedframe, he squatted beside her.

"Could *this* be a princess bedroom, Brynnie girl?"

She shook her head. "Ugly."

"Ohhh. Okay. We'll keep looking." Little chance they'd find a *pretty* bed in this historic military fort.

They rounded onto the fort's north wall and found the room that told of the Native Americans held here. Near the door, Brad looked past one imposing biker type to see a placard showing Osceola, leader of the Seminole resistance during the Second Seminole War. Toward the back of the room, an older couple perused the glass case protecting some kind of carving on the wall, and feet from them, a pretty young woman with long dark hair and a beautiful willowy figure read a sign depicting a Native American in traditional US military garb.

Brad led Brynn to the next sign, portraying army officer Lieutenant Richard Henry Pratt, the man who'd overseen the prisoners during the

Plains Indians' incarceration. He pulled his cell phone from his pocket to snap a photo.

As he lined up the shot, the dark-haired woman shifted toward Pratt's sign, and Brad threw her an apologetic smile. "Sorry. I'll be out of your way in a second."

Beautiful brown eyes turned his way. "Take your time."

"Uncle Bad..." Brynn tugged his pantleg. "Find the princess room."

The woman squatted to Brynn's level. "Princess room?"

Brynn ducked behind him with a whimper.

"Oh." The woman straightened. "I didn't mean to scare her."

"It's not you. She's...shy." Only she wasn't. Not usually. He dropped his tone to a conspiratorial whisper. "She thinks this is a castle, so there ought to be a princess somewhere."

An amused grin curved the pretty woman's lips.

Brad snapped the picture and, giving her one more smile, moved out of her way.

As he moved toward another glass-encased etching near the door, the idiot from the parking lot and his family ducked into the room, talking loudly, and took up station right where he was headed. Brad tried to squelch his annoyance.

Too crowded. He'd come back to the room when it emptied out.

"C'mon, my Brynn. Let's go this way." Taking her little hand again, he led her into the next room. Thankfully, the only two who occupied that room stepped into the courtyard as they entered.

Moving out of the doorway, he squatted in front of her. "You doin' okay, sweetheart?"

She held tight to Peanut, and her roving gaze reminded him of the museum security guard, Steve—ever watchful for danger.

When two of the jerk's kids darted through the doorway and startled Brynn, she lurched into his arms. The kids chased around the room a second, giggling and squealing. His curator persona kicked in.

"Hey!" His stern voice ricocheted off the coquina walls. As the rambunctious pair came to a standstill, Brynn held tight to his hand. "This isn't the place. Go find your parents before someone gets hurt."

To Brad's surprise, they slipped back through the doorway like chastised pups. Once they'd gone, he turned again to Brynn, only to find that tears streamed down her face. He clenched his teeth to keep a curse at bay.

"Aww, Brynnie." He pulled her to him. "Please don't cry." He cursed silently at himself. He should've been paying more attention. Her whole world had been in upheaval for far too long—even before she disappeared, if Trey and Jazz were using drugs to the level he now suspected. He blew out a breath. "I think maybe this is too much. What do you say we go, Brynnie Bear?"

"Home?" Her tears flowed.

He gulped around the knot that clogged his throat. "No, baby. I'm sorry. Not home."

"I want my house."

"I know. But you're gonna stay with Uncle Brad, okay?"

"Excuse me."

The words, spoken in a man's voice, came from the direction of the doorway. Probably the parking lot jerk, ready to confront him for taking charge of the situation with his rowdy kids. Adrenaline once again flooded his body.

Brad rose and turned, expecting to see the height-challenged moron. Instead, his gaze landed about chest-level on a huge, muscled guy in a leather vest. Brad looked up slowly to find a middle-aged man with a longish red beard arranged in a thick braid.

Despite knowing they were the only ones in the space, he glanced around, then back to the man. "You mean me?"

"Yes." He took a step closer. "Did I happen to hear you call the little girl *Brynn*?"

Fear sparked. Was this some friend of Trey and Jazz's—or someone associated with the pair that had held his niece? His heart pounded as he eyed his options for a quick exit. "What about it?"

"Are you her uncle?"

Behind him, the dark-haired beauty stood near the doorway, her expression curious.

Suddenly uncomfortable, he hoisted Brynn onto his hip. She latched on to his neck just as she had umpteen times throughout the day.

"What is this about?"

The big guy smiled. "I'm sorry. I'm not trying to make you nervous. I'm part of a motorcycle ministry at a local church." He tapped the vest, indicating the CHAPLAIN patch.

A church ministry? This guy?

"My group saw news reports about a little girl by that name missing in Georgia a few weeks ago. If that's you two, I just wanted to say we've been praying, and we're happy she's been found." He pulled something from his back pocket and unfolded it to reveal a newspaper clipping.

Brad noted the headline, and the tension drained from his shoulders. He rubbed Brynn's back, gratitude settling in his chest. "Thank you. That's. . .very kind. We can use all the prayers we can get."

"I shared the article with the others in the group this morning. We'll keep praying. I'm sure there's still a lot to be sorted out."

This was *not* how he'd expected the conversation to go.

"My name's Matthew Joie. Everyone calls me Matty." He produced a business card. "I run a car restoration business in the area. Don't know if there's anything you need, but I know a lot of people in North Florida and Southern Georgia. If I can be of help, please let me know."

Brad received the card and gave it a quick once-over. Joie-Rides. Where had he heard that name? "Thank you." He palmed the card.

"I'm sorry. I didn't catch your name."

"Yeah, sorry. My thoughts have scattered in a million directions since Brynn went missing." He rubbed awkwardly at his forehead. "I'm Brad Osgood."

The dark-haired beauty flinched and cocked her head at him. "Brad. Osgood?"

"Yes?"

She stared at him with a perplexed expression. The big guy, Matty, watched her with amusement.

"That's why your voice is familiar."

"Excuse me?"

"You wouldn't happen to be the curator at the Andrews Museum in St. Pete, would you?"

His thoughts spiraled. Was he losing his mind? He should remember such an attractive woman. "I'm sorry. Do we know each other?"

She flicked a glance at Matty, then back to him, her lips parted slightly. "I'm. . . We've. . .we've been playing phone and email tag. I'm Dani Sango."

The forger's daughter? Brad rocked back half a step, trying to process. She'd introduced herself in almost exactly the same timid voice. "How did either of you know where to find me? I didn't even know I'd be here today."

"Believe me. It's a total coincidence. In fact, when I got your email late yesterday, I figured you were trying to politely blow me off."

That truth hit a bit too close to home.

"But you obviously *did* have a family emergency. I'm really glad your niece is safe." Her brown eyes filled with compassion, and she gave him a bit of a bewildered smile.

"Thank you. This is. . ." Brad failed to grasp words to express his feelings.

"It's. . ." Dani held his eyes a moment, then turned on Matty, "*scary* bizarre."

The big man laughed, the sound echoing against the stone walls and high arched ceiling. "That's God, darlin'. He makes the bizarre and unexplained happen on a goose chase."

"A what?"

"A goose chase." Dani's eyes sparked with a healthy dose of disbelief. "Matty will tell you that God led us here. And since he's grinning like the cat who ate the canary, I'm going to guess he thinks God led us here so we could meet."

Matty's eyebrows arched. "All right, smarty. How else do you explain the coincidences? The family I've been praying for is the same one you've been trying to contact without luck. And we all end up in the same place at the same time? It's too far-fetched to say it's anything *except* God."

CHAPTER SEVEN

Fort Marion, St. Augustine, Florida—Wednesday, June 2, 1875

*B*roken Bow stood in a corner of the stone-walled room, staring at the desks and benches lining its perimeter. He'd finished his morning meal, so the bluecoat guards had herded him and a few others into this room to wait—for what, he had no idea. Surely nothing good.

He tugged the hot blue uniform away from his neck. How did the white soldiers wear such uncomfortable pieces? Unlike the soft buckskin shirts and leggings he was used to, this cloth chafed terribly in places. They didn't have sense enough to dress appropriately in this strange land's oppressive heat. Back home, he was used to wearing nothing but his breechcloth about camp on the hottest days. These know-nothings wore several layers of their heavy garb, covering all but their hands and faces, no matter the heat—and insisted their prisoners do the same. Every day since they'd been forced to give up their own clothes, he'd soaked these scratchy uniforms with sweat, as if he was wrapped in every trade blanket he owned. Not that he owned any now. They'd taken them away when they forced him to don the bluecoats' clothes.

It was the white man's way, taking what they'd given. The white leaders had long been promising his people plentiful food, something called *government annuities*, and reservation lands to call *their own* if the Tsitsistas would give up all claims to their ancestral lands. Their promises always dried up and blew away on the wind. The cattle the white men gave were frail and diseased, the monies from the annuities were slow to come, and the reservation lands were small and good for nothing.

Broken Bow released a frustrated breath, eyeing the guards patrolling the courtyard. White men made no sense. Their word was worth nothing. White Chief had talked with them on the long journey across the iron road about adopting the white man's way. Making corn instead of hunting buffalo. Speaking the white men's words instead of the Tsitsistas tongue. These ideas chafed as much as their stiff clothes.

Painted Sky peeked into the room and, spotting him, hurried over with his typical grin. "Your thoughts look heavy this morning."

He gave only a scowl in response.

"What am I saying? Your thoughts are always heavy."

He turned in Sky's direction. "You know this about me, and yet you *volunteered* to come to this place to be with me. What sort of fool does that make you?"

"A devoted one?"

"You should have stayed behind with our people. You could be lying beside your wife every night and teaching your children our ways."

"I came because your mind needs to be stirred or your thinking becomes like a stagnant pool. Stinking and deadly. You need me, Brother." He paused. "So, what has you troubled today?"

He huffed. "You know."

"Pretend I don't."

He dropped his voice to a whisper. "This place. These people. Their clothes." Again, he pulled at the constricting fabric at his neck. "They watch everything we do. Their interpreters report on all we say." He flung a hand at one of the white soldiers standing within view, his back to the open doorway. "They intend to root out everything that makes us Tsitsistas."

Painted Sky gave a sympathetic sigh. "This is not a surprise, Brother. Our people surrendered. White Chief has said we must adopt their ways so we can live—though he gave us the *books* so we can remember our culture."

"Stop speaking of that man as if he is your friend. White men speak only lies. They are not trustworthy. You, yourself, taught me that!"

More men, these from the Kadohadacho, Ka'igwa, and Numinu tribes, filed in, followed a moment later by a few of his Tsitsistas and Hinono-eino brothers. Each nodded a silent greeting, which he returned.

"My brother, the white settlers are coming, and their numbers are far greater than all of our peoples combined." He swept a hand around the room, indicating the men of the five nations being held at the army fort. "White Chief says he wishes us to survive, but the only way we can is to live according to the white way. You must understand this. Accept it."

"I will *never!*" He spat the words, drawing every eye in the room. He was vaguely aware that the men of the other tribes, hearing the passion in his unrecognizable words, signed to ask what was going on, and one of the other Tsitsistas responded with hand signs.

Broken Bow pinned his brother with an unbending glare. "And if you tell me you have, you bring shame upon our people. I will kill you in your sleep."

Hurt flashed in his brother's eyes. "Then you will break our mother's heart. She asked me to come with you, knowing you would not give up your warrior ways easily. But she sees that it is time to lay down our weapons and stop fighting."

Painted Sky's words lodged like a spear in his heart. "She, of all people, would not say such a thing! You dishonor her with these lies."

"They are not lies, Brother. I tell you the truth. She wants for you to stop fighting."

"No! Their path leads to death." Shaking, Broken Bow shoved past Sky and burst out into the sunshine, then toward their sleeping room, aware the soldiers watched him closely. No one attempted to stop him, and he ducked through the doorway unimpeded.

Inside, he unfastened the topmost buttons of the blue coat and the underlying shirt and gulped several breaths. When the door creaked behind him, he spun to find one of the Ka'igwa prisoners—a man a little older than his own twenty-one summers known as Red Hawk. Broken Bow eyed him as he signed something.

You speak right. The white path will lead to death.

Of course he was right. He'd seen firsthand just what atrocities the whites could commit, but— *How do we continue to fight them?* He signed the question, then continued. *We are prisoners.*

Again the door creaked, and several of his Tsitsistas brothers slipped in along with a few from the other tribes.

White Chief cuts our hair. He makes us wear the bluecoats' clothes. Red Hawk's brows rose in a question. *How can they punish us if we all refuse? We will talk to the others and—*

Once more the door creaked.

"What is the problem?" Romero spoke in the Tsitsistas tongue.

No one answered.

"White Chief wants you in the other room." He waved toward the door. "Now."

"What does he intend to do with us today?" Broken Bow pitched his chin in defiance.

"Some of the locals are coming to talk to you. They will be here soon. Go on. Quickly." He also signed the words for those who didn't speak the Tsitsistas tongue.

Broken Bow was about to refuse, but Red Hawk gave a small tick of his head toward the gathering room.

Confusion snagged his thoughts. Red Hawk wanted him to cooperate?

We go. The other man herded the group into the yard beyond.

Oh, how easily Red Hawk reneged on his bold words! Fool!

Romero stopped him at the doorway. "Fasten the buttons." He touched the open collar of Broken Bow's shirt.

He rolled his eyes but complied, following the rest back to the gathering room, now packed with most of the captives. Romero directed them to find seats and wait for White Chief and their honored guests.

Red Hawk encouraged the men to comply, and once Romero moved on, the Ka'igwa man motioned for the attention of all, signaling for two of his tribesmen to pull the doors closed.

Here is my plan. Red Hawk's hands flew as he signed the idea, and as he unfolded the idea, the room rippled with laughter.

⁓❦⁓

"Father, as we bring this program into existence today, we ask Your blessing."

Sally Jo's heart swelled with excitement at the words prayed by the lieutenant's wife, Anna Pratt.

It had taken some doing, convincing her father she wouldn't bring shame upon the Harris name by teaching the Indians at Fort Marion. The convincing had included a visit from Lieutenant and Mrs. Pratt to introduce themselves and explain the officer's intentions and that Sally Jo would be both safe and looked after during the hours she spent at the fort.

Even so, Papa had resisted. Sarah finally elicited his consent.

As Anna Pratt continued her prayer, Sally Jo looked around the group of volunteers. Sarah Mather, Rebecca Perit, Anna Pratt, Luke, and her. A good group. She darted a discreet glance Luke's way, and her heart gave a little patter when he looked back at her, a grin curving his lips. Oh, he was handsome and good. His heart was to serve and to share. Thankfully, Father Gabler had given his blessing for Luke to preach the Sunday church services to their students.

Mrs. Pratt said amen, then looked around. "Are we ready, ladies—and gentleman?" She gave Luke a deferential nod.

At the group's resounding affirmation, she led the way down the path, over the two drawbridges, and up to the pitch pine entrance. Her husband stood just outside, waiting.

"You are h-happy?" Luke whispered as they neared.

"I am. I never would have imagined this when Father Gabler told us he couldn't help us reach the mission field."

He grinned. "G-God's ways are higher than ours."

Oh, yes, they were. When would she learn to trust Him fully?

Lieutenant Pratt stepped toward them. "Thank you all for coming today and for your commitment to these men. I hope this won't be only teaching them a language or a few figuring skills but, rather, a stepping-stone to something greater." Just as he had when he'd visited with Papa, the lieutenant stated that his intentions were to teach these men a new way of life that he hoped might mean the Indians and the whites could finally live peaceably. "You'll see changes in them already, differences from the day of their arrival. They have each bathed, had haircuts, and are dressed in army-issued uniforms. Those are the easy things. What you all are endeavoring to do is the harder job, and I thank you for it. Are there any questions?"

"Do they speak *any* English, Lieutenant?" Rebecca Perit asked.

"To my knowledge, no. But we have excellent translators who are at your service. George Fox will interpret the Kiowa, Comanche, and Caddo tongues, and Rafael Romero speaks the Cheyenne and Arapaho languages. Today, we'll keep things brief. You'll introduce yourselves and meet the men, explain to them what is expected. In the days following, we'll see how quickly they respond and how much they can tolerate of the classroom." He looked around. "Any other questions?"

Silence fell, and he beckoned them to follow. Lieutenant Pratt led them past several soldiers, including Sergeant Pearson, who smiled at her and nodded. The young man's look obviously wasn't lost on Luke, as he settled her hand deliberately in the crook of his elbow. The young sergeant's expression turned to annoyance.

"What was that about?" She breathed the question as they emerged in the sunny courtyard.

"Just m-make. . .making sure he knows you're mine."

Sally Jo let it drop—for now—but when they were alone, she would reassure him he needn't be concerned with Pearson. Luke alone had captured her heart.

The lieutenant marched them to a pair of closed doors on the north wall. Through one of the grimy, iron-barred windows, the heads of several Indians came into view. As Lieutenant Pratt had stated, their long braids were gone, and any adornment they'd worn in their dark locks was removed. She'd known to expect it, but a pang still struck her at the stark reminder of what these men were being forced to give up. How would *she* feel if plucked from her home and family, forced to travel nearly a month to reach a foreign, unfamiliar destination, and told she couldn't wear her own clothes or live as she always had?

Her stomach knotted. *Lord, this won't be easy for them—or us—will it?*

"Mr. Worthing, please help with the doors." The lieutenant grabbed the large ring on the nearest door, and Luke stepped up to the other. At the officer's nod, they swung the doors open.

Sunlight flooded the room, showing the men seated at the desks, unmoving. Almost as one, the women gasped as daylight illuminated the back row—*not* men in army-issued uniforms but rather sun-bronzed backs and almost bare bottoms. They were devoid of a stitch of clothing but for small swatches of cloth or hide threaded between their legs, the short ends tucked into thin leather thongs circling each man's waist.

Sally Jo's eyes went wide, and she spun away from the shocking sight.

"Richard!" Mrs. Pratt locked eyes with her husband as she looped an arm around Sally Jo's shoulders. "Do something!" The woman darted a distressed glance backward as she started toward the fort's entrance again, dragging Sally Jo with her.

Foreign words drew her ear, and concern for Luke coiled in her middle. She twisted free to look for him. As she turned, a one of several Indians faced Pratt and spat defiant words while he attempted to walk past. Two astute soldiers stepped into his path, though other Indians spilled from the casemate door unimpeded.

Her eyes locked on Luke, still standing slack-jawed by the door, and she beckoned him. No sooner did he begin to move than soldiers came running from around the courtyard or the gun deck above.

Luke grasped her arm and rushed her forward. "Let's go!" However, the Indian who'd led the procession at their arrival had broken free and was keeping pace with them.

Fear crackled in her veins. Did he intend them harm? She eyed him with a sidelong glance, and he returned it, black eyes glittering with distrust. She managed to keep her feet to a hurried walk as sounds of a scuffle flared. Behind them, soldiers faced off against Indians. As she swung once more toward the exit, her attention fell again on the only Indian she recognized.

Arm at her waist, Luke pulled her toward the barricade surrounding the staircase to the gun deck. The Indian brave carried on, unchecked, toward the fort's exit.

"He's going to walk out without a challenge!" she wheezed.

Luke altered their course away from the brave and dragged her toward the staircase, though she watched in horror over her shoulder.

When the Indian was feet from the tunnel's entrance, Sergeant Pearson rushed from the darkened opening and, drawing back his rifle, sank the weapon's stock into the man's midsection. The Indian fell to all fours and vomited, then gulped for air.

Horrified, Sally Jo halted as Pearson brought the rifle stock down on his skull, toppling him further, then brought the rifle's muzzle to bear and took aim.

"No!" She wrenched free of Luke's strong grasp and flung herself toward the sergeant. "Don't shoot!" She caught Pearson's arm. "Please!"

The soldier jerked free, and his elbow caught her on the cheekbone. Pain and lights exploded in her head, and the world pitched terribly.

CHAPTER EIGHT

*P*ain bored into Broken Bow's head as soft light hit his eyes. Soft light like in a proper Tsitsistas tent. Was he home, asleep in his buffalo robes? He felt for the thick cushion of hides beneath him but instead found a stiff, scratchy trade blanket. He blinked again. At the stabbing pain of the light, he stifled a groan and sought the source of the throbbing with careful fingers. A large, tender knot rose from his scalp behind his left ear.

If not home and not in the stone-walled structure, where? He tried again to force his eyelids open, succeeding in getting the right one to cooperate. Again, the pain intensified with the brightness, though he squinted at the white cloth suspended high above him. One of the white man's army tents, then. Gritting his teeth, he risked a careful glance around. Swaying images of armed bluecoats stood at intervals around its perimeter. He had no recollection of how he'd gotten here.

Romero's face swam into view. "You are awake. How do you feel?"

So long as he lay still, his skull only ached. Even slight movements, and it throbbed mercilessly. And whether or not he moved, his belly threatened to expel its contents. He kept silent, hoping the feelings might pass.

"White Chief is not happy with you."

Of course he wasn't. "I expected nothing less."

"He wishes to speak to you."

"Let him speak." The man would have his say whether Broken Bow gave his consent or not.

With his belly threatening to revolt, he dared not argue.

Romero called out to someone behind him. There, White Chief spoke to the same yellow-haired woman who'd come with the group to meet them that morning. At least he *thought* it was that morning. . .

Why did this woman keep appearing? She was the same one who'd blocked his path the day of their arrival—and later that same day, entered the fort to speak to White Chief. She must be someone of significance to him. His second wife, perhaps.

The woman held some sort of poultice to her cheek. When the chief motioned, she pulled it from her face to reveal a fresh bruise forming under one eye. White Chief's face twisted into a frown.

Romero called out again, and this time the chief excused himself and approached. When he spoke his tone was somber, though Broken Bow couldn't understand the man's tongue.

Taking up station at the chief's right shoulder, Romero translated. "He is glad you have awakened so quickly. He was worried at the size of the knot on your head."

So quickly. Then it was the same day, not long after the scuffle. But this man. . .worried for him? Surely that was a lie.

"What were you thinking?" White Chief asked through Romero's voice. "Have I not been kind to you?"

Broken Bow snorted. "Kind? So like a white man to think removing a man from his home and family is kindness."

"Since you arrived, we have fed you well, let you bathe, given you clean clothes, and paper to draw on. I have not been harsh or unfair with any of you. Yet today, you and Red Hawk led a mutiny."

Despite his roiling belly, he pushed up onto an elbow and sat, only then realizing that the leg irons had been secured around his ankles again. He gulped down his stomach's urge to rebel, then lifted a glare to meet the chief's. "Eleven winters ago, on the banks of Sand Creek, bluecoats proved to me that white men know no kindness."

As Romero translated the words, the white chief's eyes widened. "That's right. I'd forgotten you were at Sand Creek."

"We acted in good faith, but the army returned to us deceit. White men make promises they don't keep. They speak of peace only to bring war. Your people have no honor. I will not submit to your ways."

"Then you prove that my impressions of you were correct. You are an instigator of trouble, and I was right to remove you from your people. I will levy punishment against you for today's deeds."

Broken Bow huffed, though the effort set his belly to churning more. "Being taken from our homes and locked in this place *is* punishment."

"Yes, but I can make it harder. You and Red Hawk will taste the consequences of your deeds."

"What consequences?"

"You will spend fourteen days in the dungeon." White Chief beckoned Broken Bow to stand. "Come. It is time."

"What is *the dungeon*?" Broken Bow mimicked the words.

"You'll see. Get up."

At the chief's motion, the bluecoats nearest the tent flaps hurried over. They hauled him to his feet, causing his trade blanket to fall, leaving him undressed but for his breechcloth. White Chief retrieved it and, after a discreet glance toward the yellow-haired woman, thrust the blanket at him.

"Cover yourself, and let's go."

Broken Bow took perverse pride in the obvious discomfort of the woman as she looked anywhere but at him, her cheeks flaming red. He wrapped the blanket around his shoulders, and once he'd situated it, the bluecoats gripped his arms again. The chief and Romero led him from the tent, pausing only long enough to speak a few words to the woman. She nodded, gaze falling on Broken Bow as they departed.

In the full sun, his head pounded so fiercely that he was at the mercy of the bluecoats to guide him. They walked him across the wood platforms and into the blackness of the cave. No sooner did they enter it than they pulled him through an opening to the right, through a second arched opening, and to a heavy wooden door.

"This is one of the fort's five dungeons." White Chief inserted a metal stick with strange teeth on the end, much like the smaller version they used to open and close the chains they bound them with, into a hole on the door. When it opened, he swung the door wide and guided Broken Bow through the opening.

Straining to see, he could barely make out the back end of the space, which stank of musty dampness.

"You will remain here for fourteen days, with two meals of bread and water a day. Either I or the doctor will look in on you at those times, but otherwise, you will have no contact with anyone outside."

Broken Bow was still straining to get his bearings in the odd space when the door clapped shut behind him, sealing him in utter darkness.

❧

Sally Jo's heart pounded as she blew out the breath she'd been holding. That man—Broken Bow, she'd been told—was intense. Magnificent and terrifying all at once. She'd been naive to think these men would all embrace the opportunities being given them from the start. Of course there would be resistance. Could a man like Broken Bow be tamed, taught different ways? *Lord, please!*

She rewet the cool compress, wrung it out, and winced as she touched it to her fast-bruising cheek again.

It wasn't right that she'd been eavesdropping on the lieutenant's conversation with Broken Bow, but the moment the interpreter said he'd been at Sand Creek, she couldn't pry her attention away. The tall brave had made a litany of fierce expressions, and despite not understanding his foreign words, there was no mistaking the venom in his voice.

She'd been young—perhaps ten—when reports of the massacre made the newspapers. Not so young she couldn't understand a great tragedy had struck in the western territories. At first, reports lauded the attack as a fair fight—a great victory for the frontier forces. As the weeks went on and eyewitnesses stepped forward, the perception changed. She still recalled Mama weeping as she read the newspaper reports of how seven hundred soldiers opened fire on a sleeping camp filled with women and children. Mama had shared many a hushed discussion with friends about the matter. Sally Jo had not understood it all at her tender age, but she understood enough that those long-ago discussions had plagued her dreams from time to time since.

As truth of Colonel Chivington's true deeds came out, the public outcry turned to justice. Only it never came. Chivington and his Third Colorado Cavalry mustered out of the service before anyone could be tried. No one involved paid any price, and bands of Indians across the Plains had taken matters into their own hands, sparking years of war for which these seventy-three men were now imprisoned.

Father. . .what tragedies they have endured. Broken Bow's venomous words are rooted in deep pain, aren't they? The weight of their mission struck her afresh. How could she, a young woman who'd spent her lifetime in cities in the easternmost states, possibly hope to understand and minister healing to these men who'd experienced little other than hardship in the western territories? *Lord, how? I don't even know where to begin. . . .*

As quickly as she prayed, the idea she'd discussed with Luke many times permeated her mind. Just as if they were on a mission field in some faraway country, she and the others must rely on God's leading and His timing. If she and Luke would have made it to Liberia or another mission field, her experiences would have differed there too. And regardless of where they were called, no one held the power to bring true healing and change through their own wisdom. Only the Holy Spirit could break down those walls.

Father, soften Broken Bow's heart, please, and show us how to minister to the pain each of these men feels.

Behind her, the soft rustle of grass alerted her to someone's approach, and she turned to see Dr. James Laird enter the tent.

"Miss Harris, forgive my absence. How are you doing?"

She pulled the compress from her cheek. "I fear my smile may be a bit lopsided until this heals, but otherwise I'm fine."

"Dizziness?"

"No."

"Feeling faint?"

"No, sir."

He prodded her injured cheek with gentle fingers, apologizing when she inhaled sharply. The doctor had her face him so he might look into her eyes. "He hit you with his elbow?"

"*Who* hit you?" Papa's stern voice crackled from the tent's entrance.

Startled, Sally Jo gripped the doctor's wrist as she whipped around.

"What in heaven's name!" Eyes wide, he crossed to her. "Did one of those Indians put his hands on you?"

"No, Papa." How on earth had he heard the news? He was scheduled to be in court today.

"Explain." His jaw firmed. "Or better yet, point me to Pratt."

The doctor rocked forward. "He's indisposed, sir. I can assure you your daughter is not badly injured. And—"

"Indisposed? Hiding out is more likely the case."

Dr. Laird's eyes narrowed. "Hardly, Your Honor."

"Papa, please." Her voice barely reached a whisper. "Remain calm."

He turned his fiery gaze from her to the surgeon. "That man assured me of my daughter's safety while at the fort, yet on her very first day here, I am interrupted in the midst of a hearing with a note saying my child has been injured. I demand to know what's going on!"

"Let me explain what I know of the situation."

Papa stalled him with a fierce glare. "Where is Pratt?"

The doctor glared right back. "Inside the fort, dealing with about ten unruly Indians."

"Then it *was* the Indians who bruised my daughter."

Sally Jo stepped between the men. "No, Papa. I got in the way of Sergeant Pearson's elbow."

"Got in the way of—" Confusion and fury mingled in his expression. He turned again to the doctor. "Where is Major Hamilton?"

Oh, this wasn't going well at all. "Papa, please!"

"Also inside, interviewing the witnesses."

Papa started toward the tent's exit. "Come, Sally Jo. *Now.*"

Her heart thundered. That tone was never good. She followed, nearly running to keep up as he stormed into the sunlight, down the east side of the fort, and made the turn along the south edge. His angry footsteps echoed over the two drawbridges, and he stopped just outside the thick pitch pine doors.

At his pounding, a fresh-faced private opened the small hatch and peeked out.

"Open this gate, Private." Papa spat the words.

"No one's allowed in or out, sir."

"My daughter was accosted inside this fort."

The young man nodded. "I seen what happened. A sad state of affairs." He shifted to her. "Right sorry, miss."

"Son, I am a federal judge, and I demand to be heard. Tell Major Hamilton that Edwin Harris is here to see him. If you refuse, I'll see to it you face charges of your own."

"Papa!" How dare he threaten the poor young man!

Wide-eyed, the private stepped back. "I'll deliver your message, sir, but I can't promise you the major will reply. He's busy investigatin' the tomfoolery what happened earlier."

"Tell him, Private. *Please.*"

After the young man closed the hatch, Sally Jo turned on her father. "What charges could you possibly have against him, Papa? He's following orders."

"I'd find something!" His eyes flashed, though he massaged his temples as he did when a court decision was pressing on him. "I'm sorry. I'm sorry." Only then did he really *look* at her, and his gray eyes filled with pain. "Oh, my girl. Are you all right?"

The unexpected gentleness in his voice brought a knot to her throat. He used to speak to her in that tender tone—before he went off to war and before Mama passed. She'd heard it all too infrequently since those events.

"I'm all right, Papa." If only he'd asked sooner.

He bent to get a closer look, then met her eyes. "So what *did* happen?" His brows furrowed, and his voice took on the sharp edge again. "And where is Luke? I told him to watch over you."

"He's inside, waiting to speak with the major. He wanted to come to the tent with me, but—"

"Tell me what happened."

"Of course, Papa." She related the morning's brief but chaotic events, and as she finished, the private opened the hatch again.

The young man, little more than a boy, lifted his chin. "Sir, the major and lieutenant will see you, but only if you. . .as the major put it. . .'stop your sanctimonious blustering.' *Sir.*"

Papa's cheeks reddened, and he hung his head. "I will."

Apologize for the unwarranted threat, Papa. Sally Jo willed him to hear her thoughts, though he said nothing more.

"Then you may enter." He stepped aside, and Papa barged into the dark tunnel. "Miss Harris, while the major knows Lieutenant Pratt has already spoken to you, he has questions for you as well. Please come in."

She entered, and once the private secured the heavy door in place, he turned to them both. "The officers will speak with you first, Judge. Miss Harris, if you'll wait here, please."

"She'll be safe here?" Papa asked.

"Yes, sir. The prisoners that partook in the shenanigans are about to face their punishment in the courtyard while the rest watch. Only Indian who'll be anywhere near this tunnel is Broken Bow, and he's locked in the dungeon." The private motioned. "Wait here, please, miss. This way, sir."

As the private led Papa down the dark hall, Lieutenant Pratt's voice echoed from the courtyard. She paced the length of the tunnel to see the seventy-odd prisoners—all fully clothed again. Some stood at attention in a military formation at the far side of the courtyard. Eight or so faced them on the near side, each standing beside a sawn log.

"All right, men," Lieutenant Pratt's voice boomed. "For your earlier prank, you'll be made to hold the logs at your side for the duration of two hours. You may not put them down or drop them before the allotted time. If you do, you'll start again."

At Lieutenant Pratt's command, those few were made to pick up their logs. In only a moment, their muscles would begin to quake furiously. By the end of two hours, they would be in agony.

Heart heavy, she turned back toward the middle of the dark hall. As she did, a mournful sound like none she'd ever heard before drew her ear. The nearer she drew to the pitch pine doorway, the louder it became. Following the sound, she ducked through an arched opening to her left, then through a second archway until she faced a heavy wooden door with an iron lock. Two small trapdoors marked the larger entry, one about head-high like the opening through which the private spoke to them at the entrance. The second, wider one was situated slightly below the waist.

From behind it, Broken Bow's voice rose and fell in a sorrowful key as he sang words in his native tongue. In spite of not understanding them, her heart lurched at the grief every note carried. She laid her palm on the door, the weight of his anguish burrowing deep in her heart.

Oh Father, help him. Please. . .

She stood another moment, listening, before the song that had brought her comfort since Mama's passing bubbled up from her depths, and she began to sing, bringing silence on the other side of the door.

"When peace like a river, attendeth my way,
When sorrows like sea billows roll;
Whatever my lot, thou hast taught me to say,
It is well, it is well with my soul."

CHAPTER NINE

Franklin Sango's House, St. Augustine, Florida—4:00 Sunday Afternoon

*M*ind. . .*blown!*
　　　　Dani parked the loaner car a few feet from where Matty straddled his motorcycle on Franklin's driveway. He pulled off his helmet and grinned at her. How in the world. . . ? There was no way to explain how the little girl Matty had been praying for just happened to be the niece of the *really* cute museum curator who might have knowledge about the weird art book she'd found, and they all just happened to meet at the fort by accident. No way except to acknowledge that maybe God had something to do with it.

She'd never put much stock in the idea of God. Until today. . .and now she had questions that wouldn't leave her alone.

Brad Osgood pulled in after her and parked, though he appeared to be deep in conversation on his cell. As she locked the car with the remote, he smiled at her but immediately looked away.

Dani looped the keys over her finger, draped her tiny purse across her body, and meandered toward Matty, still seated on his bike.

"Seems like a nice guy." He nodded discreetly in Brad's direction.

"Seems like."

"Brynn's adorable."

Dani couldn't help but smile. "She really is."

"Kinda interesting, the coincidences of us all showing up there at the fort at exactly the same time, huh?" He winked, a sly grin crossing his lips.

She folded her arms. "You're just so pleased with yourself you can't stand it, can you?"

He chuckled. "Ain't me I'm pleased with, darlin'. I love watchin' God show off. Today was all about you and Mr. Brad makin' this connection."

Dani shook her head and looked away. She wasn't about to let on just how much she'd already pondered these very things.

It would be a lie to say the guy holding the hand of a little blond sprite who called him uncle hadn't caught her attention, especially when he chatted about princesses with her. The fact he *wasn't* wearing a wedding ring. . .oh, dear heavens, yes! He had her attention. And then he'd smiled at her. Talk about mind blown. That smile! The warm blue eyes. The whole package, really. He seemed sweet and shy, full of southern charm. Everything that made her insides turn to warm butter, especially the way he doted on and protected his niece. And that endearing Georgia drawl? She could get lost in daydreams about a man like him.

Just stop, Danielle. She was an idiot. All this because a *stranger* smiled at her. The man had agreed to come back to Franklin's house to take a look at the artwork, nothing more. In fact, he said he needed to leave within the hour so he could head back to Georgia and find a hotel in order to make a morning custody hearing.

This was all just business to him, and she was a fool to think otherwise. Time to steer her thoughts to safer ground.

"So, where's your head?"

Heat flooded her cheeks. "Say what?"

"I said, *How's your head*? Your hangover. . ."

"Ooh." *How* was her head, not *where*. Her cheeks flamed even more. "I haven't thought of it in hours." Particularly after meeting Brad. "The headache's gone, but obviously the alcohol must've stopped up my ears a bit. Or maybe it was the loud motorcycle ride."

"You want to blame it on beer or motorcycles, have at it." The cat-that-ate-the-canary grin returned. "I kinda figured it was a certain handsome fella and his little niece jamming up your thoughts."

Her jaw hinged open, and the heat in her cheeks went nuclear. An uncomfortable laugh boiled out of her. "You're awful! And you don't know me well enough to talk to me that way."

"Oh, don't get your knickers in a twist. I'm teasing."

"Besides. . .*handsome? Fella?* Nobody talks like that anymore. It's *hot guy* these days."

His gaze flicked past her. "Looks like he's done."

She glanced back to see Brad step out of his truck.

Matty got off the bike and wrapped an arm around her shoulders. "Don't hate me for sayin' so, darlin', but you're an open book where he's concerned." He gave her a tight squeeze, then let go.

She rolled her eyes. Hate him? She'd been trying, but for every wall and buffer she'd attempted to put up, the giant Viking-wannabe gearhead weaseled past them all.

"Sorry." Brad shot them a sheepish look. "That was Miranda."

Miranda? Dani's stomach dropped. A girlfriend, then. She slipped the key ring from her finger and fumbled for the house key. What an idiot to have even thought—

"High school frenemy turned social worker assigned to Brynn's case."

The keys slipped from her fingers and hit the cracked cement, and she squatted to retrieve them. *Idiot! Get ahold of yourself before you embarrass—*

As Brad circled to the passenger side, Matty nudged her with his knee. She darted a glance at him as he winked and pantomimed opening a book.

"At the hospital this morning, she said she'd try to get an emergency custody hearing first thing tomorrow."

While Brad unbuckled his niece, Dani rocketed to her feet and spun on Matty.

"*STOP!*" She mouthed the word. *You're embarrassing me.*

He leaned close and whispered. "And it's *so* easy to do."

Dani pulled back, glaring.

Matty stifled a laugh and tried unsuccessfully to wipe the teasing grin from his lips. She huffed out her frustration and turned to face the truck.

"Somehow, she worked some Sunday afternoon magic and was able to get it scheduled." He lifted the sleeping Brynn from her booster seat and settled the girl on his hip, then shut the truck door. "Unfortunately, not until Thursday at four o'clock. So I don't have to leave as quickly as I thought."

Matty poked her in the shoulder, and she flinched.

"I'm sorry. You probably have to get back to work as soon as you can, don't you?" If his job was anything like her own toxic work environment, they wouldn't like him taking time, even for an emergency. "The longer you're stuck up here, the more work you're missing."

"Thankfully, the museum's been more than understanding, but I've got a lot of things to put in place. My tiny one-bedroom apartment is fine for me, but it's not gonna cut it for two of us. She'll need furniture and clothes. I either have to pilfer that from my brother's place—which is a little sketchy—or go buy new. I've got to find a preschool to keep Brynn, and I don't have a clue what to look for there. I mean, there's just. . .so much. It's overwhelming. And as long as I'm up here, I can't be down there figuring out the details."

"I worked every summer in a preschool from the time I was sixteen on into college. I could help with what to look for, questions to ask. I know we just met, but I live just across the bridge in Tampa. If you need help. . ." Dani gave a bashful shrug.

His face lit with that shy smile. "I appreciate that. And I've got your phone number, so don't be surprised if I take you up on the offer."

Her stomach fluttered like mad.

Matty cleared his throat. "Well, since you've got more time, what if you go in and grab this art book, darlin', and we all head to my place. I'll grill some steaks while the two of you look it over, talk about things."

Brad shook his head. "I don't want to impose. You both have been very kind already."

"It's no imposition. Is it, Dani?"

What was he asking *her* for? She barely knew him. Yet. . . "He does seem to be the sort to pick up strays."

"Strays?" Brad looked between them.

"Yeah. I'm the latest one to show up on his doorstep, so to speak."

"Well now you've piqued my interest."

"It's a long story, but I could fill you in over dinner."

He gave another bashful shake of his head, then turned to Matty. "You're sure?"

"Absolutely."

"All right, then."

※

"Uncle Bad?" Brynn tugged his sleeve, her voice a timid whisper. "I watch that 'mato show?"

Brad smiled. She'd eaten the small scoop of green beans, the spoonful of mac and cheese, and all but two bites of steak with little coaxing. "*To*-mato. And I don't mind, but you need to ask Mr. Matty, okay?"

Her cherubic face screwed up in distress, and his stomach clenched. What was he thinking? She'd been clingy and withdrawn with anyone she didn't know. He shouldn't expect her to ask Matty after what he could only imagine she'd endured. Yet before he could retract his words, Brynn crawled out of her chair, dragged Peanut from the corner of the table, and went to stand next to their host. Brad held his breath, and for an agonizing moment, she stood there, chin quivering.

"Brynnie Bear, you don't have—"

She tugged on Matty's sleeve. "Please, I watch the 'mato show?"

The knot uncoiled in his belly. Dani shot him an unsteady smile as Matty grinned at the little blond angel.

"You're a very brave girl, Brynn. Of course you can." Matty pushed away from the table and stood. "Please excuse us. Bob and Larry are calling." Matty extended his index finger toward Brynn. "C'mon, little one."

She eyed his extended hand, shifted Peanut to her other arm, and wrapped her fist around his finger. Matty walked her into the spacious family room, where Brynn burrowed immediately into the corner of his leather couch, Peanut clamped firmly in front of her like a shield.

Brad faced front again, gaze settling on Dani. "I shouldn't have told her to ask him."

"She's an amazing little girl, and kids are a lot more resilient than adults give them credit for." Dani smiled, and she leaned over the table, whispering. "And I don't know what it is about Matty, but he's got a way about him. You can't *not* like him." Her face reddened, and she darted an awkward glance toward the couch, then back again. "Don't tell him I said that."

She piled her silverware on top of her empty plate and stood, then reached for Matty's. Taking the cue, Brad gathered his and Brynn's plates and utensils.

"Y'all don't worry about those." Matty twisted to look their way as the theme song to the cartoon played. "I'll get them in a minute."

"Nonsense. You grilled." Dani headed toward the sink. "We'll clean up."

Following her, Brad admired her tall, lithe figure. She was a beautiful woman. And very kind to offer her help finding Brynn a preschool. But he needed to tread carefully. As beguiling as Dani's straight, dark hair, perfect oval face, flawless skin, and warm brown eyes were, he couldn't even think about his social life right now. Everything changed the moment Brynn went missing, and he was going to have to get used to that fact.

He settled beside her, and she grinned sheepishly. "I'm sorry. I shouldn't have volunteered you for kitchen duty without asking. If you don't want to help, I'll understand."

"I'm actually a genius at washing dishes."

"Oh. A genius. . ." She giggled. "Forgive me for not realizing I was in the presence of such greatness." Her mouth twisted into a teasing smile.

"Okay, maybe not. But I've done thousands of dishes in my lifetime, and it's one chore I don't mind. I even worked a second job as a dishwasher in Cawley for a while."

Pull it together, Bradley! She had him babbling like a fool.

"I don't mind doing dishes if someone else cooks, but my younger siblings always found ways to ditch on kitchen duties, so I was forever stuck with cooking *and* cleanup."

"I get that." Brad chuckled. "I could tell you stories about mine."

The minute the words were cast, he tried to reel them in again. The last thing this poor woman needed was to hear about his drug-addicted brother.

She turned her big brown eyes his way. "I'd like tha—"

"So, tell me about the ledger art."

Her smile faltered, though it returned just as quickly. "Of course. That's why you're here." She waved at the table. "I'll just grab the glasses and. . .we'll talk." She hurried off, shaking her head.

Brad clamped his eyes closed and rubbed at his badly knotted shoulders. He was such a jerk. Sure, he'd moved the conversation to safer territory, but he'd kicked the door closed in her face in the process. Just because he couldn't afford the mental real estate for even a simple coffee date didn't mean he had to be rude.

"Dani. . ."

Brad pushed off the counter as he opened his eyes and inadvertently ran into her, hands settling at her waist. The stacked glasses pitched in her hands and thumped him in the chest. For one awkward second, they both stared before she pulled out of his grasp.

Heat creeping up his neck, he reached for the glasses. "I'm sorry."

"For bumping me?" She stepped past him to deposit the glasses by the sink. "It was a stupid accident." She turned on the water.

"I meant for—"The magical sound of Brynn's laughter floated across the room, and his attention flew to the couch. His niece stood on the seat inches from Matty as the big man took Peanut, galloped the horse through the air, and draped it over his head so the legs flopped around his ears. She giggled as she snatched the toy back only to cuddle it a moment and, when Matty turned back to the TV screen, toss it on the couch between them—a familiar invitation to play again. It didn't take long before Matty reached for the horse, and Brynn hopped in anticipation.

Laughing and hopping were *good*.

Normal.

Nothing in life had been normal for far too long.

The boulder that had lodged in his chest weeks ago shifted, and he took what felt like his first full breath in forever. He tried to release it slowly, though as he did, his whole body shook.

"Hey." The rush of water silenced, and Dani came up beside him. "You all right?"

He sucked in a sharp breath and held it, fighting down the emotion that threatened. "Brynn's safe." He exhaled the words, scarcely believing it.

"Yeah. She is."

At the sound of her giggling again, he panted out a breath, then held another as waves of emotion washed over him.

"Brad, go to her."

He shook his head. "I'll break the spell."

"It's not a spell. Kids are resilient." She nudged him toward the couch, and he reluctantly moved that way, looking back halfway there. Dani gave an encouraging nod.

At the end of the couch, he watched her cuddling the horse. "Having fun, Brynnie?"

She smiled. "Peanut likes Mr. Matty."

"Peanut does, huh?" He scooped her into a bear hug and held on, relief crashing over him like waves on a hurricane-lashed beach. "I'm really glad."

Brynn was safe, and for a moment, she'd giggled. Even if the spell *was* broken, it proved the vibrant little imp he loved was still hiding in there—and with coaxing, might come into the light again soon.

God, thank You for bringing this precious girl back to me. And thank You that she wasn't hurt. . .or worse.

He had no idea how long he stood cradling Brynn, but when he loosened his grip, she lay utterly limp in his arms, her breathing even. The television was off, and Matty and Dani sat at the island in quiet discussion, the kitchen in perfect order.

Brad laid Brynn on the couch, and she rolled onto her side and buried her face in Peanut's mane. He planted a kiss on her hair, watched her sleep for a moment, then walked into the kitchen. "I'm sorry."

Matty faced him. "Nothing to apologize for. She all right?"

"Sound asleep. I'm sure for a four-year-old, this was an exhausting day." He was *thirty*-four and feeling wrung out. A quick glance out the window showed that night had fallen. "I should go. We need to find a hotel somewhere, and—"

"You don't need a hotel." Matty waved toward a hallway. "I've got more than enough room, and Brynn seems comfortable here. You're welcome to stay for as long as you need."

He stared. "Dinner and now this? It's too much."

"It's barely anything."

Dani grinned at him. "Remember, he collects strays. Besides, you haven't had a chance to look at the artwork." She indicated the countertop between them, where a fabric-bound book with black covers and a red spine lay.

Brad stepped up and lifted the cover slightly. It crackled and protested like it was brittle with age. At least the book itself didn't appear to be forged. The artwork inside. . .that remained to be seen.

"Where did you get this?"

Her eyes drifted closed, as if the truth was hard to speak. "It was among my father's effects. And before we go any further, you should know that my father was a convicted art forger."

"I know who your dad was. At least, I suspected, based on your last name. I'm very sorry for your loss."

Her eyes fluttered open. "I've had no contact with the man since I was two. His was a loss I suffered long ago." She darted an almost apologetic glance in Matty's direction, then focused again on him. "I don't know where Franklin got this book, whether it's forged, stolen, whether he bought it. If it's real, I assume it would cost a pretty penny, and to see his house, I doubt he could afford it."

Matty shook his head. "You just can't help yourself, always makin' digs at him. Can you, darlin'?"

"And you can't help defending him." She shrugged. "Look, I'm sorry if my words hurt—but he was never there when it counted. Never there at all."

"Your perception of him is all wrong." Matty turned to Brad. "I'm goin' to get a room ready for you and Brynn. I'll be back."

Once they were alone again, Dani shrugged. "I'm sorry. He wants so much for me to accept that my father loved me, but *nothing* in his actions indicate that."

Brad ached for her. Obviously, those long-past wounds were still a source of great pain. Would that be Brynn in the future? Not if he could help it.

"Anyway, that's why I was contacting you. I found your message on Franklin's answering machine, and I thought maybe you could help me figure out where this came from—and if it *is* stolen, help me return it to its rightful owner."

"I'll do my best, but can it wait? I haven't got two brain cells left to rub together tonight."

CHAPTER TEN

Matty Joie's House, St. Augustine, Florida—
Present Day—Monday Morning

*B*rad popped awake and stared at the unfamiliar surroundings. Where was he? Oh, yes, Matty's house. They'd made a bed for Brynn on the chair and ottoman in the corner, but she'd gotten scared and crawled into bed with him during the night. He glanced sideways, then bolted up.

Gone! She wasn't on the bed or the chair. . .and the bedroom door was cracked open. *Where. . .?*

He darted out of the bedroom and headed toward the kitchen. As he neared the doorway, Dani came into view, seated at the kitchen island, and Brynn's little frame came into view as she settled herself on the next barstool and plucked at Dani's sleeve.

"Good morning, little one."

When Dani wrapped an arm around Brynn, the girl deftly straddled the woman's lap, snuggling close, Peanut trapped between them.

"Well, aren't you sweet." Dani brushed wayward blond locks from Brynn's face.

Brynn was obviously feeling safe enough to seek out her usual morning mommy snuggles from the only female in the house. A good sign. Dani downed the last of her coffee, then laid her cheek against Brynn's hair.

She looked good, snuggling a child.

He snapped his eyes shut. What on earth was he thinking?

"What's the matter, sweetheart?" Dani's concerned question brought his focus back to her as Brynn guided Dani's hand to her shoulder.

He cleared his throat and stepped into the kitchen. "She wants you to rub her back."

Dani darted a startled gaze at him, and she ran a hand over her hair self-consciously.

"That's the routine she and her. . .m-o-m. . .had each morning."

"Ahh." The moment Dani began to rub her back, Brynn closed her eyes and sighed. With her free hand, Dani cradled Brynn's head against her chest and whispered to her.

They made a pretty picture. Dani's natural ease and the contentment in Brynn's relaxed posture made him itch for a sketch pad. But. . .he was being awkward, standing there staring. Heat crept up his neck.

"Thank you." He indicated Brynn, then rounded the corner of the island and parked himself on one of the barstools, an empty one between them. "Anything that gives her a sense of normalcy is a good thing, I think."

She smiled. "My pleasure."

Before he started staring again, he slid his attention to the book of ledger art, then toward her coffee mug, and his heart began to pound. Stupid idea to bring the book into the kitchen. He slid the book toward himself—far from possible spills—then rose again and washed his hands.

"So, what happened?"

Brad looked at her as he turned off the water.

With her. Dani mouthed the words while continuing to rub Brynn's back.

He dried his hands with paper towels.

Honestly, he'd expected that question the previous night. "I don't. . . really—"

"Morning." Matty strode in wearing an expensive-looking suit, his hair loosed from its ponytail and slicked down neatly and his beard combed out straight.

"Morning." Brad greeted him. Dani only stared.

"What?" The big man fussed with the knot at his throat. "Is my tie crooked?"

Dani laughed. "It's that you're wearing a tie at all."

"What, it looks bad?"

"Quite the contrary! Every girl's crazy about a sharp-dressed man."
She winked her approval.

"Ahhh. Well, thank you!" Matty made a slight bow.

"Important business meeting?" Brad gingerly moved the book to the
kitchen table, away from where they were congregating, then went back
to the barstool.

"Actually, we were *supposed* to have the reading of her daddy's will at
eleven, but the attorney's office called." He pinned Dani with a look. "The
lawyer's sick. Stomach flu. They'll reschedule sometime later this week."

"Oh." Her voice tinged with disappointment. "All right."

Matty walked around the island. "Coffee, Brad?"

"I rarely touch the stuff."

Dani shook her head. "That's sacrilege. It's the nectar of heaven!" She
thrust her empty mug toward Matty. "I'll take his share."

Brynn pushed herself up and, with Peanut in tow, headed to Matty's
side. She tugged on his pantleg. "Can I watch the 'mato show, please?"

Matty scooped her up. "Good morning, beautiful. Uncle Brad, may
Brynn watch the 'mato show?"

"Sure."

"All right, then." Matty carried her into the family room.

Once they were out of earshot, Dani turned. "I shouldn't have been
nosy earlier. I'm sorry."

"I don't mind answering. It's just. . .I honestly don't know what happened. My only sibling—my younger brother, Trey—has battled drug
addiction half his life."

Her breath caught. "Oh my word. Your poor parents. They have to be
out of their minds."

Just nod and agree, Bradley. He met her eyes, full of compassion, and—
"They're both deceased."

Her lips parted slightly. "I'm so sorry."

He chided himself to stop there, but. . . "Mom died of cancer when
we were young, and Dad was killed by a drunk driver when I was nineteen
and Trey, fourteen. His issues started soon after *I* became the parent."

Why couldn't he keep his stinkin' mouth shut?

"You raised your brother?"

In for a penny, in for a pound. "Crashed and burned in epic fashion is a better description."

"Because of his drug addiction?"

He massaged a knot in his neck. "That. And he never finished high school. Never attended college. Dad always dreamed we'd make something of ourselves. I let 'em both down."

Her warm hand settled on his forearm. "Brad, you can't blame yourself for Trey's addiction. You didn't force him to take drugs. And his failing to finish school is probably an extension of that. Those are *his* bad decisions—not yours."

He'd tried for years to tell himself that very truth. Why did it sound more reasonable coming from her lips? And why, in heaven's name, did she loosen his tongue so easily?

As the cartoon began to play in the family room, Matty approached with an apologetic expression. "Am I interrupting?"

"No. In fact, I hope you'll save me from sharing my whole life story."

At Matty's quizzical look, Dani broke in. "I was being nosy. He was telling me what happened to Brynn."

"What *did* happen?"

"My brother's battled drug addiction for years, but after he got his girlfriend pregnant, it seemed like they were getting their lives on track. They got clean, got married, had Brynn, had steady jobs. I thought he'd finally gotten the monkey off his back."

Matty grabbed Dani's mug and refilled it. "But?"

"We were seeing each other about every two months, but when I took the acting curator job at the museum ten months ago, life got hectic. I last saw them at Christmas. They were okay at that visit, but a few weeks back, a friend texted that they looked strung out. I drove up to check on them, and that's when I discovered Brynn was missing."

He glanced back to be sure Brynnie was distracted, then he settled his elbows on the countertop and roughed both hands over his hair. "The police found her at some drug dealer's house. The cops haven't given me details, so my mind just spins with crazy scenarios. Did they sell her for drugs? Did they cross the wrong people and Brynn became their pawn?

I just don't know. But it kills me that my own brother did this to that innocent child. It's the kind of thing that can really mess a kid up."

At the innocuous comment, a flood of memories swamped Dani, and she sucked in a breath. Images and sounds from a lifetime ago. Would Brynn be plagued with recollections similar to her own? *God, if You have any mercy, please don't do this to her.* She cleared her throat and stood.

"Excuse me a minute."

The barest hint of a look passed between Matty and Brad before she stepped into the hall.

"Did I say something wrong?" Brad whispered.

Gulping a breath, she ducked into the bedroom, closed the door, and went to the attached bathroom to splash cold water on her face.

Somewhat.

A soft knock at the door came. "Dani?"

Brad.

She grabbed the towel from the bar and stepped out of the bathroom, patting her face dry.

"Dani, if I said something wrong, I'm really sorry."

"You didn't."

"Then what's the matter?"

She reached for the doorknob, but before she touched it, her phone rang with an annoyingly familiar ringtone.

Really—now?

"I'll be out in a minute, Brad. I need to take this." She grabbed the device and stepped into the far corner of the room before she connected.

"Hello?"

"Danielle. Oh, thank God. You haven't answered my texts. What kind of trouble are you in?"

"Good morning, Mother."

"Don't good morning me. Answer my question."

"I've been away from my phone. I didn't know you were texting. And to my knowledge, I'm not in any trouble."

"Why is the law office of. . ." Papers rustled. "Alger, Stein, Pettinger, and Waddell calling my phone looking for you?"

Franklin's attorney called *her mother*? "Um. . ."

"Where are you? And don't tell me home, because I'm standing outside your apartment, and you're not here."

She'd hoped *not* to share the news until she was back in Tampa, if at all, but there seemed no help for it. "I'm in St. Augustine."

"What on earth for? You're missing work! Or did you finally get yourself fired?"

"No, Mom! Why do you always assume the worst?"

"Well, if you'd get your life togeth—"

"Stop, Mom." Dani glanced toward the door, lowering her voice so Matty wouldn't overhear. It wasn't her intention to be insensitive to his grief, even if she didn't share it. "Franklin's dead."

Silence. Blessed silence.

"He passed away three weeks ago, and apparently he named me in his will. Since any discussion about my father puts you and Alec in such a tizzy, I didn't say anything." Actually, it seemed like the older she got, *any* topic dealing with her put them in a tizzy, whether about Franklin or not.

"I see." Her mother's words were a husky whisper.

"I hate to cut this short, but I need to go. I'll touch base later. In the meantime—not that you've bothered to ask—but I'm fine."

Stunned silence. "You're sure?"

"Yes, Mom. Now I need to go. I love you."

"I love—"

Dani ended the call, then instantly regretted cutting her off. *Sorry, Mom.*

She looked at the six texts from her mother—each reading more shrieky than the last—then listened to the voice mail from the law office, asking for a call back. She tapped to return the call.

"Law office of Alger, Stein, Pettinger, and Waddell. Susan speaking. How may I direct your call?"

"This is Danielle Sango. Someone tried to reach me from this number."

"Yes, Miss Sango. Hugh Pettinger has taken ill and won't be able to make the scheduled appointment today."

"I heard. I understand it'll be rescheduled later?"

"Yes."

"All right. I do have a question, though. Mr. Pettinger gave me the keys to Mr. Sango's house and said it was mine. Does that include everything inside?"

"That's correct."

Dani thanked her and ended the call, ran a brush through her hair, and headed back to the kitchen to find Brad studying the open ledger book at the kitchen table. Matty was nowhere in sight.

At her entrance, he looked up, excitement in his eyes, though it quickly faded to concern. "Are you all right?"

She waved the phone. "Okay as I can be after a call from my mother. She's not the most pleasant person."

He stepped closer. "I'm sorry. For the phone call and for whatever I said that upset you."

"It wasn't really you." She shrugged. "I was very young when Franklin was arrested, but I remember it. Snapshots and impressions, not full-blown memories. Mom and Franklin yelling. Really loud. They scared me. Franklin especially. And I remember glass breaking and a lot of blood on the wall."

"Blood? Whose blood? Art forgers aren't usually violent criminals."

Her hands shook, and Brad gripped them. "I don't know. I still see light glinting on the shattering glass—and red splatters everywhere. Police tackling Franklin, guns drawn. A stranger scooping me up and taking me away."

"Wow." Brad dragged her into his embrace. "That had to be really hard."

Startled, she drew back, and he released her immediately.

"I'm sorry. I shouldn't have—"

Dani sank back into his arms with a whimper, her own hands balling into the fabric of his shirt. He held her tight, and for a span of a couple of minutes, she gulped deep breaths to stave off the emotions that fought to surface. There'd been few enough she felt comfortable letting her guard down with. Obviously *not* her mother or Alec. None of her siblings. She'd let her guard down with Rachel at times, but not even her very often. God love him, Brad didn't speak a word. He just held her, allowing her to draw strength from his warmth and nearness until the storm passed.

When she finally pulled away again, she hung her head. "I'm sorry."

"For what?"

"I'm embarrassed. I'm not the sort to fall into a stranger's arms. You must think I'm an absolute crazy woman."

"Hardly. I mean, I hugged you first. And before that, I was cryin' on your shoulder about my brother. Not my finest moment."

She quirked an unsteady grin at him. "So...maybe we call it even and start over?"

"Might be for the best."

Awkwardness still blanketing her, she motioned to the ledger art. "So what are you finding there?"

"As near as I can tell, it's authentic."

"Franklin didn't forge it?"

Brad shook his head. "The paper is old. You can tell by how brittle it is. And there's a printer's mark at the back of the book—from the 1870s."

Dani considered that. "Could he have found an old book and added new artwork to it?"

Another shake of his head. "The drawings themselves are faded."

"So you're telling me this is real."

"I'd bet serious money on it. You're sure you don't have any idea where he got it?"

She looked at the book. "No clue. But...my day's suddenly free. Want to accompany me to his house and see if we can't figure this out?"

CHAPTER ELEVEN

Fort Marion, St. Augustine, Florida—Monday, June 7, 1875

*A*s a boy, Broken Bow had learned to endure extreme heat and great cold with little resource. The long winters of his youth had been brutal. After the attack at Sand Creek, he had nearly frozen to death waiting for help to arrive. Yet somehow, the comparatively small chill in the cave where he'd been locked bothered him more.

He pulled his blanket snug around him as another shiver overtook him. The trade blanket was all they'd given him to ward off the dank, malodorous air, and after being chilled for so long, he ached for the warmth of a buffalo hide.

Darkness pushed in around him, cold and oppressive. He'd never feared silence, never feared the night. But this stifling blackness was heart-poundingly endless. If he ever made his way out of this place, he might never view a moonless night the same way again.

In the first days, he'd paced the perimeter of the cave, feeling his way through the utter blackness. He'd sung songs and told stories as he imagined being with his people around the fire. He'd sounded his war cry to forewarn his enemies that he would not stop fighting their encroaching ways. It had only exhausted him and made his throat sore.

When he could no longer find his voice, the blackness spoke to him, whispering that his enemies were coming, and there was nothing he could do. His fighting would only speed his death and that of his people. Those mocking voices grew louder until their despairing messages made his heart pound and his thoughts spin mercilessly. He wondered whether the Tsitsistas leaders who surrendered might have understood something that eluded him. But he could not give up his people's ways. Could he?

The only thing that had kept him from succumbing fully to despair was the memory of the woman who'd sung to him that first day. Why it affected him so, he didn't know. He hadn't understood her song, but the clear tones had stayed with him. The sorrowful beginning that built to a triumphal ending. That memory had become the thing that tethered his mind so it didn't fly far from him or sink forever into a pit.

He *hated* himself for finding even a shred of hope in the unintelligible song of his enemy.

A scraping sound alerted him—not soon enough—that the small, square hatch in the entrance was opening. Light stabbed his eyes, and pain shot through his skull. He jerked the blanket up to cover his face, but he'd already been temporarily blinded by the flash.

"Broken Bow, are you well?"

He made no attempt to answer.

After a moment, even more light flooded the cave, and he slunk down, putting his face to the wall, blanket over his head.

Footsteps approached. He pulled himself into a ball to ward off any attack, though none came. Only gentle hands. Someone pulled at the blanket, and he risked a look through squinted eyes. Two faces. Whose, he couldn't tell. It hurt too much to look. He pulled the blanket over his eyes again.

"You have been silent a long time."

"Romero?" His voice barely reached a husky whisper.

"Yes. White Chief is with me. Are you well?"

"The light hurts my eyes."

"They will adjust."

The chief spoke, and Romero translated. "Stand up. White Chief wishes to speak to you."

Eyes still clamped firmly closed, Broken Bow pushed to his feet, his joints protesting after so long on the cool stone floor. A bit unsteady, he leaned against the wall, clutching the blanket with one hand while blocking the light with the other.

White Chief held something out to him, nodding his encouragement to take it. He recognized the strange round vessel the bluecoats used to carry water, the same type they'd passed through the hatch with his periodic allotment of bread, and he gladly drank long of the fresh water.

"Better?" the chief asked through Romero's interpretation.

Broken Bow avoided the chief's eyes as he nodded.

"Help me understand why you acted as you did five days ago."

Five days. It felt interminably longer—at least two moons. He took another swallow of the water, then nearly spit it out. The chief had promised him a term of fourteen days. How could he endure another, longer spell in the dark?

"Give White Chief your answer, Broken Bow."

He squinted directly at the man. "How would you feel if you were taken captive and moved to a far land? If you were told you must give up your people's ways and take up your enemy's instead? Would you not rebel?"

White Chief nodded. "This is a hard thing. But try to see through my eyes. I am not your enemy. I wish to be your friend, to save your people from being extinguished at the hands of white men. If you will do as I ask, I can teach you ways that will let your people survive and live on long past your lifetime—even far beyond your grandchildren's."

Broken Bow took another swallow of water to give himself time to think. "Why must my people learn the white man's way, but white men will not learn Tsitsistas ways?"

"Again, you ask hard questions. I wish we were all willing to learn from each other. There is much your people could teach mine." He hesitated. "Here is what I hope. While at Fort Marion, I want to teach you to speak, read, and write in our tongue, teach you skills we use, like growing food and making tools. Those who will teach you are keen to learn some of your culture. This is an opportunity to keep parts of your Tsitsistas ways alive if you will only work with me."

His belly churned with distrust, and Broken Bow looked at Romero. "Can I speak plainly with this man?"

"He will listen and deal fairly with you."

His eyes adjusting to the brightness, he shifted his attention back to White Chief. "Your words flow easily. They are full of promise. But such words have been spoken to my people before—from men wearing the same blue coat you wear. Eagle Chief and Red-Eyed Soldier Chief. They promised us peace if we would wait at Big Sandy. Instead, they slaughtered our women and children. Why should I trust you when you dress just like those who betrayed us before?"

Sadness darkened the chief's face. "Will you tell me of your experience?"

"Why?" He lifted his chin. "So you can revel in the grief of your enemy?"

"I told you, I do not consider you my enemy. I hope one day I might prove to you that I am your friend."

There had been few white men to earn such a title among the Tsitsistas.

"Please, I want to understand, first so that I won't make similar mistakes as the soldiers you mentioned. Also, because it is the only way we will come to true peace."

Heart pounding, Broken Bow stood taller. "I had ten summers. Because of what happened, I almost failed to see my eleventh." His head throbbed as the memories came flooding back. "Eagle Chief—the one they called Chivington—told us he would bring peace." He adjusted the blanket around himself to ward off chills that had nothing to do with the dank air. "The men were allowed to ride a day away to hunt buffalo while the rest of us stayed at Big Sandy. We were hopeful. It was a happy time. But when the soldiers came, they surrounded our sleeping camp in the dark. I woke to loud gunfire. Screams. Outside our tent, my people ran in fear. We were not even dressed—we fled straight from our beds. When Mother and I ducked outside our tent, we heard our leader calling to come to his tent, to stand under the flags Eagle Chief had given him."

"Flags?" White Chief's glance was questioning.

"The striped flag the bluecoats carry and the all-white flag."

The chief ran a hand across his forehead, then nodded. "Go on."

"We tried to get to our chief's tent, but bluecoats rode down on us, one swinging a long blade." He indicated that it had been about the length of his arm from shoulder to fingertips.

"A sword."

His throat knotted until he struggled to speak. "The bluecoat struck my mother while she knelt and begged for mercy. He cut off her arm.

Here." Broken Bow indicated the spot below his left elbow. "They rode past, so I tried to help her to safety, but others shot us. Mother was struck once and me twice." He turned and let the blanket slide past his shoulders to reveal the two scars beneath his right shoulder blade. "We lay on the frozen ground throughout that day. Bluecoats wandered through the camp, shooting survivors and desecrating their bodies. I do not know why they did not kill us, except that Mother lay on top of me, and they must have thought her dead already."

After a long silence, White Chief cleared his throat. "I understand why it is hard for the Tsitsistas to trust white men—those of us in blue coats especially. But I ask you to give *me* a chance to show that not all white men are liars and murderers."

How could he trust? Relations between the Indian Nations and the white man's army were littered with death, destruction, and many broken promises.

Broken Bow shook his head slowly. "Now it is you who asks hard things."

"I do not do so lightly. All I ask is for you to *try*. If you will, I will release you from the dungeon immediately—nine days early."

He stared at White Chief, everything within him wanting to rage and rebel as he had for half his life. But where had such responses gotten him? Imprisoned far from home with no hope that he would ever see anything familiar again.

"I am tired of fighting. There is never an end to it." He heaved a breath. "What do you require of me?"

⁂

The Harris Home, St. Augustine, Florida—Monday, June 7, 1875

Thick silence hung in the kitchen as Sally Jo washed the few supper dishes and Luke dried them. Through the dining room doorway, Papa drank a cup of coffee and thumbed through the newspaper. Papa's natural overprotectiveness, which had worsened since Mama's death, had amplified even more since the scuffle at the fort. He'd all but demanded she remain at home while her cheek healed, though he'd been good enough to allow Luke to come by after work each day. Otherwise, Papa had taken the tack of hiding her away like a prisoner, not even wanting her to sit outside in their secluded courtyard. Did he honestly think he could protect her from any harm ever befalling her?

With the dishes done, she turned to her father. "Papa, could Luke and I take a walk? I've been cooped up here for days now, and I'd like to stretch my legs."

He glanced out the window. "It's already dark."

Sally Jo's heart sank. "Please? Mama used to go walking after dark."

Steadfast in his silence, he flipped the page without looking up.

She glanced at Luke, then back to her father. "Papa, what happened to Mama isn't—"

"Not up for discussion." The firm set to his jaw brooked no rebuttal. "With so many ships coming to the docks, there are far too many rough sorts wandering the streets. You're not to be out after dark."

Stomach knotting with disappointment, she nodded. "Yes, Papa." It was never up for discussion. Nearly five years later, and she *still* didn't understand how her mother had drowned, and her questions were met with these same tired answers.

"Sir, m-may we sit in the courtyard? Sally Jo has barely been out s-since—"

"Young man, I know."

Sally Jo grated at the sharp words. Whether because the judge was used to exerting his authority or because Luke's stammer irritated him, Papa tended to cut Luke off mid-thought. Now was not the time to address the rudeness, but if she hoped to see it change, it must be called to his attention. Soon.

Papa's voice softened. "You may sit in the courtyard."

"Thank you, Papa." She gave him a peck on the cheek, then grabbed Luke's hand to hurry outside before he might change his mind. They had almost reached the door when a soft knock came.

Her footsteps faltered. "Who in heaven's name?" She glanced Luke's way. "Please get the door while I light a lamp."

She arced toward the table, struck a match, and touched it to the wick even as Luke opened the door.

"May I help— Lieutenant P-Pratt? Mrs. Pratt?"

Surprised, Sally Jo spun. "Hello!"

The lieutenant smiled. "Miss Harris. Mr. Worthing. Good evening."

"Come in, please. To what do we owe the honor?"

Once they'd entered, a third person slipped in, smiling at Sally Jo as she approached.

"We've come to save you, dear." Sarah Mather wrapped Sally Jo in a hug. "Where is your father?"

Save her? If anyone could, it would be Mother's dear friend. The eighteen-year age difference between Mama and Sarah had never mattered—the two had been as close as sisters.

She motioned toward the door. "In the dining room."

"Edwin, dear?" Clear and sharp, Sarah's voice rang out as she charged through the doorway.

As much as she wished to watch the unfolding scene, she and Luke both turned to their other guests.

"Are you well, Miss Harris?" Lieutenant Pratt's kind eyes strayed to her cheek.

She touched the bruise. "It's healing."

"He meant more than just your bruised cheek." Mrs. Pratt gave her hand a reassuring squeeze.

"Oh, I'm fine." She attempted to put on a brave face.

Luke's stern glance startled her. "No. She's m-miserable. Her father—"

She laid a hand on Luke's arm, and once he stopped, she refocused on the Pratts. "Papa has struggled since losing my mother several years ago. He's become very. . .cautious. I think he's afraid of losing me as well, so he keeps a tight rein."

Though his words weren't clear, Papa's voice rose. Oh, he wasn't pleased. She shot the officer and his wife an embarrassed look. "I'm very sorry. I should probably look in on them." She turned to Luke. "Please, take them to the courtyard?"

He nodded, and Sally Jo ducked down the hall. *Lord, please keep Papa calm—and give him a reasonable heart for whatever Sarah and the Pratts came to discuss.* She stepped into the living room, Papa and Sarah's arguing becoming clear.

"And when are you going to give your blessing to them to marry,

Edwin? Luke moved here with that intention. He's a lovely, honorable young man."

Sally Jo stopped in her tracks, heart pounding.

"He seems nice enough, but—"

"But he stammers."

"Yes." Papa hissed the word, causing a boulder to lodge in Sally Jo's chest. "And he's feeding her ridiculous dream to go to some foreign country and minister to the poor. With only a clerical job to support them both!"

"Oh, the horrors!" Sarah's sarcastic lilt evoked the image of the sixty-year-old woman throwing her hands up in mock alarm. "Not everyone can be a judge, Edwin. The world requires teamsters and blacksmiths and clerks and judges—all."

"I know tha—"

"And you should be proud. Your big-hearted daughter feels God's call to minister to those in need. Instead, you see this as something to fear, something to eradicate from her life. You already talked Lila out of her calling to teach."

Papa forbade Mama to teach? When? She had no memory of that.

"Would you defy God again by locking your daughter away and keeping her from marrying a wonderful young man who shares her passion to serve the Almighty?"

Papa's voice quieted until Sally Jo had to strain to hear. "She's all I have, Sarah. What if she leaves and doesn't return?"

Oh Papa. Of course she would return, but probably not frequently enough to suit him.

"For such a smart man, you're not very wise, Edwin. With this behavior, you're likely to drive her away just like you did Lila."

What? Mama never left Papa.

"You've been given a boon with the Indians coming here. Your daughter has the opportunity to follow her calling here in town—if only you'll allow her. Instead, you've confined her to her own home. She's twenty, dear man. Not twelve. Treat her like the intelligent young lady she is."

There was a long silence before Papa spoke. "What do you want, Sarah?"

"First, come talk with Lieutenant and Mrs. Pratt. Hear what they have to say. Consider letting Sally Jo—and Luke, because he won't do this without her—return to teach these men. Quite frankly, Rebecca Perit and I haven't started our classes because we feel Sally Jo and Luke should be with us—so you're holding everyone up. And second, give those youngsters your blessing to marry."

Papa's voice dropped to a breathy whisper, too low for Sally Jo to catch his words.

"Then *get* to know him well enough. Luke's a bright, intelligent young man, a hard worker, and—stop rolling your eyes at me, Edwin. As someone who loved Lila dearly—and loves your daughter like my own—I'm trying to help you."

Another moment of silence. "Where is Lieutenant Pratt, pray tell?"

Sally Jo's heart seized. She shouldn't be caught eavesdropping! Ducking through the doorway, she crossed the foyer and scurried outside to find her guests.

Fort Marion, St. Augustine, Florida—Tuesday, June 8, 1875

Broken Bow sat against the west wall, eyes closed, the morning sunlight warming him pleasantly. Bits of conversation filtered into his consciousness. Discussions about food, the heat, men missing their families. And several who whispered about him. He kept his eyes closed and listened.

"Has he spoken yet?"

"Not to me."

"Not even to Painted Sky, I suspect. You would think he would at least speak to his own brother."

"Something is wrong. Broken Bow does not keep his thoughts to himself for long."

"You don't suppose they cut out his tongue, do you?"

He rolled a frustrated look at the group of five and, to quiet their speculation, stuck his tongue out. Almost as one, the group's eyes widened, and they murmured. Broken Bow rose, gathered the book he'd been given at their arrival—one of the requirements White Chief made, to keep it at hand—and stalked toward the men.

"My tongue is fine, and I have talked to my brother. I will speak to the rest of you when there is something to say."

He took a new position in the sunshine, away from their idle talk.

What could he say? That White Chief had gotten the better of him? His enemy had won—in only five days' time? The truth was humiliating.

Yet White Chief hadn't flaunted his victory. He had not reviled or goaded him. Instead, once Broken Bow was released from the cave, White Chief personally took him to bathe at the river, gave him fresh clothes, and ordered that he be given extra portions at the evening meal. The chief had even taken him up on the walls—a place no Indians were allowed without a bluecoat escort—and brought Painted Sky to see him.

They'd been given freedom to walk, enjoy the waning daylight, and to talk quietly away from the others. There, in hushed tones, he'd shared his difficult ordeal in the cave. Painted Sky had listened well. They'd been allowed to watch the sun disappear before returning to the courtyard. The unexpected kindness had humbled him so that Broken Bow crawled into his bed, ignoring everyone the rest of the night.

"Come. This way!" Romero's ringing voice snapped him from his memories, and Broken Bow found the interpreter beckoning everyone toward the same opening where all his trouble had started six mornings ago. George Fox also called out in the Ka'igwa and Numinu tongues.

White Chief appeared from the cave-like entrance, walking on the pathway around the perimeter with a group of white women and one man. He instantly recognized the man and the yellow-haired woman beside him. Those two continued to show up.

As they neared, Broken Bow lurched to his feet, and White Chief paused, the others stopping behind him.

Come. The chief signed the simple direction, then indicated the opening where Romero and George Fox waited.

He gave a hesitant nod, then started walking, though a light touch at his elbow stalled his feet again. The yellow-haired woman released his arm but turned to White Chief, who motioned for Romero. Once the interpreter came, she touched a place behind her ear as she spoke.

"Miss Harris wishes to know if you are well." Romero touched the same spot. "Your head?"

He turned on her. "Why do you ask this?"

The young man shifted slightly closer, a protectiveness in his posture. Not aggressive toward him. Only protective toward her. Interesting.

"I have been concerned since the soldier struck you. Are you well?"

He glanced from her to Romero to White Chief and back. "You were concerned for *me*?"

She nodded.

"Why?"

"The soldier could have killed you—would have, except. . ." Her face flushed.

He could believe the bluecoat nearly killed him, but what had stopped him?

"Are you well?"

Befuddled, Broken Bow looked at the smiling faces around him, then back to her. "I am."

A broad smile lit her face. "I am happy to hear this. Please, what is your name?"

A white woman wanting to know his name? Unheard of!

"Broken Bow."

She repeated the words Romero told her, then grinned. "Nice to meet you. I am Sally Jo Harris."

Awkwardness filled him, and he looked at White Chief and Romero for direction.

"Go on. Find somewhere to sit."

Glad to be released from the odd conversation, he started away but paused again and pinned her with a look. "Was it your voice I heard singing?"

"Yes."

He stared, brow furrowed, then carried on to the gathering place. Inside, Painted Sky was already seated, and Broken Bow took the empty place beside him and leaned near.

"Did the bluecoats almost kill me?"

Painted Sky pulled away in confusion but quickly seemed to understand his question. "Of course, you would not remember. The bluecoat hiding in the cave. He hit you, laid you out on the ground, and yes. . .he turned his gun on you."

After having ridden out to make war most of his life, Broken Bow had long ago faced his fear of dying, but something about the white woman's words snagged his curiosity. "Why did he not shoot me?"

A sound rumbled from deep in Painted Sky's chest. "He would have, but—" He shook his head. "You know I wanted no part of your rebellion, but when he struck you, I ran to help. Before I could reach you, a crazy white woman—maybe your age—ran to him, pulled his arm, yelled at him. I was focused on you, so I am not sure how, but he laid her out on the ground too."

He swallowed and looked at his brother. "You are saying a white woman saved me from being shot?"

As White Chief and the group entered, all conversation ceased, though Painted Sky continued discreetly in sign language. *Yes. The blue-cheeked woman.* The same woman who'd spoken to him—with the fading bruise on her face.

Broken Bow stared. What would make a white woman risk her own safety for him? It made no sense.

White Chief explained to them what he'd already told Broken Bow the previous day, that they would learn the white man's tongue and skills and, in return, could teach those who wished to learn things from their own cultures. Then, the four women and the man stepped forward to introduce themselves, starting with the older two women, followed by White Chief's woman. Broken Bow listened with only half an ear as he watched the young woman, noting again how the young man hovered protectively, his hand straying to her waist a time or two.

He'd been the one to pull her out of the way at their arrival.

And hurried her toward the exit six days ago.

So he was her man? It might explain much.

As all attention turned on her, a kind smile lit her face. "My name is Miss Harris." She waited for the interpreters to convey her words, then spoke her name again slowly, pointing to herself. "Miss Harris."

Miss Harris's man stepped forward.

"And I am M-M-Mister Worthing."

Chuckles broke out among their ranks.

"How will this one teach us to speak the white man's tongue?" one of the men on the far side of the room called out. "He cannot speak it himself. His tongue stumbles."

More laughter.

While Romero made no attempt to translate the jeering words, Miss Harris obviously understood as hurt flashed on her face.

Broken Bow scanned the room, then stood. Every eye turned his way, some with curiosity, others with an expectancy that he would stir more trouble.

He pinned a look on White Chief, then shifted toward Miss Harris and her man. "White Chief has acted fairly with me. I will listen to these people out of respect for him, including Mister War-Tain."

CHAPTER TWELVE

*B*e warned. The inside's as bad as the outside." Embarrassment hit Dani afresh as she pushed her way inside and set the ledger book on the console table beside the door.

Brad led Brynn, still clinging to Peanut, inside and glanced at the sparse furnishings. "Maybe, but it could be a nest egg if you sell it."

"Nice thought, but any proceeds will probably have to pay his outstanding debts."

He shrugged. "Hopefully not. I guess you'll know more after the reading of the will. If it doesn't *have* to be sold, you could rent it out. New flooring, fresh paint, landscaping for curb appeal—it might bring you a nice income stream."

Now *that* was a thought. "You know about such things?"

"Some." A shade of red crawled up his neck as he shrugged. "Says the guy still living in a one-bedroom apartment." He released Brynn's hand and walked farther into the house, eyeing the painting of Dali's *Christ of St. John of the Cross.*

"Wow." His blue eyes rounded, and his lips parted in surprise. For several seconds, he stared at the large canvas, completely transfixed, then pulled his cell phone from his pocket. He typed something into the search bar and glanced back and forth between the device and the painting. "At first glance, this looks totally authentic." He stepped nearer, squinting at the details near the bottom, then backed up a few steps and looked at the whole again. "It's incredible."

"So, Mr. Art Aficionado, would this fool you if you didn't know who made it?"

He stared in silence, a slow smile creeping onto his face. When Brynn wandered up and hugged his leg, his hand strayed to the girl's hair.

"I mean, his technique is beautiful. Judging only on that, this canvas is an amazing replica of Dali's work, for sure. But if you're asking me whether I think he made it with the intent to scam someone, I can't get to that place."

"Why would you say that?"

"For one, Dali is the most notable surrealist in history—melting clocks, that sort of thing."

She nodded. "I recall that much from Art Appreciation."

"This particular painting was very controversial when Dali created it in the fifties, simply because it was so traditional. The art community thought it was a publicity stunt that he'd create something so different from his usual style. They thought it. . .tawdry. This has gone on to become iconic as an excellent piece depicting the crucifixion of Christ, but if someone was going to go through the trouble of forging something of Dali's, I would think they'd choose his surrealist-styled pieces over this one. It's what he's known for."

"I guess that makes sense."

"A second reason is he flipped the whole bottom section. The lake, with the boats and the fishermen, is a mirror image of the real painting." He hoisted Brynn onto his hip, sidled up next to Dani, and showed her the real painting on his phone. Sure enough, the fisherman in the left corner of the original stood in the right of Franklin's rendering.

"He did that on purpose."

"He had to. It's very intentional. And. . ."—he indicated the corner—"this is not Dali's signature. Franklin signed his own name and the year—in Dali's handwriting."

"What?" She hurried over to squint at the signature. Sure enough, a small *FSango '93* emblazoned the corner.

"Anyone who'd purchase this and think it's real would be like the person who buys an expensive-looking watch from the guy on a New York street corner. Might look almost identical, but that Rolex is actually a *Relux* brand."

"So, you don't think he was trying to be deceptive in painting this."

"Not with this piece, no."

Shame spiraled through her, and she hung her head. "I. . .I didn't want to hear it at the time, but Matty told me Franklin painted these to practice the techniques when he was in college."

"Sounds plausible."

"The timeline fits. I was born in 1993, somewhere around Franklin's sophomore or junior year of college."

"Then Matty's probably right."

He moved on to the other pieces hanging on the walls, giving her history while pointing out the differences. On each, Franklin signed his own signature, always in the style of the master he'd copied.

Dani grinned. "Is this what you do all day for your job?"

He grumbled and shook his head. "Sorry. I guess I went a little art geek on you, didn't I?" He shifted Brynn to his other hip. "Give me a minute, and I'll cage the curator again. I promise."

"No." She touched his arm. "Please don't. It's fun, like my own private gallery tour."

"You're just saying that."

"You'll probably think I'm stupid, but I've never wanted anything to do with art. I'm the daughter of a convicted forger. I didn't want people to judge me by what Franklin did, so I've never gone to museums or paid much attention to art."

His jaw hinged open. "You're killin' me. Seriously? You've never been to a museum?"

"History museums. Science museums. Maritime and military museums. Historic sites. All yes. Art museums?" She screwed her face into a doubtful expression. "Not since I got old enough to appreciate them." Dani cleared her throat in hopes it would clear her embarrassment too. No such luck. "You're good at making art make sense, and I think I could enjoy it if I had you to explain things to me. Would you take me to a museum sometime?"

Oh, good grief. What in the world was she doing?

Brad's blue eyes sparkled with a teasing glint. "Miss Sango, are you askin' me out?"

Awash in a sea of embarrassment, she risked a look at him. "Would it be bad if I was?"

"I can't say it would be." That shy grin she was coming to like—a *lot*—returned, and he tugged her toward him. "I'd love to take you to a museum. Soon."

Just as his free arm circled her shoulders and drew her fully into his embrace, Brynn squirmed.

"Uncle Bad? I'm bored."

To Dani's dismay, he released her just as fast as the impromptu hug began, and he shot her an apologetic look. "Let's find something to keep you busy, Brynnie Bear."

Dani looked around, then struck on an idea. "That first door on the left is Franklin's art studio. Maybe he's got some colored pencils or something Brynn could color with?"

"Good idea."

She fetched the ledger book, then led the way into the converted bedroom. It took Brad only a minute to hunt down a few supplies for Brynn.

"Here, baby girl. Draw Miss Dani a picture." He set her at the drafting table, and she stuck out her tongue and began to draw.

"Why does she call you Uncle Bad?"

Brad rolled his eyes. "My idiot brother. I was up visiting them, and we got in an argument. Almost came to blows. Afterward, he started calling me 'Uncle Bad,' and of course, it stuck with her."

"I wouldn't worry too much. She'll outgrow that."

"I hope so—although it's kinda cute at this age."

"Yeah, it is." Dani carried the ledger book back to the plastic table in the corner where she'd found it. "So tell me about this ledger art."

"Are you asking about this particular art or the style in general?"

"Both?" She grinned, and when he grinned back, her heart gave a little patter. No two ways about it—the man was easy on the eyes.

"All right, but I'm gonna ask you to wash your hands so we don't get dirt or oils on the pages."

"There's a bathroom across the hall."

She led the way, and while they took turns at the sink, he explained.

"Ledger art is a narrative style of artwork that became prevalent as the Native Americans surrendered to the army in the 1870s."

"Narrative? Like—a story?"

"Yes. It tells a story. You see, down through time, Native Americans would draw or paint on cave walls, rock faces, tanned animal hides. Their artwork often depicted their daily activities—battles they fought, buffalo hunts, important ceremonies, camp life. Even dating. But once they were forced onto reservations, they couldn't get their hands on the animal skins like before. So they were given ledger books—a source of paper that was cheap and easy to come by."

"That makes sense." They headed back across the hall. "So what story does this artwork tell?"

"Let's look." Brad stood shoulder to shoulder with her and turned to the first page, where several Native Americans mounted on horseback fired arrows at uniformed figures. "First, if this is what I think it is, then all of this artwork would likely have been drawn by the same artist. This is one person's take on what he or she experienced."

"Understood."

"This page shows a battle between the Native Americans and the army. The fact that this figure"—he pointed to the most prominent man on the page, shirtless with the top half of his face painted red—"is larger and at the center would probably mean it's the artist depicting himself. He's drawn his arrow flying directly at this soldier here while the soldier's bullets miss him." Again, he indicated a figure at the edge of the paper.

"You don't know which battle?"

"Without a note on this piece, it's hard to tell. It could represent any number of battles." He turned the page. "In this one, there's a few mounted soldiers meeting with a single mounted Native American, while his people wait some distance away." He pointed to a group hiding behind the hills.

"An ambush, maybe?"

"I don't think so." Brad squinted at the picture. "They aren't carrying weapons that I can see." He flipped the page and, after a moment, turned back. "This may be a surrender. One Native American spokesman steps forward to offer the surrender for those waiting safely nearby."

"Why do you think that?"

"For one, there are women and children in that group. They wouldn't be part of a raiding party. And the next page depicts a fort." He pointed out specifics about the buildings and people. "The soldiers appear to be in control. They're all mounted in formation while the Native Americans are on foot, bunched together, and without weapons of any kind."

Page by page, he described the artwork—of train rides and steamboat rides, the soldiers always seeming in control. "Look at this one." He indicated the one she'd sent him by email, with the columns of soldiers surrounding the Native men. "Remember when you walked up to the fort yesterday—that sidewalk leading to where you bought your ticket?"

"Yeah."

He pointed to the stone wall in the picture. "The fort was to your left. Matanzas Bay was directly in front of you." He indicated the blue water where sailboats bobbed.

"You're saying the person who drew these was held at Castillo de San Marcos?"

"It makes perfect sense. This art style originated there."

"Is that why you were at the fort?"

"Um. . ." The telltale flush of red started up his neck again. "Honestly? No. I hate to say it, but I *was* trying to blow you off when I emailed you back. Once I realized your father was *the* Franklin Sango, I tried to put the artwork aside and just focus on Brynn. I didn't intend to reach out again." He shrugged. "Sorry."

"So, why were you at the fort yesterday?"

"A well-meaning waitress at a little restaurant suggested it, and I thought it was a good idea. Didn't occur to me until I got there that the ledger art originated there."

Dani stared at the book, then went to the window and stared out at his truck. "Do you know how crazy this is?"

"What do you mean?"

She faced him. "I called you about strange art—something I thought Franklin forged. After playing phone tag, we both unexpectedly wind up at the fort at exactly the same time with Matty, who's been praying for you and Brynn. Through totally random events, he recognizes you in the one room that talks about the Native Americans incarcerated there. A group that might have included the man who drew this book? The chances of any two of those things happening are. . .practically zero! All of them? It's beyond impossible!"

"Okay, but what does it all mean?"

She shook her head. "Other than I think the two of us *really* need to work together on the mystery of where this book came from, I don't know. This is all so unsettling. Like something bigger than me is pulling the strings right now."

"Well. . ." He came to stand in front of her. For a moment, he stared down at her, his blue eyes warm and reassuring. "Don't freak out. I'm convinced I'm supposed to be a part of this, so we'll figure it out together."

"The same two people keep showing up in these drawings." Dani's excited voice floated down the hallway toward the kitchen.

"Oh? The artist and who?" Brad gathered two of the chairs from the kitchen table.

"I mean, two in addition to the artist. A white woman and a white man—both with blond hair."

"Is the man in uniform? Perhaps it's that Lieutenant Pratt, the guy I took the picture of when we first bumped into each other." As he started toward the studio again, motion near the front door caught his eye. He paused as Matty knocked.

"It's open!" Brad motioned him in.

"Thought I'd come check on y'all. Everything all right?"

"We're making progress. Grab a chair and come on back." He headed down the hall, and Dani met him to take one of the chairs.

"Matty's here."

She smiled up at him. "I heard. You have to see this." She scuttled off to the table again.

He followed, enjoying her exuberance.

"Look." She indicated a blond-haired couple, both in civilian clothing. "They're here and then here." She carefully turned the page, and then again, pointing out the pair on a third page.

Matty appeared, toting another chair.

"What're you two finding?"

Dani glanced back at him, a wide smile on her pretty face. "Brad's been telling me all about ledger art. It's really fascinating."

As she shared the things she was learning with Matty, Brad excused himself. He pulled out his phone and dialed the private number of a curator friend at another western art museum. The call went to voice mail. Disappointment wound through him as he waited for the beep.

"Hey Saundra, it's Brad Osgood with the Andrews Museum. Have a shot-in-the-dark question for you. Have you heard of any recent purchases of Native American ledger art? I'm not sure how recently I might be talking—so let's say in the last year. If you know of anything, could you email me the specifics at my work address? I'd appreciate it." He disconnected the call and, after pocketing his phone, rewashed his hands and returned to the studio to find Dani still enlightening Matty with her newfound knowledge. Only now, Brynn was perched on Matty's knee, Peanut firmly in her grasp.

"Found a friend, I see." Brad planted a kiss on Brynn's hair.

Matty picked up the sketch pad she'd been drawing on. "She had to show me her beautiful picture. I don't know who is more excited about artwork, though—Brynn or Dani." He winked at the latter.

Dani shook her head at him. "If you don't want to hear about it, just say so."

"I'm just teasin' you, darlin'. Tell me all about it."

If the bashful dip of her chin was any indication, Matty's words pleased her.

"I was just starting to tell Brad that these two people keep showing up in a bunch of the pictures. The first time in this one, where the prisoners are being brought into the fort. They're standing in the way of the soldiers leading them inside. Then several pages later. I'm not sure *what* was happening here."

She indicated one where several Native men, their hair cut short and attired only in breechcloths, scattered from one of the casemates. The blond pair and several other white women ran toward the entrance.

Brad squinted at the room they were spilling from. "I hadn't noticed this before." He carefully tipped the book up so they all could see. "The Native Americans inside the room are all wearing uniforms. And look here." He pointed just outside the doorway. "There's a pair of pants lying on the ground. And a shirt over here."

"Were they expressing their discontent at bein' forced to wear army duds?" Matty rubbed Brynn's back as she snuggled against him.

"Maybe. Think about it. They'd been fighting white society for years, and none more notably than the army. I can't imagine the insult it must have been to be forced to wear the uniform of the soldiers who'd killed countless members of your family and friends."

Dani's eyes widened. "Now that's a deep thought. This couldn't have been easy for them, could it?"

"No incarceration ever is, darlin'."

Matty's pointed words knocked the wind out of Brad as images of Trey and Jazz in orange jumpsuits flashed to mind. Before he'd fallen asleep the previous night, he'd debated whether to visit them, and he'd come to no clear conclusion. If he hoped for his family to get and stay clean, they'd need support. But someone had to protect Brynn, and he didn't know how to play both roles. If he had to choose. . .he'd protect innocent Brynn every time.

At the melancholy downturn of Dani's lips, he wondered whether she was grappling with the hardship of the Plains Indians more than a hundred years ago or if her thoughts focused on her father's twenty-six-year-old conviction.

"Sorry." Matty hung his head. "Sucked the helium out of that balloon, didn't I?"

Brynn looked up, eyes full of excitement. "I want a balloon, please."

Dani giggled.

"Maybe if I can get Uncle Brad and Miss Dani to go out to lunch, we can find you one." Matty winked at her.

"You don't have to do that." Brad shook his head.

"There's an excellent pizza joint not far up the road, and they give balloons to their young patrons. We head that way for lunch about every other week. That's why I stopped by. You're welcome to join us in about twenty minutes."

Dani turned brown eyes on him, then his niece. "Does Brynnie like pizza?"

"Cheese pizza." Her blond curls bounced with her emphatic nod.

She turned beautiful brown eyes on him. "We'll need to eat something. What d'ya say?"

Was Brynn ready for another outing to a busy public setting? It had proven almost too much for her yesterday. "Hard to argue with that logic."

"Good man." Matty clapped him on the back, then rose, picking Brynn up with him. "Little one, I'll see you in a few minutes when we get your cheese pizza and your balloon."

Matty handed Brynn off to him. "Why don't you drive over in about ten, and we'll head out from there."

"Will do."

Once Matty departed, Dani shot Brad an apologetic glance. "I hope you're not upset at me." She continued to leaf through the pages, stopping on one.

"No. You're right. We all need to eat."

On the page where she'd stopped, the blond woman stood outside a door, mouth open wide, a few lines emanating from her like she was calling out. The door, drawn dead center on the page at a rather severe angle, split the page in two, and on the other side, blackness. When he looked closer, a solitary figure was barely visible beneath the dark overlay.

"Do you have any idea what this is?"

Brad shook his head. "Um. . .not really. Some of these pieces may not make sense to us all these years later." He turned the page.

The next page depicted fifteen Native American men in uniform, seated at desks as the same blond-haired pair stood before them. The man wrote on a chalkboard while the woman faced the attentive men.

"That looks like. . .school?" Dani quirked a brow at him.

"I remember something about that. When we get back from lunch, I'll look."

Once more, he carefully turned the page to find a two-page spread filled with small drawings of common objects or places, with the English words carefully written beneath. Door. Wall. Fort. Spoon. Sailboat. Uniform. Item after item.

"This looks like school, doesn't it?" He indicated the page.

"Sure does."

Another page showed the Native American artist instructing the blond pair how to use bows and arrows, and still another depicted what looked like a buffalo hunt happening on a St. Augustine street. Still more pages followed with the small drawing of everyday items and their English names and, filling the last few inches of one of those pages, a drawing of the now-familiar blond pair. Beneath their pictures one caption, a little longer than the others.

Luke. Sally Jo. Broken Bow friends.

CHAPTER THIRTEEN

St. Augustine, Florida—Thursday, December 23, 1875

*P*ut that back." The storekeeper, Athol Kemp, glared at Broken Bow through the doorway to the back room.

Broken Bow returned the egg he'd picked up from the basket on the counter and put his hands in his pockets. Stepping away from the counter, he turned to view the road outside and focused on one of the Ka'igwa leaders, Lone Wolf, as he sat across the street drawing in his ledger book. Strange that he'd seen three of the Ka'igwa leaders using their day pass to leave the fort just to draw. Most times, if given the opportunity to leave the fort with a pass, the Indians shopped in local stores or provided entertainment to tourists.

"Ignore Papa."

He turned to face Mr. Kemp's daughter, Abigail, from where she arranged some kind of colorful objects on a shelf behind the counter.

"He's always a scrooge at this time of year."

Scrooge. This was not a word he'd learned in his classes at the fort.

"I heard that, Abby." Mr. Kemp stepped out and shot his daughter a perturbed look.

"I meant for you to hear me. It's Christmas, and you're as grumpy as the devil himself."

"Mind your tongue, child." He shot the young woman a stern look, then set three small paper-wrapped packages, each tied with flat, red string, on the counter.

"I'm not sure I ought to give these to you." The storekeeper eyed Broken Bow.

By now, he was used to such treatment. While the tourists who visited this town met him and the other Indian men with great interest and curiosity, the locals seemed far more fearful that they'd stir trouble.

"*Lieutena* Pratt say you give me." He tapped the instructions White Chief had written that morning.

Mr. Kemp's eyes narrowed. "Just not sure this is wise. I don't want you losin' 'em or breakin' 'em and it somehow comin' back so I've got to replace 'em."

Broken Bow pushed the note across the counter. "You write why you no give. I show *Lieutena* Pratt."

Miss Kemp sighed loudly. "Papa, stop. Broken Bow is following orders. If you don't let the man do his job, Lieutenant Pratt may forbid his Indians from shopping with us. That would be a large loss for the store."

The storekeeper stared another moment, then slid the packages across the counter. "Fine. But they'd better arrive—in one piece."

Broken Bow tucked the small parcels into the bag he'd slung across his body, then folded White Chief's note and tucked it inside as well. He gave both Mr. Kemp and his daughter a nod. "Thank you."

"Merry Christmas, Broken Bow." The young woman waved as she set to work again.

He nodded to Miss Kemp again, then ducked outside.

Christmas. Yet another word he didn't understand. Luke and Sally Jo had taken their holy book and attempted to explain this celebration to their students, but he didn't understand why the birth of one baby could cause so much happiness. In fact, much from their holy book didn't make sense to him yet. In his own culture, children were reason to rejoice. Men younger than himself were expected to marry and have children to keep their tribe strong. But his teachers said that the birth of the Christmas baby was reason for every person in every tribe to celebrate. What kind of a child could this be, that *everyone* should celebrate?

He sighed. There were many things he and the other men at the fort were not able to celebrate with their people. Births. Successful hunts. Traditional dances. Nor could they seek comfort among their own people as death came. And death *had* come to Fort Marion. Of the seventy-three men who'd been forced to travel the iron road to this place, several had died, mostly from something Dr. Janeway called *consumption*. In each case, the man's lungs had grown weak, and he'd begun to cough until he brought up blood. With every death, the hearts of those left behind grew hard, like stones in their chests. They all longed for home.

Broken Bow shook his head. The more he let his mind focus on such topics, the worse his attitude grew. He needed to finish his duties for White Chief and return to the fort. At least there he could talk to Painted Sky and others, tell stories, and remember better times.

He checked his list. He'd delivered the load of polished sea beans to the local jeweler, Ballard, who'd contracted the Indians to provide the interesting baubles. He'd taken White Chief's messages to two local businesses. Picked up the parcels from Kemp. Just one job left. Deliver papers to Major Hamilton at St. Francis Barracks. Along the short walk, people spoke to him, and he returned cordial greeting as White Chief had instructed, answered their questions, and eventually made it to the building. Once he was shown into the major's office, he withdrew the several important sheets from the bag he carried and held them out to the officer. Within moments, the man had looked them over, written something at the bottom of one, and handed them back.

"Make sure those are returned to your lieutenant, please."

"Yes, sir. I go to him now." He tucked the papers away and, once he was dismissed, stepped outside into the mild air. Turning toward Fort Marion, his gaze snagged on a familiar pair. Sally Jo perched on a short, backless chair, eyes focused on the river, and Luke stretched out on his side, propped on one elbow, a book open before him. Shoving his hands in his pockets, Broken Bow set off in their direction.

Luke happened to catch sight of his approach, and he and Sally Jo both stood, Luke gesturing in the sign language he and Painted Sky had begun teaching him.

Why are you outside the fort?

Broken Bow signed back. *Quiet down. You talk too much.*

Luke's jaw dropped open though he laughed.

Turning to Sally Jo, Broken Bow nodded at Luke. "I wish I no teach. Long time, Stumbling Tongue not silent."

Giggling, she sidled up beside her man. "No, *Stumbling Tongue* is not silent—ever—but that makes *me* very happy."

"Th-thank you!" Luke tugged her close, eliciting an adoring glance from her.

He looked again at Luke. "When you make her your woman?"

Sally Jo's cheeks reddened, but her light eyes reflected something more than the momentary embarrassment he'd hoped the teasing would bring.

Luke pulled her more fully into his arms. "As s-soon as her. . .father says I can."

"We hope he'll give his blessing in the next few days." Deep hurt peeked through her brave smile.

While he didn't understand their marriage rituals, such pain should not be part of any proper marriage custom. It brought him no happiness.

She drew a deep breath. "So why *are* you outside the fort?"

"White Chief say I. . ."—he always struggled with the word—". . . *orderling?* . . .today."

"Orderly? Again?" Her sadness fled, replaced with a wide smile.

"Order-ly." He nodded.

Luke signed again. *It's good!*

Broken Bow waved away the compliment. "White Chief make many man be order-ly. Different man each day."

She touched his sleeve. "But he often picks you, which means he trusts you."

Bashfulness overtook him, and he ducked to avoid the praise.

"You've ch-changed a lot since you f-first came. He sees that."

As Broken Bow's heart clouded with homesickness, his throat grew tight. "No change. My heart hurt for my people. Heart hurt to see home." But as much as he longed to see anything familiar, there was one thing he was glad he was missing. "Heart not hurt for. . .cold." He pantomimed a shiver.

Luke and Sally Jo chuckled.

"Well, if it ain't the troublemakers."

Broken Bow turned to see who the grating voice belonged to. At first glance, the man with shabby clothing and greasy, unkempt hair the color of a mouse's fur was unfamiliar. But there was something about his eyes.

The purpose with which the man strode toward him triggered a warning.

Everything in Broken Bow went still.

"Sergeant Pearson?" Sally Jo called out in confusion.

"Haven't been a sergeant since that uppity judge you call *daddy* got me court-martialed."

Broken Bow stared at the man's eyes. Why was he familiar?

"I know, and I'm sorry, Mr. Pearson." Sally Jo stepped into Broken Bow's view. "I never intended—"

"I see this one's learned to keep his clothes on."

Recognition came then. This was the one who'd struck him, put him on the ground.

As the man charged up, Luke tried to step in between them. Too late. Pearson crowded in, leaving no room for Luke to wedge anything but his hand between.

"S-s-stay calm."

Broken Bow *was* calm. *Deathly* calm. The familiar stillness he felt before every raid had returned.

"Shut up, you imbecile." Pearson spat the hate-filled words at Luke, though his gaze never left Broken Bow.

"Mr. Pearson, we were minding our own business." Sally Jo spoke loudly. "You mind yours, *please.*"

"I've got a score to settle, you little biddy."

As Pearson shook a finger at Sally Jo, a cold swirl overtook Broken Bow. "You not speak to my friends this way."

"Broken Bow!" Luke pleaded again.

"Or what?" The man crowded in, his foul breath fanning Broken Bow's skin. "You'll hurt me? Kill me?"

"Pearson!" Luke elbowed the man's shoulder.

Broken Bow glared. If he'd wanted to hurt or kill the man, it would've been done—twice by now.

"Just so we're clear, I'll speak to that Indian-lovin' wench however I please, you heathen." He stabbed a finger in Broken Bow's chest.

Luke tried to separate them. "Step back. D-don't touch him."

"Stop." Broken Bow flicked a warning glare at Luke. In that instant, Pearson's fist snaked out.

The punch caught him hard in the nose, rocking him backward as lightning burst behind his eyes. Broken Bow shook off the effects and loosed a fierce war cry, but before he could reach Pearson, something caught him around the ribs, and he toppled sideways into the grass. As an unexpected weight landed on him, the air rushed from his lungs.

"Stay d-down!" Luke shouted.

Instinct took over. Gasping for air, he fought, nearly pushed Luke off—but a wicked kick landed sharp against his ribs. Luke's weight collapsed against him again, and another wicked kick lodged just above his hip. Grabbing Luke's shirt, Broken Bow rolled, narrowly missing a third kick.

"Get off!" he snarled in the Tsitsistas tongue. He shook Luke fiercely and scrambled to his feet. Wiping wetness from his face, he turned toward his attacker, but bluecoats from St. Francis Barracks arrived, pointing their rifles at both Pearson and him.

"Pearson, Broken Bow!" Major Hamilton's sharp call rang out. "Enough! Fight's over."

The bluecoats surrounded them both. His breath coming in short gasps, he flicked a glance at the crowd that had formed—men and women, young and old, soldiers and not. Sally Jo pulled free of one strange man's grasp and rushed to Luke's side, where someone helped him up. Senses primed, Broken Bow eyed the crowd, noting the shock, horror, and distrust on the faces.

The major turned to one of his nearest men. "Private, I'll need to speak with these people." He waved at the whole group. "Make sure nobody leaves." He turned to a second one. "You—find several others and help him. No one but Pratt or Romero is allowed in or out."

Once the bluecoats set to work, Major Hamilton attempted to grasp his arm, but Broken Bow jerked free with a glare.

The officer held his hands up. "I'm sorry. I mean you no harm. Please... step over here." He nodded past the knot of people.

With pain lancing his side, Broken Bow limped ahead of the major, and once they stopped, the man handed him a folded white cloth from his pocket.

"Wipe your face. You're bleeding."

Broken Bow ran the back of his hand under his nose and, at the sight of blood, took the cloth.

"Tell me what happened."

"I leave you, see friends." He wiped his face, then nodded at Luke and Sally Jo. He'd thought Luke was his friend, but he'd had to fight him like he was on the other man's side. "I stop, talk. The man come up."

"Pearson."

Broken Bow gave one curt nod. "He say hard words to Sally Jo. Hit me." He pinned his focus on Luke again. "Then, that one attack. Knock me down. Pearson kick."

He uttered a perverse string of his thoughts in his native tongue, aimed at the man he'd thought was his friend.

"Broken Bow!"

He clamped down on the words and glared at the officer.

"Did you touch Pearson at all?"

He shook his head.

"Then you owe Mr. Worthing. If you'd touched that man, our courts could have sentenced you to hang."

"No talking! Major's orders."

The sharp words, spoken by the corporal—one of the two soldiers posted inside the medical tent to guard Broken Bow—only served to further fray Sally Jo's nerves. She stared across the space at Luke and Broken Bow, both shirtless, facing away from her, as they awaited Dr. Janeway to return and check them for injuries. Before they'd draped blankets over their shoulders, she'd seen the angry reddish-purple bruises that had formed on each man's side. Hopefully, only bruises—not broken ribs or internal injuries.

"Oh, sh-sh-shush!" Luke snapped the words at the soldier. "I was. . . just asking him if—"

"Silence!"

"Corporal!" Late afternoon sunlight flashed into the tent as Dr. Janeway returned from outside. "You're carrying this to an extreme." He stepped up beside Sally Jo. "Surely the major meant no talking about the incident. Don't you think?"

The corporal huffed without further response.

Dr. Janeway looked Sally Jo's way. "Are you well, Miss Harris?"

"Just a little shaken."

"In that case, I'm not sure whether to mention this."

A sigh escaped her. "My father's arrived?"

"No." He withdrew his pocket watch and clicked the cover open, then returned it to his pocket. "I'm certain that's imminent, given the hour, but no, there are four sailors outside who would like to speak with you, miss."

"Sailors?" She cocked her head. "Asking for *me*?"

"Yes. They gathered your belongings from the site of the altercation and would like to return them. If you're not up to speaking with them, I'll send the corporal out. Seems he needs more to do than stand idle inside my tent." He shot the man an exasperated look.

She smiled, then used the doctor's arm for balance as she stood. "I'll go myself, thank you."

"Would you like an escort? I can spare the corporal." He winked, eliciting a giggle this time.

"No, sir. I'll be fine."

Sally Jo slipped outside to find four men—two a bit older than Luke, one middle-aged man, and the last one a few years older than Papa. The youngest two held her quilt and basket.

"I'm Sally Jo Harris. I understand you're looking for me?"

For an awkward moment, the younger three glanced toward the oldest—a distinguished man with graying hair and a scruff of a beard. At his almost imperceptible nod, the others looked back toward her.

"Miss Harris. It's good to see you again." The young, blond, bearded one nodded.

"Are you all right, missy?" the middle-aged man asked at the same time.

"I'm sorry." She looked between them. "Have we met?"

"Ehh, after a fashion. Though I might understand why ye'd block us from yer mind, lass." The other young man's Scottish burr triggered her memory. "But maybe you'll recall ye dubbed me an...addlepated dunderhead?" He spoke the last words as if unsure.

The blond man shifted uncomfortably. "And me a doltish boor, I think."

"Boorish dolt, but. . ." Perhaps she *should* have asked for the corporal's escort.

The young Scotsman elbowed his friend. "See there? She does remember us!"

"I do. You were the three that accosted me and bruised my thumb when you grabbed my artist's palette." It had been hard to keep that mark hidden from her father. "The day the Indians arrived."

"Aye. 'Twas the day, all right."

She shifted toward the eldest man, who, up to now, had been silent. This one, she recalled, had come after the fact to check on her but, oddly, never said much. Once again, he seemed ever so familiar.

"And what business do you have with me today?"

"Very little, missy, except to make a late apology for our rude, drunken behavior."

An apology? "This is. . .unexpected, especially after all this time." She looked at each, her focus landing on the oldest man once more.

Still, he said nothing, looked away as soon as she turned her attention to him.

"And to make sure you and your friends were unharmed after today's incident." This from the blond man. "Forgive us for not apologizin' sooner. We've not seen you when we've been in port."

"Thank you for checking on us. I am thankfully unscathed, but both my friend and my beau have some bruised ribs after the episode. The doctor is attending to them now." She glanced back at the tent.

Of course, there was the question of what would happen to Broken Bow. Months ago, Lieutenant Pratt had dismissed the soldiers from the fort and began having the Indians police themselves. He'd given them uniforms, assigned them jobs according to the military system, and when difficulties like today's altercation occurred, especially when it involved the St. Augustine community, those in question would face investigation and trial within the fort by a jury of their Indian peers. The Indians had proven to be quick and stern with punishment. What repercussions would today's events bring Broken Bow's way? At least he wouldn't have to face a regular court of law.

"We'll not keep ye, lassie. We only wanted to wish ye well."

The silent man cleared his throat, and the Scotsman stepped forward to hold out her quilt. "And return yer things."

"Right." The blond one offered her the basket.

When she received the items, the silent man turned to leave.

"Wait." She looked at him, and he turned back. "You said you saw what happened today?"

Rather than the silent eldest, the Scotsman spoke. "Aye, lassie. We were comin' to offer our apology to you and your man friend for our last exchange. 'Twas hard to miss when all the shoutin' started."

She turned to the silent man. "You saw it also?"

He met her eyes for the briefest second. "Yes."

Sally Jo turned more fully toward him. "I'm sorry, what are your names?"

The quiet one cleared his throat, then indicated each man, starting with the farthest from him. "Joe Watson, Malachi Stepp, and Archie MacAuley." This time, he held her gaze an instant longer. "And Raymond Delmer. Captain of the *Mystic*."

The familiar ache lodged in her belly like a boulder. The *Mystic*. Mama's favorite ship.

She swallowed down her grief. "Thank you. As I said, I'm Sally Jo Harris. Have you all spoken to either Lieutenant Pratt or Major Hamilton about what you saw? They're taking witnesses' statements this evening. I know they'd like to hear your accounts."

Mr. Stepp shook his head. "We haven't yet, missy."

"If you'll come this way, I can make sure you get in to see the lieuten—"

"Sally Jo!" Her father's voice sent her heart into a staccato rhythm and shut down any response from the men.

The first three turned as Papa hurried over, but the captain shifted away and slumped like the weight of the world rested on his shoulders.

"Who are you?" Papa eyed them suspiciously.

Her heart jumped into her throat. "Papa, I assume you've heard what happened. These gentlemen witnessed today's events." She tried to force away her mounting apprehension. "Because Luke and Broken Bow were both injured, we left in a hurry. These men were kind enough to pack my belongings and return them." She nodded at the quilt.

"You." Papa glared at Captain Delmer, who'd moved slightly behind Mr. MacAuley. "I told you, you were never to set foot around my family again."

"Papa." When had the man ever. . . ? "I've never met this man before. Any of these men." At least not before six months ago, and barely then— had she?

Yet. . .if she hadn't, why did the captain seem familiar?

"I meant no harm." The captain's voice was quiet. "I wanted only to check on her well-being after today's altercation. That's all."

"You've caused irrevocable harm to this family, and I'll not allow you to do more. Get away from my daughter. All of you."

Mr. Watson's and Mr. MacAuley's eyes grew as wide as hers felt.

"Papa! They came to do a favor."

"Shut your mouth, child! There are things at work you don't understand."

She dropped the basket and quilt. "Then explain!"

Captain Delmer held up a hand as he met her father's eyes. "That is Lila's daughter, and she's no child."

How did he know Mama's name?

"Don't talk to me about my daughter or my wife!"

Sally Jo's mind spun. "What is going on?"

The tent flaps behind her rustled, and several bodies spilled out of the canvas structure.

"Don't worry, Judge. I'm going. And you have my word—I won't seek this young lady out again." His expression hardened then, and he pointed his index finger straight at Papa's chest. "But don't you dare, for one minute, try to lay the blame for Lila solely at my feet. You are as much—or more—to blame as I am."

Papa hit Captain Delmer square in the jaw, and the captain stumbled backward. Almost fell. Mr. Stepp caught him as Watson and MacAuley formed a barrier between the two men. Dr. Janeway and a young private rushed to pull Papa back.

"That's enough!" the surgeon warned.

Strong arms pulled her into the warmth of a shirtless, blanket-wrapped embrace.

"You four! It's time you go!" Janeway jabbed a finger toward the docks.

"And you." He turned to Papa.

"No!" Trembling, Sally Jo resisted the urge to burrow deeper against Luke and instead faced the crowd. "Tell me what is going on here!" Everyone went silent as she turned on Captain Delmer. "How do you know my mother?"

Delmer once again hung his head.

"Papa?" She turned his direction, though he had averted his eyes as well. "Someone speak! Don't I deserve to know about my own mother?"

Silence hung so thick it almost choked her.

"Speak!"

"Your mother and I had an ongoing affair for years," Delmer grunted.

Again, MacAuley and Watson's faces registered surprise, though Mr. Stepp only closed his eyes in resignation. A murmur ran through the group, and no one seemed to breathe.

An affair—with a ship's captain? Mama had always been enamored with the big vessels, especially when the *Mystic* came to port. Memories of her putting on a new dress. . .her best dress. . .and leading Sally Jo by the hand down to the docks when she was ten, eleven, twelve. Too young and naive to know better.

Papa stood stone-faced.

"Oh Lord, help. It's true, isn't it?" She bored holes into her father with her staring.

Dr. Janeway snapped a glance around the group. "Maybe you ought to continue this in the tent."

"I won't continue anything." Papa turned on Captain Delmer. "And you won't either, you—"

"Stop it, Papa!" her voice shrilled.

"Let's go, young lady! Home. Now." He clamped onto her hand and attempted to drag her toward him, but Luke dropped his blanket and grabbed each of their wrists.

"No, sir! Release her."

Papa looked first at Luke's hand on his arm, then to Luke's flinty face. "You stammering little simpleton. Who do you think you are?"

Luke stood tall and met Papa's eyes. "Sally Jo's future husband. Let. Her. Go."

For a tense instant, Papa and Luke stared each other down before Papa finally loosed his viselike grip on her hand. As soon as she was free, Luke pulled her to him and held her tight.

"I'm done here." Papa stormed off several steps.

"Captain, sir." Mr. Stepp looked at Delmer. "You gonna press charges against this. . .boorish dolt, was it?" He glanced Sally Jo's way, and she gave a tiny nod. "This boorish dolt for hittin' you?"

Papa's footsteps faltered, and he turned back. "You wouldn't dare."

The captain faced him. "You hit me. Seems within my rights. But I might be persuaded not to if you'll stay and talk to your daughter."

The most hateful expression crossed Papa's features, and he studied every face in the group.

Dr. Janeway folded his arms. "I might be made to forget what I've seen under such circumstances."

The others nodded in agreement.

Delmer spoke again. "We can either tell her together, Judge, or I'll tell her myself, but she deserves the truth."

Stomach roiling, Sally Jo pulled free of Luke's embrace, then marched to the tent and held a flap open. "Papa?"

"I will tell you whatever you want to know. But not here. And not with him." He flung a hand in Delmer's direction. "Come home and we'll talk."

She narrowed a glance his way. "If that's how you feel, go, but I am not going with you. We'll have this conversation here or not at all." Sally Jo shifted toward Delmer. "Captain?"

Without hesitation, Delmer walked toward the tent, pausing to retrieve Luke's blanket. After handing it over, he stepped through the open flap.

Panic in his eyes, Papa stood absolutely still before he forced himself toward the tent.

Janeway went to the opening. "Broken Bow, gather your things and come here so I can check your ribs."

As the Cheyenne brave reached the entrance, he looked Sally Jo straight in the eye. "You are well?"

She swallowed down a sob and shook her head. "No."

His eyes darkened, and he looked toward Luke, his concern evident.

"Move along, Broken Bow." The corporal herded him through the opening.

"Miss Harris?" The doctor caught her eye. "We won't be far, in case you need us."

She nodded, then ducked inside, Luke right behind her.

Once the tent flap settled into place, she reached for her beau's hand and approached Delmer and Papa. "Somebody start. How did Mama have an affair?"

The captain drew a deep breath. "You were there the day it began, miss. It was the last year of the war, and you were maybe nine at the time. It was all so innocent at first."

"Innocent! You are anything but!"

Delmer gave Papa a harsh look but continued. "Lila brought you to the docks to take in the scenery. The two of you were standing in the same spot where you like to do your artwork now, and I happened to be walking past. It was you I noticed first. Your mother and I struck up a conversation, and we found each other to be good listeners. She was lonely and hurting after the long separation from your father. We talked of how we both hoped the conflict would end soon. That was all. Just talk."

"I wrote your mother often." Papa's attitude was building into a boil. "She knew I longed to be home with her just as much as she was missing me."

"Once the war ended, we ran across each other very accidentally the next time I was in port. She told me how hard life was with a soldier just back from the war. Again, very benign. But with each successive visit, I'd find her standing in that spot, so I'd walk by, say hello. The conversations grew longer. She began finding ways to leave you with a friend or leave home once you were tucked in bed for the night. The talks moved aboard the *Mystic*. She was unhappy in her marriage—the war changed a lot of men, him included." He nodded toward Papa. "I was tired of the long nights alone. One thing led to another."

Papa bristled visibly. "She was not unhappy."

"Women content in their marriages don't seek solace in another man's bed."

Papa flinched so hard, Sally Jo drew back.

Luke settled himself behind her and caressed her shoulders. "I'm here."

"Lila said she became even more disillusioned after you became a judge. She wanted to teach, and you told her such things were beneath the station of a judge's wife."

"Lies! All lies."

Sally Jo sucked in a sharp breath. "Are they, Papa? Months ago, when Sarah was at the house, she said you prevented Mama from following her call to teach. That didn't make any sense to me—until now."

"Lila told me that was the first of many things your father deemed 'beneath' her station. She felt trapped."

"I know that feeling." Her chin quivered, and she leaned back into Luke's chest.

"What do you have to complain about?" Papa's brown eyes flashed. "I've provided you everything you need, child."

She pulled away from Luke then. "You've provided everything but the truth! You've conveniently omitted telling me this part of Mama's life. You've withheld your blessing to keep me from marrying Luke. Goodness, Papa—you didn't even want me to teach at the fort. Just like what you did to Mama."

Papa took on the look of a caged animal, stressed and searching for a way out.

She looked again toward the captain. "You said Papa shouldn't lay the blame for Mama's death solely at your feet." Her voice quavered. "But how is Mama's drowning anyone's fault?"

"He killed her!" Papa jabbed a finger at Delmer.

The captain grabbed Papa's coat lapel. "We both did, you—"

"Stop it!" Luke waded between the two, his blanket abandoned again.

Seconds of agonizing silence filled the tent, and her tears began to flow.

Luke pushed the two men apart "T-tell us what happened."

Captain Delmer scrubbed a hand over his face. "We were finally found out when the judge followed Lila on one of her evening walks. She said he confronted her when she came home, told her exactly where she'd walked, how long she'd been aboard my ship. Lila said he threatened to divorce her, leave her penniless. To keep their daughter from her."

"I never would have done those things. I loved her. I just wanted her to stop seeing you."

The captain turned an icy stare Papa's way. "She didn't know that. She was terrified when she came to me that next day." Looking again toward Sally Jo, he continued. "Your mother told me everything, begged me to marry her. And I would have except. . ." Once again, he dropped his gaze. "I was already married."

Her knees went soft, and she collapsed into a nearby chair.

"We fought. She said I'd betrayed her because I'd never told her about my wife. She was so distraught, she ran from my quarters and, before I could stop her, she jumped overboard."

"But Mama couldn't swim!"

An agitated breath rattled from Delmer's chest. "I went in after her, but the water was murky and the current strong. Once she went under, she never came back up until it was far too late."

CHAPTER FOURTEEN

*B*roken Bow chafed as the doctor prodded his side. Before traveling the iron road, he had survived countless raids and battles. Been wounded badly enough he'd traveled to the edge of this life—and returned. But Major Hamilton insisted the white doctor check on him after the attack. Other than to bloody his nose and make him angry, Pearson had done nothing.

But standing here while he was prodded did allow him to stay near the tent. He couldn't hear the words being spoken inside, but the heatedness and torment—particularly in Sally Jo's voice—was evident. He didn't understand what was going on—just that his friends were upset and the two men who'd entered the tent with them had something to do with it.

"You're bruised, but none of your ribs are broken."

As the doctor straightened and attempted to take his face in his hands, Broken Bow drew back, startled.

"I was told you were hit in the face. Yes?" The man's eyebrows arched.

He nodded.

"Then let me look."

Chafing more, Broken Bow submitted to the further inspection. When the doctor touched a particularly tender spot on the bridge of his nose, he grabbed the man's wrist.

"Done!"

"Almost."

He shook his head. "You done."

Broken Bow stepped back, snatched his shirt from the ground where he'd set it, and pulled the still-buttoned garment over his head. Once he'd tucked it in, he reached for his uniform coat and hat.

"You might have a mild concussion. I'm going to recommend Pratt allow you to rest a couple days before he puts you back to work."

Before Broken Bow could grumble about the coddling treatment, voices rose from inside the tent. Every sense on alert, Broken Bow shifted toward the entrance, but Dr. Janeway, the corporal, and one of the other men blocked his path.

"Move." If Luke or Sally Jo was in trouble—

"Stop it!" Luke's voice rang out, sharp and clear through the tent walls—no stumbling. Then everything went deathly still inside.

"Go with the corporal. Back to the fort."

Broken Bow shook his head. "My friends inside."

"Your friends will be fine. Go." He flicked a glance at the bluecoat corporal. "Take him, now."

The short, bony boy—barely older than those who guarded the Tsitsistas herds—attempted to exert a firm hold on Broken Bow's arm as he led him away. Did they think this child would be any match for him? He stood at least a head taller and was far thicker through the chest and arms than this...twig. He could easily subdue the scrawny bluecoat—even with his side aching and his head pounding.

But breaking free, even to return to check on Luke and Sally Jo, would not be wise. It would break the trust he'd built with White Chief and might make people believe he was guilty in the attack Pearson committed against them.

No. He had done nothing wrong. Despite his concern for Luke and Sally Jo, he must act honorably with White Chief. Surely by now, Major Hamilton would have told him the circumstances. If so, he might be able to convince the chief to let him return to the tent.

The bluecoat corporal walked him over the first bridge. Before they reached the second, Broken Bow tugged gently to free his arm. "Let go."

"I have to take you in the fort."

He shook the coat he was still holding. "I wear."

The boy's eyes widened, and he released his grip.

It took only a moment to pull on the coat and button the brass buttons, though in all the wrestling he and Luke had done, one was now missing.

As soon as he'd finished, the boy gripped his arm again and marched him inside to a closed door within the east wall. He knocked, and one of the Ka'igwa men opened it.

"Let Lieutenant Pratt know I've brought Broken Bow."

The Ka'igwa man nodded and pulled the door closed, but not before Broken Bow caught sight of a familiar face seated directly across from White Chief. *Pearson*. His posture didn't indicate a man facing trouble. He leaned back in his chair, one ankle resting on the opposing knee, and his arm slung across the back of an empty chair.

Why was his attacker here? The image of the greasy-haired man set his belly on edge, particularly after the major told him that if he'd even touched Pearson, he could have been tried in white man's court and hung.

How was that fair? He'd been attacked!

White Chief stepped out, shutting the door quickly.

"Sir, I need to know. . ." The scrawny corporal attempted to force Broken Bow forward with him, though when he didn't flinch, the boy tottered back. His blemished cheeks grew red. "Um, where do you want me to put this one, sir?"

"For goodness' sake, Corporal, let him go." White Chief waved at the boy's hand gripped tightly around Broken Bow's arm. "I'll speak with Broken Bow a moment. Wait there until I call for you." He motioned to the staircase leading to the gun deck.

"Yes, sir." The corporal stalked off.

For a moment, White Chief looked Broken Bow up and down, then shook his head. "You look a little worse for wear. Are you all right?"

"Worse for wear?" He tested the words, unsure of their meaning. Broken Bow looked at the blood on his coat and pants, the grass and dirt stains adorning his knees. He smoothed his rumpled garments into slightly better position and stood at attention. "I sorry, White Chief. I clean. Make right."

"No." A slight smile curved the corners of White Chief's lips. "At ease."

Broken Bow relaxed again.

"You misunderstand. Worse for wear means. . .never mind. Just. . .are you all right? Are you hurt?"

"No hurt." Maybe he could convince the chief he didn't need days of rest like the doctor suggested. "I go to bunk? Get new clothes?"

"Don't worry about that. We'll get you fresh clothes soon, but I need to speak with you now."

He nodded. "Speak."

White Chief's face grew grim. "I talked to Major Hamilton about what happened between you and Mr. Pearson."

"Then you know. I do nothing."

"I believe that is true."

He nodded at the chief.

"But I've also spoken to Mr. Pearson, who has lodged a complaint that you threatened him."

"What is. . .threatened?"

White Chief closed his eyes, almost as if it hurt him to speak the words. "He says you promised to do him harm."

Broken Bow drew back as if slapped. "No! I no say. No. . .threatened. Pearson say bad things to Sally Jo!"

"And I trust that that's what will come out of our investigation, but we do have to investigate. Talk to everyone."

"Yes. Talk. . .everyone! I no do threatened!"

"We will. I promise you, but. . ." The man's expression turned apologetic. "I am going to need to put you in the dungeon until our investigation is done."

"Dungeon?" His heart stalled at the difficult memories of the black cave. "I do no wrong."

"It's a formality, Broken Bow. Just while we complete our investigation."

He shook his head, the motion causing his skull's throbbing to magnify. "Why you punish me? I do no wrong!"

"You're not understanding. It's a formality. A. . .a rule. It won't be for—"

"Foolish rule!" Lightning coursed through his body, and he paced, glaring at the chief. For the second time that day, he spewed vile Tsitsistas words liberally.

At the tumult, other Indians appeared, lining the walls of the gun deck as well as spilling from rooms around the courtyard. He was vaguely aware that White Chief ordered the corporal to find Romero. Not long afterward, the interpreter appeared with Painted Sky.

"Broken Bow, take a breath and let's talk." Romero waved to the far side of the courtyard.

"There is nothing to say!" He flung a hand at Pratt. "White Chief does not act honorably. I did nothing wrong, yet he will put me in the black cave."

Romero translated, and the chief shook his head.

"I won't put you in the dark."

"Lies! You said you will put me in the dungeon!"

Again, Romero translated.

"In the dungeon, yes. But with a lamp. A cot. Blankets. Your book and paint sticks. Other books to read. You will have normal meals, and you can talk to Painted Sky and others when they are not on duty."

His thundering heart slowed a little, but he still glared. "Why do you put me in the dungeon even with these things. I haven't done anything. I didn't threaten Pearson, and I never touched him. He speaks lies."

White Chief glanced at the crowd, then lowered his voice. "This short confinement gives me the chance to talk to everyone. Hear what they say happened without you being able to talk to them. This is important to my investigation."

"You said I *could* talk to others."

"You will not be allowed to speak with any witnesses—Miss Harris, Mr. Worthing, or others. But you can speak to those who didn't see it."

He moved in, crowding Pratt. "This is not right. I did not do what I am accused of."

White Chief nodded. "I know, and I will prove that you didn't do this as quickly as I can."

"What about Pearson? He says I threatened him, but he struck me. He kicked Luke. Spoke badly to Sally Jo."

"We'll look at that too." He blew out a breath. "Broken Bow, I know it feels like I'm betraying you, but have I done wrong to you up until now?"

He thought for a moment. "No."

"Then please trust me in this too."

Broken Bow stared at the faces of the men who'd gathered—and at Pearson's face as he smirked from the other side of the window. "What you ask is hard, but show me the dungeon with cot, blankets, lamp, and books, and I will go. Not happily, but I will."

Help. Lord, help.

Sally Jo wrapped her arms around her middle and prayed that one phrase over and over. It was hard to breathe. The revelations of these past minutes had left her both numb and heartsick.

"All right, young lady. You've heard it." Papa trembled visibly. "Let's go. We'll talk further at home."

At the pleading look she shot toward Luke, he snatched his shirt from the cot and pulled it on as he went to her side. "We. . .can't leave, s-sir."

"She's my *unmarried* daughter. She'll go where I tell her to go."

Sally Jo shook her head. "Lieutenant Pratt needs to speak to us about Broken Bow."

"To hades with Broken Bow!" She flinched as Papa roared the words.

Captain Delmer lunged up from the cot where he'd sat, and sunlight flashed as Dr. Janeway and the private entered.

"Judge Harris!" Janeway snarled. "You've overstayed your welcome. Get out."

"I'm trying. If you'll tell the lieutenant I'll bring my daughter by later to wrap up any business she has, we'll be on our way."

A humiliated Papa was not a safe Papa. If he removed her out of this tent, particularly without Luke, there was no telling what might happen. She didn't *think* he'd harm her, but. . .deny her seeing Luke? Ship her off to live with one of his sisters up north? Move her somewhere far from this whole repugnant situation, where she couldn't further besmirch his reputation by digging into the past. . .that, he might do. Probably would.

Panting, she looked at the doctor. "I don't wish to go with my father."

The doctor stood taller as he faced her father again. "You heard the young lady. I'll say it again. Please leave."

"Sarah Josephine Harris, now." Papa stabbed a finger at the ground in front of him.

"Call me whatever name you want." She clamped on to Luke's arm and pulled herself up, quivering in trepidation. "I'm not going with you."

"Private." Dr. Janeway eyed the young soldier as he circled to Papa's far side. "Please help me escort Judge Harris toward his home."

The soldier gulped visibly but held the tent flap open. "Sir? This way, please."

"I'm quite capable of finding my own way home." His mortification complete, Papa took one more look around, then stormed out.

The doctor followed Papa but paused at the entrance. Turning back, he faced Captain Delmer. "You too. Out."

Delmer strode out without so much as a glance her way. Fine by her. She never wanted to see him again nor his ship. She would likely never paint or draw another scene by the docks now that she understood Mama's fascination. It wasn't the grand ships she'd loved. It was him. And Mama had brought her, as a young, impressionable girl, along to her trysting place, made it seem innocuous and enjoyable. Oh, the duplicity.

"Sally Jo?"

One look at Luke's concerned face, and sobs overtook her. He pulled her close and held her tight, whispering soothing words. She clung to him, bunching his unbuttoned shirt in her hands.

She'd been betrayed. Mama had taken her to church until the very last Sunday of her life, professing a deep faith in God and a happy marriage to Papa, all while seeking love with another man. And Papa's harsh, unbending ways led—at least in part—to Mama taking her life, but he'd let her believe her mother's death was an accident.

"Are. . .you all right?" Luke whispered the question against her hair.

"What am I supposed to do now?" Her words came out in a hoarse whisper.

He cupped her head in his hands, settling his forehead against hers. "I'm s-sorry, love."

"I can't go home. I'm afraid Papa won't let you come near me anymore. Or he'll send me to live with one of his sisters, or to a convent, or something. Somewhere where I can't reach you and you'll never find m—"

Luke kissed her soundly, stalling her words and her reeling thoughts. Electricity crackled across her lips, and she gasped. He paused, pulled back, looked at her ever so briefly, then swooped in again with a passion.

For one heavenly moment, her fears calmed, and while her pulse still raced, it raced with exultation not trepidation. When, seconds later, he broke the kiss and once again settled his forehead against hers, hands still cupping her face, she was breathless and weak-kneed.

"M-marry me, Sally Jo."

"I've already told you I will once Papa—"

He shook his head against hers. "He'll n-never give his blessing. We just need to do. . .this."

She pulled back, wide-eyed. "Without his consent?"

"It. . .won't come. You just s-said you're afraid he'll keep us apart. Once we're m-m-married, he won't be able to."

"But. . ." Her trepidation tried to reassert its hold. "You see how everyone treats Papa. They all fear him. Where will we find a minister in St. Augustine who would marry us without his blessing?"

"We'll go n-north. . .to Jacksonville. Or f-farther if we have to."

She stared. "When?"

"Leave first thing t-t-tomorrow. Get married on Christmas."

Hope sprouted in her heart with the idea. "Yes!"

CHAPTER FIFTEEN

Joie-Rides Restoration, St. Augustine, Florida—
Present Day—Monday Afternoon

Speak, Danielle.

She'd wanted to say something before they'd left for lunch—while Matty was at Frank's house—but the words wouldn't come then either. Why was it so hard?

"Thanks for driving, Brad." Matty nodded from the large backseat as Brad pulled into a parking space in the Joie-Rides parking lot.

Brad put the truck in park. "Thanks for lunch. Seems like a nice group."

"Some of 'em are pretty rough, but they're good people." He leaned forward and poked her in the shoulder. "Hold this, darlin'." He thrust Brynn's balloon toward her. "So it won't escape when I open the door."

Dani received the balloon, and Matty exited and shut the door gently. When he peeked toward the sleeping Brynn, Dani also twisted to see if she'd awakened. Still out cold. She gave Matty a thumbs-up.

The big man stepped up to the driver's door as Brad put the window down. "Y'all headin' back to Frank's house?"

"Yeah. We're trying to figure out where the ledger art came from."

Matty turned his attention to her. "You're awful quiet, darlin'. What's on your mind?"

"Just. . .thinking." Pondering what Brad had revealed about the artwork hanging in Franklin's—Frank's—house and the stories she'd heard over lunch regarding the man who'd fathered her. "Do you know where the book came from, Matty?"

"Wish I did, darlin'."

"That's too bad." Brad fidgeted with his to-go drink in the cupholder, his arm brushing hers. "The drawings look authentic, but if we can't prove the provenance. . ."

"In your industry, I'd imagine that's a problem." A coy grin crossed Matty's face. "Y'all need to pray and go on a goose chase in the house."

Dani squirmed a little. "I, um. . .I don't think I'm qualified like you are."

"There's nothing any more special about me than you." He nodded at her. "Y'know, darlin', it's so simple even Little One back there could do it. All you do is ask, then listen."

"Listen for what? It's not like God speaks."

"Oh, He speaks. Not in a booming, audible voice, but He most definitely speaks." Matty cocked his head. "What you listen for is in here." He tapped his head and chest. "Thoughts, impressions, feelings. An idea that won't leave you alone. Your eye keeps gettin' drawn back to somethin' or someone. Just be still and tune in to those quiet prompts."

Brad glanced her way, obviously gauging her reception of what Matty said.

Dani shook her head at him. "I appreciate the instruction, but I don't know about all this."

"Just throwin' it out there, darlin'. Do with it what you want." He tapped a fist on Brad's door. "I'll let y'all know when we're wrappin' up, and we'll figure out what to do for dinner."

Brad gave her a sidelong glance, then looked back at Matty. "Dani and I can figure that out, since you bought the pizza."

"All right. Deal."

Matty started toward the building, and Brad put the truck in reverse.

"You don't mind that I volunteered us, do you?" He coasted backward.

"No." Her gaze drifted again toward Matty. "Will you wait a minute?" Dani unbuckled her seat belt. "I need to say something to Matty."

"Sure." Once Brad parked the truck, she handed him the balloon.

"Matty!" She slid out into the sweltering June heat, leaving the door partially open so she wouldn't wake Brynn.

He turned back at the edge of the Joie-Rides building. "What's up?"

"I, um. . ." She stuck her hands in her back pockets. "I think I owe you an apology."

"For?"

"I've been really hard on you about Frank's art—about Frank, in general."

His brows arched. "Go on."

"When Brad saw the paintings in the house, he was able to show me, through the eyes of a knowledgeable art guy, that there are a few things that make it seem maybe Frank *wasn't* trying to forge those paintings." She detailed the signatures and the mirror-image portion.

Matty grinned. "You realize I'm tryin' real hard not to say I told you so."

"I figured. And I wouldn't blame you if you did. I don't know anything about the paintings he was arrested for, but at least those don't seem to be what I thought."

"Thank you, darlin'. Good of you to say so."

A knot lodged in her throat. "And. . .I was listening to the stories everyone was sharing about Frank at lunch and at your church yesterday, and. . ." She tried desperately to swallow the tears threatening to erupt. "If I can make myself listen without seeing him as the father I never knew, he sounded like a really great guy." Her voice dropped to a hush.

Stunned, Matty pulled her into a giant bear hug. "Your daddy was the best, darlin'." His voice rumbled against her ear. "He had the biggest heart you'll ever find."

"For everyone but me." A sob rocked her, and she leaned into Matty. "Why didn't he ever come back? Why didn't he want me?"

He held her tighter. When he spoke seconds later, his own voice was husky. "He wanted you, Dani. Desperately. It ate him alive that he wasn't there for you."

"But why wasn't he?"

A deep growl rumbled through him, and he shook his head. "Lord Jesus, how do I keep my word at a time like this?"

"Your word?" Her heart stalled. He was keeping secrets from her—about her own father? She pushed back to stare at him. "Your word on *what?*"

He closed his eyes and gritted his teeth. "I can't say. I've been sworn to secrecy."

"By who?"

"Frank."

She huffed and wiped her tears. "Matty, Frank's dead. All bets are off. You kept your promise for his lifetime."

"It wasn't for *his* lifetime. It was for mine—he said I could never tell anyone."

Anger roiled through her. "Including the one person it matters to most?" She backed up a step, studying the pain in his features. "Looks like this secret is eating you alive too, but you'd honor a promise to a dead man before the living!"

He heaved a breath. "All I can say is the truth will come out."

"When? Because I've been waiting for twenty-six years for answers."

Again, his eyes clamped shut. "Soon enough."

She laughed contemptuously. "So says the secret keeper."

He wouldn't meet her eyes.

"Fine. Whatever." She walked halfway to Brad's truck but rounded on him again. "Y'know, all my life, Mom, Alec, and Grandpa Dale said Frank was a self-centered, unscrupulous crook. A low-class grifter. I've lived with the pall of being an art forger's daughter—always looked at like a third-class citizen by my private school classmates and the hoity-toity types my family runs with. And you have information that could help me begin to make sense of that part of my life I've always loathed, but you'd rather keep a promise to a dead man. Fine! Keep your secrets." She punctuated the last line with a curse and turned toward Brad's truck.

"Darlin'."

"I'm done!" She stalked away, tears streaming.

"Dani!"

She climbed into Brad's truck again.

"Are you all right?" Brad's eyes held deep concern.

"Would you please drive me somewhere?"

"All right." He guided the truck out of the parking space and onto the road. "Where?"

She gulped down several breaths. "I don't care. Just drop me somewhere and—"

"Drop you somewhere?!"

"I'm going to call my best friend. She'll take me home."

He hit the brakes, coming to a dead stop, and Brynn's balloon floated forward from where he'd secured it in the backseat. Once he'd thrown the truck in park, he batted the balloon out of the way and turned to her. "Dani, what's going on? What just happened?"

"You and Brynn don't need this. You don't need my brand of crazy on top of everything you're going through. Just take me somewhere where I can wait for Rachel, please."

"No! I'll take you somewhere, but I'm not leaving you." He put the truck in drive, then brushed her hand, resting on the center console. "Let me worry about what Brynn and I need." He stared to drive again.

They rode in silence until her tears abated and her breathing became more normal. Then Brad reached over and, eyes darting between her and the road, rubbed a hand over the back of her head, letting it settle at her neck.

"Are you okay?"

Silent, she nodded.

"What happened?"

She rested her elbow on the window ledge and rubbed her temple. "I was trying to apologize for how hard-nosed I've been about Frank. I told Matty that between your info about the paintings and the stories the Joie-Rides guys told about him, if I could disconnect their stories from the no-good bum I call *father*. . .he sounded really nice."

"I had the same thought. My dad used to call guys like Frank the 'salt of the earth.' Not rich or notable, probably flew under the radar most times. But the kind you could call at all hours, and they'd show up with a smile and give you the shirt off their back."

"Exactly. Except Frank never showed up for me." Another hiccupping sob bubbled forth.

Brad grasped her hand. "Dani, I'm sorry."

The unexpectedness of the comforting gesture startled her, and she resisted the urge to pull away.

"I can't imagine the hurt that caused you."

Boatloads.

She stared at his hand wrapped reassuringly around hers and wiped at the lingering wetness on her cheeks. If this train wreck hadn't run him off, she really needed to get herself under control before she spooked the poor man for good. She gulped a couple of breaths and fought her emotion back into submission. "Apparently, Matty knows why Frank never came to see me, but he'd rather not tell me to keep a promise to Frank, even though Frank's gone. That really upset me."

"I don't understand. Did he explain?"

Dani tucked her hair behind her ears. "Only to say everything would be revealed soon."

"What does that mean?"

"In Matty-speak? Probably whenever we stand at the pearly gates or face God's wrath. . .or whatever comes next."

He grew quiet. "So you don't agree with Matty's religious beliefs much."

"It's not that I don't agree. I don't understand. My family's never attended church, so I don't get the attraction."

"You said earlier that you feel like something bigger is pulling the strings."

"Yeah, but is that God or some cosmic accident or—" She shrugged. "Is this a bunch of mumbo-jumbo or something real?" Dani brushed imaginary dust from her jeans.

"Do you believe in God?"

"Yeah, although this world seems mighty screwed up to say He wants to be involved with us. And I really don't know if I believe anyone can have the kind of relationship with God that Matty describes." She glanced sideways at him. "What do you think?"

"I'm a little more used to the idea than you. Mom professed a deep faith in God, always made sure we went to church. After she died, Dad took us to church as often as he could, but he was busy. Since he passed, I've been pretty disillusioned. Losing both parents by age nineteen, Trey's addiction problems, him getting Jazz pregnant. But in sheer desperation, I begged God a couple of days ago to give me some kind of good news about Brynn. Half an hour later, Lieutenant Lipscomb called with the news she'd been found."

"Really?" Her heart pounded a little faster. "And you think that was

God answering your prayers?"

"I'm going to choose to believe it was Him." He squeezed her hand. "And then there's the whole thing of how we met."

"Yeah. I still can't wrap my head around it all."

"Speaking of. . ." Brad jutted his chin as the Castillo de San Marcos came into view. He pulled into the parking lot and found an empty space.

Her smile grew. "Why'd you come here?"

"Couple of reasons. First, I don't know St. Augustine, so I brought you to the one peaceful place I knew. The grounds are like a park. Beautiful green grass, sparkling water, room to walk around. And second, I thought maybe the gift shop might have a book about the time the Native Americans were here. It won't prove how Frank got the artwork, but it might help us understand the art better—add some credence to its authenticity."

"Thank you." She wiped her eyes again. "I appreciate you bringing me here."

"Wait right there."

"Okay?"

He cut the engine and circled around, opened her door and Brynn's, blocking them into the space of a small coat closet. Brad offered her a hand and, once she'd unbuckled and climbed down, he pulled her to him and held her. The spinning in her mind and chest further slowed.

"I know you wanted me to leave you here." He pulled back to look her in the eye. "But it's not my style to leave a damsel in distress. And we've both got some crazy going on."

"Some?" She scrunched her nose. "Brad, I've got it in spades."

"And I don't?"

"Your crazy is because you're doing something really important. You're taking care of Brynn. You're going to give her a good life. Me? I'm just a mixed-up little girl in a grown-up girl's body."

His lips parted, and his brows arched slightly.

"You don't need my crazy piled on yours. That's a whole 'nother level of cray-cray!"

"Dani, whose life isn't crazy? I spent a *lot* of time yesterday afternoon convincing myself that I couldn't afford the mental real estate of a woman in my life right now, but—"

"Not this woman. The fact that I just had a Chernobyl-level meltdown should prove that."

"Stop! Quit trying to hold me at an emotional arm's length, please. You just said something really important."

"I did?"

"Yes. You know how you said it felt like we were supposed to work on the mystery of this artwork together?"

"Yeah."

"I just had a similar moment." He closed his eyes, brow furrowing. "Dani, it doesn't matter how well I raise Brynn. That job should be my brother's, but he's royally messed up his life, and that's forever changed hers. She might face the same questions and feelings you have with your dad's arrest."

"Ohhhh." The statement drove home like a spike through her heart.

"I'm still scratching my head over the way we met, but what if God put us together so I can help you discover the truth about this artwork, and you can help Brynn and me navigate the pitfalls we might face on the road we have to walk?"

She drew a shaky breath. "So my brand of crazy might actually be useful?"

"Well, I wouldn't have wished it on you, but now that you've lived through it, maybe something good can come of it. And goodness knows, I'm in way over my head raising a little girl."

Dani wobbled a smile at him. "You don't have anything to worry about. You've got great instincts."

Her cell phone vibrated in her purse, hanging forgotten against her hip. Brad released her, and she pulled the device from its pocket.

"It's Matty." Wide-eyed, she shoved the device at him. "You answer it."

"Dani. . ."

She handed him the phone, then slipped past Brynn's open door toward the back of his truck. At the tailgate, she turned to see him click into the call.

"Hey Matty, it's Brad." He scowled as he slipped past Brynn's door too. "Yeah, she's safe. We're in the parking lot at the fort."

Dani shook her head. "Don't tell him where we are!" She gritted the words in a whisper.

He shot her a stern look while covering the microphone. "If you want me to talk, don't get mad at what I say." Brad pulled his hand from the phone. "Yeah, she was pretty upset. Wanted me to drop her off somewhere."

"Oh my—" She threw her hands up.

Just as quickly, he wagged a finger at her with another scowl. "She said she was going to call her friend to drive up and get her." He jerked the phone from his ear before slowly bringing it back into place.

"Of course I didn't! What kind of a man would I be if I left her?" He stared at her as he listened a moment, then nodded. "Looking right at her, three feet away." Another pause, then another nod. "Hang on."

Brad stepped nearer and held the phone out to her. "He's worried and wants to talk to you."

Swallowing hard, she eyed the device—perhaps too long, because Brad stepped nearer still.

"You really freaked him out. Please take the phone."

Trembling, she brought it to her ear. "Hello?"

"Thank You, Lord Jesus." Matty's breathy whisper crackled with relief. For a moment, all was silent, then his deep voice rumbled across the line. "Darlin', honest to God, I was not tryin' to torque you off. There's a reason I can't tell you what you want to know. But it will come out, and it'll be this week."

Heart aching afresh, she fought—unsuccessfully—to keep the emotion from her voice. "I don't understand, Matty."

"I know you don't. But please, come back and talk to me. I've got something that might help. Please, darlin'?"

She nodded. "All right."

As Brad drove back to Frank's place, Dani looked at the books he'd bought from the Castillo's store, more to keep her hands busy than anything else. Her heart and mind were spinning with too much apprehension at seeing Matty to focus on what any of them said.

"Peanut!" Brynn wailed from the backseat, sounding half-asleep. "Where's Peanut?"

Dani twisted to look at the little girl. "Hang on, Brynn." She returned the books to their bag and, unbuckling, turned and knelt on the seat. "Don't worry, sweetie. We'll find your baby."

"I tied the balloon around her and dropped her on the seat earlier," Brad whispered.

She found Peanut on the floor and handed the beloved animal over. "Here you go."

The little sprite buried her teary face in the crocheted mane, her upset easily put to rest for the moment. Dani gave Brynn's arm a reassuring rub before she faced front and buckled in again.

If only her own heartache were so simply attended to. But twenty-six years of questioning why her father didn't want her—didn't love her—and now never would? Not so easily fixed.

When they arrived at Frank's house, the tow truck Matty used to haul her Kia to his shop was parked in the driveway. Matty and the driver talked for a moment, then the driver climbed into the cab as Matty hoisted a large plastic bin from the back and headed toward the front door. The truck rolled out of the driveway and headed away from the shop.

As Brad parked, Matty placed the heavy bin on top of two others like it, stacked near the entrance, then faced them.

Dani blew out a shaky breath. "He's gonna be so mad."

Brad brushed her forearm. "He's not gonna rip your head off, Dani. He sounded more worried than angry."

If it were Mom and Alec, *they* would rip her head off—give her two long earfuls, then the permafrost treatment for days.

Why did she even care? She barely knew Matty. He shouldn't have that much pull in her life. But she did care. He'd terrified her the first moment they met, but soon after that, the man had made her feel. . .safe. Something no other guy in her life had managed to do so effectively or quickly.

"Go talk to him." He cut the engine. "I'll get Brynn and the books, and we'll be right there."

She climbed down, closed the door, and approached Matty. Unwilling to risk a look, she stopped a couple of paces short. "Before you read me the riot act, I'm sorry."

Matty engulfed her in another bear hug, and her tears flowed again.

She sobbed silently against him for minutes and cursed herself for letting her emotions run so rampant around two virtual strangers—especially emotions stemming from her issues with Frank. But the tighter Matty held her, the safer she felt to release it.

"Brynn, no."

A little arm circled her leg, and she pulled free of Matty's embrace to find Brynn leaning against them both.

"Sorry!" Brad squatted nearby as he tried to draw his niece back.

Brynn tugged at Dani's pantleg. "You wanna hold Peanut?"

Something between a laugh and a sob bubbled out of her, and Dani hoisted Brynn to her hip. "You're so sweet, baby." She sniffled and tried to wipe away her tears. "You keep Peanut close to you. I'm gonna be okay."

The little sprite laid her head on Dani's shoulder and cuddled the horse.

"Are you?" Matty's rich voice drew her attention from Brynn. "Gonna be okay?"

She heaved a breath. "I always manage to beat my feelings back into submission eventually." She shot him another apologetic look. "You're not mad?"

"At the circumstances? The amount of hurt you're carryin'? Yeah, I'm mad. But at you? No."

The words calmed her. "Thank you. That means a lot to me."

He wrapped an arm around her and planted a kiss on her head. "I do hope one day you'll be able to get past it once and for all." He let her go. "Where's the key to the house, darlin'?"

She handed it to him, and as he turned to unlock the door, Brad approached.

"I'm so sorry. I was trying to keep her entertained, but she got away from me." He reached for Brynn.

Dani twisted away. "I've got her."

"Fine, then." Brad held up his hands in surrender and started to turn.

"Hey." Dani caught his arm, and he faced her again. "Thank you. For talking me down off the ledge. I probably had you kinda freaked out too."

His lips twisted into a comical expression, and he bobbed his head as he held up his hand, indicating a *little bit*.

Embarrassment wound through her. A handsome guy. Smart. Noble enough to take in his niece—*and* he seemed kind of into her too. At least into her enough to want her help with Brynn. Yet she'd melted down in epic fashion right in front of him—more than once! *Way to self-sabotage, Danielle.* She'd need to be on her best behavior for forever with both men to make up for this insanity.

"I'm really sorry, Brad. I owe you big."

Standing on tiptoe, she leaned in to give him a quick peck on the cheek, though as she did, Brynn lifted her head, smacking Brad in the cheek. He twisted away and, rather than grazing his cheek, Dani's lips brushed his mouth.

Her heart thundered, and she drew back with a startled yelp. His eyes as wide as hers, Brad stared for one stunned second, then ducked in for a second chaste kiss. A tiny nuzzle of his mouth on hers—but lightning zinged through her, and her pulse went to warp.

"You're forgiven." He pulled away and, for half a breath, stared, amusement on his face, then he turned as Matty stepped out of the house, having taken the first bin inside. "Need help?"

"That'd be great. Grab an end."

They each hoisted the second bin and headed into the house.

Holy Moses. Her pulse thrummed, and her head spun. What just happened? She certainly hadn't intended to kiss his lips—but there was no mistaking the fact that he'd intended to kiss hers. It had all happened so fast, and she'd been too stunned to kiss him back, but even so, she'd felt the heat—like a spark to gunpowder. Man, she'd liked it.

But...did he feel the same, or was this some ploy to string her along, get her help with his niece—a glorified, built-in babysitter. Knowing her luck with guys, that's all he was thinking. *Not* what she was looking for. Not that she'd been looking for *anything* when this whole crazy week began.

When they reemerged, Matty looked across the yard and flung his hands wide. "You gonna stand in the sun all day, or are you comin' inside?"

"Um, coming in." She put Brynn down and led her through the door. The guys placed the third bin next to the first two under the front window. She glanced Brad's direction first and saw that same amused smile hiding just beneath the surface as he met her eyes. What in heaven's name did that smile mean? Was he toying with her, or had he felt the same electricity?

Matty popped the top from the nearest bin and set it aside with a clatter. The sound broke the spell.

"So, what is all this?" Dani waved at the new additions.

"Your daddy's life—prior to the point he gave his heart to God." He popped the tops from the other bins to reveal tons of file folders, photo albums, and odds and ends. "You want to know about his college days, life with your mom, his arrests, court transcripts, photos of his artwork—you'll find it all in these boxes."

One hand strayed to the top of her head as Dani stared at the treasure trove of information. "Why do you have this?"

"Frank was going to get rid of it all, said he didn't want anything to do with his old life after God grabbed hold of him. I told him that wasn't a good idea—he might need some of this down the road. So we stored it at Joie-Rides, out of his way but accessible if he ever needed it. If it can give you some peace of mind, darlin', I'm glad we kept it."

Was this guy serious? Was he offering honest answers? One way to tell. "Arrests—plural?" She knew of only the one.

"A couple of drunk and disorderlies before he met your mother, the arrest for forgery afterward." Matty shrugged. "He was a partier for a while back in the day."

Okay. . .a good start. "So there was good reason for me to think he was a drunk?"

Matty roughed a hand over his mouth. "He wasn't an alcoholic, if that's what you're askin'. But a couple of times while he was drinking, things got out of hand."

Out of hand, how? But there were so many other questions to ask. "Were you there when he met my mom?"

"No. I didn't meet Frank until he was serving time, well after he met Jessica."

"You met him in prison?"

A coy grin crossed Matty's face. "I met him on the inside, but not like you're thinkin'. I wasn't a resident, I was a teacher. My pop and I taught classes on car repair, mechanic skills. Life skills they could carry out into the world after release."

She bit her lower lip and laughed. "Seems like a Matty thing to do."

He winked. "Frank did tell me about how he met Jessica, if that's what you're askin'."

"I've heard her side, but she rarely ever speaks about Frank unless it's in the negative. To paint him as an angry drunk, remind me of the forging, how he never came back for me. I've always wondered what they saw in each other."

"Um...that's..." Matty squirmed.

She waved a hand. "I already know they got pregnant with me during a drunken one-night stand." She strayed a glance at Brad. If her bajillion emotions and the tidbit about her conception didn't scare the man away, he was either a saint or a user. "Just...was there anything more than physical attraction?"

Matty clamped his eyes shut, and when he opened them again, a thinly veiled rage rested there. "That is not the kind of thing you tell your child!"

"Mom didn't tell me that. My grandfather did." She shrugged and cleared her throat. "Nicest man in the world except toward me. I'm pretty much *persona non grata* in his eyes."

He gritted his teeth so hard, his jaw popped under his beard. He shook his head, then walked into the kitchen. The refrigerator door opened. When he didn't return immediately, Dani looked Brad's way and followed.

"Matty."

He stood, back to her, with the refrigerator door open, still shaking his head. "I'm sorry, darlin', but *that* upsets me."

"Well, thank you for your outrage, but I've lived with it all my life. I'm used to it."

He plucked three Dr Peppers from inside and slammed the door, though he still didn't turn. "You shouldn't be. He's treated you like a pariah because Frank was your father." He turned. "That's wrong on so many levels."

"Yes, it is, but you can't change the past. I long ago resigned myself to the fact he'd never love me like he does my half-siblings." She approached and laid a hand on his solid arm. "Please. Just tell me about my parents.

Did they ever love each other?"

He whispered something—maybe a prayer—and exhaled a long breath. With another shake of his head, he handed her one of the sodas.

"They were opposites in every way. He was a poor kid raised by a single mom. Insanely creative and talented, but with no means to pursue those talents. Your mom had a wealth of money and opportunity at her disposal."

Matty rounded into the other room and set the other Dr Pepper on the table for Brad. "Frank had met some art professor—somebody Knox—who saw his talent and was trying to help him earn money to attend college."

Knox. She'd heard that name in the past few days. . .

"So your daddy had a couple of pieces in this art show the professor helped him get into. In walks Jessica with your granddad. If I remember correctly, I think Knox was a client of Dale's. Frank and your mom started makin' eyes at each other across the room, then talking through the evening, and he eventually invited her out."

"And Frank got her drunk and she wound up pregnant with me, so they eloped."

Matty huffed. "He told me it was her buying him rounds. But whatever. The end result is the same. Your granddaddy was ticked. Frank ruined all his plans for his daughter's future. Apparently, he intended for her to marry a doctor or something."

Dani gave a sardonic chuckle. "Grandpa Dale redeemed that part, I guess. Alec is a prominent neurosurgeon."

Matty rolled his eyes. "Yeah, what a peach."

She furrowed her brow. "Excuse me?"

"Never mind. They moved into a tiny, rent-controlled apartment. Frank took as many shifts as he could waiting tables, picked up side jobs. Knox helped get him into college—art major, on a partial scholarship. Frank was painting to build a portfolio. His hope was to get into more art shows, earn extra money. But the time away from your mom took its toll. Apparently, she complained about being left home alone with an infant while he was working or painting or studying. I don't know this for sure, but I suspect she thought life with an artist would be exciting and glamorous, and instead, it was hand to mouth, a real hardscrabble existence."

"Mom always said Frank left us to go off and party with friends." If what Matty said was true, she'd been fed a lifetime of lies.

He huffed. "Somewhere in these boxes, you'll find proof to the contrary. There's paystubs from the restaurants he worked for." He plucked an old photo album from the nearest box and showed her a page of four-by-six photographs of various paintings. "He took pictures of the artwork he created, each one date-stamped so you can see when he made it. You might even find sales tickets for the art pieces he sold. He took his marriage seriously and tried to make something of himself. Worked hard to provide you and your mom some kind of a life. It wasn't anywhere close to what she was used to, but he tried."

Early in her life, she'd believed the monstrous picture her mother and grandfather painted of Frank, but in the past couple of days, she'd begun to question some of it. Matty painted a far different picture.

"What happened the day he was arrested?"

"What do you mean?"

She shrugged. "I told Brad this morning, I have nightmarish memories from that day."

"You remember it? Darlin', you were two."

"I remember Frank screaming at Mom. Glass breaking. Cops tackling him. And blood splattered across the wall. Did the police shoot him or—"

He looked toward the ceiling, and something between a laugh and a groan bubbled out of him. "No, darlin'." He sighed. "I really don't want to do to you what others have done. Maybe you need to find the arrest record and—"

"Matty, please! Don't make me dig for answers. If you know, just tell me."

He popped the top on his soda and took a long swallow. "Lord, forgive me if this is wrong. The day he was arrested, that Professor Knox fella told him he'd sold a couple paintings. A few hundred bucks' worth. He was excited to tell your mom, so he came home early and...um...found her... entertaining another man. A med student."

Her stomach dropped, though it took only an instant to put the pieces together. "Alec."

The irritation in his hazel eyes told her she'd guessed correctly.

"Frank threw him out, and your mom and Frank argued. She grabbed a jar from the kitchen and threw it at your daddy. He was holding you at the time, and it hit him in the shoulder. If she'd missed by an inch, it could've hit you in the face. That torqued him off, so he put you down, picked up the jar, and narrowly missed hitting her when he threw it back. He launched it so hard, it shattered a mirror, and the jar exploded. Tomato sauce. Everywhere." The same groaning laugh came again, and he drank again. "But the police were there to arrest him, and when they heard the shattering glass and saw the red splatters, they busted down the door and came in a lot fiercer than they would have otherwise."

She considered the story.

"Your mother never told you about that day?"

Dani shook her head. "Anything regarding Frank is a taboo topic—unless, of course, they can twist it to make him look bad. Now that I realize Mom and Alec were hooking up while she and Frank were still together, it makes a lot more sense why." She wandered over to the couch.

As Matty thumbed through the contents of a bin, Brad scootched down to sit beside her. For the second time that day, he took her hand.

"Welcome to your crash course on my messed-up life. Everything about it is crazy."

Brad twined his fingers between hers, and he lifted her hand to his lips. "We'll figure it out together."

A moment later, Matty walked toward them, a file in hand.

"Just so you know I'm not lyin', darlin', here's the arrest report." He handed over the folder, then sat in the nearby chair. She and Brad read through it, the document confirming Matty's account, even down to her mom having been with Alec when Frank came home.

She heaved a breath. "Thank you, Matty, for telling me the truth."

"You can always count on me for that, darlin'."

It seemed she could—which left so many areas to rethink and so many long-held assumptions to reevaluate.

Matty Joie's House, St. Augustine, Florida—Present Day—Monday Evening

Once Brad and Dani finished cooking homemade tacos, they called Matty and Brynn, ate, and afterward, Matty shooed them away while he cleaned up. Brad grabbed the bag of books and parked himself in a chair with a good reading lamp next to it. There was just one problem.

Dani had gone to help Brynn start the DVD, and within minutes, they were curled up, Brynn in Dani's arms, both completely zonked. It was darn cute, but how was he supposed to keep his focus with that view?

For the hundredth time, he pulled his attention from the attractive sight and attempted to read about the incarceration of the Plains Indians. The book had good information, a detailed history of people and events, if he could just keep his focus.

He skimmed over the long journey from the western territories to Fort Marion, starting in wagons, then moving to a train, a brief steamboat ride, another train, and finally the arrival at the fort. The description of their march into the fort echoed the piece in the book. He also read of the plan to educate the men in hopes of helping them integrate into white society, of how St. Augustine citizens stepped up to teach them blacksmithing, farming, cobbling, and other life skills. As he read about the locals who came to the fort to teach them academics, two names snagged his attention. Brad stole one more long look at Dani curled around Brynn, then walked into the kitchen where Matty was reading that morning's paper.

Brad checked the opposite end of the island for cleanliness and, to be on the safe side, wiped it down with a damp paper towel. After washing his hands, he retrieved the ledger art from the entryway table and brought it to the kitchen island.

Matty folded a corner of his newspaper down to watch as Brad carefully leafed through the pages. "What're you up to?"

"I guess I'm comparing notes."

The big man laid the paper aside. "And what're you finding?"

He gently turned the book toward Matty and walked him through the pages in comparison with the events in his newly purchased history book. Brad carefully turned each page, his movements unhurried. "So just before lunch, I saw a page with a couple of names written on it." He flipped a page, then another and stopped. "Here. 'Luke. Sally Jo. Broken Bow friends.'" He pointed to the picture of the familiar blond-haired pair, then turned back to the history book.

"And from this book. . . 'Among the St. Augustine residents who volunteered to teach the Indians were Sarah Mather, Rebecca Perit, Anna Pratt, Sally Jo Harris, and Luke Worthing.'"

Matty's eyebrows arched. "So these two"—he pointed to Sally Jo and Luke's likenesses—"were the teachers, and Broken Bow, one of their students."

"Exactly."

"And this is Broken Bow's artwork."

"Bingo."

"I still can't figure why Frank would have it or where it came from."

"That's what we need to find out."

"You didn't search Frank's house today, did you?"

Brad shook his head. "Not really. Dani got so upset right after lunch, and we spent the afternoon talking with you."

"Hopefully, tomorrow will be more productive." Matty pinned him with a serious look. "Thank you for keeping her safe today."

"You have to know I wouldn't have left her." Yeah, she kind of freaked him out with all the tears, but at the same time, they riled up a protectiveness in him that he'd not felt for a woman in...goodness, had he ever? "Besides, I didn't want to have to face you if I had."

"No, son." A low chuckle escaped Matty's mouth. "You would not want to know the trouble you'd face." His grin teased, though the hardness around his eyes forewarned of his seriousness.

Message received, loud and clear. As if he needed to be told. He had no intention of hurting the beautiful young woman.

"So. . .does your book have an index? Can you see if it specifically mentions Broken Bow and what happened to him?"

"Now that's a thought." Brad skimmed the index and found Broken Bow's name and a list of corresponding pages.

CHAPTER SIXTEEN

Fort Marion, St. Augustine, Florida—Saturday, December 25, 1875

Two days, and he'd not yet been released from the dungeon. Broken Bow sat on the cot, staring at the things he'd brought with him. His drawing book and paint sticks. A Bible. A fresh shirt. He had blankets for warmth, a lantern for light. They'd brought him healthy amounts of food and fresh water. But he was still locked away—for what?

Because Pearson had attacked him, spoken bad things about Sally Jo.

White Chief had come more than once to reassure him that he was working on setting him free. But because today was a day of celebration, he said it might take a few more days before he could finish his work and release Broken Bow.

And he'd not seen Luke or Sally Jo since leaving the medicine tent after the attack, no matter how often he'd asked. White Chief said he would send them as soon as he could, yet they'd made no appearance. Given how upset Sally Jo was, it was concerning.

A sharp knock came at the dungeon's door, and he turned to find a face on the other side of the small hatch. His first time in the dungeon, they'd kept it and the food slot closed. This time, the hatch remained open and people spoke through it often.

"Broken Bow?" Romero's voice broke the stillness. "Someone wishes to speak to you."

He lunged off the cot, instantly sorry when pain shot through his bruised ribs. For a moment, he braced a hand against the wall as he caught his breath.

"Are you unwell?" Romero squinted at him.

Broken Bow drew a cautious breath, then paced to the dungeon's door, hope increasing that his visitor might be one of his friends. It would be good to at least see that they were unharmed. "It is nothing. Who is here?"

Romero shuffled aside, and Miss Mather stepped up. His hopes crashed.

"Merry Christmas, Broken Bow."

He nodded a greeting. "Miss Mather."

"I hope you are well in spite of your surroundings."

He chafed in these surroundings. His irritation grew relentless. But Romero would correct him if he spoke too aggressively of his frustration. Better to be silent.

"Mr. Worthing and Miss Harris asked me to bring you something."

He furrowed his brow. "Why they not come?"

"They've written to explain why they can't be here." She held up a folded paper with a round decoration on it. "And they asked me to make sure you received your Christmas gift." She hoisted a lumpy bag into view.

"Christmas gift?"

She nodded. "They are honoring you as their friend by giving you a gift in remembrance of our holiday, Christmas." She attempted to fit the paper and gift through the narrow food slot, but when the lumpy bag wouldn't fit, Romero opened the door, then stepped back.

Miss Mather stiffened her spine and cleared her throat, obviously bothered by the musty stench as she handed him the items. He took them. On the opposite side of the paper from the decoration, Broken Bow's name, written in Sally Jo's neat handwriting, adorned the page.

He waved the paper at her. "This say nothing. Only my name."

She chuckled and, taking the paper, slid her finger under a flap trapped beneath the decoration. "You have to break the wax seal to find out what it says." She pantomimed the action, then handed it back to him.

Broken Bow shook his head and broke the disk.

Smoothing the paper, he found more of Sally Jo's handwriting.

Dear Broken Bow,

Luke and I were told you have asked to speak with us.
It will be several days before we are able to see you. We

*have left St. Augustine to get married. We plan to wed on
Christmas Day and return soon after. We promise to visit
once we return. Please accept this Christmas gift from us,
and forgive us for not being there to give it to you in person.*

*Sincerely,
Sally Jo and Luke*

Broken Bow read the note slowly, then again to be sure he understood. "Luke make Sally Jo his woman?"

She dipped her chin. "Yes."

It was about time they married. He'd expected it long ago. A broad smile overtook him. "Is good."

She held out the bag. "This is the Christmas gift they sent."

Broken Bow untied the rough twine from around the top of the bag. Peeking inside, the smile reasserted itself as he withdrew one of several oranges. The tangy-sweet fruit was a favorite. He must find something special to give in return.

"Merry Christmas, Broken Bow."

The last time he'd seen Luke and Sally Jo, he'd intended to ask them the meaning of this special day, but once Pearson attacked, his questions were forgotten. Maybe Miss Mather would share.

"Christmas hard to..." He tapped his head. "Hard to know. Why one baby so...mean big?"

Miss Mather pondered his words. "You're having a hard time understanding Christmas and why one baby means so much?"

He nodded.

"The baby, Jesus, was the Son of our Creator, God. And He came so He could give every person a very special gift."

"What He give?" He held up the fruit. "Orange?"

The woman laughed. "No. Something much more special. He gave us life."

Confusion ruled. "My mother give life to Painted Sky, me. Not baby."

She laid a warm hand on his arm. "I'm not explaining myself well." She peeked toward the cot. "Bring me your Bible, please. Mr. Romero?" She turned toward the translator, standing off a few feet. "Can you help me, please?"

Broken Bow deposited the bag of oranges and the message from Sally Jo and Luke on his cot, then picked up the book. Perhaps he shouldn't have asked. The explanation of this baby and their special day had a confusing feel.

"How well can you read?" she asked, and Romero, who'd taken up station beside her, interpreted her words into the Tsitsistas tongue.

Broken Bow shrugged. "Luke says I read well. The holy book is difficult at times though." He waved the Bible at her.

Romero translated.

"I can understand that. I'm going to tell you some very important things and then let you read the story for yourself. But before you read it, begin by asking God for help understanding, and He will give it."

At Romero's translation, Broken Bow heaved a breath. This was going to take work.

She took the Bible from him and opened it to where the words started. "When God created the world, it was perfect. There was nothing bad in it. The people He created were perfect. No bad in them. Their hearts were full of light. If nothing changed, they would live forever with the Creator, God."

"Creator was here—with the people?"

"Yes. At that time, He walked among His people. They could see Him, and they knew Him. He wanted their friendship."

He drew back, eyes widening. "They had big medicine!"

"I understand why you would say that, but they were no different than you or me."

It was hard to imagine. Those people had to have been very special for Creator to walk among them. How could she say they were ordinary?

"There was also an evil spirit, the devil. His heart was full of darkness, and he led the first man and woman to disobey God's rules. When that man, Adam, acted against God, it tainted him and his woman, Eve, from then on. They were no longer perfect inside. There was now darkness—or sin—in their hearts. And they passed that darkness on to every baby they bore. This darkness separated them from God, and there was nothing Adam or Eve or anyone else could do to restore that relationship back to the perfectness they had before."

"This devil is no good. He broke everything."

"You're right. He is pure evil."

"So did the people make their way back to Creator?"

A wide smile lit the woman's face, and she turned in the book to a place about halfway through. "Man couldn't do it on his own, which is why Jesus had to be born. God wanted to restore His relationship with people, but for that to happen, blood had to be shed. Perfect blood with no darkness or sin in it. So God sent His Son, Jesus, in the form of a baby."

He listened intently to Romero's translation, his mind snagging on the need for blood to be shed. Luke and Sally Jo had tried, on various occasions, to tell them stories from the holy book, both during class and church services. That part sounded familiar to him, though he'd never fully understood it.

"This *devil* caused the first man and woman to carry darkness in their hearts here." He pointed to the front of the holy book. "And it took all these pages for Creator to fix the darkness—by sending His baby Son? Why not send a warrior to fight the devil and kill His enemy?"

"Because of what I just said. In order to restore His relationship with people, perfect blood with no darkness had to be shed. God is perfect, and His Son, Jesus, is perfect. Creator sent Jesus as a baby. He grew up, and there was no darkness in His heart. The devil tried, but he couldn't trick Jesus into sinning. Throughout His life, Jesus did many very special things, things that only God could do. Things like make a man with weak legs be able to walk. Or make blind eyes see. One man had his ear cut off, and Jesus touched it, and it regrew."

His mind spun. Such fantastical stories! "How?"

"Jesus was God in the form of a man. All the things Creator could do, He could do."

His heart stalled. "You're telling me He made someone's ear grow back?"

"Yes, and many other amazing miracles."

A cloud shadowed his heart, and homesickness filled him. "I wish Jesus was real and here today. I would take Him to Mother and ask Him to make her arm grow again."

Miss Mather's eyes filled with tears, and she pressed her lips together.

"He is real, Broken Bow. Listen to the end of the story. Jesus loved and helped people, but bad men took Him and beat Him. They tortured Him in horrible ways until He didn't even look like a man. And then they killed Him in a way meant for the most shameful sinners."

He looked at Miss Mather, then Romero, and back again. "They did this to Creator's Son? And He *let* them? Why? Why would He not use His great medicine to kill them?"

"Because Jesus chose to become the willing sacrifice. Someone had to pay for all the darkness in people's hearts, and He was the *only One* who could—because He was the only One with no darkness in His heart. So He let these men kill Him to pay the price for everyone else's sin."

"So His death was not a thing of *weakness* but of bravery."

"Yes! Thank You, Lord. You're understanding me. When He died, Creator took all of His anger over all of the darkness in people's hearts, and He placed it on Jesus so *He* paid the price for it, not everyone else."

Broken Bow listened intently to Romero's translation and nodded slowly. "I think I understand."

"Jesus' closest friends thought that was the end, their friend was gone. But after three days, Creator brought Jesus back to life. He overcame death and won the battle against the devil. And because His blood was pure, it was what was needed so that Creator and Man could become friends again. The Bible tells us that once that job was done, Jesus left earth and went to heaven, where Creator lives. And He is preparing homes for us. One day He will come back to take us with Him. But while we wait for Him, He sent us a Helper. If we ask, the Holy Spirit will live in us and help us with all the same power that Creator and Jesus have."

She seemed sincere, but. . . "Miss Mather, this story is hard. I don't know about it."

Miss Mather nodded. "It is hard to believe at first. That's why I want you to read it for yourself. Here." She handed him the open Bible. "The Gospel of Luke tells from Jesus' birth all the way to His death and His coming back to life. Will you read it?"

"Luke." He received the book. "Like my friend?"

"The Gospel of Luke is written by a different man, but with the same name. Your friend, Luke, was named after him." She tapped the open book. "This Luke lived long ago and talked to those closest to Jesus, then wrote down their stories."

He nodded. "All right. I'll try to read it. But this book is hard for me to understand."

A wide smile overtook her. "Remember what I said. Pray before you read. God will help you understand, and I am praying He will show you the truth."

"All right. I will do this for you, Miss Mather. And because the story is called Luke."

Judge Edwin Harris's Home, St. Augustine,
Florida—Monday, December 27, 1875

Sally Jo held tight to her husband's hand as he led her into her father's courtyard, but the nearer they got, the harder her heart pounded.

"Wait!" She dug in her heels and drew Luke to a stop.

When he turned, Luke's expression was full of understanding. "Don't be. . .anxious. I'll be right b-beside you."

"This won't go well." It couldn't possibly. Papa had been embarrassed when Mama's affair came out. He'd have been even more humiliated when his only daughter didn't come home since. And now she was arriving to collect her things. He was a smart man. Surely he'd already surmised what they'd done—and if he hadn't, he'd soon know.

The door opened, and Papa stared out, eyes wide and unshaven face haggard. His breath hitched, and he sagged against the doorframe.

Sally Jo's heart lurched. "Hello, Papa."

"I'm glad you've returned." His voice fairly shook. "I've been beside myself with worry." He flicked a glance from her to Luke and back. "Come in, Sally Jo. Now."

When she made a timorous move toward the door, Luke's grip tightened. "Judge Harris."

Her feet stalled.

Papa made no acknowledgment of Luke at all.

"Sir, we've come for S-Sally Jo's things."

"I've been waiting for you to return. We need to talk about what happened."

A wave of nausea gripped her. "Are you going to answer my husband, Papa? Please?"

Though his blank expression didn't change, his face paled visibly, and he leaned all the harder against the doorjamb as he closed his eyes. "Husband." When he opened his eyes again, they remained unfocused. Distant. "You married without my blessing. This isn't how things are done."

"I didn't want to marry Luke without you, Papa. We sought your blessing, but you wouldn't give it."

"Maybe I would have."

Luke stiffened. "You tipped your hand when you called me a stammering s-simpleton."

Papa heaved a big breath. "You shouldn't have married him. He's wrong for you."

Irritation prickled through her, and she stood taller. "Why, Papa? Because Luke stammers? Because he doesn't work a prestigious enough job to suit your fancy? Or because we both dream of going on the mission field to spread God's Word?" When no answer came, she pressed on. "Luke couldn't be any more right for me, Papa. I'm sorry you can't see that. Now, may I please enter and get my things?"

Papa rubbed his forehead as if to rid himself of a fearsome headache, then waved as he stepped out of the way. "They are your things."

Luke eased forward, once more tightening his grip on her hand. "Thank you, sir."

Papa made no move to block them, and they took the staircase to her second-story bedroom. Sally Jo held her emotions in check as she packed clothing, her favorite books, Luke's many letters, and other beloved items. Neither spoke as she shoved the items into the bags they'd brought. When they had all they could carry, they descended again.

Papa sat on the bench near the door, face pale and eyes hurt. "Do you have everything?"

Again, a wave of nausea rolled over her, and she set her bags down. "Papa—"

"Do you have everything?" He spoke more firmly.

Her shoulders slumped, and she fought down her emotion. "As much as we can carry."

"Then be on your way. I have things I need to do." He tipped his chin up, opened the door, and nodded toward the courtyard.

"Papa, please. I love you. Might we talk about this?"

"I love you too." His eyes welled with tears, something she'd never seen. "More than you know, child. But you've made your choice. Go on."

Luke approached him. "Please d-don't do this to her. She needs you, sir."

For once, Papa met Luke's gaze. "Why? She chose you."

"She chose to get married. Why can't she have both of us, sir?"

Papa moved around Luke and carried the bags she'd put down into the courtyard.

For a moment, Luke stared, looking as flabbergasted as she felt. Then he shifted one of the two heavy bags he carried under his other arm and settled his free hand at her back. "Come, Sally Jo."

At his whispered word, she exited, her breath hitching as she brushed past Papa. She turned one last time to face him. "I love you, Papa."

He closed the door without a word.

⁂

Fort Marion, St. Augustine, Florida—Tuesday, December 28, 1875

Luke looked at her as they approached the fort. "Are you all r-right?"

He'd asked her that same question at least twenty times since leaving her father's house the previous day. How should she answer? Fatigue pulled at every muscle. Her mind spun with questions. She was numb, but at least she could breathe, unlike the moments immediately after Papa closed the door. She'd expected him to be angry, maybe even try to force them to annul their marriage. She hadn't imagined he'd be so distant. He'd just released her and shut the door. Perhaps permanently. That hurt far worse than his anger ever could.

Maybe she was beginning to understand Papa's concern with what others thought. Since leaving his house, it seemed everyone stared, as if they judged her—wrongly—to be the worst of sinners. She'd not meant to sin against anyone, least of all Papa. But this was her life, and she had a right to make her own decisions.

Lord, this isn't what I wanted. I wanted Papa to respect my husband, to respect my choices. I suppose in a way he is, but I never dreamed he'd be so cold.

"Sally Jo." Luke led her over the first of the fort's drawbridges and stopped beside the ravelin, the ancient triangular structure built long ago to protect the fort's entrance from direct cannon fire. "Please answer me. Are you all right?"

"What do you want me to say? I lost Mama five years ago and Papa yesterday. My heart is crushed."

His eyes clouded, and he faced her directly. "You're not s-second-guessing our marriage, are you?"

That stung like a slap to the cheek.

"No." She gave an emphatic shake of her head. "Goodness, no. You're the only thing that makes any sense right now, Luke."

He stared deep into her eyes, then pulled her into the opening of the ravelin's stone staircase. Moving onto the first step where the stone wall shielded them from view, he once again stared deep into her eyes.

"I'm sorry." He leaned in and kissed her tenderly. "I n-never wanted this to happen to you." He attempted a second kiss, this one more lingering, but she broke it quickly and slipped into his arms instead.

Head on his shoulder, she inhaled deeply. "I don't doubt for one minute that marrying you was the right thing, but I am unsure of something."

"What?"

She held him tighter. "I'm not sure about teaching anymore."

"What?" Luke tried to pull away, but she wouldn't let go, too afraid he'd be angry with her.

She'd lain awake half the night thinking—about Mama and Papa, Papa's rejection of Luke, about everything in her life. "I'm just not sure what we're doing here. Are we having any impact?"

This time, he fought free and settled his hands on her shoulders. "Yes! Our f-friends are learning English, and they're. . .acquiring skills. We're teaching them good things."

"But what kind of a difference is any of this going to make? Will they honestly be allowed to integrate into our culture?"

He blinked. "We have to trust God f-for that. We may never see the. . .

impact we make when we follow God's leading."

"After all that's happened these last few days, I'm having a hard time discerning where God is. I need time to make sure we're doing what's right. Sometimes it's so hard to continue on blind faith alone."

He watched her for a moment. "You're not ready to teach today."

She shook her head, and his shoulders slumped. "I'm not sure I'm ready to teach at all."

"I s-suppose it is unfair of me to expect you to after so many big events these last several days. But we're here. Let's at least talk to the. . . lieutenant about when we'll restart our classes."

"Or *if.*" She lifted a timid glance toward her husband.

Pain flashed in his eyes, but he simply wrapped his arms around her again. When he did speak, his voice was quiet. "We need to see Broken Bow while we're here."

It would be far easier if they could slip inside and speak to Lieutenant Pratt, then slip out again. But word would reach Broken Bow that they'd come and not seen him—and as much as she was questioning things, she didn't want to hurt anyone else. "You're right. We promised."

"Yes. It's important we keep our word."

She allowed Luke to lead her off the ravelin's staircase and over the second drawbridge. Once they were let through the pitch pine doors, he tucked her hand into the crook of his arm and led her into the courtyard. No sooner did they step into the sunlight than they found Lieutenant Pratt at the base of the staircase, talking to Painted Sky and another of their students. All three men turned their way.

"Mr. Worthing. Miss Harris." The lieutenant walked their way, the others following. "I hope you had a pleasant Christmas."

Sally Jo smiled as Luke's chest puffed.

"The best, s-sir. Sally Jo and I got married."

Pratt's eyes widened. "Married? I wasn't even aware you'd officially become engaged!"

Behind him, Painted Sky and the other man grinned.

"The opportunity came s-suddenly, and we took it."

"My heartiest congratulations." Pratt pumped Luke's hand. "My Anna will be so excited." He turned to Sally Jo. "I'm sure your father is very pleased, Mrs. Worthing."

She somehow kept her smile from faltering, all while attempting to clear her throat of the knot that threatened to choke her. "I hope so, sir."

"I'm sure he is."

She could only nod.

"Lieutenant, might I speak with you while Sally Jo visits with Broken Bow?" Luke shifted a glance to her. "Would th-that be all right?"

Surely the request was meant to save her the embarrassment of his explanation of what had transpired these last days and why they were requesting a hiatus from teaching.

The lieutenant produced a key from his pocket. "You've come at a good time. I was about to release him from the dungeon."

"Only just now?" Her question slipped out unbidden.

"My investigation took longer because so many were busy with the holiday."

"I didn't mean to be rude, sir. I hadn't thought how Christmas would slow things."

"Unfortunately, it did, but there's good news. I can finally release him *and* recommend Mr. Pearson be held accountable for the incident." He led them toward the dungeon. As they walked, Painted Sky signed to Luke, indicating his happiness at their marriage, and Luke thanked him.

Pratt grinned. "You and Broken Bow have taught Mr. Worthing well, Painted Sky."

The Cheyenne chuckled. "Stumbling Tongue teach more good when he talk with hands."

Luke was the first and loudest to laugh, followed by Lieutenant Pratt. Sally Jo grinned herself, though when her thoughts shifted to how her husband's tongue didn't stumble when he kissed her on their wedding night, her cheeks grew unbearably hot. She took Luke's arm again, hoping no one would notice.

They reached the dungeon, and the officer unlocked the door and swung it wide. "Broken Bow." The Cheyenne brave climbed off the cot, looking half asleep.

"White Chief." He came to stand in front of the doorway, his short-cropped hair mussed slightly.

"My investigation is complete. You are free to return to your normal duties."

"I do no wrong?"

"According to my findings, you did nothing wrong."

He seemed to shake off sleep then, and he stood a little taller. "Thank you, White Chief." He shifted a look around at the other faces, settling finally on Luke and Sally Jo. "You marry now?"

"Yes." She nodded. "We're married now."

"Is good. I happy." The genuineness in his dark eyes made her believe him.

"Thank you, f-friend." Luke wrapped an arm around her waist.

"Broken Bow, get your things." Lieutenant Pratt nodded toward the cot.

Painted Sky slipped inside to help carry his brother's personal effects. Once they'd gathered everything, they all departed for the courtyard again. There, the lieutenant gave Broken Bow leave to put his belongings away and enjoy some free time while Luke went with the officer to talk.

"You go with us?" Broken Bow nodded toward the gun deck.

"Yes, I'll walk with you." At the top step, Broken Bow handed off a couple of his things to Painted Sky and spoke in Cheyenne to him. The older brother hurried toward the wooden barracks they'd built along the north wall while Broken Bow nodded in the other direction. He and Sally Jo started to walk, though neither spoke until they'd passed several of the other Indians.

Once they were alone, Broken Bow turned to her. "Your eyes sad. You not happy be Luke's woman?"

Emotion welled into a boulder-sized knot in her chest. "I'm very happy to be Luke's woman. He's good to me. Other things make me sad." She fought to chip away at the boulder. "Tell me how *you* are."

A smile tugged at his lips. "I good. Very good."

Sally Jo squinted up at him. "You *are* the man that was just released from the dungeon, aren't you?"

"This time not same."

"No, you had a lamp and your drawing book." She nodded toward the ledger and paint sticks he'd kept with him. She narrowed a teasing glance his way. "And clothes."

Broken Bow laughed. "Yes." He sobered. "Miss Mather see me Christmas."

"She brought you your gift?"

"Yes. Thank you for oranges." He patted his stomach. "Miss Mather tell me about Christmas. How that baby grow up. Die. Come back from die."

Excitement sprouted in her chest. "She told you how Jesus died and rose again."

"Yes. She tell me, then I read Luke book." He revealed his Bible tucked beneath the ledger book.

"You read the book of Luke?"

He quirked his brows. "I have much time. . .read. Read more. Read *more*."

Sally Jo giggled. "You read a lot, obviously."

"Then I read. . ." He shut his eyes as if working to recall something. "If you say with mouth Jesus Lord and believe God raise from dead, you save."

Her jaw hinged open, and she stared. "You read all the way to Romans?"

A slight nod. "Jesus make me clean here." He tapped his chest. "Light live here."

Tears spilled down her cheeks. "Have you told Lieutenant Pratt?"

"Tell you, Luke first."

She reached for his arm and started toward the stairs to the courtyard. "Well, we need to tell the lieutenant, quickly." Before her husband said something she might regret.

CHAPTER SEVENTEEN

Fort Marion, St. Augustine, Florida—Monday, April 3, 1876

*A*s the sun began to brighten the eastern sky, Broken Bow paced the gun deck, his heart heavy and his thoughts spinning. It was not unusual for him to dream. Since his youth, his nights had been filled with images of many things. But after Miss Mather's visit in the dungeon and the change his prayer to Jesus had made, the dreams were different. More vivid.

For at least the last moon, his dreams had grown disturbing. Normally, he could awaken and shake the images quickly enough, but of late, they lingered. Worse, as he'd watched the Ka'igwa and Numinu men he'd dreamed of—the very same ones he'd seen around the plaza, drawing, on the day of his altercation with Pearson—they acted odd. Secretive. Often pulling aside to whisper among themselves. Any happiness they might have shown in this place had waned, and they now chafed at the slightest orders or expectations.

After much prayer, he'd decided to speak with White Chief about the dreams that echoed into reality. As the predawn sun further brightened the sky, he positioned himself along the gun deck's western wall to watch for White Chief's arrival. When the sun crested the horizon on the far side of the fort, the chief finally strolled into view.

As the officer made the turn to cross the first drawbridge, Broken Bow caught the chief's attention. When the yellow-haired man lifted a hand in greeting, Broken Bow nodded, then discreetly signed to him.

Can I speak to you? Alone.

White Chief reached the end of the drawbridge and gave a single curt bob of his head.

Broken Bow made no outward acknowledgment but headed toward the stairs, smiling and nodding to the other men who'd risen early to watch the sunrise. He reached the courtyard as White Chief turned out of the tunnel from the entrance.

"Good morning, Broken Bow."

"Good morning, White Chief."

"It looks like a glorious sunrise this morning. Would you like to step outside and watch it with me?"

"Yes. I like much."

White Chief led the way to the water's edge, and they both faced the rising sun.

"What's wrong?" The chief kept his focus on the morning's spectacle.

He whispered a silent prayer for help explaining his concerns. "I have many dreams. From last moon." Broken Bow glanced toward the other man but quickly looked back to the sunrise. "Dream of White Horse, Lone Wolf, Dry Wood. In dreams, they make trouble. Bring death to fort. I see in dream. . ." He reached for the English word. "Head and bones." He crossed his forearms into an X shape ever so briefly before he folded them against his chest. He'd seen the head and bones on bottles the doctor kept in his medicine tent.

White Chief swung a startled look his way but covered his surprise with a laugh, and Broken Bow smiled at him, hoping anyone watching from above might think they were just having a friendly conversation.

As the chief faced the sunrise again, he spoke softly. "You saw a skull and crossbones in your dream?"

"Yes. Three men from dream—they act no good when I awake. They plan something. Do not know what."

The chief nodded slowly. "They've been acting strangely for several weeks. And a bottle of poison has been stolen from the doctor's supplies. It was marked with a skull and crossbones."

Broken Bow turned a passive look his way. "Same day Pearson attack, I see three men from dream in town." He waved a hand at the sunrise. "All sit different place. Draw town in books. Streets. Stores."

White Chief closed his eyes and blew out a loud breath. "I've been keeping watch on these men you mention." He opened his eyes again.

"And I've noticed a lot of drawings of the town in their ledger books. I thought it odd. Unlike their earlier drawings, there's no significant event happening in those pictures. Just the town."

"White Chief think they do no good?"

He put his hands into his pockets and nodded. "They may be plotting an escape—or worse, with that bottle of poison going missing. I will notify Lieutenant Colonel Dent that something concerning is going on."

"You want I take him message?" He wasn't yet sure of the man who'd replaced Major Hamilton as post commander. White Chief said he was the brother of President Grant's wife—whoever that was. But if his carrying a note to the man would help White Chief keep peace in the fort, he would gladly run that errand.

"No. You've done more than enough. Pretend nothing has happened other than you watched a beautiful sunrise with me. Then pray and trust me that we will get to the bottom of it."

"Yes, White Chief." He turned again toward the last vestiges of the brilliant sunrise and watched the pinks and oranges fade into morning.

✦

Fort Marion, St. Augustine, Florida—April 4, 1876

"Mrs. Worthing, a word please?" Mr. Romero interrupted Sally Jo in the middle of her reading, beckoning her toward the classroom's doorway.

She lowered her book. "Can it wait? I'm in the middle of a passage."

"Forgive the intrusion, but no."

Unusual.

She glanced at her students' faces. Most had turned to look at Romero. "Broken Bow, will you finish reading to the end of the page, please?"

He rose, expression grim as he paced to the front and took the volume. She indicated the spot where she'd stopped, then she stepped out into the courtyard, squinting against the sunlight.

As Mr. Romero led her toward the east wall where Sarah Mather and Rebecca Perit also stood, he glanced her way. "Is your husband here today?"

"Luke is home, under the weather."

He stopped once they reached the other women. "Ladies, please dismiss your classes immediately and ask them to prepare for their noon meal. Then gather your belongings and vacate the premises. Quickly."

"Pardon?" Miss Perit scowled.

"There's a situation Lieutenant Pratt needs to take care of, and it will be best for everyone if civilians aren't here."

Sally Jo's heart lurched, and she shifted a concerned glance toward Sarah.

The older woman nodded. "We will, Mr. Romero. When will we be allowed to return?"

He nodded toward the tunnel. "I will have that answer for you as you leave. Ten minutes. No more."

Dread shivered through Sally Jo as he walked across the courtyard. She faced the other women. "What is going on?"

Sarah watched Romero's retreat. "I don't know, but it can't be good. Do as you're asked. Dismiss your students and pack up, and once you leave, tell only Luke about what happened here." She turned Sally Jo's way. "No one else. We don't want rumors spinning out of control."

They hurried off to their respective classrooms.

When she returned, Broken Bow glanced up.

"Gentlemen." At her soft call, all eyes turned her way as she returned to Broken Bow's side. "Class is dismissed early today. Well done. I'm very proud of each of you and the strides you're making. We'll pick up with more of this the next time we meet."

"We done?" One man squinted at her.

"For today. Please pack your things and prepare for the midday meal. I will see you all soon." *Lord, please. . .let me see them soon! This is a bit frightening.*

The majority of her fifteen students gathered their belongings and were gone in a cloud of dust, just like children. However, Painted Sky and Broken Bow lingered, as was their habit.

Sally Jo stacked the books she'd carried into the fort that morning. "Go on now. Take your books up to your bunks and get washed up for your meal."

"You no talk to me, Broken Bow today?" the elder brother asked.

She straightened, facing both men. "I wish I could, but not today. I was told I need to dismiss you all and go." Her gaze lingered on them each a moment.

Broken Bow's brow furrowed, and recognition registered in his eyes. He grabbed the last two books and shoved them into her bag. "Yes, go now. Talk later."

The words held a finality that knotted her stomach. Would this be the last time she saw Broken Bow and Painted Sky? *Lord, no, please! They are my friends—my husband's friends.*

Between Luke's stammering and the fact she was Judge Harris's daughter, she and Luke had struggled to form close friendships. Oddly, Broken Bow and Painted Sky were two of the most accepting people they'd met.

Broken Bow scooped up her bag and held it out to her. "Go."

She took the bag. "I will see you both soon."

Broken Bow nodded. "Soon."

He gave her a gentle shove toward the door. She stared at him for a moment, then gave him a brief but firm hug. When she pulled free, his eyes were wide, startled. She turned then and, approaching Painted Sky, repeated the process. Obviously uncomfortable, he wiggled free more quickly and nodded toward the fort's entrance.

"Go."

Sarah and Rebecca exited their classrooms at the same time, and the three moved toward the tunnel across the courtyard.

True to his word, Romero met them near the exit. "The lieutenant is unsure when you'll be allowed to return, but he'll send word to each of you."

Sally Jo turned a concerned gaze on Sarah, but the elder woman simply nodded and herded them through the pine doors. Once they stepped into the sunshine and crossed the first drawbridge, her heart stalled as Lieutenant Pratt, armed with a pistol on his hip, and a line of soldiers, each armed with a rifle and bayonet, stood at the ready.

Oh Lord Jesus, this can't be good.

CHAPTER EIGHTEEN

Matty's House, St. Augustine, Florida—Present Day—Wednesday

*D*ani emerged from her borrowed room, still clad in her oversized sleep T-shirt and capris but with hair and teeth brushed. Barefoot, she padded into the kitchen to find Matty and Brad deep in conversation at the island. Brynn sat between them, sleepily cuddling Peanut.

Brad smiled. "Morning."

"Don't bother." Matty's tone was teasing. "She won't speak before she drinks a potful."

Dani rolled a perturbed glance his way, then forced a smile. "Morning. Both of you."

At Dani's sleepy greeting, Brynn's head lifted, and she watched Dani pour and doctor her coffee. Once she sat on the remaining barstool, the blond sprite plucked at her shirtsleeve, and Dani helped her get settled in her lap.

"Carry on. Didn't mean to interrupt." She took a sip and began to rub Brynn's back.

"I was just filling Matty in on what I read last night." He held up one of the books he'd bought at the Castillo's store. "Our artist was a twenty-one-year-old Cheyenne, Broken Bow, who survived the Sand Creek Massacre a decade before. Because of that experience, he joined the Dog Soldiers, who fought heavily against the settlers going west. That's why he was sent to the fort."

She blinked, trying to process the information and took another sip of coffee to wake herself up.

"His time at the fort started out rough, but he mellowed quite a bit.

Became a favorite of Lieutenant Pratt and his teachers—the blond couple we keep seeing in the ledger book. Luke Worthing and Sally Jo Harris."

She savored another sip. "That's quite a change."

"He became quite the student—excelled in his studies, read anything he could get his hands on. Even helped foil an escape plot by the Kiowa prisoners."

"Really?" Matty leaned around her.

"Yeah. He took information to Pratt, confirming what the lieutenant suspected. The culprits of the proposed plot stole a bottle of poison and spent a good deal of time mapping the town in their ledger books to plan their escape routes. Their plan was to either travel back to their homeland, live out the remainder of their days in the woods, or die in the process, but Pratt was able to squelch it before it happened."

Dani turned her attention to the snuggle bug in her lap and brushed Brynn's hair back from her sweet face. "And they all lived happily ever after?"

"Not at first. Prior to this plot, the prisoners were given a fair amount of freedom. With a simple pass, they could walk alone into town to sell handmade goods to tourists, buy from the local shops, or run other errands. But the local papers spun this episode into a full-blown uprising, and for months, the residents lived in fear of the Indians coming to rape, pillage, and murder them in their beds. So for a while the Indians weren't allowed out except when escorted by military guard, though they did finally get their freedoms back."

Matty chuckled. "Sounds like today's reporters."

"Isn't that the truth." Dani rested her cheek against Brynn's hair and enjoyed the homey, idyllic atmosphere. When had her own family ever drunk a cup of coffee together? She couldn't recall a time. And snuggles from a sweet little sprite while chatting with her handsome uncle? She could totally get used to this. "So what happened to Broken Bow?"

His blue eyes sparkled for a moment, and he made no attempt to answer. Then he seemed to shake himself and cleared his throat. "I, uh...I don't know yet. I got tired about that point. I'll read more tonight before bed, but we probably ought to spend our daylight hours searching for where this artwork came from. Unless you have other plans, that is."

"That sounds good."

Brad leaned forward to see past her. "Matty, is there a washer and dryer over at Frank's place? I need to wash something for the custody hearing tomorrow afternoon."

"Actually, I need to do some too." She hadn't dreamed she'd spend so many days here.

"Yeah. Definitely. Speaking of the hearing, it's at four tomorrow?"

Brad nodded.

"Anyone gonna be there with you to lend moral support?"

He shrugged. "I haven't asked anyone."

"Well, if you want company, my day's wide open tomorrow after lunch."

"I'll go too." Dani sat straighter, though sheepishness quickly overcame her. If Brad *was* stringing her along, she'd played right into his hands. "If you want extra company, I mean."

"Thank you. I'd really appreciate it if you both came. Honestly, if I let myself think too much about this hearing, I tie myself in knots, worrying whether the judge is going to hold me accountable for Trey's issues."

"Brad. . ." She gripped his hand. "You have a good job. You proved long ago that you're willing to do whatever it takes to care for those you love. And you're crazy about your niece. I'm no expert, but I can't imagine the judge *not* awarding you custody."

He roughed a hand over his hair. "But Trey—"

"Son." Matty's voice took on a tone that didn't allow for argument. "Trey made his own choices. Quit wallowin' in your self-doubt and listen to Dani. She's speaking truth."

Brad nodded. "Thank you both. I know you're right." He caressed her fingers with his thumb, then gave her hand a squeeze. "I'm gonna get cleaned up." He stood. "C'mon, Brynn."

The little sprite grunted her displeasure.

Dani turned a sheepish look his way. "If you put her clothes on my bed, I'll help her get changed."

"You sure?"

"It's a simple thing."

His shy smile warmed her. "Thanks."

He headed toward the hall but turned back. "What about the reading of the will? You don't even know when that's going to be. Shouldn't you stay close in case they call?"

Matty waved the concern away. "Rescheduled for 10 a.m. Friday."

"Really?" She turned toward Matty. "They didn't tell me!"

"Have you checked your phone? The attorney's office texted this morning."

"Oops." Dani's cheeks warmed. "I'll look once I get back to my room."

Brad chuckled. "I'll go grab a quick shower."

Dani sipped her coffee and rubbed Brynn's back, but her gaze trailed after him. Tall, nicely built, handsome, smart. Held a good job. Sweet and caring. Doted on his niece. Man, he was the stuff a girl's dreams were made of.

Beside her, Matty cleared his throat and pantomimed opening a book.

She gave him a playful shove. "Would you stop. I'm not *that* obvious, am I?"

"Not to his face, darlin', but you sure had a dreamy look in your eye as he was heading down the hall."

"You love to embarrass people, don't you." She drained the rest of her coffee.

"Teasin' you has been the highlight of these last few days." His grin full of mirth, he took their mugs to the sink.

"You're incorrigible."

He set the mugs in the sink and walked back. "No, I'm observant—and not too shy to comment about what I see." He bent until they were eye to eye. "By the way, he watches you the same way when you're not lookin'. He's just as smitten."

Was he?

Frank Sango's House, St. Augustine, Florida—Present Day—Wednesday

Dani pushed Frank's door open and stepped inside, Brynn and Peanut gripping her hand. "So what should I be looking for?"

"To prove provenance?" Brad stepped in, shut the door, and set aside the laundry baskets Matty had loaned them. "A receipt would be great!"

She chuckled. "Pipe dream much?"

"You asked."

"Anything else?" She resisted the urge to toss out her usual snide comment about Frank. This new perception that he might not have been as crooked as she'd always believed would take some getting used to.

"Any kind of a publication that talks about the book. Newspaper or magazine articles, an auction catalog, that kind of thing."

"All right." She motioned toward the hallway. "The door just past the bathroom was his office. I figured I'd start there. You coming, or. . . ?"

"I thought I might look through whatever's in these bins." He waved at the storage totes. "It's probably a long shot—everything's pretty old in there—but you never know."

"That works." She focused on her shadow. "Brynn, honey, I think Uncle Brad has some fun things for you to do out here."

"Yep, c'mon, Brynnie Bear." He held out his hand, and she went to him.

Dani waved at the little girl, who waved back with a timid smile.

After tomorrow, Brad and Brynn would probably head back to St. Pete to sort out a larger place to live, childcare for Brynn, and other issues. It was going to stink not seeing them each morning—especially when Brynn made it her habit to come seeking snuggles until she woke up.

It felt good to be needed.

Dani opened the office door carefully. She'd looked in here on the day she'd arrived. While it wasn't hoarder-level cluttered, there were stacks of papers, folders, and magazines everywhere. She turned on the light and stepped inside.

"Where do I even start?" She looked around.

Matty's off-the-wall comment about doing a goose chase in the house came to mind, and she huffed. What was it about that man that she was actually considering it?

"Pure stupidity." Yet the idea wouldn't leave, so she glanced toward the ceiling.

"I really don't know what I'm doing here. You never seemed to take interest in me, so I've never paid You much mind. But, um. . .my last fortune cookie said that 'necessity is the mother of taking chances,' so

I'm taking a chance. If You *are* real, and You *do* care, *and* Frank came by this artwork honestly, then show me the proof." She heaved a breath, embarrassed at the absurd prayer. *"Please."*

She bit her bottom lip and added one addendum. *And if it's not utterly stupid of me to ask, show me if Brad really* is *smitten like Matty says. . .because I really don't want this to be one-sided on my part.*

Dani cringed. She was asking for disappointment. For her, relationships had always gone wrong, to the point she'd pretty much given up, vowing that the right guy would have to fall into her lap.

Just like Brad.

The thought came so quickly, it almost took her breath away.

The man *had* fallen into her lap and stayed by her side every day since.

She stood, flabbergasted for a moment, then shook her head. "Quit being stupid, Dani. Get to work."

She hung her tiny purse on the doorknob, then turned toward the desk, bumping a hard-sided suitcase beside the door as she did. It tumbled into the vacuum cleaner next to it, causing a racket. An instant later, Brad looked in.

"You okay?"

Dani bent to right the suitcase. "Yeah. Just letting my inner klutz free."

He grinned. "You have that problem too?"

"Several times a day." She set the case beside the door.

As she faced him, a goofy grin overtook him, and his blue eyes sparkled furiously.

Her heart pounded. Good gravy, his eyes were mesmerizing.

She finally broke free of his spell and waved a hand. "Anyway, nothing to see here."

Brad stared for another moment, and only when Rachel's special ringtone sounded did he glance toward her purse, a red flush crawling up his neck. "I. . .um." He reached to caress her hand. "I couldn't disagree more, but anything I say is going to get all twisted and. . .I'm—" He stopped when Rachel's tone sounded again. "Your purse is ringing, so I'm gonna head. . ." He hooked a thumb toward the living room.

Heat and a most delicious giddiness tangled within her, and she nodded. "O-okay."

Shoving his hands in his pockets, he backed into the hall, gaze still firmly on her until he bumped the opposite wall. He winced, and his face bloomed a deeper red, drawing a giggle from her. Brad walked away, rubbing his head as he disappeared. Dani somehow resisted the urge to see if he looked back.

What in the world? Her heart pounded and, jaw slack, she glanced toward the ceiling. Oh, this was getting weird. Delightful, but weird.

Shaking off the moment, she pulled her phone out and made for the desk, though she must have brushed the suitcase again, for it toppled forward.

"Oh, good grief." She righted it and looked out to find Brad peeking down the hall. "This stupid suitcase has a mind of its own."

He laughed, warm and easy.

She pulled the rolling office chair to the corner of the desk. Punching the text app on her phone, she muted the device and read Rachel's message.

Haven't heard from you in days. Back home yet? You OK?

Hey, Boo. Sorry I've been incommunicado. Things are OK, just nuts.

How'd the reading of the will go?

Lawyer was sick. Moved to Friday @ 10am. Still in St. Aug.

Sure you're OK? Staying @ Franklin's? Hotel? What about that weird art book you found?

Dani hesitated. Telling Rach she was staying with Matty would send her into full alarm mode. She'd skip that until she could talk to her friend rather than text.

Don't know about the art book. Art hanging on the walls are not forgeries.

Dani dug into the nearest pile. Folders of old utility bills, mortgage statements, and the like. Her bookkeeper's mind couldn't help but note that he paid on time or early, kept a low balance on the one credit card she found, and paid it off each month. And he paid more than the minimum on his house payments. Facts that flew in the face of the narrative she'd believed her whole life. To make more room, she set that stack on the floor beside the vacuum cleaner and, not wanting another run-in with the suitcase, backed away slowly.

She pulled the next stack to the edge of the desk, this one just a conglomeration of different magazines. Individual copies of collectible car magazines, motorcycle magazines, art magazines. There appeared to be no rhyme or reason other than newest to oldest. She pulled out an art magazine and opened to the table of contents.

Her phone's screen lit up.

NOT FORGERIES? THEY'RE REAL?

FRANK PAINTED THEM IN COLLEGE. TO PRACTICE TECHNIQUE.
BRAD THINKS FRANK WASN'T TRYING TO BE DECEPTIVE IN PAINTING THEM.

She scanned the table of contents. Nothing about Native American artwork, though her eye snagged on a name. *S. Daniel Franklin.* The name Frank signed on his email to Brad. She checked several others, finding articles in each under that name.

So Frank wrote for several magazines under a pen name?

The phone's screen illuminated again.

BRAD?

Oh, crud. Dani bit her lip. She hadn't even thought what mentioning him might stir up.

SORRY. BRAD OSGOOD.

ANDREWS MUSEUM CURATOR.

YOU TALKED TO HIM?

Again, how in the world to explain Matty's goose chase and everything that had happened since she'd arrived via text messages? She'd save it for a phone call.

YES. NICE GUY. TELL YOU MORE WHEN WE CAN TALK.

There were at least five twelve-inch-tall stacks of magazines lining the back edge of the desk, and S. Daniel Franklin authored at least one article in every one she checked.

"Hey Brad!" She grabbed several magazines and headed toward the door.

"Yeah?"

As she neared the exit, the magazines slipped out of her grip, hit the wall, and toppled the suitcase again.

"Are you kidding me?" She grabbed the three wayward mags and snatched the suitcase up. Brad stood at the hall's end, staring.

"You okay?"

"Yes, but this kamikaze suitcase is trying to kill me."

He laughed as she set the carry-on at the end of the coffee table.

"You keep it out here, or it might do me in."

"We can't have that."

Brynn craned her neck toward the hard-sided case. "Uncle Bad, I can play with that?"

"Sure, baby. Go ahead." He set it near her and returned his attention to Dani. "So did you find something?"

"Not the provenance, no. But it is interesting." She sat and opened the first of the magazines to the contents page. "Does this name ring a bell?"

"Um. . ." He stared a moment, then his brows arched. "That was the name Frank used to contact me."

"Exactly. And look here." She opened the other magazines and pointed to the appropriate titles and their author.

"Frank was a freelancer for magazines."

"Yeah, and it looks like he was pretty prolific. There's stacks of magazines in the office!"

Brad narrowed a glance at her. "Could he have been looking for a quote for an article he was working on about ledger art or something?"

"That would sure put a different spin on him contacting you under that name."

From where Brynn sat beside the now-open suitcase, she made a soft whinny and galloped Peanut inside the bag.

Dani grabbed his wrist. "She's playing!" She barely breathed the words, her heart going into a gallop of its own. "She hasn't done that except for that very brief moment at Matty's the other night."

Brad's expression held a mix of shock and relief. "I've been praying she'd come back to herself." He turned a misty-eyed glance Dani's way but quickly looked back to Brynn. "She's usually got such a vivid imagination."

She nodded.

"Uncle Bad? Peanut's hungry. She wants oats."

"Oats." He glanced at Dani. "I don't know if we have any oats, baby."

Dani tightened her hold on his wrist. "Are Brynn and Peanut both hungry?"

"Just Peanut."

"Okay. Let's see if we can find oats." She hurried into the kitchen, returning with a small plastic bowl she'd found. "Here." She pantomimed pouring something and handed the bowl over. "Will that do?"

Brynn set it in front of Peanut, then petted her mane. "Put the oats in the barn, Miss Dani."

"Where, baby?"

"In da barn!" She pointed to the other side of the suitcase.

"Oooh. In the barn." She unzipped the nylon divider. A magazine and some random papers lay strapped in the bottom, so she removed those and pantomimed putting the oats away.

"Thank you."

She kissed the girl on the cheek. "You're welcome, sweetheart."

When she returned to the couch, Brad had settled his elbows on his knees and cupped his clasped hands in front of his mouth, eyes pinned on his niece.

Dani sat beside him. "You okay?"

Obviously overcome, he leaned against her shoulder. "It's a good moment."

Yes, it was—and she liked sharing it with him. Would she have such a chance in another day or two? It was terrifying to think how quickly she'd grown used to all this. . .waking up to Brad and Brynn, spending her day with them, going to sleep with them on her mind.

The fear that she was about to get her heart broken—badly—grew.

Sitting back, Dani tried to push the defeated thoughts away, flipping through the items she'd taken from the suitcase.

A boarding pass with Frank's name—dated four months ago.

A folded paper—which, when she opened it, was a printout of an email with an address highlighted halfway down the page.

A glossy magazine with another folded paper peeking out the top. When she tugged it loose and looked at it, her jaw went slack and her hands shook. Picking up the magazine, she looked more closely. "Brad! A Native American Art auction catalog. . .and a receipt."

✦

"You prayed a fortune cookie as a prayer?"

Brad almost laughed at Matty's question. Almost. The same could not be said for the big man, whose guffaws billowed like giant waves.

"Is that wrong?" Dani's hands still shook. "When I tell you I don't know how to pray, I mean it. If I did something wrong, tell me."

Brad shot Matty an annoyed look. She was obviously freaked out, and this guy had the audacity to laugh? "Calm down. God wouldn't have answered you if you did."

Matty collected himself, though his laughter was obviously ready to burst forth without notice. "No, darlin'. It might be unconventional, but you prayed as honestly as you knew how."

"And God answered."

Her face a mask of disbelief, Dani stared at the receipt and auction catalog, open to the page showing Broken Bow's ledger art. "I don't believe it. *God* got all up in my business and answered *me*."

"Yes, darlin'. You dared Him to, and He told you He's real and wants your heart."

Her brown eyes grew large. "What does that even mean—He wants my heart?"

He sat forward, eyes focused on Brad. "You mind if Dani and I sit out back and talk?"

"I'm not going anywhere." *Just. . .don't laugh at her. Not when she's freaking out.*

Matty rose and, reaching for Dani's hand, helped her up. They disappeared through the sliding glass doors to a decent-sized screened porch with a comfortable outdoor furniture set. He'd not realized any of that was there.

He picked up the auction book and receipt. Dani had been so astounded at finding them—but any answers he'd tried to give her had fallen on deaf ears. She wanted to hear from Matty.

Who could blame her? Matty was unabashedly open about his faith and lived the things he spoke in ways few others he knew did.

At one point in his young life, Brad had been that way. Excited about God after attending an elementary-aged church camp. But within the year, his mother died. He'd never quite recovered from that blow, and when a drunk driver killed his father, he'd all but buried his belief.

Lord, if I'd kept my faith, would Trey have fallen into drugs? If I'd turned to You more, would it have saved him? Maybe not. . .but it surely wouldn't have hurt. His gaze drifted to Brynn. *I don't want to mess her up too. I'm sorry for all the years I've doubted You or pushed You aside, tried to do things on my own. I need You back in my life, please. Guide me.*

He sat back and waited for some feeling, some change. But. . .there was nothing. No angel choirs singing. No ray of sunlight shooting through the ceiling. Just the status quo.

After a moment more, Brad cleaned up the mess on the coffee table and gathered the papers he'd been perusing from Frank's old files. "I hope *You* heard that, Lord. I meant it."

He returned everything to its rightful place, set the provenance with the book of ledger art on the kitchen table, and grabbed some of the photo albums and loose photos from the bins.

Page after album page contained photos of Frank's art, from photos of the whole piece to close-ups of particular elements, including the signatures. Matty was right. Frank was gifted. His original pieces were amazing, drawing the eye with color and composition. His copies of the masters were flawless and convincing but for the intentional discrepancies he painted into the pieces—which, come to think of it, were probably the reasons for the close-up photos. He'd documented each difference with pictures.

Which ones had he been convicted of forging?

Curious, Brad laid aside the photos to look through the files. The entire middle bin contained documents relating to his arrest, investigation, trial, and plea deal. Somewhere in there, surely, he'd find the photographs he was looking for. He glanced out the sliding doors. Dani was still deep in conversation with Matty.

"Brynnie, you okay?"

She turned and smiled. "Me and Peanut have fun, Uncle Bad."

"Good girl."

She disappeared again into her toddler imaginings, allowing him time to dig. He pulled the first of several folders and, sitting on the floor, flipped through the reams of papers.

Half an hour later, the sliding doors opened, and Matty and Dani reentered the house. Matty departed to prepare for a lunchtime appointment, and Brad turned to Dani.

"You okay?"

"I'm really good."

"What happened?"

"Honestly? I don't know." She shrugged. "Matty tried to explain God to me. I'm still confused, but after we talked awhile, he asked if I wanted to pray with him, so I did. It was the weirdest thing. It felt like someone poured something really soothing over every inch of me—filled me with complete. . .love. And acceptance. I've always carried such shame because I was Frank's child, but right now, it doesn't matter." Her cheeks took on a red tinge. "You probably think I'm crazy."

"I do *not* think you're crazy." He pulled her into his arms. "I'm so happy for you, Dani." The fact that her mother and grandfather threw such shade at her for being Frank's daughter was unconscionable. She couldn't help who fathered her.

She melted against him, and he held her. This woman fit so easily in his embrace. Taller than average, her head rested against his shoulder rather than hitting somewhere in the middle of his chest. Her warm breath teased his neck, sending delicious shivers through him. His mind strayed to the accidental-on-purpose kiss they'd shared the day before, and he contemplated trying another one—less accident, more purpose. All he had to do was dip his chin, and he could taste her lips again. Only when he made a move in that direction, she stiffened.

"What is that?" Dani squinted toward the boxes near their feet.

"What?"

"The picture." She wiggled from his arms to stare at the open files.

Crud. Was she upset he'd gone poking around? "I was letting my inner nerd out. Looking at the albums of Frank's paintings, and I got curious which pieces he supposedly forged. Are you upset?"

"No. Look at anything you want." Rather than the file, she retrieved the photo album. "But this piece hangs behind Grandpa Dale's desk in his law office."

The photo depicted a tranquil apple orchard with a young man standing on a ladder in light-colored pants and a striped shirt. Nearby, a young woman in a pale green dress watched him with a serene expression.

"This artwork is copied from one of the artists in the Tonalism movement."

"Tonalism movement?" Her face became a mask of confusion. "You're speaking Greek."

"No, I'm speaking art. Um…" He thought for a moment. "You've seen the painting known as *Whistler's Mother*?"

"That old, frowning crone dressed in black with a doily thing on her head?" She drew a circle in the air above her hair.

Brad gaped before a frustrated laugh burst out. "You are blowing my mind."

"What?"

"You have much to learn, young Padawan. That description borders on sacrilege."

"Okay." Her smile was a mix between embarrassment and surprise. "I've already told you, you must take me to a museum and teach me."

He wrapped her in another embrace. "And I will—*soon*. I can't, in good conscience, let you languish in this state." Brad reluctantly let her go. "But back to the point. The painting you so badly described, *Whistler's Mother*, is the best-known example from the Tonalism movement. This painting looks like the style of a contemporary of Whistler. Joseph DeCamp."

"But if Frank painted it, why would Grandpa Dale hang it in his office? He *hates* Frank and anything to do with him."

"I can't answer that."

"Neither can I. It doesn't make any sense for him to keep such an obvious reminder of Frank so close." Dani leafed through further album pages, eventually stalling on another. "This one's hanging in Grandpa Dale's game room at his house."

The Impressionist painting depicted men playing billiards in the style of Jean Beraud.

"Why would my grandfather have two—and maybe more?—pieces of Frank's artwork hung prominently in his home and office?"

"Good question."

Dani kept flipping pages, stopping on occasion to study some of the photographs.

Meanwhile, Brad snatched up a batch of photos still in the developer's sleeve and started to flip through those. However, they weren't photographs of Frank's artwork. These were candids from some event at a studio or gallery.

"Oh my." Dani craned her neck to see the photos he perused. "My mother was younger than me there." She indicated the attractive, tanned blond in the white sleeveless dress.

"Yeah, and there's Frank." He indicated the young man with the mop of long, dark hair, dressed in black jeans, a form-fitting white T-shirt, and leather jacket, eying the blond hottie from a distance.

She whipped around to look at him. "How do you know? You've never seen him before."

"His mugshots were in the files."

"Oh." Dani shuffled through the photos. "I think this might be the art show where they met. Look at the date stamp." She indicated the marking in the lower right corner. "This was March, and I was born in December the same year." She stalled at one where Frank and her mother stood face-to-face, an obvious spark zinging between them. "That's nine months, almost to the day." She shivered.

"Oh, awkward. Have you ever seen these before?"

"No. Remember? All things Frank were taboo in my mom's household."

"Right. So who is this guy?" He indicated a slim, prematurely balding gentleman in baggy slacks and a garishly colored, printed button-down. "I've seen him in a bunch of these photos."

"The gallery owner, maybe?" She arched a brow.

"Maybe. I'd say ask your mother, but. . ."

"Yeah, that's not going to happen." Dani flipped through a few more.

"That's Grandpa Dale." She held up a photo of a distinguished man in his fifties, shaking hands with the possible gallery owner. "And no—I'm not going to ask him either, but he's obviously someone Grandpa Dale knew—or met. Maybe Matty would have an idea."

She grew quiet, then looked at him. "So how much does art sell for? I mean, obviously things like the *Mona Lisa* are priceless, but how much does this kind of art sell for?"

"It all depends. Who the artist is. How old the piece. The medium. The size. Matty said yesterday that Frank sold a couple of his original pieces back in the day for a couple hundred bucks, but his forgery case was memorable for the number and value of forged pieces. Probably, if you dig into these files, you'll find what they all sold for."

"What about ledger art? It doesn't look like much. Is it valuable?"

"Well, we have *that* answer." Brad rose and went to the kitchen table, where he'd left the auction catalog. Pulling the receipt from between the pages, he scanned to the bottom, then flipped the page over. He blinked and looked again.

"How much?"

"Um. . ." He swallowed, then met her eyes. "Close to forty thousand dollars."

The air rushed out of her so quickly, he could swear she'd been punched. "Say that again."

"Forty. Thousand. Dollars."

She mouthed the figure. "Shut up!" She walked to his side to look herself. "Why? That's. . . I barely earn more than that in a whole year! I know he was an art guy, but what would possess a man who lives in a rundown little hovel to spend his wad on that kind of art? Brad, this makes no sense!"

CHAPTER NINETEEN

Fort Marion, St. Augustine, Florida—Friday, June 30, 1876

hite Chief studied Broken Bow's fingernails, then turned to consider a Numinu brave's hands as well. "You men know this is a tough decision if I'm resorting to checking the length and cleanliness of your nails to break the tie."

Broken Bow smiled, and they both chorused together. "Yes, White Chief."

He'd seen the chief employ such methods many times in their weekly competitions. When two men had equal marks for attending daily classes, weekly church services, fulfilling assigned duties, and keeping bunks and uniforms neat, the chief checked the length of their hair and fingernails.

"Congratulations, Broken Bow. You win this week's competition."

Equal parts cheers and groans sounded from the men standing in formation behind them. The Numinu brave gave him a reluctant nod and congratulations.

White Chief continued, "Now that things are settling down after our little. . .*uprising*. . ." He pinned a fierce look on the Ka'igwa ringleaders who, until only recently, had been relegated to wearing leg irons. "I feel comfortable reinstating camping privileges to the weekly winners." That announcement produced cheers. "Broken Bow, once you've packed your things, I'll walk you to the dock, where you'll sail to Anastasia Island."

"Thank you, White Chief." The news warmed him. It had been a long while since any of them had been allowed out of the fort, especially camping on the barrier island across the river.

"The rest of you are dismissed. Enjoy your free time."

The group broke ranks. Some headed off while others huddled around Broken Bow and the other man, congratulating or consoling, as the case warranted. White Chief waited until the knot of people thinned, then motioned for Broken Bow to follow.

He excused himself and followed the chief.

"Congratulations." White Chief spoke only when they'd sat on the well in the corner.

"Thank you, White Chief."

The officer dropped his voice, despite everyone having filtered out of earshot. "This is, in part, reward for your help with the escape attempt. Your information was very valuable."

Broken Bow nodded. When the bluecoats had arrived that afternoon, White Chief had pulled the Tsitsistas leaders, Eagle's Head and Heap of Birds, behind closed doors and asked for their help, and both men had pledged their assistance—to the death if need be. Initially, it had upset Broken Bow that he was not included—had he not proven his allegiance?—but Romero assured him it was a calculated move to protect Broken Bow from retaliation. It still needled him, but he understood White Chief's intentions.

"I know I don't have to caution you. The St. Augustine residents were in a holy uproar over the false reports. Be careful, but enjoy your time away."

"I make White Chief proud."

"You already do." The man nodded toward the stairs. "Go on. Pack up."

Once Broken Bow had gathered a few belongings, White Chief met him with a knife, bow, and arrows. Broken Bow tucked the knife in his pack and slung the bow and arrows across his back, then followed White Chief through the pine doors. As they walked toward the docks, Broken Bow shared his plans to sleep long, hunt, draw, and read.

He paused as they reached the end of the docks. "White Chief think I, others, go home—ever?"

"Back to your people?" White Chief also stopped.

"I pray for Tsitsistas, Hinono-eino, want to tell them of Jesus. What He do in here." He laid his palm over his chest.

White Chief nodded, though there was sadness in his eyes. "I have high hopes. One day."

A cloud veiled his heart. "White Chief words and face no match."

"Only because I have no control over when you men might be released—or what will happen when you are." He heaved a great breath. "Of the seventy-three men who came here, you are one who has embraced what I have attempted to teach. The Broken Bow who marched into Fort Marion a year ago is not the Broken Bow who stands before me now. You could do much good if you returned home and shared your new faith and knowledge—but my requests have not been met favorably. Yet. I won't stop trying. Don't you stop praying."

Broken Bow smiled. "Thank you, White Chief."

Beside the small sailboat, they said their farewells. As the boat's owner navigated away from the long dock and past the larger ships, Broken Bow caught sight of two familiar faces aboard the *Mystic*. At the sight of the gray-headed man who'd upset Sally Jo and one of the young men who'd been with him, Broken Bow's heart slowed with dread. Luke and Sally Jo had never explained to him what happened that day—only that it was a personal matter—but he'd seen the hurt that man caused. The gray-headed man watched him intently and bobbed his head, the motion almost too slight to notice. Broken Bow cocked a look at him, confused, then returned the slight motion. Odd. He didn't seem threatening, but he was one to watch. If he could save Sally Jo another wound, he would.

The boat's owner dropped him safely on the other shore. He thanked the man and, after slinging his belongings across his shoulders, started south toward their camp.

When he reached the campsite, his heart sank. A tent was already erected and a fire blazed, though no one was in view. Crouching along the edge of the marsh, he watched. What should he do? In his homeland, he would simply find another camp, but he was a prisoner with a two-day pass. White Chief expected him to stay in *this* place. He dared not betray his trust, given the possibility of Romero or a bluecoat coming to check on him.

Nothing stirred until, finally, two forms appeared over a small rise on the far side of the camp, walking hand in hand. Broken Bow squinted, then began to laugh. At the sound, Luke and Sally Jo scanned the area until he emerged from the marsh grasses.

"There you are!" Luke started toward him. "W-we've been expecting you for an hour."

"Why you here? White Chief no say my friends come."

Sally Jo's face lit with a huge smile. "He's been planning this for weeks now to reward you for your help, and he thought you'd enjoy some company, so here we are."

He met them at their tent. "White Chief, Luke, Sally Jo play tricks."

"You're n-not upset, are you?"

"No. Is good."

"Then help the man get settled." Sally Jo gave Luke a gentle push.

Working together, the men set up his tent in minutes, and Broken Bow stripped out of his uniform jacket, then exchanged his army-issued footwear for his moccasins. With those tasks done, they relaxed on the sand.

Sally Jo brushed grit from her pale green dress. "When Lieutenant Pratt brings you down here, do you do anything special, Broken Bow?"

"White Chief make us march. We do duties. He inspect—tent, uniform, same as fort. He also give much freedom. Men collect sea beans, shells. They hunt, fish." He searched for an English word, then signed it when he couldn't come up with it.

"R-r-race?"

"Yes. Race." He shot Luke a teasing grin. "Thank you, Stumbling Tongue."

The other man gave him a playful shove, and they all had a hearty laugh.

"Tsitsistas race Ka'igwa. Numinu race Hinono-eino."

"Oh! Competitions between the tribes."

"Yes. Run far, come back. Also, when water low." He hovered his hand above the sand. "Men find, eat. . ." Again, he searched for the word, but with no sign for the one he was looking for, he tried a different tack. "Shell. Open shell. Eat inside."

Luke's eyes lit with understanding. "Oysters."

"Yes. I like oysters."

"And what are we going to eat tonight?" Sally Jo shifted a questioning look between them both. "The tide's in right now, so I doubt it'll be oysters."

"I hunt."

"I'll go too." Luke turned on her. "You want to c-come, Sally Jo?"

"I'll be fine here. I may draw a little, try to capture the sunset."

The same dread Broken Bow had felt as he noticed the gray-headed man across the river returned, eclipsing his heart. They each went to their tents, and Luke produced the bow and arrows Broken Bow had made for him. When he approached, Broken Bow gathered his own weapons and spoke in a hush.

"You stay. Watch over Sally Jo."

"Why?" Luke's brow furrowed.

He stood. "The day Pearson attack. At medicine tent, gray-headed man and three others come, talk to Sally Jo. I see that man today. At docks."

"Delmer is the *M-Mystic*'s captain, But he's no. . .threat to her."

He scowled. "He upset her."

"Upset her, yes. But he won't h-harm her."

Behind them, Sally Jo drew near, humming softly as she crouched at the entrance of their tent.

Luke nodded at the bow in Broken Bow's hand. "Is that all you need?"

He retrieved the knife White Chief had given him and tucked the leather sheath into his belt. "Yes."

"Then let's get going." He approached his woman and kissed her soundly, then stared deep into her eyes. "I love you."

Her cheeks flushed. "I love you too. Now go find supper or we'll all be hungry tonight."

"We won't b-be long." Luke paused. "If you have any problems, the r-rifle is in the tent."

At her nod, Luke headed out of camp, motioning Broken Bow to fall in. When they reached the rise where he'd first seen his friends, Luke spoke again. "I appreciate your concern for Sally Jo, but Delmer wouldn't h-harm her."

He glared. "Why you say?"

Luke fidgeted. "Sally Jo's mother was m-married to her father but was 'visiting' Delmer. They were. . .in love. Sally Jo didn't know this until that day by the tent."

Broken Bow closed his eyes. No wonder she'd been upset—and reluctant to tell him why.

"He no danger to Sally Jo?"

Luke shook his head. "He and his f-friends came to check on her after the s-scuffle with Pearson. He was. . .concerned for his lover's daughter."

Broken Bow blurted his thoughts in the Tsitsistas tongue, unsure how to express their full breadth in English. "This Delmer. Have no honor. Take another man's woman."

"I agree. But I d-do think his intentions were pure that day. I doubt he would have r-revealed anything, except Sally Jo's father came while he was still there."

It made much sense. Her father's arrival had forced a confrontation. "Is why she not speak to father?"

"And why we m-married so suddenly. Delmer has kept his p-promise to leave her alone."

A man like that—his word wasn't good, but Broken Bow could see why Luke would doubt him as a threat. He motioned. "We hunt."

They moved inland, slipping into the piney woods. Since their first successful camp here, he'd often slipped into these trees and chest-high palmettos to listen to the birds and wind or to search for the razorback hogs that rooted for food in the dense ground cover. It had become a favorite pastime while on the island.

Nocking an arrow, he crept along a faint game trail, Luke taking a larger, man-made path that angled him farther inland still. They moved slowly, bows ready, easing through the fan-shaped palmettos. Not an easy task since the stiff plants rattled fiercely when moved. Broken Bow leaned his shoulder against one of the tall pines. Luke also stopped some twenty feet away, and they both grew still.

Minutes ticked by, and some distance in front of them, the palmettos rustled. He scanned for the waving of the fronds, though another sound snagged his ear from completely the opposite direction. Eyes fixed on the first, his ears strained for the second.

"I'm telling you, I saw that blasted Indian on a boat headed this way. Just gettin' him alone would be enough." The whispered words chilled Broken Bow. "But to find the judge's daughter is just beyond this ridge? I bet the two of 'em's together!"

His heart stuttering at the implication, he leaned around the tree until he found three men beyond the edge of the woods.

"Like mother, like daughter?"

"Yeah, steppin' out on her husband."

He shifted back down the path for a better view. As he squinted through the palmettos, one of the faces came into sharper focus.

Pearson.

"I'm tired of the two of them messin' up my life. Caused me to spend time in jail after our last run-in. Been waitin' to give 'em their comeuppance."

He had no idea what *comeuppance* was, but it couldn't be good. Broken Bow threw a prayer heavenward, then sounded a call toward Luke that his tribesmen would easily recognize. His friend, though, was not trained in the ways of the Tsitsistas. Luke's eyes remained pinned on the area ahead.

Broken Bow looked again toward Pearson and friends, but they'd moved off, slinking along the backside of the sandy dunes toward Sally Jo and camp. His heart lurched, and with another whispered prayer, he drew his bow and fired his ready arrow at a tree some ten feet in front of his friend. The projectile sailed, silent and true, and struck the tree with a *thwap*. Luke ducked, startled, then whipped around. When their eyes met, Broken Bow stood tall so Luke could see his signs over the vegetation.

Trouble in camp.

Dropping his bow and quiver so he wouldn't be tempted to use them against Pearson, he ran. Down the game trail and out of the woods. He sprinted up and over the sandy ridge and made it back to the camp before the three men emerged.

Sally Jo startled when he skidded to a halt near her. "What in heaven's na—"

"Pearson comes." He spat the whispered words and pinned his eyes on the dunes.

"What?"

"Stay behind me."

"Where is Luke?" Her voice pitched toward panic.

Yes, where *was* Luke? He scanned the path he'd taken. No sign. He should have been—

"P-pearson!" Luke's voice rose over the dunes.

At the sound, Broken Bow lunged up the nearest hill and found his friend, bow aimed at the former bluecoat who, along with his two companions, held knives at the ready. The three faced Luke.

"Drop them." Luke nodded toward the nearest.

None of them moved, so Broken Bow kicked the sand, showering it over the middle man. All three glanced up, Pearson's eyes going cold at the sight of him.

"Do what he say!"

For one tense breath, no one moved.

"Put 'em down." Pearson nodded, and the other men obeyed. But as Pearson moved to toss away his blade, his hand snaked out. Sunlight glinted on steel. Luke grunted, fingers slipping from the bowstring.

At the sight of his friend falling, instinct took over, and with blade in hand, he launched himself from the dune. He caught Pearson by the neck, dragged him close, and readied to plunge the knife between his ribs. The sight of Sally Jo cradling Luke as she sobbed stayed his hand for the briefest moment.

He raised the knife again, but something smacked him hard across the back of the head, and everything faded into oblivion.

Sarah Mather's House, St. Augustine, Florida—Saturday, July 1, 1876

Luke was gone. Never would she feel his arms around her. Never would she feel her toes curl when he kissed her. Grow frustrated at his speech difficulties, then chide herself for her impatience. She would never bear his children or minister on a mission field beside him. They would never face life together again. She was utterly alone.

Why would You take him from me? Why so soon? And if he had to go this way, Lord, why couldn't Pearson and the others have taken my life too?

The bedroom door cracked open, and Sarah peeked in. When Sally Jo lifted a numb glance to her friend's face, the woman pushed the door wide and placed a tea tray on the nightstand. "Sit up, dear."

Sally Jo shook her head.

Sarah sat and petted her hair. "Speak to me, please."

"I don't want tea."

"You've had nothing since yesterday. You need to keep your strength up."

"Why?" It would be so much easier if she simply let herself slip away.

"Lieutenant Pratt came by some hours ago. You were asleep. He's very concerned for you, Sally Jo, but—"

She shook her head. "I'm not ready to see anyone."

"He came bearing news."

What was bigger news than Luke Daniel Worthing's death at Pearson's hands?

"Broken Bow is in difficult shape. Two stab wounds, broken bones, bruises."

At the mention of her husband's best friend, some of the haze cleared and her mind honed in on Sarah's words. With the strength she could muster, she pushed herself up.

"He's fighting but—" The woman's words cut off quickly.

"But what?" *Oh Lord, what?*

"After the escape attempt and now Luke's death. . .there are those in the community calling for. . ."

The fog cleared more, and though her mind spun until she felt sick at her stomach, she sat taller still. "Calling for what?"

Sarah's voice grew thick. "For Broken Bow's execution. And I don't know that it can be stopped."

"Oh, Lord Jesus, no." She fell into Sarah's arms. "He was trying to help Luke—protect me!"

"The residents are up in arms because—"

"The escape attempt. I know." She pulled back from her friend's embrace.

"No. They're in an uproar because. . ." Sarah blew out a frustrated breath, then grasped her by both arms and turned a heated look on Sally Jo. "Were you and Broken Bow meeting there alone?"

"What? No!" She wrenched free. "What are you. . . ? Is that what people think?"

"There are rumors flying that you and Broken Bow were alone together and that Luke found you, and that's why he was stabbed. He confronted Broken Bow."

"No!" she shrieked, her stomach roiling. "They went hunting for our supper, and Broken Bow returned very suddenly. He was in camp only long enough to tell me Pearson was coming before—" A wave of nausea hit her, and she shoved Sarah off the bed and darted to the washbasin. With nothing in her stomach, she leaned heavily on the stand while she dry heaved. Sarah came to hold her hair back, then guided her to the bed once she was done.

Sally Jo sat heavily. "Please believe me. Broken Bow didn't stab Luke. It was Pearson!"

Sarah poured tea and handed her the cup. "Drink."

She took a swallow, then another. "Please! Tell me you believe me."

"Yes, child. I *had* to ask. But I couldn't imagine you'd break your marriage vows."

Like Mama did. . .

"You and Luke were so obviously in love. Anyone who saw you together would know that. And knowing Broken Bow, I can't believe he would betray you, Luke, or the lieutenant to do the things he's being accused of."

"Sarah, he did nothing wrong!" Her voice went hoarse. "He doesn't deserve to die."

"No, he doesn't."

"But what can I do?"

Sarah wrapped an arm around her shoulders. "Pray. Think. Leave no stone unturned in trying to help this young man. And go see him. He needs to know you don't blame him."

"Blame *him*? Of course I don't!"

"I know." Sarah patted her hand. "Drink your tea, dear."

She took another swallow, though it was tasteless. "Do you think you can get Lieutenant Pratt and Lieutenant Colonel Dent to come here?"

Sarah twisted to look at her. "Now?"

Sally Jo nodded. As much as she didn't want to relive yesterday, they needed to hear the truth.

Relief washed over Sarah. "There's my brave girl. Yes. I'll collect them now." She exited the room but turned. "Finish your tea and get the hairbrush from my vanity. Even if you don't put it up properly, you can neaten your hair."

Sarah's purposeful footsteps faded as she reached the front door and departed. Sally Jo tried for the thousandth time to fill her lungs. The air never quite reached the bottom. But she breathed out a prayer, a desperate request for strength and wisdom, then swallowed another gulp of her tea. Rising, she padded to Sarah's room and brushed her hair.

A few moments later, a soft knock came at the front door.

Wouldn't Sarah let herself in?

She headed down the hall and peeked out the nearby window, then she pushed the door open to look out.

"Papa?"

"Oh, thank goodness." He hung his head. "I've had a hard time finding you. I thought you and Luke rented a room at Canton's boardinghouse."

At the oh-so-normal mention of her husband, her emotions roared up. "We do." *Did.* Without Luke's income, she didn't know where she'd live soon.

"No one there could tell me where you were."

She swallowed around the knot in her throat. "Sarah didn't want me to be alone."

He lifted his gaze, eyes sad. "You should come home. It's where you belong."

Was it? She was in no place to discern such a thing. Not with every shred of her absolutely numb, frozen on the inside—so frozen she wondered if she'd ever feel again. But she *had* to keep plodding. For Broken Bow's sake.

Hadn't Sarah said something about leaving no stone unturned? Had God possibly sent her father so she could solicit his help?

"Papa, I have a favor to ask."

A twinkle of hope sparked in his eyes. "Anything."

"Rumor is Broken Bow may be. . ." She sobbed. ". . .may be executed for Luke's death."

"I've heard." He reached for her hand, though something didn't feel right. The minute he touched her, she pulled free, her mind reaching to lay hold of the feeling just out of her grasp.

"Broken Bow is innocent. He didn't do what people are saying."

Papa gave no reaction.

"Can you help me show he doesn't deserve to be execu—"

"Did you?"

She cocked her head. "Did I what?"

"Did you do what people have said you've done? Did you meet with that Indian alone?"

The question had rocked her when it came from Sarah's mouth. Her friend knew better than to think her capable of such a deed. Even more, her own father should know that, though given his unbending history and nature...

She wouldn't have thought it possible, but she went even colder inside. "What do you think, Papa? Am I capable of such a thing? Is that how you raised me?"

"Your mother raised you."

"And Mama was unfaithful, so therefore I must be too? Is that what you're implying?"

His silence spoke volumes.

Sally Jo shook her head. "You've come to the door on the day after my husband was murdered, and other than to mention his name in passing, you've offered no condolences. No caring. And you have the audacity to ask me if I was unfaithful. Never, Papa. Not one time has any impure thought crossed my mind. I love Luke with my whole heart, and there will never be a day I don't. Until you can understand that, we've nothing more to discuss."

She closed the door and locked it, then plunked down on Sarah's hall tree, wholly unsure her legs would hold her.

How much later Sarah arrived with the two officers, she had no idea, but she unlocked the door and let them in.

Sarah astutely pinned her with a concerned look. "Are you all right?"

"Papa came by." She whispered the words.

When the other woman's eyes rounded with hope, she shook her head. "The relationship is hopelessly broken." She turned to Lieutenant Pratt. "How is Broken Bow?"

His face was lined with stress. "Not well. Dr. Janeway is caring for him, but we've moved him within the safety of the fort so he won't be as vulnerable to—" His words stalled.

An attack by *concerned* citizens, surely.

"I would ask how you are," Pratt whispered, "but I think we all know."

Sarah guided them into the parlor and invited the men to sit. They all took their places, Sally Jo on a small settee with Sarah, the men facing them from chairs opposite a small table. As clearly and concisely as she could, she recounted the events of the previous evening and answered their questions with all the detail she could recall.

"And you're *sure* it was Pearson who stabbed him?" Pratt asked.

"Yes, sir. There was no mistaking him."

"Who is this Pearson?" Lieutenant Colonel Dent asked.

Bile rose in Sally Jo's throat. "Walt Pearson, former sergeant under your predecessor's command. Broken Bow and I had a run-in with him the first day we went into the fort to teach, sir."

"Run-in?"

Pratt recalled the incident and how, ultimately, Pearson had been removed.

"And you've had two altercations with him since that point?"

Sally Jo laid her head on Sarah's shoulder. "Is that not enough to show a pattern?"

"Show a pattern? Yes. Stop an unjust execution?" Dent shook his head. "That remains to be seen."

Sarah sat forward and pinned Dent with an expectant look. "Your brother-in-law is the president of the United States, sir. Are there not some big strings you can pull?"

Dent returned the look. "Again, that remains to be seen. I have inquired."

"Well, then, I think we're done here." Sarah rose, and the men rocked to their feet.

Fort Marion, St. Augustine, Florida—Monday, June 3, 1876

Sally Jo wrung water from the cloth and laid it across Broken Bow's forehead. In his restless sleep, he gave an involuntary shiver and a low moan.

"Shh. It's all right." She caressed the back of his hand, and for an instant, his swollen eyelids fluttered open, then closed again. He settled for only a moment before unintelligible words came to his lips.

As she dried her hands on the nearby towel, she sang the first verse of "It Is Well with My Soul," then lit the lantern to combat the growing dusk. Retrieving Broken Bow's well-loved Bible, which lay open on the edge of his cot, she skimmed for the verse she'd last read and began again.

" 'But what saith it? The word is nigh thee, even in thy mouth, and in thy heart: that is, the word of faith, which we preach; that if thou shalt confess with thy mouth the Lord Jesus, and shalt believe in thine heart that God hath raised him from the dead, thou shalt be saved.' "

Lord, I know Broken Bow's eternal salvation is secure, but please don't let him die a prisoner—especially for crimes he didn't commit. Save him, Father, please!

A soft scuff drew her attention to the doorway, where Lieutenant Pratt and Dr. Janeway stood.

She offered them a sad smile. "He seems more settled when I sing or read to him."

Pratt came to watch him sleep. "It's good you've come, especially given your own loss."

The ever-present lump in her throat grew. She'd arrived early the morning before—just as the lieutenant himself had walked up from town—and she'd not left. Sitting with her friend had been her saving grace, the thing that kept her mind from spiraling into the dark pit of Luke's death and kept her plodding forward. "I need him as much as he needs me right now."

The officer flicked a somber glance at the doctor. Janeway stepped outside and pulled both doors closed as Pratt retrieved chairs from along the wall.

Dread filled her as the men sat. "What is it?"

"I've spoken to Lieutenant Colonel Dent. There won't be help from the higher ranks or the president on behalf of Broken Bow."

"Oh, Lord, no. They would sacrifice his life—for *what?*"

Janeway angled a glance away, his tone bitter. "To keep the peace, I think, ma'am."

"The residents are calling for justice on behalf of your husband's death. They want Broken Bow's blood."

She sat straighter and folded her hands atop the Bible. "It should be

Pearson's blood that mollifies the crowd!"

Pratt cleared his throat. "I've gone over this in my mind so many times. I was the one who sent Broken Bow to the island. I proposed the plan for you all to meet him. And now I am all but helpless to save his life."

"All but. . ." Janeway grunted the words, then turned a stern look on the lieutenant. "Tell her, sir. Please. She might have an idea to make this work."

"Make what work?"

Pratt brooded a moment, then met her eyes with a piercing look. "What I am about to say must stay between us."

Sally Jo nodded. "All right." She closed the Bible in her lap and placed her hand on the cover. "On my honor, sir—I won't say anything to anyone about this."

"Broken Bow asked me just before he went to the island whether I thought he might ever return home. He longs to share Christ with his people. His transformation is nothing short of miraculous—and I so wish to give him that opportunity."

"I've thought the same thing." If only there was a way.

"In the aftermath of the Kiowa escape plot, we blindfolded the ringleaders and marched them around the courtyard until they dropped. We put them back in their respective dungeons, and the good doctor injected them with something to make them sleep. To the Indians, it appeared they were dead. The soldiers carried their bodies out and transported them to the guard house down the street, where they served two weeks in solitary confinement—away from the view of the others. The Indians were quite impressed with my miracle-working powers when I brought the ringleaders back to life upon their return to the fort."

Sally Jo nearly chuckled. She'd heard the awed whispers about White Chief as things had begun to return to normal. "How does this apply to Broken Bow?"

"I've lain awake these last several nights pondering whether there's not a way to use the same ploy to save Broken Bow's life. Make him appear dead. Dig a grave in a hidden spot on Anastasia Island—just as we've done for other Indians who died here—and transport him out of here." The lieutenant's shoulders slumped. "Faking the death and digging a grave, I can handle. But how do I transport a badly injured man back to his homeland without people seeing him and raising an alarm? A wagon will take too long, and it would be torturous, if not deadly, in his present state. I couldn't put him on a train in his condition. And even if we spirited him out of the fort until he had time to heal, a single Indian man would garner notice on a train at any time."

She met Pratt's eyes. "That is a dilemma, sir."

"As a longtime resident of St. Augustine, you must know people, Mrs. Worthing. Is there anyone you trust to solicit help?"

Sally Jo clicked through the people she counted as close friends and came up with only one name—Sarah. And as dearly as she loved the woman, she would not ask her to be party to this. She was too well established in the community. Too many counted on her. As for herself. . .Luke was gone. Her mother was dead. Her relationship with her father was. . . unsalvageable. Everyone else was too cautious to befriend the judge's daughter on any level beyond pleasantries.

Her mind shot down a rabbit trail, and for a split second, she let herself explore the idea. She couldn't ask him, could she? Sally Jo pondered but quickly shoved the thought away.

Not an option. Was it? "Lord, help us. . ."

"Sally Jo?" Broken Bow's soft call brought her around, and she set the Bible on the edge of the cot as she reached for his hand.

"I'm right here."

His gaze drifted around the room and landed back on her. "Luke?"

Oh Lord, help. Tears welled in her eyes, and she smiled her bravest smile. "Luke is just fine." And he was—walking beside his beloved Savior. "Please, rest. Get better so you can go home soon."

The lieutenant stabbed at her with his finger, but other than flicking a warning glance his way, she pressed on, suddenly sure of what she needed to do.

"You have important work to do there."

"Home?"

"Yes. Back to your people. Close your eyes and rest. Get your strength up. We've a long journey ahead."

His eyes drifted closed again, and within minutes, his breathing indicated he slept.

When she finally released Broken Bow's hand and stood, the lieutenant met her with a stormy gaze. "What are you doing? You've promised him something none of us can deliver."

"Please don't be angry. I know how to get Broken Bow safely away, but we'll need to move quickly. It will happen within the next day or two. Maybe even tonight."

"How?"

"Leave that to me." She darted a look out the window, noting that full darkness was moments away. "I need to speak with someone, then I'll return with more news."

"It's getting dark. Do you want an escort?"

Sally Jo shook her head. "It's better if I do this alone."

His demeanor reluctant, Pratt saw her out of the casemate and to the fort's pine doors. "Please don't leave for home, sir. I doubt I'll be long. Call Painted Sky to sit with his brother." He'd been there for much of the past two days but had gone to sleep after their evening meal. "If my suspicions are correct, their time together will be short."

She ducked out into the night. As she walked, she picked up several small pebbles and tucked them into her palm. Once she reached the docks, she hurried to the *Mystic*. In the darkness, she could make out the forms of several men on the deck, scurrying about. Taking one of the small rocks, she aimed at a man and hurled it. It struck the wood deck and skittered across it. Missed. Before the man got too far beyond, she slung another stone and this time must have hit him.

"Hey!" He turned, glaring down at her. "What do you think you're doing?"

"I'm sorry. I need to speak to Captain Delmer. Is he on board?"

The fellow leaned over the railing. "Who's askin'?"

"Tell him Lila's daughter." That would grab the captain's attention.

The man huffed, then stomped off. Moments later, the captain's silhouette hurried down the gangplank and stopped feet from her.

Even in the dark, his eyes flashed. "You should not be here."

"No, I shouldn't, but I'm desperate. May I speak to you privately, please?"

"About?"

"Privately?"

Delmer hesitated, then waved her up the gangplank.

Heart pounding, she grabbed her skirt and scurried ahead of him. He motioned her toward the stern and through a doorway, which he closed.

"Are you trying to stir up trouble with your father?"

"My father and I no longer speak, Captain. I eloped with my intended on Christmas Day because things were so broken between us."

"You sayin' I caused all that?"

"I said nothing of the kind. Things were horribly broken before that, but everything came into sharp focus during that conversation with you. Luke and I married two days later."

"I can't say as I'm surprised, but I am sorry." He bobbed his head. "And. . .congratulations on your marriage."

"My husband is dead." She closed her eyes and drew a breath, her legs going soft. "He was murdered."

Delmer caught her arm and guided her toward the nearest chair. "Murdered?"

"On Friday. Right over there." She motioned toward the island across the river.

His jaw went slack. "You're the one the town's buzzing about."

She nodded. "Just so you know—the rumors are not true. I was not meeting with Broken Bow alone. The same man who attacked us at Christmas murdered Luke and has spun this story to see Broken Bow hung, which is why I need your help."

"Out of respect for your mother, I'll do anything I can. But what type of help are you thinking?"

"I need a discreet way to get Broken Bow out of St. Augustine—somewhere far enough away so that we can reach his people without drawing the attention we'd garner here."

"You want me to break an Indian out of jail and take him home." A sardonic smile spread on his lips. "You'll make it so I can never return to this port again."

"Not true. Broken Bow is fighting for his life. It will be easy enough to make it look like he's died and was buried here. No one will be looking for him."

"You want me to take on the responsibility of a badly injured man."

"I'm leaving too. I'll care for him if you can provide us the means to get away."

"You'd give up your whole life to rescue this Indian?"

"My life ended when Luke died. Broken Bow was my husband's best friend, and he's about to be murdered for a crime he never even thought about committing. I have to do this."

He stared at her for a long moment, then ground the heels of his palms into his forehead. "I may regret this, but all right. *If* you can make this happen tonight. We sail at dawn."

"Done. And thank you. You're saving a good man's life."

CHAPTER TWENTY

Frank Sango's House, St. Augustine, Florida—Present Day—Thursday

Since Matty had wall-to-wall meetings until early afternoon, they'd taken their good clothes to Frank's house to change before leaving for the hearing. While Dani brushed her hair and applied a fresh sheen of gloss to her lips in the bathroom, Matty's voice floated down the hall from the direction of Frank's kitchen.

"So have y'all figured out any more about this Native American artist?"

Brad answered back, also from that side of the house. "Kind of a strange story. Luke and Sally Jo—Broken Bow's teachers—got married around Christmas of 1875. After that whole thwarted escape attempt the next spring, Broken Bow was one of the first Indians to be given a pass to leave the fort on his own again, and he met up with the teachers on Anastasia Island."

Dani smoothed her navy slacks and adjusted her shimmery gold sweater. Definitely one of her more classic looks. It would do for Brad and Brynn's custody hearing.

"There was a former soldier who Broken Bow had some scuffles with during his year at the fort, and the last one happened when he and his teachers were camping that weekend. Luke was killed by the guy, and Broken Bow was badly wounded. He succumbed to his injuries a few days later, and they buried him in a secret grave."

"That's awful. What about the woman?"

Dani fluffed her hair one last time, snagged her hairbrush and lip gloss from the counter, and headed down the hall. "Sally Jo disappeared.

No one could find her the morning after Broken Bow's death." When she emerged from the hallway, both Brad and Matty stared with silly grins on their faces.

"Uncle Bad, Miss Dani's real shiny."

The schoolboy grin faded from Brad's lips, replaced by a more appreciative once-over glance. "She's a very beautiful woman, Brynn."

Her cheeks warmed. "It's one of my work outfits. Business casual and all that."

Matty chuckled. "Darlin', you rock it."

"Thank you both." She looked at Brynn. "Can I brush your hair, baby?"

At the girl's nod, they sat on the couch, and Brad excused himself to change. "Anyway, Sally Jo disappeared."

"Never to be heard from again?" Matty took up his usual station in the nearby chair.

"That's where it gets really odd." Dani brushed a section of Brynn's hair, careful not to pull too hard. "The book says she returned to St. Augustine years later, *very* pregnant. She went to visit her estranged father, a federal judge in the city, and tried to make amends. While she was there, the story came out that Broken Bow hadn't died that night in 1876. In fact, she'd found a way to spirit him out of the fort and the city, get him back to his people, and for all the years she was gone, they'd ministered about God on the reservation. And eventually fell in love with each other and married."

"So, the baby was Broken Bow's child?"

"According to her." She ran the brush through the next section of Brynn's hair.

"He didn't return with her?"

Dani shook her head. "I can't help but feel for this woman. Her mother died years before the Native Americans came, she had a difficult relationship with her father, her first husband was murdered, and her second—Broken Bow—died of unknown causes on the reservation, which is why she returned home. But not long after she arrived, she went into labor and died of complications herself." She didn't just feel for. She identified with this woman. They'd both been through a lot.

Matty's brows shot up. "That's a lot for one gal to go through."

"Yeah. And she couldn't have been more than my age when she died. Maybe younger."

"So, did her baby survive—and did her daddy raise it?"

"We don't know what happened to the baby. According to the books we've read, she's buried next to her first husband in one of the cemeteries around here—but there is no indication that there's a baby buried with or near her."

"That's a wild story."

"Right?" She paused to work a difficult tangle from Brynn's hair, then continued. "Broken Bow and Sally Jo's story is tragic and compelling. I found it really interesting to read about them, but I'm still not sure why Frank would spend that kind of money for this art."

Matty shrugged his massive shoulders. "Frank didn't spend money frivolously. Especially that much. If he bought it, there was a reason."

She gave Brynn's hair another swipe, then had the girl face her. "I bought you something." Dani produced a darling headband adorned with pink ribbon roses from a paper bag.

The girl sucked in an excited breath.

"Want to wear it?"

Brynn bit her lip and nodded, and Dani arranged it in her hair.

"How do I look, Mr. Matty?"

"Adorable, little one. And now you and Peanut both have flowers in your hair." He indicated the horse's mane.

Brynn crawled into Matty's lap and snuggled against him.

Dani rose and tossed the paper bag in the trash, then snatched the pack of loose photos she'd been looking through the afternoon before. "I was going to ask you, do you know who this man is?" Dani held out the photograph of Grandpa Dale and the prematurely balding man.

He took it. "Where'd you get this, darlin'?"

"Brad pulled it out of one of the bins." She moved nearer to him and fanned the photographs. "I think this is the art show where Mom and Frank met."

"You're right. He showed me these before." He flipped the picture over to reveal Frank's handwriting in faint ink on the back. "Looks like it's art professor Jamie Knox, the one I mentioned the other day—helped

Frank get into college, brokered a lot of his art sales."

Dani snatched the photo and laughed. "I never thought to look on the back."

"Of course you didn't. You're the selfie generation. Everything's digital."

She smiled sheepishly. "I resemble that remark!" Looking again at the back of the photo, she spoke the name. "Jamie Knox. I saw that name recently."

"Probably in those files." Matty jutted his long beard, which he'd combed out that morning, toward the storage totes.

"Before you brought the files. If memory serves, it was the first day. Right after I got here—even before Gray ambushed me." She mentally retraced her steps and, remembering, jumped up to retrieve the thick file from near the answering machine.

She turned the pages inside so they were facing the right direction.

"That's right." Dani retook her seat. "James Kenneth Knox died five years ago, but before his death, he also spent time in prison for forgery."

Brad reemerged, his hair combed and wearing a green golf shirt and khakis. As soon as he entered the room, Brynn hopped down and ran to him.

"Uncle Bad, look!" She touched the pink roses adorning her hair.

"Wow, Brynnie, where'd you get that?"

"Miss Dani gave it to me."

He scooped the girl up and, at his appreciative smile, Dani shrugged. "It was a dollar at the grocery store. Just the kind of thing to make a little princess's heart happy."

"Exactly the kind of thing this clueless male wouldn't think of. Thank you."

"Hey. Flowers. Ribbons. Frou-frou. Tea parties and tiaras. I got you covered."

Matty looked at his watch and cleared his throat. "We'd better get a move on. Don't want to be late."

Brad's easy smile drained. "Right."

"Hey." She closed the file folder and went to Brad's side. "Don't get apprehensive. This is all going to turn out fine."

He nodded and drew a deep breath. "I know. Just. . .really nervous. Thank you both for going with me."

"Brad!" Miranda Dempsey waved, then gathered her overstuffed briefcase. "You made it."

As soon as she spoke, Brynn glued herself to his leg, and his heart lurched. He'd mistakenly hoped he'd seen the last of the timid behavior. "Miranda."

She glanced around at the others, then back to him. "How are you? How's Brynn?"

"Um." He scooped his niece up, and she buried her face in his neck. "Truthfully, I think we're both nervous."

"Okay, take a deep breath and relax. There's absolutely nothing to be nervous about."

He tried to release the tension from his shoulders. "That's what they keep saying." He turned toward Dani and Matty. "Miranda, these are my friends. Dani Sango and Matty Joie." He nodded at each. "Miranda Dempsey is an old friend and now our caseworker."

Miranda nodded. "Pleasure to meet you both."

"I don't know how this is supposed to work, so if it's not okay for them to be in the courtroom during the hearing, they'll wait outside."

"Judge Elscott is very accommodating in these types of cases. We'll be in his chambers. It'll be very informal. I can't imagine he'd turn your friends away. Personally, I think it'll help your case for him to see that you have a support system."

Dani nudged him. "Told you."

"Uncle Bad, can we go home now?" Brynn whispered.

"In a little bit, baby." He turned back to Miranda. "Where's Lipscomb?"

"Hung up on a case. I have his statement, so if he doesn't show in time, it'll be all right."

They chatted another moment before they were shown into a small but comfortable office with rich green carpet, built-ins full of leather-bound books, a neat desk, and several options for seating, including a couch.

"Mr. Osgood, please, come in." The judge waved them into the chambers, and Brad guided Dani with a hand at the small of her back. The judge offered them seats, and as Brad moved toward one near the front of the desk, Brynn chose that moment to reach for Dani, who took her and headed for the couch.

"Miranda, why don't you pull a chair over from the table. Mrs. Osgood, you're welcome to sit here if you'd like." The judge motioned to the other chair in front of his desk.

"Oh. Um." Embarrassment wound through Brad as he looked at Dani.

She looked toward the judge. "I'm nobody special, Your Honor. Just a friend lending moral support."

Brad whipped around to face her more fully. "That's not true."

Stunned silence hung in the air before the judge spoke. "Would you like to explain?"

He turned back to the judge. "Dani's not my wife. We met four days ago, but we've both lived a few lifetimes since then, seen each other through some rough spots, and. . ." He turned to her. "Without question, she's somebody very special to me."

The judge's eyebrows arched in surprise. "Forgive my mistake. Miss. . . Dani? You're welcome to sit in the place of spouses or *very special people* if you'd like."

It was exactly where she belonged. Side by side with him. Brad locked eyes with her and mouthed a single word. *Please?*

Eyes glistening with unshed tears, she rose at Matty's gentle nudge and took the seat offered. "Thank you, Your Honor."

As she settled Brynn in her lap, Brad sat and twined his fingers with hers.

The hearing proceeded from there, with Miranda providing case history, statements from Trey and Jazz requesting Brad take custody of Brynn, as well as Lipscomb's written statement of Brad's character during the search for his niece. Miranda added information of having known Brad much of their lives and how he'd taken on raising Trey after their father's death. With very few questions, the judge signed the paperwork assigning temporary custody of Brynn to Brad.

Minutes later they walked out, and Matty took Brynn, who'd fallen asleep. Reaching the main hallway, Miranda turned as Matty headed off a short distance to a nearby bench.

"That was a bit of unexpected drama." Miranda shot them a flirty smile, though it mellowed to something more serious. "You really do look like you belong together. I'm happy for you both."

"Thank you." Brad hung his head. "I figured you'd give me grief, say it's too soon."

"Me, give you grief?"

"After all the ribbing you dished out in high school? Yes!"

Miranda laughed. "Good grief, I must've been a terror! I'm so sorry. You won't get grief from me. My husband and I married after dating just two months. Ten years later, we've got four kids, and we're happier than ever."

"Thank you for that."

"I'll call, help you get set up with a caseworker in St. Pete who'll be able to help with permanent custody. In the meantime, keep my number handy if you have questions."

"I will. Thanks, Miranda."

Once she'd walked away, Dani turned the prettiest brown eyes his way. "You totally took my breath away in there. Did you mean it?"

"Did I sound at all indecisive?"

"No."

He drank in her beautiful features, then bent and claimed her lips. She stiffened in surprise but quickly melted against him, her hands straying to caress his shoulders. He pulled her closer still, and she melted all the more. He sunk a hand into her thick hair and deepened the kiss, his heart pounding with desire. When, a moment later, he finally pulled away again, he rested his forehead against hers and caressed her cheek.

"And did that feel like I was questioning anything?"

She shook her head, breathless. "No."

"Rest assured, Dani, I meant every word."

CHAPTER TWENTY-ONE

Matty Joie's House, St. Augustine, Florida—
Present Day—Thursday Evening

*B*rad received the freshly cleaned glass from Dani and dried it, his attention straying from her to the kitchen island, where Matty had papers spread across the wide surface. "What's all this?"

"A folder from Frank's place. Dani pulled it out just before we left this afternoon, and I wanted to take a closer look."

"The one with the art professor's obituary?" She rinsed the last glass, then handed it to Brad. "What's in it?"

His eyes focused on a paper, Matty spoke like his attention was only half on the conversation. "A lot of things."

"Like?" Dani turned off the water, patted her hands on another dishtowel, and went to the island, where she read over his shoulder.

Matty looked up. "Like probable proof that Frank was *not* guilty of the forgery."

"What?" Brad dried the last glass and set it aside, then joined the two.

"It snagged my attention earlier when you said Knox also did time for forgery."

"Yeah, that's attention-grabbing!" Brad slung the dishtowel over his shoulder. "What's the likelihood that a professor *and* his student both were forgers?"

"Frank's got pages of notes—with documentation—that could show this professor was setting him up."

Dani shifted to look at him. "Like, enough to get a new trial and clear his name?"

Matty frowned. "No darlin'. He took a plea deal. There wouldn't be a new trial under those circumstances, even if he was alive."

Dani pressed her eyes closed. "Right. I should know that." Her grandfather was an attorney, after all.

"So, what exactly do you have here?" Brad skimmed the obituary, then replaced it.

"Well, if I'm following Frank's notes, this Knox character was getting Frank to create art in the style of whatever painter. Sometimes as a friendly challenge—'paint me something in the style of Van Gogh' or whatever. Other times as a class assignment."

"Okay?"

"He was also brokering the sales of some of those same pieces."

Dani sat. "You said Frank was selling pieces he'd painted while he was in college."

"Yeah. To get extra money for you and your momma. Knox came to him with the idea."

"So it *wasn't* Frank's idea to begin with?" Brad sat on Matty's other side.

"Back up. No. Frank wanted to sell his art—but he was a poor kid with no connections. This professor was a bigwig—at least in comparison—with plenty of contacts. It was a lucrative partnership for both."

Matty retrieved a stapled packet of papers with a typed list on top. "At some point, Frank logged all of the sales Knox helped him make here. The piece, amount it sold for, date it sold, and photos—both Frank's portfolio photo and the police crime photos for the ones he was charged with forging. On the supposed forgeries, he's also listed how much he supposedly received for them." He flipped the pages to reveal photographs matching the names on the list.

"Wait!" Dani caught Matty's wrist. "Turn back one."

Matty complied, and she took the packet of papers. "Brad. This is the same picture I recognized yesterday." She indicated the Jean Beraud–inspired painting of men playing billiards.

He looked more closely. "Yeah, it is."

"What's that mean, darlin'?"

"While looking through Frank's albums yesterday, I noticed that he'd painted this painting." She stabbed the photo. "One just like this hangs in my grandfather's game room at his house. And. . ." She flipped backward, then forward until she found the other. "And this one hangs over his desk in his law office."

Matty took the packet and looked at the list, comparing it to the two photos. "Neither appears to be one he was accused of forging. So those were just straight-up sold."

Matty picked up another stack of papers. "This is the documentation on the supposed payments for the forged pieces."

Dani looked at the faint photocopy. "Wire transfers." She met Matty's eyes. "May I?"

He handed her the stack, and she leafed through it.

"I have a problem here." Brad reached for the list of sold paintings, flipping through to the billiards painting. He produced his cell phone and brought up the camera, zooming in over the corner where the signature was. "This photo shows Frank's name clearly displayed in the corner—unlike these others." He flipped to one of the paintings Frank was accused of forging, showing Matty the discrepancy between the portfolio photo and the police photo. "Dani mentioned this yesterday. Her family so hates Frank that they won't even speak about him, and yet we're supposed to believe her grandfather would hang Frank's art in his home or office with his name for everyone to see."

Matty sat back, folding his hands over his stomach. "That's a really good point. From all I've learned about Dale Taglund, he'd be too proud to display anything associated with Frank."

As if she hadn't heard a word they'd said, Dani turned, her mouth open. "This doesn't add up. All of these wire transfers came on different days from the same account. What could that possibly mean? That Frank had a black market fan who bought anything and everything he painted, no matter the style or artist he supposedly forged?"

They all sat in silence for a moment as the pieces sank in.

"So what are we saying here?" Brad looked at Dani and Matty. "This Knox guy was taking Frank's paintings, changing the signatures in the corner, and brokering sales as if they were real?"

"You're the art guy." Dani turned wide brown eyes his way. "Is that plausible?"

"Given the fact that Knox served time for forgery later in life, yeah. I think it is, but why didn't any of this come out at trial?" Brad looked again at the photos. "This seems like more than enough to cast a reasonable doubt."

Matty scrubbed his face in frustration. "It never got past the first day of trial. Frank was young, poor, and, I hate to say it, stupid. He had a public defender, and when he couldn't answer where all this money was coming from. . ." Matty tapped the wire transfers Dani still held. "Frank got spooked. Figured he was going to put his mom in the poor house *and* lose the case, so he took a plea."

Brad turned to her. "Dani, this is bugging me. Do you have photos of either of those paintings your grandfather's got?"

She thought for a moment, then shook her head. "Not with me, no. I was the hated grandchild, so I didn't go poking around in Grandpa Dale's—" Her brown eyes rounded. "His website. He's got a picture of himself at his desk on his website. You have a computer, Matty?"

"Of course! C'mon."

Once Brad checked on Brynn, who'd fallen asleep watching the 'mato show, they went to Matty's office. With a few keystrokes, she brought up the website for Taglund, Moore & Petersen, Attorneys at Law. A couple more clicks, and she was at a page showing her grandfather in a relaxed pose at his desk.

"Can you zoom in on the corner of the painting?"

She looked up at Matty, who reached around her, zoomed in, and recentered on the corner where Joseph DeCamp's—not Frank's—name was written in block letters at the bottom.

"The signature's forged!"

Law Office of Alger, Stein, Pettinger & Waddell, St. Augustine, Florida—Present Day—Friday

"Mr. Joie, Miss Sango, right this way." The receptionist stood at the mouth of a hallway.

"Um, am I allowed to bring my. . .boyfriend and his niece back with me?" She shifted a timid glance Brad's way, then back to the receptionist.

"Bring whomever you'd like."

"Thank you."

Brad helped Brynn from her chair, and they followed the heavyset woman to an office where the attorney's desk sat empty, but one other person occupied a chair facing it. At their entrance, she turned, and Dani recognized the woman from Matty's church.

"Lana." Matty gave her a warm kiss on the cheek. "Good to see you."

"Mattyyyyyy." She gave a toned-down version of the church greeting as she hugged him.

"I trust you remember Dani."

"Of course." Lana turned her way. "Good to see you again."

"Hi, Lana." She reached for Brad's hand. "Um, this is my boyfriend, Brad Osgood, and his niece, Brynn. Lana goes to Matty's church."

"It's a pleasure." Brad smiled as he wrapped an arm around Dani's shoulders.

Lana arched a brow at Matty. "Is this. . . ?"

"The same family we were praying for. Dani and I met them on the goose chase."

The woman's smile broadened. "And you two are dating?"

Warmth spread through Dani. "As of four yesterday afternoon."

"Now there's a story I can't wait to hear."

The attorney who'd given Dani the keys to Frank's house entered the office. "Forgive my delay. I'm Hugh Pettinger, for any of you I've not met. If you'll take your seats, we'll get this done."

While they'd talked, the receptionist had added chairs for Brad and Brynn, arranging them in a semicircle, so they each sat with Matty and Lana occupying the outside seats.

"Let me start by giving my condolences to each of you. I've worked with Frank Sango for a number of years now, and he truly was a wonderful man."

A knot welled in her throat, and Brad grasped her hand.

"I plan to keep this brief, so I'll do as little talking as I can. Mr. Joie, Franklin Sango requested that you be the executor of his will. Are you willing and able to fulfill those duties?"

"Yes, sir."

"Mr. Joie and Miss Quint. You two were Frank's closest confidantes. Given the unusual circumstances of Miss Sango never having known him, Frank requested that you both assist her by answering any questions she might have about his life. Are you agreeable to his wish?"

"Yes," both chorused in unison.

"Wait." Dani leaned to see Lana. "How exactly were you and Frank connected?"

"Longtime friends, and within the last year, I became Frank's girlfriend."

A million thoughts came to mind, but she clamped down on all of them. "Continue."

"All right. Miss Sango, before you leave, I'll provide you a copy of the will for your reading pleasure. Before I explain what your father has left you, there's a brief video I'd like for you to watch."

"A video?" Was she in high school again? Random!

Pettinger opened a laptop, turned it to face her, and pointed to a button. "When you're ready, start the video by hitting that button. It's about five minutes long. We'll all step out—"

"What is this?" This felt absolutely juvenile and moronic.

Matty stood but touched her arm. "Darlin', this is where you get the answers you've been askin' for. Hit PLAY and watch."

Pettinger and Lana left, and Matty grabbed Brynn and Peanut and followed.

Brad turned to her. "Do you want me to go too?"

She shook her head slowly. "I don't know. Stay." She twined her fingers into his. Behind them, the office door closed, and she reached for the button.

A black screen came up, which resolved into a picture of Frank's screened room. A second later, Frank—older with short-cropped hair and a dark, five o'clock shadow—sat in front of the camera.

He smiled, swallowed, then looked straight into the lens. "Hi, Bean."

At the nickname he'd called her all those years ago, a tidal wave of memories washed over her. Nothing concrete. Quick images, like snapshots.

"Forgive me. I'm, um. . .I had something all planned out to say to you, but right now, I've got so many thoughts in my head, I don't even know where start. So, um. . .I'll start with this. Baby girl, I love you. From the depths of my soul, I love you, and I've never stopped."

A sob rocked her, and Dani leaned heavily on the arm of the chair. Brad scooted closer and slipped an arm around her.

He fell silent, a moment, then carried on. "I want you to know I did not forge paintings. Every piece I made had subtle clues to show it wasn't authentic. I always signed my own name, left other clues throughout the painting. How some of those signatures got changed is. . .well, I'm pretty sure who framed me. I documented all my paintings on film, and on the backs of every photograph, I wrote down the clues I left. I tried to be smart about it, Bean. But I messed up. I didn't fight. I thought the best thing for everyone—you, my mom, me—was to take the plea, do my time, and put it all behind me."

"I was really naive in that regard. Once I got out, I tried to come see you. Your mom had divorced me long ago, and I couldn't find you. Didn't know her married name. So I went searching for you through the one channel I knew. Your grandfather's law firm. The day I showed up, I thought things were going pretty well when I was shown into his office. Like I said, I was naive. Dale hated me, and I should've realized it was all a big setup."

Dani leaned into Brad.

"Your grandfather gave me an ultimatum. I could sign away my parental rights, never try to see you again, and walk out of his office with $300,000 in hand—and the knowledge that you'd be provided for, for the rest of your life. Or, if I pursued trying to find you, your grandfather threatened to dummy up charges against me—have me put back in jail. And he would cut you off for the duration of your lifetime. He told me I had to decide then and there. No going home to think about it. If I left his office, the offer was gone."

Frank hung his head. "I'd already messed up your life once, Bean. I was fresh out of prison with no idea how I was going to support myself, much less you. I was in a very low place, and I made what I thought was the right decision. Honestly, in that moment, I thought you'd be better off without me, so I signed away my rights."

He held up a document, written on Grandpa Dale's law firm letterhead, that showed Frank's signature and the date. In his other hand, he showed a photocopy of a check in the amount of $300,000, made out to Franklin Daniel Sango.

Dani punched the button that started the video, and the screen froze.

"Brad, this is evil! My grandfather purposely drove my father out of my life."

"I don't even know what to say right now."

She reached for the computer, but rather than starting the video again, she zoomed in and read the document frozen on the screen. Shifting the view to look at the check, she read it—and stalled on the routing number.

"Brad!"

"What?"

A soft knock came at the door, and Matty dared to peek in. "You done, darlin'?"

She wiped her tears. "Matty, come here!"

Dani leaned in and squinted, and when Matty approached, she pointed. "You're not going to believe this. The routing number on the check Grandpa Dale gave Frank is the same number as all those wire transfers we found last night."

"You remember the account number?"

"I'm a bookkeeper. I remember numbers easily—and I'm telling you, that check is the same account those wire transfers came from! I think Grandpa Dale funded the forgery scheme!"

Brad twisted to look at Matty. "Didn't you say Dale and Knox worked together?"

"Not worked together. Frank once said Knox was a client of Dale's."

"Right. So. . .we know Knox was eventually convicted of forgery himself. If Dale was ticked at Frank for ruining Dani's mother's future, and he knew of Knox's penchant for forgery because he was his attorney, then Dale could have employed Knox to change the signatures on the paintings, just to get back at him. Dani just proved the same account that paid for the art is tied to Dale here." He stabbed a finger at the computer screen. "Would that be your grandfather's style, Dani?"

Matty shook his head. "That would answer a lot of questions."

"Yes, it would be his style." Tears welled in Dani's eyes again. "And, in my experience, if Grandpa Dale *had* done such a thing, he'd be arrogant enough to keep those two paintings as trophies."

Brad turned to her. "Are you okay? This has to be—"

"Nuts? Cray-cray?" She heaved a breath. "I told you, my family's not easy."

"Yeah, well. . .neither is mine. We'll get through it together." He looped an arm around her shoulders, pulled her close, and planted a kiss on her temple.

"Finish your video, darlin'." Matty nodded at the computer, and Brad punched the button to start it again.

"I didn't want your grandfather's money—not for me. So I started planning how I could provide something for you even if I never got to see you again. I took that $300,000, and I've grown it into a nest egg for you. It won't replace the years we lost, but I hope you'll understand that my heart has always been to see you taken care of. I went about it in the wrong way—and that's been the biggest source of shame in my life, Bean. But I've tried to make up for it in the only way I knew how."

His lips twisted into a sad smile. "There are a million other things I need to tell you, but for this video, I think I've said enough. I'll make more, and I hope one day you'll see them all. Maybe it'll give you some small idea how much I love you. So until next time, I love you, Bean. Bye."

When she didn't move, Matty reached over and stopped the video.

"Who's him?" Brynn pointed to the frozen image of Frank as he rose from his seat.

"That's my daddy, Brynnie."

There was a knock on the door, and Pettinger and Lana reentered.

"Are you all right, Miss Sango?"

"I. . .my head's kind of full, but thank you for showing me that. It answers so many questions."

Pettinger turned the computer toward himself, clicked a few buttons, and after a moment, removed a thumb drive, which he handed over. "The remainder of your father's videos are on this drive. It's yours."

She received the treasure and fidgeted while he closed the laptop. "So, all that remains is for me to explain your inheritance. In a nutshell, the will says that you are the sole heir to your father's sizeable estate, which includes his home, the fifteen acres it sits on, his half of the Joie-Rides Restoration and Custom Detailing business, his collection of seven classic cars and twelve classic and modern motorcycles, his bank accounts, and the recent addition of the book of Native American ledger art."

"What?" She gaped at the man. "Repeat that!"

He rattled off the list again, though she still had trouble grasping all he said. But two things in particular snagged her attention. She turned on Matty.

"You said Frank worked for you!"

"When did I say that?"

"The day we met?"

"Uh, no, darlin'. I never said he worked *for* me. He worked *with* me— as my partner. Equal shares."

"Partner? Partner!"

"Yes. And you can either join me in the business, or I'll buy you out at a fair price. Your choice."

She closed her eyes, her heart pounding. How did she even begin to make such a decision? "I don't. . .I don't know."

"Take a breath. You don't have to make the decision *now*, darlin'. You've got all the time in the world."

She stared for long seconds, mind swimming, then finally looked at Pettinger again. "What about the ledger art? Why did Frank purchase it?"

"I'll answer that." Lana shifted her chair to see her better. "A couple of years ago, Frank did a few of those DNA tests. They all came back saying he had some small percentage of Native American heritage—particularly Cheyenne. He didn't know how to research his genealogy, so he enlisted my help. We were able to trace his family line back to about the 1880 mark—when one of his relatives was adopted from an orphanage in very southern Georgia. The only information they had on the child's origins was the mother was named Sally Jo, and the child was obviously Native American. We hit a wall at that point. Then, about a year ago, we were at the fort, where I picked up a book about the prominent women of St. Augustine and discovered the story of Sarah Josephine Harris, who taught the Plains Indians incarcerated at Fort Marion in the 1870s. She was commonly known as Sally Jo. And—"

"She married a Cheyenne brave named Broken Bow after years of ministering with him at the reservation."

Lana's lips parted. "You know Sally Jo's story?"

Dani smiled at Brad. "A thing or two, yes."

"Well, she is your great-great-great-grandmother, I believe. And Broken Bow was your great-great-great-grandfather. Frank watched art auctions just for the love of it. When he discovered that his ancestor's ledger art was up for sale, he had to buy it, fully intending for this piece of your past to be another foundation stone in your future."

EPILOGUE

St. Augustine, Florida—Present Day—Two Months Later

 $\mathcal{T}$ he familiar Jaguar convertible rolled into the church parking lot, and Dani hurried off the porch toward the car. Before she reached the passenger door, both Mom and Alec climbed out.

Mom shot her a sheepish grin. "Sorry we're late. We got a little turned around."

Dani smiled. "Glad you were able to make it."

"What exactly are we doing here, dear?"

"I told you—going for a motorcycle ride." She gave them both the once-over, noting their jeans and comfortable shirts. "Thank you for taking my advice and wearing suitable clothes."

The two exchanged pensive looks but nodded.

She had to give them credit. Once she'd presented them with the evidence of Grandpa Dale's involvement in framing Frank and the document he'd made Frank sign to give up his parental rights, their tune had changed. As they'd talked through the history, they admitted they'd both been just as duped into believing the worst of Frank as she had. And when she'd shared some of Frank's sweetest videos with Mom, true healing had started to come. . .something she never thought she'd see.

"C'mon inside." She took her mother's hand and led the way, coming to settle at the back of the church as Matty made his announcements.

"Danielle, who are these people?" Alec whispered. "Are they safe?"

She chuckled. "They're my friends. They may not fit into your country club lifestyle, but they're as salt of the earth as you'll find."

"We're gonna get this goose chase started in just a minute," Matty called out. "Dani's leading the charge today, so fall in behind her."

"Goose chase?" Her mother leaned in to whisper the question, as wide-eyed and freaked out as Dani had ever seen her. "What is that lunatic-looking man talking about?"

"But first. . ." Matty turned on her. "Dani, you want to share?"

"Be right back." Before either could speak, she darted down the main aisle and stood beside Matty at the microphone. "So, you all know that because my dad took a plea deal, there could never be a retrial. But a lot of you also know I've been kicking around applying for a pardon."

Murmurs rippled through the crowd.

"His attorney, Mr. Pettinger, is helping me with the process, and we'll have the paperwork together soon to get that rolling, so please keep it in prayer." Her throat grew thick, and her eyes stung with unshed tears. "I'd really like to see my father pardoned."

Ear-splitting whistles and applause went up, and several shouted out their support.

"All right. Let's pray, and we'll get this goose chase started!" As Matty bowed his head and led them in one final prayer, she stepped off the stage and returned to Mom and Alec, who, surprisingly, offered her encouraging hugs in response to her announcement.

Once he closed his prayer, Matty headed for the sound booth, turned the sound system and lights off, then caught her eye while the group filed out. "You ready to lead your first chase, darlin'?"

"Ready as I'll ever be." She waved Matty nearer. "Matty, meet Jessica and Alec Neely—my mom and stepdad. Mom, Alec, meet Matty Joie—my business partner."

Both her parents dropped their jaws, though Alec recovered a little quicker than Mom.

"Pleasure, Mr. Joie." He extended a hand in greeting.

"Matty. Everyone calls me Matty. And the pleasure's mine. I think the world of your girl here. She's learning the business fast and challenging me to move in some new directions."

Mom nearly beamed. "She's an amazing young woman."

"That she is!" Matty turned on her. "All right. We're holdin' up the show. Let's do this, darlin'."

She led the way out of the church, and Matty locked up.

At their bikes, she pointed Mom to Matty's side. "Matty's got the more comfortable bike for first-time riders, Mom, so you'll be with him. It'll be like riding in an easy chair."

She shoved a helmet toward Alec. "And you'll ride with me." Once they both donned their helmets, she straddled her bike and patted the seat behind her. "A couple tips. Pretend you're a spider monkey on my back. Hang on tight, lean into the curves, and trust me."

He took the offered seat. "Uh. . ."

Dani reached back, grabbed her stepfather's wrists, and wrapped them around her waist. Once she revved her bike to life, the rest of the group followed suit.

Heart rate increasing, she lifted a nervous glance toward the blue sky. *Okay, Lord. . .it's a goose chase. Where are You leading us today?*

She set out, Matty falling in beside her, and the rest lining up behind. Dani turned right out of the parking lot and headed down the road. At each intersection, she paused, waiting for a direction, and twenty minutes later, they pulled into the municipal parking garage in St. Augustine's historic district. Once she'd parked, she tapped Alec's arms, seemingly glued to her middle, and he sat up.

"I can't decide if that was exhilarating or terrifying." Alec's eyes were wide as he pulled his helmet off.

She gave him a firm pat on the shoulder and laughed. "It's both."

As Mom climbed down with help from Matty, her saucer-sized eyes reflected sheer panic.

"You all right, Mom?"

"That was an experience." Unsteady, she scrambled toward her husband's side.

Matty sidled up next to Dani as she pulled her tiny purse from her saddlebag. "Where to, darlin'?"

She led the way out to the street and glanced left and right, unsure of a direction. *Lord, where?* As her gaze strayed across the street, her uncertainty fled. "There!" She pointed toward the Castillo de San Marcos.

"The fort?" Matty arched a brow at her.

"The fort."

As the group crossed the street and headed down the sidewalk toward the entrance, Mom found her voice again. "I thought you said your young man, Brad, was going to be up here this weekend?"

"Something came up at the museum. He and Brynn weren't able to make it this weekend. But I promise, next weekend, we'll come by and you can meet them both."

"We'd like that. I'll make sure your brothers and sister are home."

As they got in line to pay, she noted Brad had texted.

On your goose chase?

Yes, but maybe I'm missing you, not really hearing God's leading. I wound up back at the fort.

Missing you too! Long-distance relationships are for the birds. When you get in the fort, call me. Have some news.

News. . . ? She didn't know whether to cringe or cheer. They'd been awaiting the museum's leadership decision about the curator position, and kept promising the decision was close.

Call in a couple. About to pay now.

She tucked her phone away and, at the sight of Park Ranger Carlos Delgado, she grinned.

"Hey, Dani." He waved. "Welcome back."

"Hey, Carlos." She flashed her annual pass. "I need a couple day passes for my parents." She paid their fee, then led them across the two drawbridges.

She'd been back to the fort several times since the reading of Frank's will. Looking around the place through the lens of Broken Bow and Sally Jo's history gave it a sense of reality that she'd never experienced before. It was no longer just a historical site. Now it was *her* history—her ancestors' story.

"Dani, I need the restroom," Mom whispered.

She nodded. "Right there. Past the stairs. I'll call Brad while I wait for you."

Mom scurried off, and Alec and Matty headed for the casemates, so she pulled out her phone and called Brad. The call rang in her ear, and an instant later, Van Morrison's "Brown-Eyed Girl"—the special ringtone Brad assigned to her on his phone—played from somewhere nearby.

Dani spun, looked around, and out of the dark tunnel, walked Brad and Brynn, hand in hand, Brynnie holding tight to her crocheted horse.

Her heart gave a huge flutter, and she hurried across the distance, launching into Brad's arms.

"I thought you said you couldn't come!"

"Well. . .that's not *exactly* true."

"Obviously." She pulled out of his embrace and hoisted Brynn to her hip. "Hi, baby. How are you and Peanut?"

Brynnie shook her head. "Jellybean."

"What?"

Brad roughed a hand over the horse's crocheted mane. "She renamed her horse Jellybean."

"Oooh." Dani grinned. Hopefully, a further sign the sprite was healing. "Well, how are you and Jellybean?"

"Good." She cuddled against Dani's shoulder. "We missed you, Miss Dani."

"I missed you too, Brynnie!" She kissed the girl, then turned on Brad. "So what *are* you doing here? How'd you know where to find us?"

A cat-that-ate-the-canary grin crossed his lips. "I didn't. I let God lead me on my own goose chase today. Actually, I've done that every weekend I've not been with you."

"Okay?"

"I've been asking God to show me how. . .when. . .to move forward with our relationship, and, um. . .I felt like it would be time when we wound up at the same place on our respective goose chases."

"What are you saying?" She shifted Brynn to her other hip.

He dropped to a knee as he produced something from his front pocket. "Danielle Shae Sango, will you marry me?" He popped the top on a ring box, revealing a beautiful round-cut diamond ring.

"Oh my—" She was vaguely aware that a crowd had gathered, though all her focus was pinned on Brad. "Are you serious?"

"Do I look serious?"

She nodded, mute.

"Then will you marry me?"

For one breathless instant, she stared, then nodded. "Yes, I'll marry you!"

When he stood and pulled her into his arms, the gathering crowd cheered, and he claimed her lips. Her heart pounded as electricity crackled from the top of her head all the way to her toes. Was this really happening? With her free hand, she bunched the material of his golf shirt and pulled him a little closer, breathing deep of his woodsy cologne as he deepened the kiss. Brynn wrapped her arms around their necks, nuzzling into the intimate moment with a giggle.

"You found da princess, Uncle Bad!"

They both pulled back, laughing.

"I guess I did, silly girl!" He pulled Brynn from Dani's arms and set her down. "Stand right here, please."

Still breathless, Dani watched as he opened the ring box and, this time, removed the sparkler and slid it onto her hand.

"Wait. What about the museum? The curator position. . ."

"Oh." A flush crept up his neck. "That was the news." He shrugged. "They offered me the position, but I turned it down."

"What're you going to do for a job?"

From behind her, Matty's voice boomed. "You're the boss, darlin'! Hire the man!"

She twisted to find Matty with Mom and Alec as well as various other church members and strangers.

"Well?" He arched a brow at her. "Can I have a job?"

Dani pressed her lips together and nodded. "All right. You're hired. For what, I'm not sure, but we'll figure that out later."

He pulled her into another big hug. "I love you!"

"I love you too. But how am I ever going to top this goose chase?"

"Oh, I think God's got plenty more surprises in store for us."

AUTHOR'S NOTE

Hello, Readers.

As always, thank you so much for taking time to read one of my stories. It is such an honor to know that there are those who read and enjoy the tales I spin.

I wanted to take a few minutes to clarify some of the historical facts and details that went into the creation of *Love's Fortress*. First, the characters. Several of the historical timeline characters are real. We'll start with Lieutenant Richard Henry Pratt. From the time of the surrender of the various Native American tribes, he was put in charge of investigating which men were most responsible for the troubles. He was thorough and meticulous in his research of their backgrounds and their deeds during various conflicts. He knew the men who had stirred up the most trouble on the reservations, and it was his recommendation that these seventy-three men be shipped to St. Augustine's Fort Marion. But from my research, his heart truly was to see these men be able to integrate into life among their white counterparts, so he formed many innovative ideas on how to make that happen. He fought hard for the men whose lives had been entrusted to him, and they came to respect him greatly during their three years at Fort Marion. In fact, many of them followed him to his next post, the Carlisle Indian School in Carlisle, Pennsylvania, after their release from Fort Marion in 1878. Of course, we have likely all heard of the many atrocities that have and are continuing to come out in regard to Native American residential schools. I will make no further comment about that topic, since I haven't researched it thoroughly enough to understand it all, but I feel I would be remiss if I didn't mention that Lieutenant Pratt was the founder of that school and many of "his Indians" willingly went there after their release.

Sarah Mather is another historical figure. Miss Mather was a fireball from all I understand of her. At age sixty, when the Native Americans first came to the fort, she already had a long history of teaching and championing the causes of the underprivileged around her. She moved to St. Augustine from Massachusetts in the late 1850s, and in her many years in that town, she was credited with running a school to educate the Black community after the Civil War's end, as well as helping start churches and homes for the aging among that same community. While I depicted

Sally Jo Harris as being one of the first masterminds behind the plan to educate the Native American prisoners, it was actually Sarah Mather who approached Lieutenant Pratt with the idea to educate the Plains Indian men. She and Lieutenant Pratt remained good friends even after he was transferred out of St. Augustine, and she continued to champion the Native American cause long after the Plains Indians were released.

One humorous story that I couldn't find a way to include in *Love's Fortress*: While teaching her Native American students at the fort one day, Sarah caused quite a stir when she was attempting to coach her students on how to make the "th" sound properly. To her students' horror, she removed her dentures—something none of them had seen before—and tried to explain by indicating where to place the tongue in relation to the teeth. Lieutenant Pratt heard a ruckus from her classroom and went to see what was up. He found at least one of the men covering his eyes and calling out in broken English, "Miss Mather no good!"

Rebecca Perit is the third historical figure I included. While she was mentioned only in passing in my story, she was another great influencer in St. Augustine during the late 1800s. She and Sarah Mather—both of whom never married—were lifelong friends and dedicated to teaching and helping those in need. The two formed a powerhouse team to help the underprivileged in their town.

Other real people, mentioned mostly in brief or passing fashion, are Major Hamilton, Lieutenant Colonel Dent, Dr. Laird, and Dr. Janeway. Very little of my research focused on them, other than mentioning them by name, so any inaccurate depictions of these people are due to my own fictionalization of them, not because of any detailed research.

Broken Bow is purely fictional, though I took a sampling of various men, events, and stories from my research and made his personality and actions a mash-up of what I'd read. Most notably, I modeled him after Cheyenne warrior Okuhhatuh, or "Making Medicine." This man was a Cheyenne Dog Soldier who was sent to Fort Marion because of his involvement in the capture of a German immigrant family on the Plains before the Cheyenne surrendered. The family of nine was captured, and both parents and the oldest (adult) children were murdered. The middle children—preteen and teenaged daughters—were raped and carried off by some of the men. And the youngest children, who were still in single digits, were given to the Cheyenne tribe to raise as their own. When Lieutenant Pratt discovered Making Medicine's involvement in this case, he became one of the men chosen to be incarcerated at the Florida fort. And, as depicted in my story, out of sibling loyalty, Making Medicine's brother, Little Medicine, volunteered to accompany his brother to Fort Marion. The thing I love most about Making Medicine's story is that during the summer of 1875, a family of tourists came to see the ancient fort (something the tourists could easily do by asking for a pass from St. Francis Barracks, a few blocks down the street). The Pendleton family— George (who would later become a US senator) and Alice, along with their daughter, Jeanie—struck up a conversation with Making Medicine while there and in the process shared the Gospel with him. They were able to lead him to Christ during that visit, and it forever changed the trajectory of Making Medicine's life. Upon his release in 1878, he adopted the name David Pendleton Oakerhater (David for the Biblical king, Pendleton for the family that led him to the Lord, and Oakerhater because that was the English pronunciation of his Cheyenne name) and asked to return to the Cheyenne reservation in Oklahoma. There, he found much success in sharing the Gospel with his people.

A couple of the incidents from *Love's Fortress* are more or less factual. The escapade where the men stripped down to their breechcloths and embarrassed Lieutenant Pratt in front of his team of teachers was, in fact, based on truth, though it didn't happen in quite the same way as depicted in the story. Pratt quickly discerned that "his Indians" needed activity and purpose, so early on in their stay at the fort, he began having them do physical training and drills in the courtyard. After a short time, they seemed to be falling into a proper routine. They were an impressive sight, and Pratt was proud of their accomplishments. Some of the locals (many of them women) were quite interested to see the goings-on within the fort, so one day Pratt turned from overseeing the morning exercises, opened the pine doors, and invited these locals in. But in the brief moment he'd turned away, some of the men stripped down to even less than their breechcloths (in fact, they wore only a string around their waists!) and continued their drills. Imagine the shock and horror when these Victorian-era women emerged from the tunnel to see several naked men exercising in the courtyard. And imagine Pratt's embarrassment at his charges having gotten the better of him! Oh, he had his hands full with this bunch!

The Kiowa escape attempt was another true event. While I depicted Broken Bow having some involvement of the foiling of that event, in truth, it was solely Pratt who discovered the plot and squelched it. The Kiowa leaders (with help from the Comanche) began mapping the town and various escape routes in their ledger books. Pratt noted changes in their behavior and secretive whispers exchanged between the men involved. Once he was fairly sure of what he was dealing with, Pratt brought in the troops from St. Francis Barracks to put the plot down. As mentioned in the story, the night he foiled their attempt, Pratt marched the three ring-leaders around the courtyard, blindfolded, until they were so exhausted, they dropped. Then the post surgeon injected them with a sleeping agent, seeming to render them dead, and they had the "bodies" carted away from the fort. The ringleaders were held in solitary confinement in the guardhouse down the street for two weeks, and other Kiowa men were punished within the fort, demoted, or otherwise dealt with. When, after two weeks, Pratt returned the Kiowa chiefs to the fort, there was quite a stir among the other prisoners because of how he'd brought the three men back to life! While Pratt kept the escape from becoming any kind of major event, the local newspapers spun it into quite an "insurrection," which caused a great stir in the local community for months afterward. I'd like to note that, in the three years of their incarceration, no one ever escaped. Sally Jo spiriting Broken Bow away from the fort is purely a fictional convention for the story's sake.

I also tried to weave in small details of daily life in the fort. Things like a local jeweler contracting with the Native Americans to gather and polish "sea beans" from Anastasia Island. Or the fact that the prisoners would be allowed to make and sell other wares—bows and arrows and ledger art among them—to the locals and tourists. These men were quite industrious, and while some sent money home to their families on the reservation, they also kept a good portion for their own enjoyment. They did quite a booming business with the local stores, purchasing various foods and knick-knacks with the money they earned from their "curio" sales. They also held various cultural events at the fort, anything from powwows to "buffalo hunts"—carried out with cattle from area ranches and performed by riding the worst of nags from the local livery stable. They did archery exhibitions in the street and would teach anyone who wanted to pay the money how to shoot a bow and arrow. Outside of the brief span when the escape attempt shut down their comings and goings, the Native American men were usually free to leave the fort to wander into St. Augustine's shopping district by simply asking for a pass. And while some people attempted to stir up trouble, the men actually proved to be very careful in their dealings with everyone outside the fort. They seemed to know their reputation—and that of *all* Native Americans—rested on how they presented themselves, so they were very subdued and respectful during their three years at Fort Marion.

Twice during this story, I have Sally Jo sing a verse from the song "It Is Well with My Soul." If you know your music history, you'll know that the song wasn't published until 1876—a year after my story is set. However, the song was written three years before its official publication, and I'd guess it was performed in that three-year span at various events. So, while it might seem I've made a mistake in my research, I am trusting that Sally Jo might have had opportunity to hear the song performed before its official publication.

Lastly, I'd like to address the "goose chases" from the contemporary timeline. The idea for this plot element came from the book *Wild Goose Chase* by Mark Batterson. Batterson suggests that following the "Wild Goose" (or Holy Spirit) can be a true adventure if we let Him lead us—and I couldn't agree more. I'm far from an expert on this, but I am trying to learn to be more open to the Spirit's leading, and I hope this element in the story might encourage you also to step out and let the "Wild Goose" lead you into grand adventures. I think we all have great things in store if we'll let go and truly let Him lead.

Thank you again, dear readers, for taking the time to read *Love's Fortress*. Of the various books I've written, it was by far the most challenging one on so many levels. But I am going to trust that God was in the midst of those struggles, and hopefully He will use this book to speak to you.

Jennifer

Jennifer Uhlarik discovered the Western genre as a preteen when she swiped the only "horse" book she found on her older brother's bookshelf. A new love was born. Across the next ten years, she devoured Louis L'Amour Westerns and fell in love with the genre. In college at the University of Tampa, she began penning her own story of the Old West. Armed with a BA in writing, she has won five writing competitions and was a finalist in two others. In addition to writing, she has held jobs as a private business owner, a schoolteacher, a marketing director, and her favorite—a full-time homemaker. Jennifer is active in American Christian Fiction Writers and is a lifetime member of the Florida Writers Association. She lives near Tampa, Florida, with her husband, teenage son, and four fur children.